OTHER SIDE
of
HEAVEN

Also by William James in Orbit

THE SUNFALL TRILOGY
Book One: THE EARTH IS THE LORD'S

THE SUNFALL TRILOGY
Book Two

The
OTHER SIDE
of
HEAVEN

William James

ORBIT

An *Orbit* Book

First published in Great Britain in 1993 by Orbit

A CIP catalogue record for this book
is available from the British Library.

ISBN 1 85723 127 9

Typeset by Leaper & Gard Ltd, Bristol, England
Printed in England by Clays Ltd, St Ives plc

Orbit
A Division of
Little, Brown and Company (UK) Limited
165 Great Dover Street
London SE1 4YA

CONTENTS

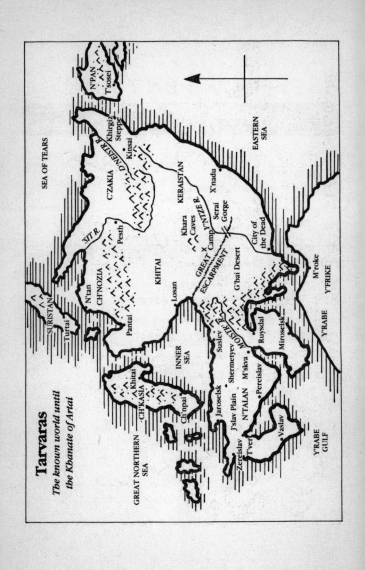

Tarvaras
The known world until the Khanate of Artai

The Voyage of the Sunstealer

The Khanate of the Golden Clan of the Altun

Chart showing principal bloodlines and family relationships.

The names of characters appearing in the books of the SUNFALL trilogy are indicated by capital letters.

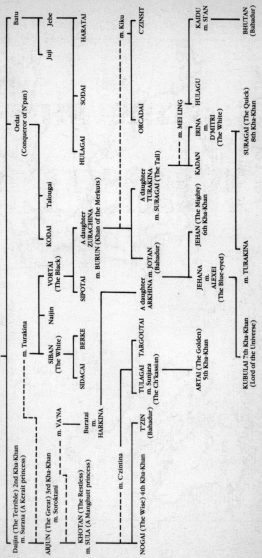

Note: Broken lines indicate second marriages and subsequent step-relationships.

The
OTHER SIDE
of
HEAVEN

PROLOGUE

Death of a Khan

In the splendour of the Golden Circle, the centre of the centre of Kinsai, the nobility had assembled to pay final respects to Nogai the Wise, Lord of the Known World, Fourth Kha-Khan. His body had been wrapped in layers of tissue of gold, and now it lay upon its funeral pyre in the great oval ceremonial bowl. On the beaten gold of the dais four gates had been erected. They faced north towards the Khirgiz steppe and the Sea of Tears, south towards the province of Keraistan, east where lay the islands of N'pan, and west to face the city of Pesth and the setting sun.

Only the western gate had been left unsealed, so that the spirit of the dead Kha-Khan would depart towards Heaven. Jehan wondered if the continued observance of a custom which was founded surely on pure superstition implied that the Yek were losing their ability to discriminate between ceremony and meaningless ritual. If God truly existed, then certainly it was insolent presumption for any man to attempt to define Him in terms which related to human preoccupation. And if there was a Paradise, it was unlikely that it lay beyond the sun.

Jehan was wearing the fancy gold coat of the Altun, and its collar made his neck itch. He waited until no one appeared to be looking, and then loosened the wire fastenings at his throat. Then he stretched his neck and turned his head from side to side to ease the soreness.

The Khans were all standing in a group under an awning which had been raised to extend the cover of the portico which provided access from the inner

3

courtyard to the vestibule of the Golden Yurt, the palace of the Kha-Khan. Nogai's brother T'zin, and his half-brothers Tulagai and Targoutai were in the centre of the crowd at the front, and they were flanked on either side by Siban and Burun. Siban was a son of Daijin the Terrible, who had been Kha-Khan before even Jehan's father was born. Once Siban had been a candidate for the Dragon Throne, but his aspirations had been shattered by Nogai's election. In the space of twelve years he had become an old man. His hair was snow white, and his skin was pouched and seamed so that he looked as if he had lost flesh. Burun was Jehan's grandfather, and he had been the chief instrument in the elevation of Nogai to the Khanate. In reality he was only Khan of the Merkut Clan, but during Nogai's lifetime he had been the virtual power behind the throne. Siban and Burun were friends when it suited them. They were of similar age, but no one would have known it. Burun's physique was altering slowly as he grew older and it was true that he had gained weight, but he had the vitality of a man half his age.

Everyone was wearing the crimson scarf which signified mourning. The women, Jehan's mother and sister among them, were crowded into the arcade which ran along the eastern side of the courtyard, and most of them were wearing gowns trimmed with the same colour. The setting sun cast a red haze over everything, and considering that cremations were always conducted at about the same hour it was easy to understand why red was the universal signal for death.

Jehan could see his father in the throng behind Burun, but he resisted the impulse to wave. Jotan was the Khan of a province which had once been the country of the Alan people. He was also Burun's heir.

4

When their eyes finally met it was Jehan who looked away first. He envied his father his immense self-possession. Jotan always knew exactly how to behave, was never at a loss in any situation, and he was renowned throughout the Khanate for his statesman-like abilities.

'Name of God, fasten your collar.' Kadan nudged Jehan with his elbow.

Jehan made a face, and then pretended that he had not heard. It was hard sometimes to remember that his cousin was only thirteen. Already Kadan was as tall as most Yek adults, and although he possessed Altun red hair and clear grey eyes, in everything else he resembled his father, the alien whom men called Suragai the Tall.

'This is a funeral,' Kadan muttered. His tone was one of amused reproof. 'Have you no respect?'

Jehan pursed his lips. If they had been able to talk aloud, he would have silenced Kadan by pointing out that strictly speaking he was not entitled to be in the front rank of mourners at all. Suragai was after all only a S'zltan, Burun's vassal and chief advisor.

'Be quiet whelp,' he whispered.

He did not turn his head, but out of the corner of his eye he saw Kadan grin. If they had been conversing in anything other than muttered asides Kadan's response would have been cheerfully disrespectful. Probably he would have countered Jehan's point about his rank by observing that they were both great-great-grandsons of Daijin. Certainly it would have been difficult for either of them to claim pre-eminence.

On the dais the Shaman was laying out Nogai's totem, and the seals and insignia of his reign. The emblems had been defaced on the instant of Nogai's death, and until the installation of a successor every

5

official communication which originated from the Golden Yurt would be sealed with the talisman of the vacant throne.

Automatically Jehan switched his attention to the separate canopy under which stood the Kha-Khan elect. Artai the Golden was a youth of seventeen summers who had been raised exclusively in the rarefied atmosphere of the court. Selected as a possible candidate during the reign of Arjun the Great, Nogai's predecessor, it had been Nogai's controversial decision to continue the young nominee's training and to name him heir.

Jehan watched Artai's smooth features for some sign of expression. The eyes with their huge golden irises met his for an instant, then swept on without apparent recognition. Jehan frowned. He mistrusted Artai, and he believed with all his heart that the implementation of Nogai's will was a serious error of judgement.

All over Kinsai the gongs began to be struck. At first the noise was a confused clamour. Then the beat steadied. It became a metallic throb which seemed to enfold everything within its range so that Jehan could imagine that every heart in the city was pulsing in time. Everywhere the people would be stopping whatever they were doing. They would stare towards the setting sun, and they would uncover as a last homage to Nogai.

The Shaman accepted a burning torch from an acolyte. He walked three times around the cremation bowl, then touched the torch to the pyre. At once the scented, oil-soaked wood burst into flame. A puff of grey smoke was pushed into the air by the rising current of hot air. The light breeze which had sprung up blew the smoke westward, and it dispersed as quickly as it had come into being.

6

Everyone made the invocation, but even as he spoke the words Jehan thought that he did not believe that the smoke was an omen. He did not think that Nogai's spirit was even now commencing its journey towards Heaven, and he guessed that the Shaman had deliberately waited until the evening wind was in the right quarter before touching off the pyre. The Shaman were trying to establish themselves as priests of Yek mysticism, but only adherents to the cult of Sufi accepted that there was such a thing as spiritual power on earth.

The Shaman was bowing to Artai now. In theory nobody was supposed to leave before the Kha-Khan elect, but already Burun and most of the other Khans had started to turn away. Artai's expression was outraged, and when Jehan saw it he grinned.

'Of course there is time.' Burun's tone was bland. 'Until the election is confirmed by the assembly of the Khans, Artai is only a nominee. He has no power.'

Several of the Khans who were in the room nodded sagely, but Jehan guessed that no one was yet really serious about overturning Nogai's will. He selected a pear from a bowl on the table, and used his d'jaga to quarter it. The meal was supposed to be a social occasion, but with so many nobles gathered in Kinsai to elect a Kha-Khan it was probably inevitable that even the most incidental conversation would turn to the question of the succession.

'Who can we elect if not Artai?' Jotan was sitting three places down from Burun. He rocked his chair back against the stone pillar at his shoulder as he spoke.

The question was rhetorical, but two minor Khans who had claims through their direct descent from the third son of the Ancestor looked as if they expected

7

to be named. Jehan hid a wry smile.

'Oh, well,' Burun was gesturing as if to indicate his impartiality, 'I was only asked for constitutional advice. Everyone knows that I support Artai.'

Jehan watched the faces of the others who were seated around the long table. It was clear that a few of them at least doubted the sincerity of Burun's declaration.

'The Merkuts already control a tenth part of the known world,' someone observed sourly. 'Is that not enough?'

There was an embarrassed silence. Jehan tried to see who had spoken, but it could have been any one of a group of lesser Khans who were sitting at one end of the table.

For a moment it was as if Burun had not heard. He was pouring wine into a cup. Then he raised his head. 'It is the duty of every Khan to further the interests of his clan.' His tone was mild. 'If the Merkuts have found advancement, then it has been paid for in service to the Khanate.'

No one spoke. Slaves entered the room with another course, and for a moment the mutter of conversation became commonplace. Jehan guessed that Burun knew who had made the remark, and thought that whoever the man was, he would not like to be in his place.

A smooth-faced Y'rabe heaped freshly steamed k'va onto the platter in front of Jehan. The staple was a grain similar to rice, although its smell was yeasty and it was coloured like straw. When Jehan spooned a portion of stewed meat from a bowl onto it, the juices soaked into the k'va and stained it brown.

Jotan's chair came forward with a crash. The noise made heads come up all along the table.

'Is there a Khan who is not motivated by the desire to advance his clan?' Jotan's voice sounded harsh.

8

Burun appeared to concentrate on the meat on his plate for a moment. 'True,' he observed prosaically. 'But every Khan is bound by the Yasa. There must be order in the world. The throne should not lie vacant, and thus Nogai's will should be obeyed.'

There was no response. Jehan thought that none of those present wanted to be the first to express his reservations, and he wondered how much of what his grandfather had said had been sincere, and how much had been for effect.

'Are we then to be ruled by a child?'

It was Siban's son Sidacai who spoke. His words produced a mutter of agreement.

Artai's age was not the matter under discussion. There had been virtual peace during the twelve years of Nogai's reign, and as a result the Kha-Khan elect had never been to war. Even if he had desired it, there had been no opportunity for him to prove himself in the eyes of men like Sidacai for whom the ability to command was the only true measure of excellence.

It was clear that Burun knew what was being implied, but his answer took Sidacai's question at face value. 'As to that, Artai will grow older. And in the meantime he has wise counsellors to whom it is to be hoped he will pay heed.'

Jehan was tempted to point out that once a Kha-Khan was enthroned his power was absolute, but he said nothing. Burun knew the Yasa as well as anyone.

'Counsellors.' Sidacai sneered the word. 'Merkuts, you mean.'

'Among others.' Burun seemed unoffended. 'But so that you will not accuse me of self-interest, let me say that I will not be among them. I have neglected the overlordship of my feudal lands for many years in the Kha-Khan's service, and I intend to devote myself now to that purpose.'

9

'Eh?' Sidacai's face reflected his amazement. 'You're retiring from court? I don't believe it.'

'Nevertheless.' Burun's tone was calm. 'I have Artai's agreement.'

The announcement produced a variety of reactions, but it was clear to Jehan which Khans thought they had the most to gain by supplanting Burun as the power behind the throne, for they were the men who were loudest in expressing their regret at his departure from active involvement in the administration of the Khanate. It was not Jehan's place to speak, but he guessed that Burun intended no such thing. If he was retiring from public life, then it was for good reasons. Jehan smiled grimly. Burun never did anything without a good reason. He caught his father's eye, but there was no answering smile. Jotan's face was set in a frown of concern, and suddenly Jehan realised that his father had not known what Burun was going to say.

It was still dark when Jehan awoke. The house was still, but as soon as he sat up a page appeared in the doorway.

'Noyon?'

Jehan reached out and turned up the lamp which floated in the bowl beside his bed. He put his feet on the floor and stood up. He could not remember the name of the page, who was a member of his grandfather's household. 'Light some more lamps, will you?'

'Yes, Noyon.' The page moved around the room.

It was the season of rain, and the rustling sound of a light shower against the shutters filled the whole chamber.

'Send Joden Bahadur to me.' Jehan picked up a robe. 'Thank you. I'll dress myself.'

The page hesitated. 'Joden. Is he the –'

'– The tall dark officer who commands my escort.'

'Yes, Noyon.' The page hurried away.

Jehan had been sleeping naked. Clean robes had been laid out on a rack, and his boots were lying to one side. He hopped awkwardly on one leg as he pulled on the silk hose.

'Lord.' Joden came into the room. He picked up the mantle and helped Jehan into it. 'Are we going somewhere?'

'Yes.' Jehan picked up his sword. The page hurried to wind the broad silk sash around his waist, and when the task was done Jehan settled the scabbard so that it was at an exact angle. 'We're going with my grandfather. Get your men ready.'

'Oh.' Joden looked amused. 'We've been waiting for your command. They're down in the ward.'

'I see.' Jehan wondered if Burun had said something to an orderly, and thought not. 'In that case attend me.'

He went out of the room and walked along the passage. There were sentries at the doors of the rooms which were occupied by his mother and grandmother, and they saluted as he went past. The page trotted nervously ahead. He held open the door so that Jehan could enter the hall.

The house was one of several which Burun owned in different cities around the Khanate. The hall had a ceiling which was also the roof of the building, and it was surrounded by galleries which led to each floor. Jehan could hear the rain striking the tiles above his head. Apart from an enormous circular table and three stools, the hall was unfurnished. A rich carpet had been laid out in the centre of the polished floor. Its fringes had been teased out, and Jehan could see the gold threads which glittered among the cream and brown which were the principal colours. Burun was sitting at the table, and Jotan was pacing the

11

space across the carpet. Jehan stopped in the doorway, and at once they both looked in his direction.

'Good morning, Noyon.' Burun smiled. 'Did you sleep well?'

'Morning?' Jehan grinned. 'Grandfather, it's the middle of the night.' He bowed to Jotan. 'Good morning, Father.'

Jotan nodded. Then he walked over to the table and sat down beside Burun.

Burun glanced at the page. 'Sihan, get my grandson something to eat.'

'Yes, Lord.' The page went away.

'Joden, wait in the ward,' Jotan said.

The officer looked questioningly at Jehan. Jehan nodded, and Joden left the room.

Jehan sat down on the third stool. The page returned with a platter of cold meat. Jehan cut a slice from the meat with his d'jaga, then peeled slivers from the slice and ate them.

'You're coming with me to Keraistan,' Burun said. 'Your father thinks you ought to remain here.'

Jotan snorted. 'I think both of you should stay. Surely you don't want to go now, anyway. Not in this rain.'

Burun looked sideways, his face impassive. Jotan stood up again, and he paced to the doorway and back. Jehan peeled another sliver of meat. It fell onto the table and he extended his talons, impaled it, and put it into his mouth. He chewed slowly, letting the juices run over his tongue.

'Artai won't be enthroned for over a month,' Burun said. 'I have business on my estates. I haven't seen my steward since last year.'

'Hah!' Jotan gestured. 'Country affairs. You're deserting the seat of power to concern yourself with farms and small judgements.'

'You choose to interpret it that way.' Burun's tone was unyielding. He reached across and pulled the platter into the centre of the table. Then he tore a piece of meat from the haunch.

'You are needed here,' Jotan appealed.

'Am I?' Burun looked up sharply.

'You know you are. If you leave court we will be supplanted. Artai will listen to whoever flatters him the loudest. You know that.'

Jehan reflected on his father's statement and thought that it was accurate enough. Artai loved flattery. When he looked up he saw that Burun was watching him.

'What do you think I should do?' Burun asked.

Jehan hesitated. 'Khan, you will do what you think best, without my advice,' he responded at last.

Jotan laughed bitterly. 'That's true enough.'

Burun ignored him. 'I am asking for your counsel, Noyon. When I announced that I was retiring from court, you said nothing. Now tell me what is in your mind.'

The rain had stopped. Jehan sheathed his d'jaga. Then he met Burun's stare squarely.

'Khan, I am not privy to your reasons, but I imagine that you do not wish to be associated too closely with Artai's reign. The Merkuts hold fiefs in every part of the Khanate, and my father's overlordship of the Alan country ensures that the interests of the clan will not suffer. The news that you are retiring has lessened the antagonism which existed between the Merkuts and other clans. Now that they no longer fear your influence some of the Khans will become careless. You can go ahead with whatever you are planning without interference.'

Burun looked impressed. 'I always said you were

brighter than your father. So tell me what I am planning.'

Jehan was sure that his expression was transparent. 'Khan, I would not care to guess.'

Burun showed his teeth in polite disbelief. 'You have learned the most important lesson of all, Jehan. Always conceal what you know. Never reveal more than you must. Good. I am pleased with you.'

Jotan was watching impassively. When Jehan caught his eye, he nodded. 'I'm still not convinced,' he said. 'But I've never known you to be wrong. Very well. Go. You have my permission.'

Burun looked pleased. He stood up, and Jotan bowed formally to him. 'Father, look after my son.'

'I will,' Burun said. He crossed the room and went outside.

Jehan stood up. Jotan was watching him again, his expression brooding.

'Burun is right,' he said suddenly. 'You are the cleverest of us all.'

Jehan felt absurdly pleased. He had always felt that he was overshadowed by his father's presence and achievements.

'You know what Burun intends, of course.' Jotan was adjusting his mantle as he spoke.

Jehan nodded. 'He means the next Kha-Khan to be a Merkut.' He watched his father for a reaction. He was not sure how much Jotan knew or guessed about Burun's plots and schemes.

It was as if Jotan had frozen into immobility. 'Name of God. Are you certain?'

'No.' Jehan restrained a laugh. The awe on his father's face was comical.

'Name of God.' Jotan shook his head. He walked slowly to the door, then stopped and looked back. 'Be careful until I see you again.'

14

'Father, I will.' Jehan followed his father outside.

The escort filled the courtyard. Most of the troopers had swathed themselves in cloaks, their lances at rest. The covered area of the ward was not big enough to hold all of them, and those who had been unable to shelter from the rain were trying to dry the metal of their harnesses. An orderly led Jehan's bay out of the shelter of the archway which led to the stables. The st'lyan was covered with a blanket, and Joden whisked it away and in almost the same motion boosted Jehan up into the saddle. The animal backed up a few paces, ducking her head nervously until Jehan had the reins under control. The sweep of her great gilded horn endangered a pair of servants who were loading a pack animal, and they flinched as the st'lyan tossed her head.

Burun clapped Jotan on the shoulders. 'Don't worry. We'll be back in no time.'

Jotan nodded. Jehan guessed that he was hiding his true feelings. Burun turned away as if he had noticed nothing. He pulled himself into the saddle of a grey mare, and stabbed his feet into the stirrups.

'Are you taking the coast road?' Jotan was looking past Burun at Jehan as he spoke.

Burun shook his head. 'We'll take the road across the plain.'

Suddenly everyone was mounted. The troopers began to ride out of the gate in double file. Jehan urged his st'lyan through the crowd, and he was followed by Joden. They fell into line four or five pairs from the front of the column. The paving of the streets outside was wet and slippery, and the noise of the hooves passing over the stones rang off the gables of the houses.

'It's a three-day ride,' Joden said. 'Do you know where your grandfather intends to sleep tonight?'

'No.' Jehan shook his head. 'There are inns aplenty. I travelled this way once when I was a child.'

'In the Old Khan's time.' Joden was watching the pair of riders ahead, using his reins judiciously so that he did not start to overtake. 'Now there was a man.'

Jehan wondered if Joden had been eavesdropping while he was waiting outside. He watched the officer's olive-skinned features, but it was apparent that Joden meant nothing more than a statement of fact. Everyone spoke of the reign of Arjun as if it was the greatest time in history. Certainly the Khanate had expanded to cover the whole of the known world, and Yek arms had been unbeaten in the field for a period of over thirty years. They were still unbeaten, but the fact was less important now because there was no one left worth fighting.

'Artai will be Kha-Khan now.' Jehan was glad that he had spoken softly.

'Lord?' Joden's face was blank.

'Nothing.'

Jehan turned his head, then stood in the stirrups to stare back down the column. Burun's standard was close to the rear of the main body. His staff were clustered around him, and when Jehan saw Suragai he guessed that Kadan was somewhere close by.

'This is a strange time to be leaving Kinsai,' Joden said.

Jehan turned back. They were passing other great houses now, and he saw how the sentries marked who was in the column by the banners. If Burun wanted to convince the other Khans that he was serious about retiring from court, there was probably no better way than to absent himself on minor business at a time when everyone else was jostling for position around Artai.

There were a few people on the streets, and when

they saw the Merkut totem on the standard they stepped politely to one side. Most of them bowed.

'It's a good time,' Jehan said. 'The weather is mild.'

Joden made a face. 'Oh. I wasn't talking about the weather.'

Jehan grinned. 'I know.'

Kinsai was built upon a volcanic plug which stood up out of the centre of the plain. No one had ever been permitted to build outside the walls, and there was a single causeway which wound down to the flat land below. As soon as the head of the column had passed through the gates, groups of scouts and outriders galloped ahead. About a hundred men who were being commanded by one of Burun's older officers dropped back as soon as they had descended to the fields, and soon Jehan could not see them even when he stood in the stirrups.

'Rear guard,' Joden said. 'Your grandfather is being cautious.'

Jehan was not surprised. Keraistan was settled land which had been at peace for over twenty years, however it would have been remarkable if Burun had travelled anywhere without observing a few precautions.

The column rode into a crossroads, and at once the pace slowed. When Jehan reined out to the side to see what was causing the delay, he found a Shaman with two acolytes coming the other way. The man was dressed in blue vestments, and his beard was curled in the style of the people who lived in the far south of the continent. Several of the troopers were bowing in the saddle, and one muttered an invocation. Jehan caught the Shaman's eye and nodded politely. Then he rode on.

Shortly before nightfall they rode down the side of a

17

hill and stopped at a staging inn. The road ran through groves of trees, and the land all around was lush and fertile. Two rivers had their source in the area, and there was good grazing for hundreds of vèrst in every direction.

'Is this your grandfather's land?' Joden asked.

'Yes,' Jehan nodded. 'We have been on a Merkut fief for about four hours. Most of our st'lyan are bred around here.'

Merkut colours decorated the inn, and its keeper was waiting anxiously outside the door. The lamps had been lit, and there were slaves to guide the animals to their stabling.

When the innkeeper saw Jehan, he bowed. 'Noyon, I had no word of your grandfather's coming until the scouts arrived. I have a caravan of Y'frike staying overnight, and there are some nobles who have been travelling in the south, or I would have reserved the best rooms –'

Joden dismounted. He caught the bridle of Jehan's mare, and Jehan swung down from the saddle. At once a slave ran forward and took both sets of reins.

'The Khan is over there,' Jehan pointed. 'Speak to him if you have a problem.'

'Yes, Lord.' The innkeeper looked disappointed. Jehan guessed that he had been expected to intercede, and he grinned. If the inn was full it would not matter. Except that it was the season of rain, Burun would be just as happy to sleep beneath the stars.

Burun sidestepped his st'lyan out of the crowd. He dismounted, then threw his reins to a waiting slave. 'What's this, Gurai? I'm told you have no room for me.'

'Lord –' the innkeeper began nervously.

'Well, no matter.' Burun brushed dust from his robes, and it was as if the innkeeper had never

18

spoken. 'I have too many men with me, in any case, for you to be able to accommodate them all. Send a servant to show my aide where they may camp. I and my officers will use your public room. I suppose you can feed us?'

The innkeeper looked relieved. 'Oh, most certainly, Khan.'

'Good.' Burun nodded with an economy which seemed to end the conversation. He walked past everyone into the inn.

Most of the men were dismounting now.

'Officers.' Joden looked pleased. 'That means us. Come on.' He followed Burun inside.

The inn was built in the old style. For those who were shy about sharing their pleasures or their sleep with others, a wooden arcade around three sides of the main room supported a gallery at first-floor level off which opened private chambers. Oil lamps blazed in profusion, and there was an enormous stone hearth where the cooks laboured. The musicians were nomad gypsies from Khitai, the flat steppe which stretched for thousands of verst across the continent. They flooded the centre of the floor with noise and colour, and danced in the footsteps of tumblers, a harpist, jugglers, and a trainer of animals who seemed to have introduced most of his stock into the inn for the diversion of the travellers. The walls were hung with silks and damasks which had seen better days. The material was bleached and stained in places, and the variety of the colours clashed with the hues worn by the occupants of the room.

Jehan, seated at one end of a long low table of some dark wood, found his eyes dazzled by the blaze of marching lights, his senses drugged by the smells of spices, mulled wine, and the heat from the fat-spitting cook fire. Burun had vanished. Joden was arguing with a portly butler, and the rest of the column's officers were already spread around the room, mingling with the throng which packed the inn to capacity.

'Food.' Joden returned suddenly with a laden platter. 'At least the cook knows what he's about.'

The meat was venison which had been roasted on one of the turning spits, drowned in a gravy which made Jehan's mouth water. A serving woman was laying out bread, salt, cups for wine, and a flask which was designed to satisfy twenty men rather than two. Jehan sliced the meat and forked it into his mouth with his talons. Suddenly he was seized by an un-believable hunger.

Burun slid into the seat opposite. At once a slave brought a clean platter and more wine. His grand-father had changed into clean robes, and Jehan was abruptly conscious of his dusty mantle and travel-stained boots. Slicing venison with his d'jaga, Burun said, 'Enjoy the food, but finish quickly. There is someone for you to meet.'

Jehan was caught by surprise. 'Oh?'

Burun was studying the other tables. 'You don't think I followed the road across the plains for the good of my health, do you?'

'It's shorter than the coast road. I thought maybe you were in a hurry.' Even as he spoke, Jehan realised that the timing of Burun's journey had been far too opportune.

Burun grinned crookedly. 'I've never been in that much of a hurry in my life. Have you finished yet?'

'I can eat later.'

'Then suppose you follow me.' Burun signalled, and the innkeeper came suddenly out of the crowd.

'The room is ready, Khan. You have it for an hour. It is the fourth from the top of the stairs.' A key appeared in the man's hand. 'You know the stairs, Khan?'

Burun snorted softly. 'I remember they exist. I'll find the room. Jehan, come along.' He took the key out of the innkeeper's hand.

Jehan rose, and then he hesitated. He was experiencing an overwhelming sense of wariness, and it occurred to him to wonder why Burun was involving him in something which was clearly secret. Already Burun was crossing the packed common room, and as Jehan started after him he realised that a divide had been crossed. The bond of trust was a fragile thing, and it could only survive so long as he believed that Burun's actions were for the best.

A narrow passageway leading from the far corner of the room gave access to a flight of back stairs. The stairway was dark and winding, and brought them eventually to a portion of the first-floor gallery which could not be seen from below. Panelled wooden doors along a corridor bore numbers in Syraic script. Burun unlocked the fourth and went inside with Jehan at his heels. The door was on some kind of spring, and it slammed shut behind them.

The chamber was dark, lit by a single oil lamp. It held a bed which was uncurtained, and there was a table, a mirror, a rack for arms, and on a cushioned bench against one wall sat a man who was apparently only a little older than Jehan. He was tall, golden-haired with tawny skin, and in addition to the silver-grey clan staining which was tattooed onto his eyelids there was an unusual gold caste mark high on one cheek.

Jehan recognised him at once. 'Alexei. What are you doing here?'

'Spying for your grandfather, it seems.' The observation was made drily, as if the discovery was not an

21

altogether welcome one. Suragai's eldest son bowed to Burun. 'Khan, I did not expect your presence.'

Burun, apparently impervious to Alexei's tone of voice, located a flask and cups beneath the table. He poured wine, and in silence he offered Alexei a full cup. Jehan noted the frozen politeness which seemed to exist between the two, and he wondered if he had at last encountered someone who was not completely in awe of the legend which surrounded his grandfather. Alexei was an offworlder like his father, and it was rumoured that the two did not get on. Suragai served Burun as close counsellor, but Alexei was an intimate of the court of the Kha-Khan and was reputed to spend his days in the company of the younger Altun. He kept the kind of household which was otherwise proper to an heir to the Dragon Throne, and his behaviour with a number of ladies of the court was the scandal of Kinsai. A score of feuds with enraged husbands or fathers went unsettled only because Alexei had no talons, and could not therefore be engaged in kanly, the Yek form of duel to the death which was fought under strict rules with the retractable claws which grew from the finger ends of the True People.

Still in silence Burun hitched himself smoothly onto the edge of the table. He lifted his own cup and drank. Alexei inspected the cup in his hand as if he suspected the contents. Then he drank.

'I chose this place because I wanted you to know who you had been serving these last five years,' Burun said into the stillness. 'Who did you think was keeping you in such princely state? Nogai?'

Alexei looked startled. After a moment he nodded.

'– A natural assumption.' Burun sounded satisfied. 'You were friends, after all. But the reports you sent came to me, and the honours you received came from my hand. Would you have accepted them if you had known their true source?'

Jehan watched Alexei's expression, and grinned at the sudden antagonism he saw there.

'Khan –' Alexei gestured. '– It would have depended on what I was being asked to do. In the event I was requested only to write letters about the doings of those of the Altun with whom I was regularly in contact –'

'– As a result of which a number of possibly troublesome conspiracies were prevented,' Burun finished smoothly. 'Surely you knew what effect your reports had? I never took you for a fool.'

Alexei flushed angrily. 'Khan, if it is any business of yours, of course I knew. I thought that I was serving the Kha-Khan.'

'And so you were.' Burun's answer was soft. 'And so you were.'

Jehan picked up the third cup from the table, filled it from the flask, and drank. He was not sure why he was present. Burun and Alexei were ignoring him as they sparred, and he did not like the sensation that there were events here which involved him and were at the same time out of his control.

Alexei stretched out his legs. Then he laid down his cup and stared at Burun. 'So why am I here? And what proof have I that you are my master?'

'That you are here at all ought to be proof enough,' Burun said.

'Not necessarily. You could have intercepted a letter or letters. I did not identify myself, but it would have been easy for you to work out who was the author. Nogai's death is a perfect opportunity to bend me to your service. I cannot after all ask him for the truth of the matter.'

Burun showed his teeth. 'A fair point. You are

cautious. Very well, I believe you are returning to Kinsai?'

Alexei looked down at the polished wood of the floor between his boots. 'You are well informed, Khan.'

'Not at all. Anyone who is anyone is going to the capital for Artai's enthronement. I will return there myself in due course.'

'– But not yet.' Alexei made the observation innocently.

Burun's expression was unreadable. 'No,' he said. 'Not yet.'

Jehan guessed that Alexei knew the real reason for Burun's journey, and reflected that it was becoming ever more certain that his grandfather's announcement of retiral from court had been a blind.

'– In the meantime –' Burun gestured. '– I offer you the means to ingratiate yourself with the Kha-Khan elect. It is now the bronze month. In two weeks' time a group of the Khans will co-ordinate the activities of their tumans to impose martial law upon Kinsai. They intend to confine Artai within the Golden Yurt, and to permit his installation as Kha-Khan on condition of his acceptance of a petition to appoint one of their number supreme military leader of the Khanate. The nominee will of course become the effective ruler, and the Kha-Khan will be nothing more than a figurehead.'

'I'm surprised they don't simply overturn Nogai's will.' Alexei made the observation calmly.

'Hunh.' Burun nodded. 'They could take that course. But they are by no means certain that they have the support to win an election. This way at least the form of the Yasa will be preserved.'

Jehan thought that he ought to be appalled by the conversation. Minor breach of the Yasa was commonplace enough, it was true. But there was an element here which conflicted with everything upon which the Yek way of life was based.

Alexei seemed to consider. Finally he said, 'I am trying to persuade myself that this revelation to me is not also of great advantage to yourself.'

Burun smiled gently. 'Of course I stand to gain. The moment he hears about the plot, Artai will call on everyone he knows to be loyal for protection and aid. Probably he will beg me to defer my retirement from court. Whatever happens the interests of the Merkut clan will be furthered by the removal from influence of the faction which has instigated the affair.'

Alexei nodded. 'It is Sidacai, of course.'

Burun looked at his hands, then laughed softly. 'I said you were not a fool.' He started to name the conspirators, listing the numbers of men involved and the times and places, while Jehan wondered how he had come by the knowledge.

A scant half hour later Alexei stood up. He nodded briefly to Jehan, walked to the door, then turned. 'My reward from Artai could make me independent of you, Khan.'

'Yes.' Burun did not appear to be disturbed by the prospect. 'It is to be hoped that the Kha-Khan elect will be generous. But do you know of a better way for me to demonstrate that you are already my servant?'

Alexei smiled. 'You would have to say that, of course. Spare me further proofs, I beg you. I do not think that I can sustain the role which you are creating for me.'

Burun did not smile, and his answer was perfectly serious. 'Have no fear. We are well matched. Will you speak with your father before you leave?'

Alexei's expression was a mixture of amusement and exasperation. 'And have the master of your spies wonder why he did not know that his son was your agent? I think not.' He went out.

Burun poured more wine. He drank slowly. Jehan listened for the sound of Alexei's footsteps receding along the passageway outside. He shifted restlessly.

'You wonder why I brought you here,' Burun said. 'Think of it as a lesson in the politics of power.'

Jehan flushed. He laid his cup aside, then walked to the door and opened it. When he looked back, Burun had not moved from his perch on the table. Jehan closed the door gently. Then he walked along the shadowed corridor towards the light of the gallery.

Suragai said, 'My son was here.'

Jehan sipped k'miss and tried without success to compose his features.

'Don't bother to deny it.' Suragai sat down at the table. 'Your officer saw him riding away, and told me.'

Jehan wondered at Joden's lack of discretion. He looked up. 'He had business with my grandfather. Don't ask me to tell you what it was about.'

'Oh.' Suragai looked amused. 'I won't. I only wanted to see what you would say when I asked you.'

Jehan wondered if Suragai knew that his son was one of Burun's spies. Probably he did, and concealed his knowledge. Only a fool gave away everything he knew.

Burun came across the room and sat down. Jehan waited for Suragai to say something about Alexei, but he did not. Burun's attention was fixed upon a group of men who were sitting at an adjacent table. Most of them wore Arcutt clan tattoos, their eyelids shaded emerald green.

'Mark me,' one said. 'This youngling will make a ruin of the Khanate, and it is Nogai's doing. We ought to have elected Siban.'

26

The men who were facing in Burun's direction seemed to become aware that they were under scrutiny. A slave brought wine, and Burun took a cup and sipped from it.

'Your pardon.' Burun raised his eyes and stared at the man who had spoken. 'I don't know your name.'

The Arcutt paled visibly. 'Atagai,' he said. 'I am a lesser Khan of the Seljuk Arcutt.'

'Hunh.' Burun nodded evenly. 'I know your lord, of course. Well you are on my land, and here you may say what you please – what you believe. But so far as Nogai is concerned, I think you are mistaken.'

A second man so like the first that they had to be brothers spoke quickly. 'Nogai's success as Kha-Khan was surely due to his counsellors, Lord. Men such as yourself –'

The overt flattery made Burun show his teeth in a grim smile. 'They did not call him Nogai the Wise for nothing. When he asked for my advice, I gave it. But if it was his grandfather who made us great in war, yet so it was Nogai who showed us how to rule in peace.'

The man who had named himself as Atagai sat up. 'Nogai is dead,' he observed coldly. 'It is Artai who concerns us now. I think he's a boy, guided by rogues who want nothing more than their own advancement.'

Burun seemed to consider a retort, but it was Suragai who spoke first. 'Artai's counsellors are men such as he you named first,' he said. 'Siban for one –'

Another of the Arcutt flushed angrily. 'It was not Siban Khan to whom my lord referred.'

Suragai looked at the speaker calculatingly, and the man's eyes dropped.

Burun chuckled suddenly. 'Peace,' he said. 'As I said, you may speak as you please here. Even if I were still a counsellor to the Kha-Khan, and in fact I am not, I would take no offence.'

The news was clearly a surprise. 'Khan, I meant no insult.' It was the man called Atagai who spoke.

'Hunh.' Burun stared. 'I think you did, but it matters not.'

The Arcutt went crimson. 'Khan, I would be happy to offer you satisfaction.'

Burun sat back. 'No doubt. But as I have said, I take no offence. Why should I kill you?'

There was no immediate answer. Jehan wondered if the incident had been deliberately staged. The Arcutt could not have failed to know who Burun was before starting to speak.

'Well.' Suragai stretched so that his size was apparent. 'We don't have to fight seriously.' His tone was idle. 'But we might have some sport.'

'Sport?' Several of the Arcutt looked interested.

'Yes.' Suragai looked across the table. 'For instance we could wrestle.'

Burun was grinning. 'Yes.' He nodded. 'So we could.'

News of the proposed match communicated itself rapidly around the inn. The innkeeper appeared, looking concerned for his furniture, and was drawn aside by an aide. Gold coins changed hands. One side of the floor was filled with Y'frike, tall dark-skinned men from the continent to the south. At first their only concern was to wager upon the outcome of the contests, but as soon as they realised that Burun was prepared to back the wrestlers of his side with considerable sums in gold koban against possession of the sleeping quarters which had been reserved by the travellers who formed the opposition, their interest became more practical. A caravan master who was nearly Suragai's equal in size and stature began to remove his robes. His muscles rippled in the light of the lamps, and Burun laughed aloud.

The chamber was transformed. With the tables pulled back and sawdust sprinkled to soak up the wetness of the spilled wine, an improvised wrestling ring was packed on every side by an audience which was hotly partisan. The Arcutt were riding with only a small escort, but all of them were in the crowd. The Y'frike, distinctive in their midnight-blue *kefiyah*, were a complete side of the square, and Merkut troopers and their officers held their lances horizontally to keep back the press of bodies.

Burun tossed a heavy leather satchel to Jehan. 'Your job is to pay any winner from the other side. Also you take a key from anyone who loses.'

'I would rather fight.' Jehan weighed the satchel. It was heavy enough to contain a year's tithe from Burun's southern domains.

'I expect you would.' Burun nodded appraisingly. 'Very well. If there is a challenge from someone who is of suitable size and weight, you may give the bag to Hodai. But be careful if you fight the Arcutt. You realise this was planned?'

Jehan was not surprised. 'I wondered.'

'I'll fight last.' Burun's voice was calm. He was watching the Arcutt Khan as he spoke.

'You think the man Atagai means to disable you?'

'I think he'll kill me if he can. Don't worry, Noyon. I was well warned. Why do you think Suragai suggested this?'

In the ring the Arcutt noble who had defended Siban was already circling a Merkut officer, the commander of Burun's own tuman, whose name was Arghatun. Both men were stripped to the waist, stalking each other on stockinged feet, their arms outstretched to make the first hold. The noble leapt, and Arghatun grappled, twisted, and there was a cry and a crash. The Merkuts in the crowd cheered.

The throw was agreed fair. The Arcutt yielded up a key and retired to the far side of the room, shaking his head. Arghatun, grinning, began to dress again.

Burun's aide Hodai took on the brother of the Arcutt Khan, a man with more art to his wrestling than sinew, and threw him swiftly. Jehan added a second key to his collection.

Joden threw, apparently for the fun of the encounter, a young Y'frike caravan guard and a junior officer of the Arcutt escort. Neither of them had room keys to give up, but they were wildly cheered for their sportsmanship, and retired bruised but cheerful.

The Y'frike caravan master climbed into the ring and stood waiting. There was a delay while Suragai disrobed. His back was criss-crossed by old scars, and the men who saw them muttered in awe. Y'zan, the commander of Suragai's guard, was holding his master's garments as he stood beside Jehan. 'This will be worth watching,' he said.

It was apparent at once that the Y'frike was no novice. His feet scarcely left the timbers of the floor as he sidled forward, and he offered as little of himself to a hold as was possible. Suragai pattered in lightfooted, his speed taking everyone by surprise. One foot scythed out, catching the caravan master on the right calf. The man gasped and went down on one knee. Then he rose and charged. The crowd roared, but Suragai was no longer in the same position. Instead he had thrown himself to one side. Catching a reaching hand as it went past, he whipped the Y'frike round, then let go. The dark-skinned bulk spun away, and the shaft of a lance shattered as the caravan master hit the crowd.

Jehan expected Suragai to move in and finish the

bout, but the offworlder waited patiently for his opponent to recover. The Y'frike got up slowly. There was a bleak kind of respect in his expression now, and before he came forward again he seemed to nod as if he was acknowledging an equal. His first move was a feint. An arm came out, but as Suragai moved to one side he was charged, his guard beaten aside. The Y'frike stooped, clasped, and drew the offworlder into a muscular embrace. His hands were locked across Suragai's back, and the watching Merkuts groaned.

Then the lamentation became a gasp and finally a roar of appreciation. Slowly, unbelievably, the offworlder was expanding his arms inside the bear hug which enclosed them against his chest. The Y'frike strained, his eyes wide with disbelief as his locked hands were forced apart. Suddenly Suragai bent and turned. The caravan master went down with a crash which shook every timber in the inn.

Jehan, who had not wagered, found himself wishing that he had accepted the shouted odds which had been offered at the instant when Suragai had been enfolded in the Y'frike's embrace. The offworlder was bending down to help his opponent to his feet, and the Merkut troopers who had backed him were going wild.

A third key was added to the collection in Jehan's possession, and there was a pause while everyone who could still afford it called for wine.

The excitement which had heralded the start of the wrestling had died a little now. It was as if it was accepted that the match involving Suragai was the high point. Suddenly Jehan saw that the Arcutt Khan was climbing over the barrier of lances. Burun was already disrobed. Then the floor was clear, and on it was the Khan of the Merkuts, solid and well-built but clearly aging, facing a man who was perhaps ten or

31

fifteen years his junior. Burun's face was solemn, his eyes thoughtful. He had stripped to his hose, and now he seemed to be prepared to wait for his challenger to attack.

Suragai, still only partly clothed, shouldered his way to Jehan's side. 'This is as it was planned, Noyon.'

'Is it?' Jehan pointed, surprised that his voice was so steady. 'The Arcutt has oiled himself. My grandfather won't be able to gain a hold.'

'Well.' Suragai seemed to be untroubled. 'Not at first maybe.'

The match began at great speed, and it was clear that the Arcutt wanted to disable his opponent quickly. Burun's opponent was of almost equal height, and while he had no advantage of weight, he was obviously younger and fitter. He moved in fast, and there was a flurry of blows which aroused a mutter of comment. If Burun was troubled he did not show it. He backed out of range, blocking methodically, busy in the face of Atagai's impatience. Occasionally he caught at a striking hand or foot, and then there was a thud as he returned blow for blow, but he was never able to maintain his grip, and always the Arcutt drew back with a grunt, then came on again.

All at once Burun appeared to trip. The wave of comment ceased as the Arcutt charged, and in the same instant Burun had recovered. His hands were full of sawdust, and he showered Atagai with the stuff and danced away.

The watching crowd was shouting comment and opinion again. With his oil coated by fine sawdust the younger man was susceptible to a variety of holds. He shook his head as if to clear his vision, turned to locate Burun, and came forward once more.

With a space of no more than a length separating them, both men seemed to pause and there was a moment of silence. The Arcutt was breathing with a queer whistle which was oddly disturbing. It was as if every breath was catching at the back of his throat, and as he circled to the left Jehan was aware that the match was on an equal footing. The contestants had no weapons against one another other than their hands and feet, their speed and stamina, and the obvious strength of their muscles. Burun was no longer showing his age, and Atagai was moving slowly and cautiously, an odd light in his eyes.

The Yek only ever wrestled for sport. The races of the True People – the Yek, the N'Pani and the Ch'noze – were all equipped with talons which made any form of hand-to-hand combat a potentially deadly affair. Thus in wrestling almost anything short of the clawed slash which could open flesh to the bone was permitted, and it was apparent that both Burun and his opponent knew every trick. A thumb sliding into an eye was the answer to a knee lock. Burun's head jerked back at once, but Atagai's hands came up and caught at the older man's scalp lock. Burun's outstretched hands saved him from being thrown face first onto the floor. He rolled, lashed out with one foot, and the Arcutt gasped and fell back.

It was an escape which was only just good enough. The two men closed at once, grasping one another around the shoulders. Burun's breathing was fast, and his complexion was livid beneath the bronze tan which was the result of a life spent beneath the red sun. The Arcutt fought for a lock and found it. Setting his arms in the same full hug which the Y'frike caravan master had applied in the previous contest he slowly increased the pressure in an attempt to crush Burun.

Burun's face became darkly congested. His hands seemed to search for a new hold, and then he caught

33

at the pads of flesh which covered his opponent's shoulder blades. With his talons still retracted he gripped and wrung until Atagai cried out and loosened his hold. At once Burun seemed to force the encircling hug aside. He slid to one side, and his two clasped hands met at the back of the Arcutt's neck. His knuckles whitened. A vein was beating rapidly in Burun's temple, and then inexorably the Arcutt's head began to bow towards his chest.

It was at that moment, with the watching crowd holding its collective breath at the unlooked-for spectacle, that Jehan saw that Burun was speaking softly to the man who was helpless beneath his hands. The words were inaudible, but it was clear that the Arcutt understood. His bloodshot eyes widened, and then his lips seemed to compress as if he was biting down on his answer. Burun spoke again, but his question received no reply, and at last he seemed to be satisfied. His grip relaxed by a fraction, and then, just as the Arcutt was drawing his first shuddering breath, Burun's hands slid beneath Atagai's chin, and he pulled up and back.

There was an audible click, and then the man who was secured by Burun's interlocked arms slumped limply onto the sawdust.

The expression in Burun's eyes was perplexed as he released his hold and stepped away. 'Name of God, that was careless. I've broken this fellow's neck for him.'

There was an instant of frozen silence, and then the room exploded. The disbelieving jeers which met Burun's statement became hysterical whoops as the Arcutt's decease was confirmed. His body was lifted and borne away.

No one seemed to think that it was appropriate to approach the nobles of the Arcutt party for the key to the dead man's room. Forced forward by the press of the crowd, Jehan saw only that their faces looked sick. Merkut officers were clearing a space round Burun. A cloak was thrown around his shoulders, and with Suragai hustling spectators aside they escaped into the quiet of a passageway.

'Why did you kill him?' The words were out of Jehan's mouth before he could stop them.

Burun looked up. Already his breathing had eased and there was only an intense tiredness in his eyes. 'I asked him to tell me who had sent him.'

'And did he tell you?'

'No.' Burun laughed harshly. 'That is why I had to kill him. Now when I move against them, my enemies will think that he told me everything. My other sources will be protected.'

Jehan was not sure that he understood. He was about to pursue the subject, then something in Burun's expression warned him that he had over-stepped his right to question. Suragai was at Burun's shoulder. He had not spoken, and his expression was sombre, brooding. Suddenly Jehan guessed that the offworlder was probably the only person apart from his grandfather who actually knew what was going on, and in that moment he felt anger, and then fear and mistrust. As a boy he had liked Suragai, but that was before he understood the alien's function. Probably Suragai was deeply involved in the intrigue which was at the root of everything. It was in that instant that Jehan vowed that if he ever became Khan of the Merkuts, then on that day Suragai would be dismissed to some remote outland fief. If it was necessary to employ such a man in order to remain Khan, then it was likely that the power which resulted was tainted and not worth having.

Suragai's eyes were still watching, and Jehan

looked quickly away. He was sure that his emotions were plain, and he feared the offworlder's ability to read them and to interpret their intent.

It was in the afternoon two days later that they rode up the steep path to Burun's fortress of Zr'nadai. Like Kinsai the keep was situated on a plug of volcanic rock which stood up out of the surrounding countryside. Here however the summit was only large enough to accommodate the walled enclosure, and the town had been constructed around the base of the rock so that the houses spread out across the fertile valley.

The grass was bright green, but each spike was tinged with a spine of light blue. The air smelled richly of the sharp scent which came from the sap and needles of the tall, black-barked pine trees. The fortress was constructed of dark red stone, and it seemed to float in the air above a sea of pines.

Burun's banners were flying from the tower, and the men of the garrison were lined up along the rampart which was on either side of the gate, their lances at the salute. The troopers at the head of the column trotted their st'lyan briskly into the courtyard. There were people leaning out of every window in the inner wall, and when they saw Burun they cheered. Jehan's mare reared nervously at the noise, and he hauled on the reins to bring her under control again. When Burun dismounted the people cheered again. He walked into the middle of the yard, and at once his steward came out of the crowd which was waiting beside the door.

'Lord.' The man bowed respectfully. 'It is good to see you well.'

Burun laughed drily. 'Well. Hah, you should see my bruises. Natan, you are growing grey in my service.'

The steward nodded and smiled. 'More silver than

grey, Khan. You have not changed.'

'Hunh.' Burun snorted. 'We are all older.'

The people were beginning to disperse now. The cook was chasing the scullions back to work, and only a few serving women loitered at one of the windows, aware that the eyes of the troopers were upon them. Jehan dismounted and threw his reins to one of the grooms. Officers had already started to allocate quarters and stabling, and the courtyard was emptying fast.

'The harvest was good.' Natan spoke again. 'But Khan, I'm glad you're here. There are some matters for you to settle, and there is a dispute to be heard.'

'Yes.' Burun nodded. 'Do you know my grandson?'

The steward bowed to Jehan. 'Noyon. You came here once with your father.'

Jehan remembered. He had been five or six at the time. 'That's right. You made me a bow –'

'– And you shot a p'tar for practice, and it went wild. We had to kill it.'

'Yes.' Jehan felt himself going red at the memory. 'My father gave me such a beating. I couldn't sit down for a day.'

He remembered the enraged pack beast – a larger and coarser version of the basic st'lyan stock, although it lacked a horn – and the feel of the bow in his hand. The satisfaction which he had felt as his child's arrow found its mark in the animal's rump had changed to terror as it had bellowed, and then had commenced kicking its stall to pieces.

'Every boy gets at least one good beating in his life,' Burun said. He clapped Natan on the shoulder and together they walked towards the door. Jehan followed. A serving woman lingered artfully beside the door as he passed, and he ignored her carefully.

The hall inside the keep had a high ceiling, and the

37

furniture was old and blackened both by time and by exposure to the heat and smoke from the fire which burned in the enormous hearth during the cold months. The gloomy shadows reminded Jehan of the games he had played here as a child, and the other less happy memory was banished at once and he felt strangely comforted.

'We are clearing the land which lies at the far end of the valley,' Natan said. His finger traced an area on the map. 'It is going very well. It will be under the plough next year.'

'Good.' Burun glanced up. 'How much have you cleared? Remember the Yasa.'

The law permitted only a set amount of forest to be cut and cleared for cultivation, the area being determined in proportion to the number of people who lived on the land.

'We have cleared a hide. I have sokemen who were your slaves before they were freed, and I think they may be trusted to work land which is so far removed.'

Burun nodded. 'Very well. Remember to notify the Kha-Khan's bailiff. Once you have a crop he will assess the revenue.'

Natan rolled up the map. Jehan thought that he was going to raise an objection, but the steward only nodded. 'Lord, I will.'

Somewhere out among the trees which surrounded the slopes below the keep a bird called thrice. Burun's head came up, and then he turned back to the fire.

'There was a writ from Kinsai to restore jurisdiction over the land on the west bank of the river to the Kerait clan.' Natan pored over a page of the ledger which he had drawn onto his lap. 'Shall I do it?'

'God, no. Are they still on about that?'

38

The steward shrugged. 'Strictly speaking the land on the west side is theirs.'

'They forfeited it years ago.'

'Yes, Khan. But every case I have which concerns the place, the Khan of the Keraits claims belongs to him. I judge them anyway, and he can do nothing. But he has collected old men who will swear that such-and-such a matter was always decided by the Keraits. I am collecting men who will swear the opposite.'

'Hunh.' Burun gestured impatiently. 'I can deal with this before the Kha-Khan when things are more settled.' He picked up a cup from the table, and filled it with k'miss.

Jehan thought that he had passed the land in question on the journey to Zr'nadai. A small Kerait fief lay almost isolated by a bend in the river. As the bend grew wider, etching the bank away on one side and depositing silt on the other, land was being lost by the Keraits and gained by the Merkuts.

'Sinan has an accounting of the tithes which were sent to Kinsai,' Natan said. 'But I can find my own tally if you wish.'

Burun shook his head. 'No. I'll catch up with Sinan.' He drank.

Outside the keep the same bird call sounded again. This time it was Natan who looked up, and Jehan wondered if the cry was real, or if one of Burun's agents was signalling to be let in at the wicket gate which was set into the wall at the steepest part of the rock.

Natan stood up. 'Khan, I ought to go down –'

'Yes.' It was as if Burun knew the reason for the interruption without being told. 'Leave all this until tomorrow. Go now.'

The steward bowed deeply. 'Good night, Khan. Good night, Noyon.' He hastened out of the room.

39

Jehan rose. He poured k'miss into a cup and drank. The spirit which was distilled from fermented mare's milk was Burun's favourite drink, but Jehan thought that he preferred wine. He peered out of the narrow window into the blackness below the keep wall, but he could see nothing. When he turned back, Burun was watching the flames rising from the hearth.

'How long are we staying here?' Jehan made his tone casual.

Burun looked up. 'Are you bored already?'

'I'm not sure why you wanted me here.'

'Oh.' Burun looked amused. 'As to that, I wanted you out of Kinsai when the plot against Artai was discovered.'

'Not my father?'

Burun made a face. It was as if he thought that an explanation ought to be unnecessary. 'Jotan is the first person Artai will go to for help. I thought that you might have noticed that every other member of our family is absent from the capital. There is no one else for Artai to trust.'

'Oh.' Jehan felt foolish. He looked away.

'You are troubled of course.' Burun's voice was tranquil. 'If you want me to explain what is going on, I will. But it would be better for you to work it out for yourself. In this instance, as in every other, innocence is your best protection.'

Jehan considered the argument. The Khanate was riddled with intrigue, and only by demonstrating a lack of intimate knowledge could a person hope to avoid the implication of guilt by association.

'I'm the grandson of a Khan. Will anyone believe I know nothing?'

Burun grinned. 'If they know anything about me, they will.'

There was some truth in the remark, but Jehan was

unable to raise an answering smile. Burun's reputation for the devious use of his feudal power was at the root of his concern.

'I don't like what is happening to us.' Jehan watched Burun's face for a reaction. 'Things used to be so much simpler.'

'The issues used to be so much clearer,' Burun said mildly. 'We are a race bred for war and conquest. Now that there is no one left to fight it is difficult for us to occupy ourselves. The Yasa never prepared us for a time of peace when there would be no prospect of military employment. Whereas once a Khan could advance the interests of his clan by gaining new territory, now he is forced to compete with his own kind. And yet the Yasa says that we may not make war upon one another without the permission of the Kha-Khan.'

'The Yasa is broken every day.' Jehan was aware that the objection was ridiculous even as he spoke.

Burun made a face. 'Let us say that we use common sense to amend the laws which are no longer applicable to our situation. The Yasa is altered frequently by the agreement of the people, but it cannot be disregarded. Without the law there would be chaos.'

Somewhere in the keep a door slammed and there was the sound of muttering voices suddenly silenced. The room was oppressively warm, and Jehan struggled to shake off the feeling that he was being kept out of affairs which ought to be his concern. He tried to concentrate on the sense of what Burun was saying, as if winning the argument would alter the whole situation.

'The point is that we are being forced to change before we are ready,' Burun said. 'The Yasa was never constructed for a situation like ours. Nogai knew that, but even he could do little.'

'Surely Nogai was a bad ruler.' Jehan picked up the

41

idea. 'For he failed to introduce changes in the law at a rate which would keep pace with the needs of the people.'

'That's an idealist's approach.' Burun frowned. 'I never took you for one of those.'

Jehan sat down. He could think of nothing to say.

'In the first place it is not the Kha-Khan's responsibility to introduce changes in the law.' Burun picked up the flask of k'miss and drank from it. 'His task is to rule according to the Yasa. Nogai was the best man for the time. If he had lived, I would not be running conspiracies like threads around the Khanate to keep it together.'

'– Conspiracies which support Artai.'

Burun put down the flask. 'That's right. I haven't asked for your opinion about that because I know you don't like him.'

Jehan felt himself flush. 'Are you telling me that you do, Khan?'

'Oh.' Burun laughed grimly. 'I think he's spoiled. He listens to the voice that flatters him the loudest. He has a temper like a cat's, and if we give him too much power, he will use it to destroy us. He has been brought up too much by women, and he has absorbed their ways.'

'– And yet you support his claim to the throne.'

'It was Nogai's will,' Burun said. His eyes were opaque.

'– To give absolute power to a boy whose temper, by your own admission, we cannot trust? Khan, you can do better than that.' Jehan was amazed at his own temerity. Burun was watching him appraisingly, and he looked quickly away.

'It's true that we give the Kha-Khan all the power when we elect him.' Burun spoke after a moment. 'But he cannot rule without the acquiescence of the people. There are some safeguards.'

Jehan allowed his features to display amusement. '– And so you will deny that Artai's rule is supreme? That's a breach of the Yasa, if ever there was one.'

'The Yasa be damned.' Burun growled the reply. 'In this matter as in everything else, every Khan will do what he thinks will serve his interests best, and the Yasa will have nothing to do with it.'

'Obviously.'

Jehan was not sure if he had won a point by gaining such an admission. In his heart of hearts he knew that probably Burun's approach was right.

Burun picked up the k'miss flask again. Suddenly he looked up. 'As with everything that Nogai did, it will all turn out for the best. Artai may not like us, but for the moment he is forced to trust us and to rely upon us.'

'– Because of the plot which you revealed to Alexei.'

'Exactly.'

Jehan reflected that Burun had betrayed a conspiracy to impose exactly the kind of limitations upon Artai's power which he had just admitted were necessary. 'You absented yourself from court so that he would turn to my father for help.' The deduction was obvious.

Burun shrugged. 'Your father is a statesman. Also he is half Altun. Artai will find it easier to trust another member of the Golden Clan.'

Jehan nodded slowly. There were implications which still troubled him. '– You knew about Sidacai's intentions as soon as they were formed –' He stopped.

The k'miss flask was still in Burun's hands. He looked at it as if he did not know how it had got there, then laid it aside. 'I am drinking too much.

Perhaps it is because I am getting old, but I like to drink more. Do you remember when I settled matters with Vortai?'

'Yes.'

'Then you ought to remember that Siban tried to have me condemned for breaking the Yasa. He alleged that I made war on another Khan without permission.'

Vortai had been Burun's father-in-law. The feud between them had been long and bitter, and it had ended with Vortai's death and the disappearance of his son Sipotai in the radiation-poisoned wastes of the G'bai desert.

'I remember that you timed your actions to co-incide with the death of the Kha-Khan.' Jehan met Burun's stare squarely. 'Arjun's death meant that Siban's accusation could never be _proved. And it seems to me that Siban was obliged to accuse you. It was his duty under the Yasa.'

'You've been listening to your father,' Burun commented tartly. 'No one believes that I had authority.'

Jehan suppressed a smile. There was no one alive other than Burun who knew the truth about the episode.

'So far as Siban was concerned, it is true that he had a duty under the law.' Burun gestured. 'But in the event that was not his reason. He hoped that the Merkuts would be disgraced, and that his way would be cleared so that he could ascend the throne. He even tried to bargain with me.'

The logic of Burun's argument was difficult to follow. 'And Sidacai is Siban's son,' Jehan said. 'So now he will be condemned. It does not seem to me that there is a great deal of difference between the two cases.'

Burun showed his teeth, but there was not a trace

44

of humour in his eyes. 'There are a few similarities, yes. The fact makes my revenge the sweeter, although I doubt that you are capable of appreciating that point.'

Jehan guessed that Burun was perfectly capable of instigating the plot which was about to cause Sidacai's downfall. There would be no evidence to connect him with it, of course. 'You are saying that the end justifies the means,' he said. 'Is that what the Yek have come to?'

Burun's expression was remote. It was as if he was staring at something which lay in the middle distance. Then he seemed to hear Jehan's question. 'One day you will be a Khan,' he said. 'Then you will understand.'

Jehan did not know how to reply. 'If Artai is as unsuitable as we both believe, none of this may matter,' he observed lightly.

A sentry's voice called the hour of the watch, and the answers from the guard posts came distantly, like an echo. Burun stirred the fire with an iron poker, and a coal fell into the hearth, showering sparks.

'If Artai lives longer as Kha-Khan than Nogai, I will be surprised.' He spoke softly.

Jehan wondered if the penalties which applied to talk of the death of a ruling Kha-Khan also related to reference to his successor elect. He stood up, avoiding Burun's eyes.

'The headaches.'

'Yes.' Burun nodded. 'Nogai had them as you know. Sometimes he was blinded by the pain. It is the curse of Daijin's line.'

Jehan shivered. 'Daijin was mad.' Suddenly he was aware of his own lineage.

Burun gestured dismissively. 'I know. You are thinking that you are also descended from Daijin.

Both your father and your mother carry his blood. But if you were afflicted, you would know it by now.'

Jehan was displeased to discover that he was so transparent. The majority of the Altun were descendants of Daijin, and perhaps one in four had inherited the genetic defect which resulted in the condition which the Sechem now diagnosed as an incurable brain tumor. In its early stages, presence of the affliction was characterised by occasional blinding headaches.

'And do you think Artai is sane?' The question was one which had occurred to Jehan many times before, but he had never uttered it aloud.

Burun seemed to consider. 'You know him as well as anyone. There have been times when he appeared unbalanced, but consider his upbringing. His tantrums were never discouraged, and perhaps it is not surprising that they have continued past childhood.'

Jehan wondered if his thoughts were still plain upon his face. He had seen Artai at his worst – the fits of uncontrollable anger, the convulsions and vomiting – and he feared for the Khanate in such unsteady hands.

'You support him because you think he can be controlled.' He watched Burun's face. 'What if you are wrong?'

There was a moment when Jehan thought that Burun was going to outline his true objective. Then suddenly it was as if he had changed his mind.

'Trust me.' Burun's tone was soothing, and he spoke like a parent addressing a restive child. 'Only trust me. Everything I do is for you.'

Jehan experienced only mild frustration. He had not really expected a straightforward response. 'You told my father the same thing once.'

Burun's face was suddenly wary. 'Oh?'

'Yes. In front of Pereislav, before the attack. The Kha-Khan had just sent you absolute authority in the war. My father wanted you to use the power to bargain with Nogai – to obtain terms for your support of him when everyone else was against him. You refused.'

Burun seemed to relax. 'I expect I did. But I voted for Nogai in the end. You know I would never have revealed what I intended. And what I said was true then, as it is now. Everything I do is for my children.'

There was no answer to that. No matter how the argument progressed, Burun had the ultimate justification for his actions. Jehan crossed to the door. Then he stopped and turned. 'But you never consult us.'

'Eh?' Burun looked mystified. 'What do you mean?'

Jehan thought briefly before he answered. It was important not to reveal too much knowledge. He opened the door. 'Whether or not we agree with your methods, Khan, is immaterial. What matters is that none of us are sure that we want the same things, or that they are worth the price you would have us pay.'

The morning was full of the arrangement of petty details which, added together, ensured the continued governance of the fief. Jehan followed Burun through an inspection of granaries, but when a group of town elders appeared to discuss matters as varied as the licensing of moneyers and the establishment of standards for the milling of flour and the brewing of ale he became bored and slipped away.

'You will have to attend to such things one day.' Kadan made the observation with obvious amusement.

'Don't remind me.' Jehan scowled. He ignored the salute of a sentry, and tramped steadily along the

47

rampart in the direction of the yard which gave access to the stables. 'I used to think that one kept a steward so that the responsibilities of governance could be delegated to him.'

Kadan was ambling easily at Jehan's side. His long legs matched his cousin's pace without effort. 'Oh, well –' He started to speak, then broke off.

'Yes?' Jehan glanced sideways. Kadan only hesitated when he was remembering to be diplomatic. Probably he had been the recipient of another reminder from his father about the difference between his status and Jehan's.

Kadan looked only a little embarrassed. 'I think a Khan is supposed to demonstrate interest,' he said finally.

It was the kind of thing Burun would have said. 'Huh.' Jehan snorted. 'You ought to be the heir, not I.'

'Kadan Khan. People might have trouble saying it.' His cousin's tone robbed the words of offence.

Jehan's mouth twitched, and then he grinned. He clapped Kadan on the shoulder. Every step he took away from the chamber in which his grandfather was closeted with the town elders seemed to lighten his spirits. The thought of the responsibilities which lay in the future was a shadow which it was easy to disregard.

There had been a light shower of rain about daybreak, and now that the sun was high the paving stones of the keep were beginning to steam gently.

'Why do you find feudal affairs so restricting?' Kadan asked. 'They are your birthright, after all.' A pair of servants were coming along the rampart. They bore bowls filled with fruit and ice, and Kadan stepped nimbly to one side as they bowed in mid-stride, then ran on.

'Blame my father.' Jehan started down the stairs to

the yard. 'He took me to war before I was your age. I grew up expecting that my life would be spent with the tumans.'

Kadan pursed his lips. 'I've never fought in a war, so I wouldn't know about that. Your father doesn't strike me as the kind of man who would enjoy war.'

Jehan glanced sharply at his cousin's face, but there was no malice there. 'You're right. He doesn't. That's why he's so good as a statesman. Unfortunately it is not a quality he ever tried to develop in me.'

The stables were dark and cool. Long lines of boxes sheltered under an arched stone roof. A trough for water ran the length of each wall, and there was an orderliness which could only have been brought about by great attention to detail. Jehan let the door bang, and at once a guard came out of the shadows at the far end of the nearest passageway.

'Hold! Who goes there? Identify yourselves!'

Jehan realised that he was little more than a silhouette in the red light which shone past his shoulder through the slats of the door.

'Jehan Noyon. Let me pass.'

The trooper came along the space between the rows of stable boxes. 'Oh. I'm sorry, Noyon. Who's that with you?'

'Kadan Noyon. Ortai, your eyes must be failing.'

The veteran grounded his lance. 'Maybe they are, Noyon. None of us are getting any younger.' He saluted Jehan, then eyed Kadan up and down. 'Name of God, Noyon, when are you going to stop growing?'

'Oh.' Kadan grinned. 'In another drem or so maybe.'

Jehan chuckled. A drem was a thousandth of a verst. Such a growth would make Kadan the tallest man in creation.

The trooper spat left and right. It was a thing men did in the presence of evil. 'That wouldn't surprise

49

me. Alien blood can't be reckoned, they say. No offence, Noyon.'

Not many people would have cared to remind the sons of Suragai that their father was not human. Jehan watched Kadan's face, but his cousin absorbed the remark placidly. 'None taken. Where are our st'lyan?'

'Over there, Noyon.'

'Thank you.'

Jehan's grey was in the first box of a row. When he edged in past her she sidestepped and tried to crush him against the timber wall. He fisted her in the side, and she screamed and her horn rattled against the wooden manger, then she settled once more.

Kadan watched from the doorway. 'If I didn't know better, I would swear that animal was only half broken,' he said.

'Everyone says my st'lyan have bad manners.' Jehan forced the bit into the mare's mouth. 'This one was my grandfather's gift. All his beasts are wild.'

'I know.' Kadan laughed. 'My father has a chestnut of the same breeding.'

'The big one. I've seen her. It's the steppe cross that makes them so fierce.' Jehan looked across the top of the loose box and saw that the sentry was returning to his patch of shadow. 'You were remarkably forbearing there. Don't insults mean anything to you?'

'If I were to rise to every wrong word, I would never be done fighting.' Kadan's response was calm. 'Ortai is a simple man, and he spoke out of fear and superstition.'

'Hunh.' For all that he had spent a great deal of time in Kadan's company, it was the first time Jehan had ever thought specifically about the alien part of his cousin's origins. 'In any event no one can say that you are not human.'

Kadan flexed one hand thoughtfully. 'That depends upon what you mean by human,' he said. Because his mother was Burun's daughter, he had been born with talons. Their silver tips flashed, then retracted.

Jehan was suddenly embarrassed, and he wished that he had not mentioned the subject. Quickly he turned back to the task of saddling the mare, and after a moment Kadan went into the next box to attend to his own beast. He hummed tunelessly while he worked, and Jehan thought that alien processes of thought must be very strange. He tightened the st'lyan's girth, and then led the grey outside.

'Why was the building abandoned?' Kadan asked. He reined his mount around a small tree which was growing in their path. 'It is not all that far from the town.'

Jehan shrugged. They had ridden almost to the southern end of the valley to inspect a collection of old buildings which Burun intended to offer to the Sechem. In the distance the keep was a red mass on its hilltop. There were animals grazing the steep slopes to one side of the wall. 'A failed commercial venture. Some outlander persuaded my grandfather that he could weave haigus in sufficient quantity to make it worthwhile to carry the stuff for sale to X'nadu.'

'And did he?' Kadan looked interested.

'For a season. His goods were no better than others which were being made closer to market, and those, since they did not have to travel so far, sold for less.' The trees beneath which they were riding were tall with broad copper-coloured leaves. Jehan reined in for a moment, then gestured. 'Let's ride along the river.'

Two tributaries of the river joined near the end of

51

the valley. One came down from the hills and flowed quite fast. The other was part of the meandering mainstream, and it moved in lazy curves across the plain.

'Do the people fish here?' Kadan handled his mare with perfect economy.

'Some of them.' Jehan nodded. 'There are huts along the river bank.'

'Yes. I see them. Is that a ford?'

'It had better be, or we will have to go back upstream.'

The slower-moving portion of the river veered around a low hill, and when they emerged from the trees Jehan saw that there was a flat barge tied up against the far bank. A stone house nestled by the side of a knoll, and to one side stood a yurt, clearly abandoned.

'I didn't know the Keraistani dwelled in yurts.' Kadan gestured at the sagging framework. He stood in the stirrups, and shaded his eyes from the sun with one hand.

'They don't usually.' Jehan saw that someone had tied ropes across the river between sturdy trees so that the barge could be drawn back and forth. 'My grandfather settled a few Ch'noze here, years ago. Maybe this is one of them.'

'In any case he's built himself a house,' Kadan observed.

'That's not all he has built.' Jehan kicked his st'lyan into a trot. 'Come on. Let's see if he'll ferry us across.'

The construction of the barge and its attachments was too sound to be unskilled work. One rope ran through a block and tackle which was hitched to the trunk of a tree. The ends of the rope were fastened to the barge, and another rope ran through a kind of frame so that even if the pulling rope broke the conveyance would not be carried away downstream. While Kadan shouted across the river to attract the attention of the men on the other side, Jehan examined the workmanship. The Sechem had designed a similar system of blocks and pulleys for the drawbridge of the keep. If a fisherman brought his catch to the kitchens he might have seen the device and copied it.

One of the men on the far bank was loosening a mooring rope attached to the barge. He shouted something.

'What did he say?' Kadan turned. 'I can't make him out.'

Jehan listened. The language was Yek, but the vowels were being sounded Ch'noze fashion. 'Something about the animals. He says we can't take both of them across at once. The barge won't take the weight. We'll leave yours tethered here, and come back for it. Mine won't take kindly to being tied up.'

Both of the men from the other bank were hauling on the pulley rope now. It groaned with the strain, and the ungreased pulleys shrieked.

'Should I wait here?' Kadan dismounted.

'No. Come with me. I'm curious to see what he charges.'

Jehan walked down to the edge of the bank. It shelved steeply into the water, and he judged that there would be sufficient depth under the keel of the barge to prevent it bottoming when it accepted the weight of a st'lyan.

One of the ferrymen jumped down into the waist-deep water to hold the prow of the barge steady. The other bowed to Jehan.

'Lord, I remember you. You are the son of the son of the Khan.'

Jehan searched his memory and a name emerged.

53

'Ronen. Now I know you. I thought you were a fisher-man.'

The man looked guilty. 'Well, Lord, part of the ford was washed away the year before last. The river can be crossed easily enough in the dry months, but during the rains –'

'Yes.'

'– I thought it was my duty to help travellers.'

'I see.' Jehan thought that the absence of a proper fording place should have been reported. It would have been no task to deposit more stone. 'And what is your charge for ferrying us across?'

Kadan was leading Jehan's mare down to the edge of the bank. The grey shied nervously as her hooves hit the timbers of the barge.

'Nothing, Lord.'

'Oh? Surely people give you something?'

'Well, sometimes. Just as a token, Lord.' The ferryman's expression was nervous.

Jehan stepped off the bank onto the prow of the barge. The timbers of the vessel were old and well weathered, and he wondered where such a craft might have been obtained. 'And do you still fish?'

The man who was pulling himself out of the water was much the younger. Possibly he was the ferryman's son. Together they began to haul on the rope. The flow of the river aided crossing in this direction, and the barge moved across swiftly.

'Yes, Lord. I still fish. The Khan's steward takes my tithe from my catch.' The barge grounded against the opposite bank as the ferryman spoke. Kadan led the grey off onto a patch of pebbles, and at once the light-ened craft lifted under the force of the water flowing against the keel, and the ropes groaned with the strain.

'And what do you give the Khan for the use of his

river? A tenth of your tolls, is it?'

The ferryman went white. 'Oh, well – you must understand, Lord –'

Jehan had not imagined that Ronen had told the steward about his piece of private enterprise. 'A tenth is fair, is it not?'

The man's shoulders seemed to sag. 'A tenth, Lord.' He nodded.

Already the barge was halfway back across the river with Kadan on board. The pulling was being done by the younger man, and by two youths who had come out of the stone house to assist him. Jehan waited until the craft bumped back against the bank below him, and then he led Kadan's mare off onto dry land. The arms and shoulders of the pullers were slick with sweat, and their faces were turned away.

Jehan felt in his wallet. The smallest coin he had was valued at one thousandth of a koban. He decided that no one would dare charge more than that, and held it out. 'Here. I shall tell the Khan's steward to expect your tenth on settling day.'

'Yes, Lord.' The ferryman's expression was wooden, but he bowed. 'Good day, Lord.'

Kadan was already mounted. Jehan pulled himself into the saddle, and followed him up the slope and into a grove of trees.

'For a person who is not interested in feudal governance, you show a surprising attention to petty detail.' Kadan reined in until he was riding at Jehan's side.

'Do I?' Jehan considered. It was just as Burun had said. The people were changing, and the Yasa was not keeping pace. It was difficult to enforce laws when people had got used to ignoring them. He thought about his conversation with Ronen, and wondered if he had played the tyrant. He decided not. The tribute system was at the basis of the economy. If it was allowed to lapse, everything else would fail.

Among the trees the ground was uneven. There were a few small clearings, but they were covered by tangles of briars.

'This is poor ground.' Kadan reined aside to avoid an outcrop of rock. 'Why did your cloth merchant build here?'

'He wanted to be close to a source of clean water.'

'Oh.'

There were signs that some trees had been cleared, and Jehan guessed that the buildings were close by. A bird rose up out of a thicket, and both st'lyan shied.

'I suppose it will suit the Sechem. They like isolation.' Kadan sounded doubtful.

Jehan grinned. 'It was your father's idea.' Because Suragai was bred from a race which employed science for everything, he was constantly followed by Sechem and Engineers. Strange devices were always being produced, and the prohibitions of the Yasa had been amended many times to permit their general use.

The ground started to slope downward. Jehan let his mare stretch out, and she hurtled down a narrow defile. A low stone wall had been built across it, and he yelled to warn Kadan. The grey gathered herself, then leapt. Her hooves clattered on the stones on top of the wall, and then she was clear. The ground beyond the wall was dead level – grass over cobblestones. Jehan glanced back and saw that Kadan was crashing along in his wake. He reined in hard, and the st'lyan almost sat down on her rump. Kadan wrestled his animal to a halt. He was laughing breathlessly.

'That's a good mare.' Jehan kicked his feet free of his stirrups. 'I thought she was too docile to have much spirit.'

'She's not as wild as yours.' Kadan swung down

from the saddle. 'But she's just as strong.'

There was a well in the centre of the yard. Jehan hauled water from it with a leaking wooden bucket, but when the st'lyan tried to nose past his shoulder he shoved her head away. 'No. You're too hot.' He drank, then scooped up water in his palm for the grey. Her rough tongue scrubbed at his hand.

'What a place.' Kadan was looking around at the buildings.

'It's worse than I expected.' Jehan nodded.

There was one large structure which had lost part of its roof, and there were four or five others, all much smaller. Two of them had collapsed, and the rest were in ruins. The cobbles underfoot were covered with grass, and most of the visible stonework was green with moss and lichen. Jehan could see rotted timbers which looked like loom frames through a gap in a nearby wall. He led his mare around the yard so that she could cool down.

The towering face of the largest building cast a shadow over most of the yard, and something about the place made Jehan uneasy. He felt instinctively that he was being watched, and he wondered if maybe a traveller had found his way to the spot, and feared to be accused of trespass.

Kadan was giving his mare water. Jehan pulled a rough cloth from one of his saddlebags, and he worked it over the grey's shoulders, across her flanks, and down in between her legs. Her hide felt dry and cool, and he led her to the well and allowed her to drink her fill.

'Are you going to look inside?' Kadan took the reins of both animals to tether them.

Jehan nodded. He took his bow out of the case on his saddle bow, and nocked an arrow. Kadan raised an eyebrow.

'At least draw your sword.' Jehan could not shake off the feeling that someone was watching. 'There could be a wild animal in there. Anything.' He put his shoulder to the front door of the largest structure and forced it half open. The wood squealed in protest.

There was a kind of hall inside, and three narrow passages led off from it. Nothing movable remained. Either the last occupants had taken everything with them, or else people had come later and had stolen everything which was not fastened down. The grey stones were cold, and the air was dusty and hard to breathe. Jehan walked quietly along one of the passages, his bow half-drawn. The silence made the back of his neck prickle. At the end of the passage there was another door. It was massive, made of dark wood bound with iron. Jehan forced it a handspan out of its frame, and then it gave suddenly and crashed back on its hinges.

'Jehan?' Kadan's voice carried down the passageway.

'Here.' Jehan went through the doorway. Another corridor stretched away into the shadows. Dark spaces pierced the wall at intervals. Nothing moved and he chided himself for his caution.

A faint sound whispered in the dust behind him, and he whirled so that the club which was smashing down struck his shoulder instead of his head. The blow knocked Jehan down, and a wash of pain along his arm made him cry out. Desperately he flung himself to one side, unable to see what was attacking him. The club crashed into the wall beside his head. His bow was on the paving, useless. He clawed urgently at his d'jaga. A huge shape was looming above him. He slashed with his talons and kicked out frantically, catching his assailant in the groin. The blow knocked his attacker the width of the passage.

Jehan tried to rise, but he could not. The dark shape was already getting up slowly. The lump of wood held between its hands looked enormous.

Kadan burst through the door into the passage. He unsheathed his *jusei*, the great sword of the Manchu, and swung in one uninterrupted stroke. The attacker's head bounced and rolled on the paving, and a fountain of blood sprayed out which splashed Jehan. He struggled into a sitting position. It hurt even to breathe, and he felt sick.

'Here.' Kadan was trying to help him to rise. The corridor whirled in a kaleidoscope of colour.

'I can't. My arm's broken.'

'Oh.' Kadan scooped Jehan up as if he was a child, and carried him out of the darkness into the yard.

Jehan thought about the distance he would have to ride to get back to the keep, and he shivered. His right arm was numb. He had never suffered a serious injury before.

'It's not your arm. I think your collar bone is broken.' Kadan was feeling down the flesh of the shoulder. He drew the arm on the injured side up and across. Jehan gasped, but at once the pain eased.

'You'll have to set it and bind it in place.' Jehan looked up. 'Can you do that? Otherwise they have to break it again when we get back to Zr'nadai.' The thought made Jehan's stomach churn. Yek bones healed very quickly, but the speed of the process meant that injuries had to be treated with a degree of urgency.

'Probably.' Kadan's tone was prosaic. 'Lie flat.' He made deft adjustments to the position of Jehan's arm and shoulder, and then bound the result with strips torn from his mantle. Jehan's tongue felt like leather and there were beads of sweat on his brow, but he thought that the break would set correctly.

Kadan went away. When he came back he was carrying a flask of wine from Jehan's saddlebag. 'There is no one else,' he reported. 'I thought maybe there were others.'

Jehan drank. The wine trickled across his tongue, and he shivered again. He could still smell the blood which had splashed across his face. 'I'm glad you're a monster.'

Kadan grinned. 'I'll take that as a compliment.' He took the flask and corked it. 'Do you think you can ride?'

'In a little while.' Jehan was worried because he felt so weak. He ought to be recovering faster than this. 'Was it a man that attacked me?'

Kadan grimaced. 'A kind of a man.'

'Oh.' There were fewer mutants every year, but some were still born to each generation, particularly in land which lay close to the G'bai. The Yasa permitted them to remain alive, but they were not suffered to breed, and most became outcasts.

'He had no ears. That was why he never heard me coming. You must have surprised him.'

That was probably true. No mutant would attack two armed men unless he was cornered. Jehan indicated the flask with his free hand, and Kadan uncorked the flask and held it to his lips. This time the wine was warming, and Jehan felt better.

'Will you be all right?' Kadan got to his feet. 'I'll be right back.'

'Yes.' Jehan felt embarrassed by his cousin's concern. He realised that if he had stayed at the keep, accompanying Burun through the feudal round, the incident would not have happened.

Kadan was doing something to the saddle of Jehan's grey. Jehan watched and saw that he was rigging a frame which would support a rider. When he had finished, Kadan came over. 'How do you feel?'

'I'll be all right.' Jehan tried to stand up, but his injury unbalanced him and he almost toppled onto the strapped arm. Kadan supported him just in time. He boosted Jehan gently into the saddle.

'I'll send someone back to bury the mutant later.'

'You'll have to send troopers.' Jehan used his free hand to pull the grey's head round. 'The ordinary people won't come here.'

'Yes.' Kadan nodded. 'We'd better take the long road back. There is a path through those trees.' He rode carefully alongside, and Jehan guessed that his cousin was waiting for him to fall off. Abruptly he remembered why he had come here, to see if the place was safe and suitable for occupation by the Sechem, and he smiled grimly.

By morning the bones of his shoulder were beginning to knit, and Jehan was managing with a simple sling to support his arm on the bad side. A Sechem attached to Suragai's staff had pronounced himself satisfied with Kadan's efforts at setting the fracture, and he had given Jehan a foul-tasting concoction to drink to prevent the onset of the fever which sometimes accompanied the commencement of the accelerated healing process.

'You were lucky,' Burun said. 'If you had gone there alone –'

'I didn't.' Jehan knew that his answer sounded curt. He eased his arm in an attempt to get rid of the dull ache which persisted across the width of his right shoulder. 'Peace, Grandfather. I'll live to plague you yet awhile.'

Burun grunted. The great hall of the keep was packed with people, most of whom had come to get judgement in one lawsuit or another. Everyone had heard that Jehan had been injured, and the dais on which Burun sat was heaped about with gifts of cordials or other comforts, all of them prepared by townswomen with unmarried daughters and one eye to Jehan's bachelor status.

Burun's steward came out of a small crowd at the rear of the hall. 'Khan, the next case is ready.'

'Good.' Burun sat forward. 'Is this the matter you told me of, Natan?'

'Yes, Lord.' The steward nodded. Then he turned and motioned two groups of people to come forward.

Jehan was about to leave the dais, but Burun's hand detained him. 'Stay. I want you to hear this.' Burun turned and spoke to Natan. 'Very well. Have them name themselves, and then let them tell me why they have come to me for justice. Which of them is the complainer?'

An elderly man in a good coat and breeches took two or three paces forward. Two other younger men, clearly his sons, remained where they were. Every glance they directed at the members of the other party was a scowl of hatred.

'Lord –' The complainer bowed deeply. '– My name is Asugai. I am a farmer on your mesne and I sell haigus wool to the merchants who manufacture cloth. I bring the suit which is before you.'

'I see.' Burun glanced at the second group. 'Then it is against you, Haratai, that the complaint is being brought. Is that your son you have with you?'

The defendant was a big man, muscled like an ox. His clothes were rough, and he still wore his carpenter's apron. He ducked his head respectfully. 'Yes, Khan.' The youth who stood at his back bore a surly expression on his face. His bow towards Burun's chair was a travesty.

'Very good.' Burun seemed not to have noticed the

62

scant homage which he had been paid. 'You, Asugai. Tell me why you are here.'

'Lord, I ask for your judgement against Haratai, here present, for he has burned one of my barns, and it was full of haigus wool.'

'Indeed.' Burun turned. 'How say you, Haratai? Are you guilty?'

The carpenter flushed. He placed his feet apart, then spoke. 'Lord, it is a fact that Asugai's barn was burned. But in truth, Lord, the barn was not his but mine, for I had built it for him, and he refused to pay me.'

The announcement produced angry shouts of denial from the farmer's side, and in a moment there were partisan cries rising from every part of the hall. Burun held up his hand, and after a moment there was silence.

Burun glanced sideways at Jehan. 'See what you can do with this. I give it to you. Judge it on my behalf.'

Jehan swallowed. The plaintiff looked belligerent, the defendant resolute, and suddenly there was absolute silence in the hall.

Jehan cleared his throat while he thought about what to say.

'You, Asugai. Do you deny that you owed Haratai payment for building your barn?' Jehan saw that one of the farmer's sons was whispering in his ear.

The farmer's smile was shifty. 'Lord, I would have paid him. I asked him to wait a while, that is all.'

'– Aye. Then arranged to sell the wool which he owed me to another for a good price,' the carpenter growled.

'Oh.' Jehan adjusted. 'So payment was agreed in haigus wool. How much wool exactly?'

'Lord, as much as would fill the barn which I built. That was the contract.'

63

'Hunh. I see. Asugai, is it the fact that you had the means to pay, and did not?' Jehan watched as the farmer shuffled his feet. The man spread his hands wide.

'Lord, it is true that I had the wool. But the wool crop this year was scarce, and I was offered nearly double the usual price for it by Oroden, the merchant with whom I trade. Is it right that I should sacrifice my profit? I would have paid Haratai in koban to the usual value of the wool, but he pressed me.'

'– And so you refused to pay him.' Jehan nodded grimly. 'The wool that was burned – was this the wool that you would have sold?'

'Yes, Lord.'

'– The same wool you owed Haratai. Even so.' Jehan eyed both men. Their eyes betrayed them. Both of them knew that they had broken the Yasa. Suddenly Jehan was aware of Burun's presence at his side. He glanced left, but his grandfather was lounging back in his chair. His eyes appeared to be closed.

'Very well.' Jehan took a deep breath. 'This is my judgement. You, Haratai, should have come to this court for justice when you were refused payment. Instead you took the law into your own hands. For that I fine you enough haigus wool to fill a barn, and you will pay that penalty to Asugai before the next day of settlement.'

At once there were opposing shouts, the sons of the farmer claiming that the compensation was too little, the carpenter that it was too much. Jehan held up a hand, and he was amazed when both parties at once ceased their protests.

'– You, Asugai, have admitted in front of witnesses that you failed to pay that which was owed, even though you had the means. You know the Yasa. The fact that you found yourself in a position to make an increased profit has no bearing on the case, and so I fine you. You will pay Haratai enough haigus wool to fill a barn.'

A few of the spectators were already laughing, appreciating Jehan's balance of one complaint against the other.

'Lord, I have lost a barn –' The farmer appealed, his face greasy with sweat.

'– You had a barn for which you had not paid. That is no barn. Now you have no barn. Is that not fair?' Jehan watched as the man searched for an answer.

The farmer studied the floorboards between his feet. Finally he raised his head, his expression crafty. 'Lord, I will give up my wool only after I receive Haratai's.'

Jehan shrugged. 'If neither of you gives the other anything, I shall consider my judgement carried out.'

'– But, Lord, I have lost all the materials which went into the barn –' The carpenter seemed to realise that he had neither lost nor won.

'– You burned a barn for which you had not been paid. Which is to say, you burned that which belonged to you. What you do with your own goods is your affair.' Jehan gestured. 'Is that not so?'

The carpenter's head went down. After a moment he spoke again, his voice subdued. 'Lord, I would have come to this court for judgement, but my son Hulagu told me he would get payment. I left the matter to him. I did not burn Asugai's barn.'

'Well.' Jehan registered the information. 'It seems that there is another case to be answered here. Asugai, were you approached by Haratai's son?'

The farmer flushed. 'Aye, Lord. The boy asked me for that which I owed his father, and demanded of me half as much again or he would burn down my barn. I thought he acted at the will of Haratai.'

65

The carpenter's son glowered. He met Jehan's stare defiantly. 'Lord, he lies.'

One of the farmer's sons took a pace forward. 'Lord, I was there. My father is telling the truth.'

Jehan considered briefly. The crowd at the rear of the hall stirred as if they anticipated what he would say. 'Indeed. Then Haratai it seems to me that your case is against your son, for it was he who burned the barn.'

'– And my wool, Lord.' The farmer spoke quickly.

'And your wool, as you say. Hulagu, step forward.'

The carpenter's son took a nervous pace, and then another. He seemed, at last, to sense that he was in trouble.

'My judgement against Asugai and Haratai stands.' Jehan waited for a mutter of comment to die. 'Haratai, I fined you not for burning, but for taking the law into your own hands, contrary to the Yasa. You, Asugai, I fined likewise for a breach of the law, for as you know a man must pay what he owes before he enters into any new contract. Hulagu, son of Haratai, I find you guilty of burning a barn and property which was not yours. What have you to say?'

'Lord.' The carpenter's son scowled. 'I did what seemed to me to be necessary. Asugai is a thief, and my father was a fool to allow himself to be robbed. I would have sold my father's wool to Oroden, and the profit would have been ours. Would the Khan's justice have given us so much?'

The insolence produced a growl of anger from the crowd. Jehan showed his teeth mirthlessly.

'– And yet it seems to me that your actions have brought no profit at all. Asugai has lost his wool, and your father still has not been paid. These are grievous injuries, and I shall fine you for them. To Asugai and Haratai both, you shall pay –'

'– A barn full of haigus wool,' several voices in the crowd shouted. 'Before the day of settlement.'

'Yes.' Jehan grinned. 'Let it be so.'

The people cheered. Burun was chuckling quietly.

'Lord –' The carpenter hauled his son forward, holding him by the shoulder of his jerkin. '– My son has nothing on which to distrain. How shall I get payment?'

The people roared. Apparently Hulagu was generally unpopular. Jehan held up his hands for quiet. 'Haratai, it seems to me that every parent has certain rights of recourse over his children. Since you cannot get your due one way –'

The carpenter nodded brusquely. 'Lord, I'll take my fine out of his hide.' With one hand he was already loosening the broad belt around his waist. He glanced to his right, and then ducked his head in Jehan's direction again. '– Also, Lord, if it please you, I yield my parental privilege to Asugai. It seems to me that there is a fine due to him from the same source.'

Jehan looked at the farmer, who nodded quickly. 'Lord, I would be satisfied with that.'

'Very well.' Jehan signed to the guards at the rear of the hall, and they threw open the doors. 'This judgement is ended.'

The farmer and the carpenter were joining to hustle the culprit outside. Most of the people were pushing after them to watch the beating which was clearly about to be administered.

Burun waved to a servant, and the man hastened up to the dais with a tray which held a flask of wine and cups. 'Clever,' Burun said. 'I especially liked the way you justified fining one man twice as much as was proper, and the other half what was justly due.' He poured wine and drank.

'You told me once that justice ought to be practical.' Jehan accepted a cup.

'Oh, I'm not criticising.' Burun smiled. 'I only wonder if you could apply the same principle on a wider scale. You might have to, you know, one day.'

Suragai said, 'My son wishes to serve you as I serve your grandfather.'

The sun was baking the stones of the parapet. Jehan pulled his tunic over his head. His recently injured shoulder was still awkward, and he winced as he raised his right arm, then lowered it again. 'I doubt I'll ever need a spymaster.'

Suragai said nothing. His face assumed a patient expression, and Jehan looked away. Across the length of the valley there were people working in the fields. Jehan wondered if it was the season for a particular farming task, and reflected that he knew very little about the actual process of agriculture.

'You don't like me.' Suragai spoke at last.

'Is it so obvious?' Jehan circled his arm in an attempt to exercise the muscles. The stiffness in his shoulder worried him because it was lasting longer than he had expected. He thought about what he had just said, and shook his head. 'I thought I knew you, Suragai. When I was your son's age, I liked you. But now I see that I don't know you at all. Can a man like or dislike what he does not know?'

The offworlder snorted softly. 'That's a philosopher's argument. You're using too much diplomacy on me, Noyon.'

Jehan flushed. He knew that Suragai was right, and that his initial reaction had been the honest one.

'At any rate it's my son we're discussing,' Suragai said. 'Not me.'

'Oh?' Jehan looked up. 'I don't trust you, Suragai. I don't trust what you do.'

'That's honest enough.' Suragai did not appear to

be offended. A fine surcoat covered his mantle. The material had been treated to radiate away the worst heat of the sun, and it demonstrated the low tolerance of the wearer to the extremes of temperature which were accepted by the Yek as normal.

'Shall I prove my loyalty?' Suragai's tone was tolerant. 'Your grandfather trusts me to serve him, or I would have been dead long since.'

'My grandfather thinks that he has to use men of your quality to get what he wants. I don't like what the Khanate has become. Is power worth having if it has to be gained by means which are not open or direct?'

'If you want me to debate the value of honour in the acquisition of feudal power, I will,' Suragai said after a moment. 'But Noyon, I believe it is the complexity of what we do which troubles you, rather than its essence.'

Jehan wrinkled his nose. 'Now who is presenting the philosopher's cause? How would my grandfather argue this?'

Suragai showed his teeth in a grim smile. 'Noyon, he would tell you to get what you can from every situation, and to worry about honour when you have won.'

'Hunh.' Jehan nodded. 'That's a cunning man's answer. And I seem to remember that he said something of the sort once. But what about the Yasa?'

The question appeared to perplex the offworlder. 'Noyon, I'm the wrong person to ask about Yek law –'

It was not the interpretation which Jehan had intended, and he gestured impatiently. '– If the end is just but the means are unlawful, is there justification?' Even as he spoke he knew that he was being simplistic.

Suragai frowned. 'I don't believe the Yasa forbids the exploitation of an advantage. However much it circumscribes a man's actions, he is free to advance himself.'

Jehan watched a cart which was coming up the causeway. A courier with his escort was trying to overtake, and the driver of the cart was cursing the troopers as he was forced to pull to one side of the road. 'I don't think you've answered my question.'

'You want to know if my activities on behalf of your grandfather are in breach of the Yasa,' Suragai observed. 'And you want to know if it troubles me. Noyon, I'm a simple man. My Khan commands me to act, so I do.'

'Hunh.' Jehan made a face. 'That's an unattractive reason.'

'Maybe. And according to any code of laws I've ever encountered, a man is responsible for his own actions. But is your position better?' Suragai leaned over the parapet. The courier had entered the court-yard, and he was dismounting.

'What do you mean?'

'Your approach implies an obedience to the law which is just as blind. You tried a case the other day. Both of the men who came before you had broken the Yasa, and they knew it. Existence of the law was no deterrent.'

'I dealt with them accordingly.'

'Exactly so. But also you dealt justly. Both men lost, but they did not suffer.'

Jehan thought that somehow he had lost the thread of his argument. 'You sound as if you are saying that good and evil are necessary to one another.'

Suragai shrugged. 'If every man acted towards others without regard for his own interests, there would be no need for law. Certainly without the existence of injustice, justice would not be held in such high regard.'

'My grandfather says that a Khan does what serves him best. Without regard for right or wrong?'

'Noyon.' Suragai spread his hands. 'If good and evil are necessary to one another, then perhaps it is required of a man to do a little wickedness now and again in order that his nature may not become too perfect, and thus a reproach to other men. Where better to break the law than in pursuit of the interests of the clan, which is an end, at least, which is approved by the Yasa?'

'Oh.' Jehan clasped his hands, applauding the twist of logic. 'Splendid. Almost you convince me that wrong acts are essential to civilised existence.'

Suragai bowed. 'And so, Noyon, I shall leave you. May I tell my son that you will accept his service?'

'Yes. He is my friend.'

The offworlder seemed to examine the statement. He nodded and turned away.

Jehan stretched. He did not think that Suragai had justified himself, even though he had demonstrated that his motives were sound. Burun came out of a portal which provided access from the gallery which ran round inside the wall.

'I thought I would find you here. Was that Suragai I saw?'

'Yes.' Jehan nodded. 'We were talking philosophy.'

'I'm pleased you had the leisure. It's the last you'll have for some time.'

'Oh?' Jehan straightened. 'I saw the courier arrive.'

'Yes. I have letters from Artai and from your father both. We're going back to Kinsai.'

Jehan picked up his tunic. He draped it around his shoulders.

'You see it has turned out as I said it would,' Burun said. 'Are you convinced now?'

Men were already crossing the courtyard towards

the stables, and several servants were hauling baggage in the direction of a cart. Jehan flexed his arms. The ache which had persisted in his shoulders was suddenly only a memory.

'Artai has asked you for help.'

'He is begging for my aid.' Burun's expression betrayed his satisfaction.

'Hunh. Then you have demonstrated your control of one aspect of the situation. But Khan, I don't know that it follows that everything else will fall out as you have planned.' Jehan spoke levelly.

Burun ran a hand through his hair, disturbing the elaborate braiding which secured his dressed top-knot. 'Aren't you pleased at least? Everything I do is for my children. Not one of you is grateful to me.'

'Oh, well. I'm pleased at your success, of course.' Jehan grinned at Burun's exasperation. 'But you didn't arrange any of this for me.'

Burun shook his head as if he did not believe what he was hearing, and then suddenly to Jehan's surprise he laughed. He turned away and went back through the gallery in the wall, and Jehan stood listening as the sound of his boots striking the paving stones gradually receded.

PART ONE

Artai the Golden

The Kha-Khan elect had bathed, and he was freshly scented. His hair was the colour of spun gold, and two body slaves were doing their best to comb it out so that it could be braided. It was an exercise which was fraught with difficulty. Artai was incapable of sitting still for long, and only his abnormal concern with his appearance made him submit at all to the restrictive nature of the ministrations of the Y'frike slaves. When he craned to stare down at the crowds in the great square below the palace, his head moved so that it rested upon the parapet like a decoration. The part-braided ends of his long hair escaped from the busy fingers which were engaged in their intricate task. The dusky features of both slaves assumed long-suffering expressions, and one of them pursed his lips.

'The people do not see me, or they would bow.' Artai turned back from his scrutiny of the square.

Alexei was sitting on the end of a low couch which was positioned in the centre of the room. He controlled the urge to laugh at the tinge of regret which had coloured Artai's tone.

'Magnificence, you could attract their attention.'

Artai's great golden eyes opened wide. 'Oh? How?'

'Well you could shout, or wave maybe.'

The expression which made its way onto Artai's face was familiar enough. He wrinkled his nose, half closed his eyes, and then he surveyed Alexei as if he was trying to understand a bad joke. 'That would not be fitting,' he said finally. He stared at Alexei for a moment longer, and then suddenly he grinned

75

impishly. 'Of course you are not serious, but it would be fun.'

'Yes.'

'Ishiko would be outraged.'

'Probably.' Alexei nodded. Ishiko was the Kha-Khan's major domo, a N'pani who was arguably the most powerful slave in the Khanate. He was the supreme arbiter of protocol and courtly behaviour, and it was likely that he would be put out, to say the least, by the notion of a Kha-Khan who behaved with such a lack of reserve.

It was clear that Artai found the prospect attractive. He craned over the balcony again, but finally he seemed to sigh. Then he sat down again on the golden stool which had been placed on the balcony of the chamber. Once more the body slaves began the process of dressing the golden hair.

'When I am Kha-Khan, I will be able to do as I please.' Artai was watching Alexei's face as he spoke.

Alexei considered the proposition. There were almost no restrictions on the behaviour of the Kha-Khan elect, and his wilfulness was legend.

'You disagree?' Artai's tone was petulant.

'Magnificence –' Alexei attempted an equable approach. '– There is surely more to concern a Kha-Khan than his own interests.'

'Ho!' Artai sat up straight. 'You presume to instruct me?'

Alexei stretched out his legs. He examined his booted feet for a moment, and then he raised his eyes. 'Not at all, Magnificence. Does it not say in the first *Sura* of the Yasa that the Kha-Khan is above all the servant of his people?'

Artai flushed. 'The Kha-Khan's will is supreme,' he said. 'No power on earth is greater, and the Yasa is his to do as he –'

'The Yasa belongs to the people,' Alexei said. 'It is not for a Kha-Khan to amuse himself like a selfish child.'

The Kha-Khan elect stood. The golden irises of his eyes seemed to have expanded, and with his head held too high he appeared to be staring at the ceiling. 'I am the Exalted,' he said.

Alexei looked back patiently.

After a moment Artai looked away. 'I will be the Exalted.'

'Yes.'

'– And if I am to be a great Kha-Khan, I ought to be able to recognise when I am being told the truth.' He looked down his nose. 'Even by an alien.'

'Yes.' Alexei ignored the mild insult. He showed his teeth. He had anticipated a tantrum, and he was surprised by Artai's self-control.

'Hunh.' Artai nodded slowly as if he was satisfied. He sat down, and after a moment he gestured languidly. 'I do not know if you are so frank with me because you do not care how I react, or if it is honesty which prompts you. Do you speak so to other men?'

Alexei sat back. 'Magnificence, it is too much trouble to lie.' He watched Artai for a reaction.

'Oh, well.' The Kha-Khan elect raised his eyebrows. 'My uncles and most of the other Khans take such pains when they speak to me, and yet you go to no trouble at all. I think it is rebellious of you, that you cannot be bothered to find a falsehood with which to flatter me.'

It was true that the members of the court sometimes seemed to be in competition in their attempts to gratify Artai's vanity. Alexei was amused to discover that the Kha-Khan elect was not deceived. It provided a new slant on his character. He laughed. 'Your uncles would be shocked to hear that you think that they lie,

77

Magnificence. Targoutai thinks that he alone knows the truth.'

'All of the Khans say proper things to me.' Artai waved a hand. 'But I watch their eyes when they speak, and I see what they intend. I know they do not hold me in high regard. Each of them seeks to use me for his own ends.'

'Then judge them by their acts, Magnificence, and do not listen to what they say.'

The elder of the body slaves gathered the braided ends of his master's hair and bound them together with gold wire. He twisted the queue forward and arranged it carefully. The end of the wire was studded with jewels, and the effect was that of a snake poised to strike above Artai's scalp.

'I can trust almost no one,' Artai said. He did not seem perturbed. 'Perhaps I can rely upon the Merkuts, for they cannot yet aspire to the throne. Burun loves power, but also he desires order in the land and so he will protect me. It took me a long time to understand that.'

The analysis of Burun's character was so shrewd that Alexei was startled. He avoided Artai's stare.

'Why did you decide to serve me?' Artai asked.

Alexei hesitated. 'You are the Chosen,' he said at last. He was impelled by the circumstances to provide an honest answer, but as always there were degrees of the truth. 'I served Nogai. I was his friend and companion, and it was his will that you should ascend the Dragon Throne.'

'You do not seek reward?'

'Oh, certainly.' Alexei grinned. 'I am a member of the Kha-Khan's court, and without his favour I am nothing.'

Artai digested the information. '– Then for your service to me thus far I will confirm you in the offices

78

and estates which you held from Nogai.'

It was as much as Alexei had expected. He bowed from his seat on the couch. 'Magnificence, you are generous and I thank you.'

The body slaves had finished their tasks. At Artai's back they knelt, and then prostrated themselves. As if he sensed their homage the Kha-Khan elect waved a hand in dismissal. The slaves rose and backed out of the chamber, their eyes cast down. Artai seemed to gaze out across Kinsai. It was already late morning, and the red glare of the sun was evaporating away the moisture left by an earlier shower so that the golden roofs of the principal buildings were wreathed with a mist which eddied and flowed under the influence of the heat which rose off the plain.

Suddenly Artai turned. 'Your father serves Burun in the rank of S'zltan.'

'Yes, Magnificence.' Alexei met the piercing glance squarely. The observation did not seem to require any other response.

'– And yet you are not, I think, your father's heir?'

Artai walked from the balcony across the expanse of the chamber to a marble table which stood against one wall. He was watching Alexei, his head cocked to one side like a bird examining a dubious worm. There was an odd expression on his face.

'No.' Alexei shook his head. 'My father's heir is Kadan, his son by the daughter of Burun.' He felt no trace of resentment as he made the statement. The estrangement which had accompanied his father's marriage to Turakina was an old wound, long since healed.

'– Then surely you have sworn fealty to some noble lord, and owe service for his favour?'

There was an alien caste to Artai's features as he spoke. His eyes were abnormally large, and suddenly

79

Alexei realised that both the muscles around the eyes and the jet black pupils which were centred within the golden irises were affected not at all by the light but responded rather to some inner stimulus. The discovery was unsettling, for it was commonly accepted that it was difficult to meet the impassive stare of the Kha-Khan elect for more than a few seconds. Amber gold eye colouring was unusual but not unknown. Now it occurred to Alexei to wonder why no one had remarked on the phenomenon before now. Clearly Artai exhibited at least one mutated characteristic. Possibly he possessed others which were even less obvious.

'Magnificence, I have given my oath to no man.' That much was certainly true. Even as he spoke, his last conversation with Burun sprang unbidden into the forefront of Alexei's mind.

Artai seemed to ponder. Then it was as if he had come to a decision. ' – Then I will dignify your estates of Khara Khitai with the ulus of a Khan,' he said smoothly.

Alexei blinked. As a reward for delivering the information which had led to the exposure of Sidacai's planned coup, the honour was excessive. He was thrown off balance by the casual ease with which the Kha-Khan elect was controlling the interview. Usually Artai behaved like a fractious child, his temper uncertain, his demeanour abrupt and discourteous.

'I am scarcely worthy, Magnificence – '

It was a stock reply, one which invited dismissal, and Artai treated it accordingly.

' – You are worthy because your loyalty to me is beyond question,' he said. 'It is true that there are Khans enough in the land; but there are none I dare call friend.' For a moment his look was piercing, and then he produced a rare smile. 'The Lord of the Earth

80

cannot have a common man for a companion, and so I choose to give you the rank which is proper.'

It was hard to know how to respond. Alexei stood up. He searched for a formula with which to answer, his knowledge of Artai's character combining with his just-formed suspicion to produce a chill of disquiet.

'If you were more eager for my friendship, I would not trust you.' Artai spoke softly. He picked up a sheet of parchment from the table, glanced at it, and then raised his eyes. 'Do you fear me?'

Alexei constructed a suitable reply, then discarded it in favour of plain truth. 'Magnificence, I fear your nature.'

'Hah.' The Kha-Khan elect produced a snort of laughter. 'You would fear me, if you knew my nature. But you do not, and so you only fear what you suspect my nature may be. Do you think I am mad? The blood of Daijin runs in me, it is true.'

The question was uncomfortably close to the mark. Watching Artai's expression, Alexei saw only amused curiosity, and he shrugged. 'Is a man truly mad who knows his nature, Magnificence? On this world there is scarcely a Khan who does not have a tyrant or a murderer in his bloodline.'

Artai's nose wrinkled. 'You might as well argue that a man who knows that he is mad is less to be feared than a man who believes that he is sane. Certainly the man who does not question his own sanity is mad indeed. I like your answers better when they are honest, Alexei.'

The amber stare was difficult to meet without flinching. 'It is true that I fear the part of your nature which at times you do not care to control,' Alexei said steadily. He held his breath.

The muscles of Artai's head and shoulders seemed to twitch. Then he nodded. ' – And yet you have chosen to serve me. I am satisfied.'

Alexei released the breath he had been holding. It was apparent that Artai's inquisition had been a kind of test, and that he had passed.

The Kha-Khan elect was studying the parchment in his hand. All at once he looked up. 'This is Sidacai's death warrant,' he said. 'I will sign it the day I ascend the throne.'

Sidacai was confined in one of the lower levels of the Golden Yurt. A military council had already decreed the execution of the five principal conspirators, but confirmation of the sentences of death would not be lawful until the Dragon Throne was occupied once more.

'Has Siban not petitioned for Sidacai's life?' Alexei watched as Artai rolled the parchment and laid it aside.

In fact the appeal was common knowledge. There had been no evidence to connect Siban with his son's plot to overturn Nogai's will. The Khans who had joined with Sidacai were all members of the family of Kodai, who was a grandson of the Ancestor via the line of his second son Ordai, Conqueror of N'pan. With their deaths, the Senjin Clan of the Altun would virtually cease to exist.

Artai did not turn. He nodded. 'He has reminded me that the beginning of a reign is a traditional time for the pardoning of malefactors,' he said. His tone suggested that he disapproved of the notion. ' – In truth I am ill-disposed towards mercy. I would as lief offer my own throat to the knife.'

The news was scarcely a surprise. The Yasa allowed for only a limited selection of penalties under the law. A man might be fined, in which case it was usual for him to be ordered to make payment to the person or persons who had suffered as a result of his crime. A noble was likely to be stripped of rank and privileges – reduced to the status of a commoner. For serious offences there was only one sentence – death by the knife. Imprisonment was not regarded as punishment. A person was only detained pending trial for a capital crime, or while awaiting verification of sentence.

'I have never killed a man before.' Artai was staring at the table as he spoke. He looked up, but Alexei was unable to read the expression in his eyes.

The antechamber outside Artai's apartments was hung with silks like a yurt. A long time in the past the Yek had been nomads, and even though the principal cities of the Khanate were constructed from stone, the interior decoration of many of the principal houses owed its origins to the heritage of the tent.

A group of lesser Khans stood muttering in one corner of the room, and when Alexei came through the hangings which provided access to the bedchamber they fell guiltily silent. One of them bowed, a false smile on his face, but Alexei ignored him. He strode past the lines of guards and attendants, nodded to the pair of officers who lounged at their ease in the shadow of the enormous length of midnight-blue fabric which hung suspended from the ceiling in lieu of a screen, and slackened his pace only when he was out in the long gallery which ran supported around the entire upper floor.

The inner wall of the gallery was pierced at intervals by high arched windows. These provided a view of the great central staircase. Burun was in one of them, sitting with his back to the side pillar, his booted feet stretched out along the sill so that he was perched above a sheer drop to the marble-floored hallway below. He did not move when he saw Alexei, but nodded and smiled.

'Khan, good morning,' Alexei nodded politely, but he did not return the smile. Burun wanted something, or he would not be here. Certainly he was not waiting to see Artai – the Khan of the Merkuts was so powerful that he did not have to wait for audience like other men.

There was little doubt that Burun understood the reservation which was embodied in the greeting. 'Noyon.' He nodded calmly. 'Is it a good morning?'

A Noyon was the son of a Khan, and so, strictly speaking, the form of address was incorrect. Alexei tried to decide if Burun was mocking him. If he was, it did not matter.

'If you call a morning which has seen my ennoblement good,' he said flatly, 'then it is, very.'

Burun's feet came down off the sill. 'Artai has given you a Khanate,' he said. He did not sound surprised.

'He has dignified Khitai with the ulus of a Khan,' Alexei nodded. It was difficult to avoid sounding pleased.

'Oh, well.' Burun extended his hands, studying them. His silver-tipped talons flashed, and then suddenly he looked up. 'You warned me Artai's reward might make you independent of me.' There were lines of amusement creased around his mouth and eyes.

'So I did.' Alexei guessed that he was being invited to assume that the Khanate, like the gifts which he had received during Nogai's reign, had come from Burun's hands. Briefly he wondered if it could be true, and realised that there was no way to be sure.

A line of N'pani slaves came along the gallery. Each carried an oval platter, and in the platters, embedded in snow, were the fruits of two continents. When the slaves saw Burun they hissed and bowed, then passed silently through the door to the antechamber.

'A Khanate is a responsibility,' Burun said. 'Who will you appoint to manage your estates?'

'Perhaps I should oversee them myself.' Alexei met Burun's stare steadily. He knew he was being teased.

Burun shrugged elegantly. 'Well as to that,' he said, 'it is true that the realm is at peace now. But have you considered that Artai will desire to mark his accession with some conquest – some increase in his influence?'

Alexei allowed his nose to wrinkle. 'Khan, if you are asking me what the Kha-Khan's intentions are, then I have to tell you that he has not confided in me.' The fact that the title of Khan was a military as well as a civil appointment had not occurred to him until now, but now that he thought about it, the suggestion seemed ridiculous. 'There is no one left to fight,' he said.

'A few bandits maybe.' Burun showed his teeth. 'Sometimes I forget that you are not native to this land, Alexei. The Yasa says that there must be but one Lord upon the Earth. Do you suppose that Artai has ever examined the old maps?'

'If he has not,' Alexei observed, 'then I have no doubt that someone is showing them to him even now.' He knew that his tone was tart, and saw Burun grin.

The maps held in the archives of the Sechem – the keepers of Yek knowledge and the interpreters of their law – showed two land masses of continental size on the far side of the Great Sea. Not much was known about them, and no Yek had ever visited them – the Yek were not keen sailors – it was not even certain that they were inhabited.

Suddenly Alexei remembered Tarvaras as he had first seen it – a revolving holographic projection suspended in the viewing well of the briefing amphitheatre of an Imperial survey vessel, the

Simonova – off which he and five other humans had been marooned over twelve standard years earlier. The Imperial survey had not cited a continent which was more or less populated than any of the others. In almost the same moment Alexei recalled that his father had been at the same briefing. Sergei Rostov, once Admiral of the White of the navy of the Third Empire, was now Suragai S'zltan, chief advisor and counsellor to Burun, and might easily have mentioned the survey assessment to his feudal overlord.

'Khan, I don't know any more about what lies across the sea than anyone else,' Alexei said.

Burun's expression did not alter. 'Do you think Artai will believe that?'

Alexei considered the question and then shook his head. He met Burun's eyes. 'Khan, if you want me to encourage Artai to order an expedition, say so.'

'I want you to offer to lead it,' Burun said, and smiled.

'What?' Alexei was appalled. 'Why should I?'

'Oh.' Burun gestured. 'Think of the glory.'

'Glory be damned.' Alexei frowned. He reviewed the route the conversation had taken. 'Khan, it's clear that you want me out of Kinsai. Is it my influence with Artai that troubles you?'

Burun looked mildly offended. 'There are easier ways to supplant you,' he said.

Alexei guessed that if Burun wished to discredit him with Artai he only had to link his name with any one of the intrigues which were a constant background to the life of the court. Not for the first time it occurred to him how vulnerable his position was, and he reflected ruefully that there was probably no more security or protection in the rank of Khan than there had been in any of the various honours which he had received while he had been an intimate of the clique which had surrounded Nogai. So far as the Yek were concerned any man who was not of the race of the True People – the Yek, the N'pani, the Ch'noze – was an alien, barely human, and as such was forever suspect.

'Trust me,' Burun said, and spread his hands in a placatory gesture. 'Do I not promote your interests along with my own?'

The wording of the entreaty was perfectly serious, but given the situation it was hard not to laugh. 'So much for your independence,' Alexei said.

'Hah.' The observation seemed to amuse Burun. 'Noyon, your concept of independence is like your concept of slavery – confused and badly reasoned.'

They had argued the subject before, but in the midst of a society in which slavery was a common-place, the comparison struck Alexei as one which was particularly inappropriate. He opened his mouth to make an acid retort, and then remembered that the *sura* which permitted captives to be enslaved also went to considerable lengths to provide laws for their welfare. A slave might not be ill-treated or subjected to undue hardship. The circumstances in which freedom might be won were clearly defined, and Alexei knew that he had sometimes thought that the lowest class in the Empire – the proles, who worked for pay – were no less enslaved and had perhaps fewer rights. He shook his head. 'I won't argue with you, Khan.'

'I should hope not.' Burun stood up. He smoothed the skirts of his coat, and then suddenly looked up. 'Artai will be enthroned in three days,' he said.

Now that the leaders of the conspiracy had been condemned, the remaining uncommitted Khans were falling over themselves to declare their support for Artai, their reservations suppressed. Alexei gave

Burun a hard stare. 'I never thought Sidacai would be so inept,' he said. 'Even if he had desired it, he could scarcely have done more to ensure that the Khans would support Nogai's will.'

Burun's eyes were like dark featureless pools in his face. They revealed nothing. 'Sidacai was never comfortable with the planning or the preparation for a campaign,' he said smoothly. 'He was always hasty.'

The scheme to impose military control over Kinsai had been a logistical catastrophe, and it was the utter inefficiency above all which had made Alexei suspicious. His own sources among the Altun had picked up vague hints of another conception upon which Sidacai had drawn or to which he had been led. At first he had assumed that it must be Siban, baulked from attaining the Dragon Throne, who had hoped to govern the realm through the medium of his son. Then he had realised that the originator of the plot could just as easily have been Burun – intending all the time that it should fail – achieving at a stroke the removal of effective opposition, placing Artai in debt to the Merkuts for the security of his throne.

'Artai will not pardon him,' Alexei said.

'So I have heard.' Burun turned as if to walk with Alexei towards the head of the stairs. 'It is a pity. I ever liked him.'

It was an unnecessary lie. Burun had tolerated Sidacai, no more than that. Alexei remembered Sidacai's veiled insolence – the times when he had used his status as the son of a son of Daijin to thwart Burun. He said nothing.

Suddenly Burun swung round. 'There could be a way to save him,' he said, as if the possibility had only just occurred to him. 'The Khans condemned him because it was the law, but none of them believes that he is a threat to the order of the realm. If he were absent from Kinsai for a time –' He paused delicately.

'If, for example, he were to be engaged in the reconnaissance of the Unknown Lands,' Alexei supplied. He nodded, accepting Burun's intent. 'Of course I would have to ask Artai for Sidacai to be freed into my custody,' he said.

Burun stared impassively. 'The whole world knows how the Kha-Khan elect trusts you. How can he assign any motive but an honourable one to such a request?'

If Burun had originated the plot, it was possible that he felt some responsibility towards Sidacai. Sidacai would not know that Burun had been at the back of it all, of course, and either way he would owe his life to the Merkuts.

'How do you know that Artai will let me go?' Alexei was sure that his suspicions were plain upon his face as he spoke. He remembered what Artai had said about Burun's lust for power, and how it was tempered by a desire for order.

Burun shrugged. 'Artai has elevated you. Now he will start to wonder if his trust is well-founded. When you ask him for leave to serve him on this mission he will welcome it as the solution to his anxieties, for even if you are only gone from Kinsai for a time, it will seem to him that you do not mean to impose upon his favour.'

The reasoning was convoluted in the extreme, and Alexei blinked. 'And when I return?' he asked.

'When you return he will heap you with honours,' Burun said simply. 'You will have demonstrated that you are his servant, for by removing yourself from the court at such a crucial hour you will have proved to him that he was right to trust you.' He started to walk along the gallery.

Alexei followed reluctantly. He was more than ever aware of the control which Burun was capable of exercising over the affairs of the Kha-Khan's court.

I have lived among them more than a third of my life, and still I do not understand them.

The intrigue, if one existed, was worthy of the inner circle of the Imperial court on far distant Knossos. Alexei found himself recalling events from his childhood – the dimly understood shifts of influence from one family to another, his mother the niece of the Emperor, his father a commoner and always absent on the Imperial service – and almost before he was aware of it his hand had risen to the gold caste mark on his cheek. He stroked the imprint absently. On any world in the Empire it would have been recognised with reverence as a sign of his status as a member of the royal family. Here it meant nothing.

I am the human. It is the people of this world who are alien. I must remember that.

The Yek – indeed all the races which possessed talons – were a mutation from human stock. Alexei allowed himself to dwell upon the knowledge which he had retained from that long-ago survey briefing. Every day he forced himself to recall it. Every day he became less certain that the distinction between human and alien was an accurate one.

The stairway at the end of the gallery was a cascade of white marble which descended without interruption to the jet-black floor of the entrance hall. Burun halted. 'Noyon, you must forget your origins,' he said, his tone sympathetic. 'You will never leave us.'

Alexei jerked his hand away from his cheek, then laughed to dismiss the subject. 'Khan, I am content.'

The expression reflected in Burun's eyes was candidly disbelieving.

Alexei flushed. With the Khan of the Merkuts as with his own father he found it almost impossible to conceal his true emotions. He forced himself to bow politely, and then turned away and began to descend the stairs. When he looked back he saw that Burun had been joined by a crowd of aides and counsellors. It was without much surprise that Alexei marked the towering figure of his father at Burun's shoulder, but when their eyes finally met there was no hint of response.

The garden of Alexei's Kinsai house was surrounded by a waist-high wall. Outside was the main street, and it was this feature, along with its complete lack of privacy, which made it Alexei's choice for the performance of his daily ritual of exercise. His liaisons with various ladies of the Kha-Khan's court were not a matter which he had ever attempted to keep secret, and more than one irate would-be challenger – usually the father or brother of the lady in question – had gone away with a thoughtful expression on his face after witnessing a display of alien skill at arms.

A N'pani of Alexei's household had designed the garden, and as a result there was more art than agriculture to its appearance. Raked expanses of *shinshun* – the black volcanic sand which covered great expanses of the G'bai desert to the south of the continent – were dotted with the occasional carefully pruned tree, and there were isolated rocks. Nothing else marred the garden's absolute simplicity. Alexei's favourite spot was in what he supposed might have been termed a clearing – at least it was in the centre of a circle of four rocks, each one the size of a crouching man. A tatami, a triple-woven rush mat, had been placed on the sand, and as he walked towards it Alexei saw that the slave had raked over his footprints as he had departed, leaving the surface smooth and even. He smiled sourly. The moment he went back into the house the gardeners would run out to eradicate the tracks left by his coming and going. The N'pani professed to believe that tracks in the sand were disturbances in the *wa*, or harmony, of the garden. They saw order in everything – even in the chaos of nature – and their patience was infinite.

'Give me the sword, Ordai, and then go.'

'Yes, Lord.'

The orderly was a Yek, a member of Alexei's guard, and the disappointment showed clearly upon his features. Alexei undid the wire fastenings down the front of his tunic and pulled it over his head. When he held it out Ordai took it one-handed, folding it awkwardly before tucking it under his arm. He offered the sword.

It was not a weapon which was capable of being carried on a belt or in a sash. The companies of Yek troopers who were armed with swords carried something which looked like a *spatha*, the Imperial short sword. Some had adopted the *jusei*, the 'great sword' of the Manchu, which had been introduced by Yuan, an officer on the navy staff of Alexei's father, likewise a castaway. Alexei hefted the practice sword experimentally, and Ordai stepped back. The Yek were amazed by the *chanthu*, the two-handed straight sword of the Kurgan, the personal bodyguard to the Emperor, because of its size. Only a tall man in the peak of condition could lift it, and when Alexei stood it on its point, it reached to his chin.

He whirled it at shoulder level. The guard was an inverted vee which forked away from his hands, and by rotating his wrists one within the other it was possible to convert the axis of the blade into a glittering circle.

'Go away, Ordai.'

The orderly was already backing away. Alexei knelt

on the mat, his legs spread apart, his feet together. It was the middle of the morning, and the red ball of the sun was already high in the awful blue of the sky.

He ignored the heat. The Yek were practically immune to the extremes of heat and cold which were part of the climate of Tarvaras, and even they took shelter, if it was possible, from the midday intensity of the red giant around which the world and its two moons orbited.

The exercises followed a pattern, a dimly remembered copy of the Kurgan *haiku* – a two-handed reach skyward to the left, and then to the right, a reverse, two-handed, and then the single-handed moves.

'Reach, reverse; thrust, withdraw.' Alexei muttered the formula under his breath.

There were tiny flutes – raised striations of steel – down the blade, and its swift movement through the air produced a hum of sound which rose in pitch the faster the exercises were performed.

'Reach-reverse-thrust-withdraw.'

An officer of the Kha-Khan's guard came into the street. He reined in when he saw that Alexei was in the garden, watched for a time, and then spat expressively to left and to right and rode on.

Alexei smiled grimly. The Yasa provided for the settlement of disputes and affairs of honour only between the races of the True People, for they alone were equipped with the talons with which the kanly – formal mortal combat – was fought. The law said nothing about duels between species which were not considered to be human – although that did not prevent an offended party from seeking recourse. Word of his prowess with the *chanthu* had spread, Alexei knew, and quarrels were seldom more than exchanges of acid words as a result, because were he to be challenged the choice of weapons would be his.

I will not fear them. I will live my life as I please.

Even as the thought came to the forefront of his mind, Alexei knew that it could never be that simple – that he was forced to conform to alien culture and alien reasoning.

'*Reach-reverse-thrust – withdraw!*'

The kneeling position forced him to employ every muscle of his upper body. There was none of the relief which might have been gained from a change of stance.

'Reach-reverse-circle-thrust-reverse-circle.'

The rhythm changed with the progression of the *haiku*. There was a slick of sweat along his arms and down his chest. The skin, he noted, was still tinged golden – that faint tone which signified to those in the know that he had been subjected to the bi-annual treatment of Longivex, the Imperial longevity drug which, because of the rarity of the poppy from which it was produced, was restricted to the élite, the favoured few such as the royal family, the privileged, the very rich – and he frowned as he wondered how long it would be before the absence of the drug showed in his physique and appearance.

I am thirty – no – more. A year on this world is approximate to standard, but there is a difference.

He was young by any measure, and Alexei knew that he should not feel concern. Men lived a long time on Tarvaras. Even his father did not appear to have aged greatly, although he was sixty or more years old.

Sixty? Alexei's jaw tightened. *Seventy would be closer. Name of God, he is an old man!*

Alexei revolved the blade in a glittering figure of eight, working the axis of the spin gradually across his shoulders. The *haiku* was one which ended with a downward cut, followed by a single outward thrust.

94

Another sword encountering it would have shattered on impact.

The inner contemplation of the matters which troubled him merged suddenly with awareness that the sword was an unbearable weight at the end of his extended arms. Alexei rose to his feet in a single effortless movement, twirled the *chanthu* one-handed, and speared it into the coarse black sand.

'Ordai!'

The orderly had been watching, Alexei knew, from behind the large rock beside the path. Alexei gestured at the still-quivering sword, and then strode on into the house. The exercise ritual usually calmed him, but today he felt the remnants of the anger and frustration at his situation in the tenseness of his stomach. The antechamber which he entered was filled with silent N'pani. They unwound his sash and stripped away his sodden garments. There was no taboo in this land against male nakedness, and some of the slaves were women. Alexei pretended not to notice. He stepped into the shallow copper tray which had been placed in the centre of the floor, and allowed himself to be showered – a constant sprinkling of water which was poured through a perforated funnel by one male slave, while others maintained the supply of water with buckets.

'Enough.'

Alexei stepped out of the tray onto the floor. The wood of the planks was almost white, but it had been sanded and then varnished with gums and resins until it glistened. Every spilled drop of water was a reflection. Female slaves mopped at them with cloths of unbleached fabric, and Alexei took one out of a pair of slim hands and towelled himself dry. Yek bathing involved immersion up to the neck in water which was maintained at a temperature hot enough to strip the flesh from a man's bones if he did not acclimatise himself to it gradually, and baths were communal. He had found it difficult to accustom himself to the practice, although with the right kind of company there were undoubted compensations.

The bedchamber was hung with silks which were so fine that they bruised if something brushed against them. The chamber seemed empty.

Alexei heard a whisper of sound at his back, but he did not turn. Either the lady who had been his companion the night before was leaving, in which case it would be bad manners to notice, or she intended to remain, and would return to the chamber when she was ready. Either way it made sense to maintain some degree of detachment. A woman of this world who had passed her eighteenth birthday without being contracted in marriage was entitled to go with any man she chose – but did so on her own terms. No commitment was ever implied, and it was customary to pretend, whenever she decided to depart, that her identity was unknown.

The assembly of the Khans met the same afternoon. Because his ennoblement could not be ratified until the Dragon Throne was formally occupied, Alexei was not permitted to vote. Like every other member of the court however, he was present in the circular council building. The structure was built to resemble a stone yurt – the outer wall was a continuous string of arches which were covered with felt panels, there was a planed timber floor, and there was no provision for anyone to sit down. A gallery had been suspended around the wall at the height of two standing men – the only concession to spectators. The roof was a dome of beaten gold.

The only item of business, the election of the Kha-

Khan, proceeded so swiftly and was over in such a short space of time that it was clear to everyone that it was little more than a formality. Artai's name was the sole nomination, and instead of a proposing speech by one of the Khans there was a reading by a court secretary of the portion of Nogai's will in which he expressed the wish that Artai should succeed him.

There were no votes against, and no abstentions.

'See how the Merkuts hang back,' someone at Alexei's side muttered.

A Noyon of the Seijin clan – his crimson eye shading was like a badge which identified him – made a face and shook his head. 'The whole world knows that the Merkuts have given Artai his throne,' he said.

If Burun's refusal to place himself in a position of prominence by acting as Artai's proposer was a subterfuge to disclaim his influence, then it was apparent that none of the Khans recognised it. Everyone deferred to him in the casting of lots, and after he had tossed his white counter into the bowl which was placed in the centre of the chamber there was a wild scramble for precedence.

'You were a boy when you came to us, but now you are a man.' Turakina ran the needle through the folds of material several times, looped the thread upon itself, and then snapped it off short. She laid the garment aside.

Alexei was sitting cross-legged on the morning-room floor. Irina, his half-sister and the daughter of Turakina by his father, was kneeling intently on a cushion behind him while she attempted to dress his hair Yek style. When he turned his head to look at Turakina she gave a gasp of annoyance and let go of the half-plaited queue.

97

'Your concern does you credit, step-mother, and is a compliment to me, I know. But I have no taste for marriage.' Alexei formed a smile as he spoke, lest she detect a hint of the offence in his words.

Turakina raised her eyebrows. 'You have taste enough for the fruits, I am told,' she observed tartly.

Alexei stared calmly at her, and after a moment she produced a snort of half-amused annoyance and shook her head.

'If our strangeness offends you, then a woman of your own kind might perhaps be found,' Mei Ling offered tentatively.

Suragai's second wife was a N'pani, tiny, beautiful, regal, whom men called the Golden Lotus. She had been a courtesan before Turakina had bought her contract as a gift for her husband. When he had recovered from his embarrassment, Alexei's father had freed her – on the grounds that it was improper for a woman to be bought and sold like merchandise – and with Mei Ling's consent had opted to marry her. Turakina had known from the first how he would react, but she had pretended resistance for a day and a night before giving her consent. Now the two women were inseparable, although they were quite different in nature, and complemented one another like the two sides of a coin.

The sun was setting on the tops of the distant mountains. Alexei stared out of the open end of the room, awed as always by the view. His father's Kinsai house was built upon a natural plateau which rose above the curtain wall of the city. The morning room was supported out from it on stilts, reaching into nothing so that to stand at the foremost edge of the platform was to seem to be poised above an abyss. Kinsai was constructed on top of a plug of volcanic rock which rose sheer for almost a thousand metres

98

out of an almost perfectly flat and featureless plain. In the late afternoon, with the red sun setting and the dust from the caravans crossing the plain hanging on the air, the whole edifice looked like a monolith rising out of the depths of a brooding red sea.

'Lady, I do not want a wife – any wife.' Alexei met Mei Ling's enquiring gaze, and after a moment she nodded as if she understood.

Kadan was stretched out across a couch which was placed under one of the windows which ran the length of the room. He laughed softly. 'I think I have heard this conversation before,' he said.

'– And you will hear it again.' Turakina glanced at her son, silencing him, and then she turned to stare at Alexei again. 'Noyon, I have a duty to your father, my husband,' she said. 'You ought to be married – indeed it is the scandal of the Kha-Khan's court that you are not. Is there no lady of family you will consider?'

Once, before she had married his father, Alexei had played at courting Turakina. He had not been serious, and although she had thought herself in love with him at the time he had known that it would be a mistake for them to marry – even if Burun, who was her father, had been prepared to permit such a thing.

Kaidu and Hulagu, Mei Ling's twin sons, trotted into the room. They hesitated as if they expected to be dismissed, and then hurled themselves noisily on Kadan. He rolled them on the floor, growling in mock fury, and they giggled.

Mei Ling pretended a stare of disapproval, but when she saw that Alexei was watching, she smiled.

The twins were seven years old, and it was impossible to distinguish between them. Alexei settled himself in front of Irina once more. His father's family was by now a familiar part of his life, but he felt no particular attachment to any of them. Because the Yek

99

mutation bred true, all the children had talons instead of finger nails, and they possessed both the remarkable powers of healing and the resistance to disease which were the genetic inheritance of the True People.

Turakina and Mei Ling were unfolding a sheet on the floor between them. The sheet had embroidery in gold around its border, and Turakina began to inspect it section by section, snipping at loose threads or stitching them down.

'Maybe I should marry,' Alexei said lightly. He saw Turakina's head come up. 'But one wife would not be enough. I should have two at least – three even – or else I would not be properly cared for.'

Turakina wrinkled her nose. 'If you are not well cared for, it is the fault of the master of your household,' she said primly. 'A wife is not a servant – though she ought to concern herself with your comfort, it is true.'

Irina doubled Alexei's now plaited hair forward across his scalp. She had worked strips of gold braid into the weave, and now she secured them in place. 'There,' she said.

Alexei glanced at his reflection in the mirror which was propped against a cushion. 'I still do not look like a Yek,' he said, grinning.

'The colour of your hair is wrong,' she said. 'It is the colour of ripe corn. If you were shorter, then you would look like a C'zak.'

The C'zaki were a subject people from the east coast of the continent, and so the observation was not a compliment. Alexei looked up and saw that Kadan was laughing openly.

'Are the women of your homeworld beautiful?' Irina asked, 'Or do they look like you?'

Alexei ignored Kadan's splutter of amusement. He

squinted out of the corner of his eye to look at Irina. She was about twelve years of age – standard years – and possessed the curious red-gold hair colouring of a descendant of the Ancestor.

'They are not as beautiful as you,' he said, and smiled.

She flushed, pleased.

Kadan scooped the twins up off the floor. He sat down on the couch again, a boy on each knee. 'Beauty is a matter of individual perception,' he said seriously.

It was sometimes hard to keep in mind the fact that Kadan was not yet an adult. He was already taller than most Yek, and his stature displayed the kind of lankiness which promised both strength and agility. Alexei glanced at him, but said nothing.

'Beauty is less important than character,' Turakina said, as if she believed it.

Alexei showed his teeth in the pretence of a smile. 'If you say it, step-mother, then of course it must be so.' He guessed that Turakina had been engaged in yet another attempt to negotiate a match on his behalf, and wondered which family had been involved. It was half a year, he thought, since she had last broached the subject of his bachelor status.

Turakina frowned at the sarcasm in his tone. 'Noyon, I do not intend to argue with you,' she said severely.

'Good.' Alexei nodded as if the news pleased him.

Almost all Yek marriages were arranged. A contract was a matter for agreement between the respective parents, although the participants were consulted and there was a provision in the Yasa which prevented particularly women from being married off without their consent.

To submit to Turakina's intent would be to surrender his freedom. Alexei remembered what

Burun had said about the definition of independence, and he smiled grimly.

The yard at the front of the house was paved with flagstones. The sound of hooves ringing on them echoed through the house, and hearing them both Turakina and Mei Ling rose. Alexei turned.

His father came into the room. He was dressed Yek style in a loose tunic and breeches, and he had on a surcoat which was stiff with gold embroidery. The hilt of a *hiranu*, the short sword of Manchu manufacture which was carried as an alternative to the *jusei*, peeped from his waist sash. His hair was dressed in a manner which was appropriate to his rank.

'It's done,' he said. 'The time is set.'

Kadan sat up straight. 'Artai's enthronement?'

'Yes.' Suragai was carrying his gauntlets in one hand. He cast around for somewhere to put them, and at once Mei Ling took them and gave them to a waiting servant. He smiled at her. 'Lady, you adorn my house,' he said, then looked past her at Turakina. 'Lady, I am happy to see you.'

It was a formula, one which Alexei had heard his father use many times before, and yet he saw both women smile.

Turakina had on a gown into which were woven gold and silver threads. Her hair was long, and it was impossible to tell the place at which it merged with the fabric. She said, 'Then tell me, my Lord, how many times you have thought about me this day.'

Alexei saw his father produce a rueful smile.

'In truth,' Suragai said, 'I did not think of you at all. But were you not here to greet me I would miss you.' He held out his hand to her, and she took it, laughing.

'My Lord,' she said, 'your answer is always the same.'

102

'And why not?' Suragai was looking past her at Alexei as he spoke. 'It is always the truth.'

It seemed to Alexei as he considered it that a great deal of effort must be required to sustain such a relationship, and he could not imagine how his father could be bothered with it, or how the women could be content.

'Artai is to be enthroned the day after tomorrow, at the tenth hour.'

They were standing together at the very edge of the platform on which the morning room was constructed. The sun was setting, and the extent of the plain was lost in a crimson haze. Alexei stared out over the view, and wondered why his father had caused his house to be built in such a style.

'I had heard the day, but not the hour,' he said.

'I know.' Suragai nodded. 'Burun spoke to you. I ought to congratulate you on your elevation, I suppose.'

Alexei snorted softly. 'Spare me, please.'

He saw his father shrug.

'As you wish.'

It was how most of their arguments started – the sudden stirring of discord caused by their lack of understanding of one another's attitudes – an incautious word which stubbornness would not permit to be retracted.

Alexei took a breath, then exhaled slowly. He gestured, one-handed. 'Forgive me. I did not intend to sound churlish. Are you pleased for me?'

His father seemed to consider. 'Of course I am,' he said at last. 'And if I sound reserved, then it is because, having risen so high, we both have further to fall.'

They had been speaking quite naturally in Yek.

Alexei glanced back over his shoulder. Turakina and Mei Ling were still examining the sheet, and Kadan and Irina were playing with the twins beside the door. He switched to Anglic. 'You don't trust Artai.'

'I fear him,' his father said bluntly. 'It is Burun I do not trust.'

Alexei opened his mouth, then closed it again. It was on the tip of his tongue to observe that Burun was no more or less trustworthy than he had ever been, but he realised suddenly that he would be stating the obvious. No one – no one who was not of Burun's own blood – knew so much about him. 'Why do you serve him?' he asked softly.

'Oh,' Suragai chuckled. 'He rewards me – I owe him my life – he would kill us all if I did not – how many answers do you want me to give you?'

'Necessity.' Alexei knew he was making a face as he spoke the word.

'Is that wrong? Why do you make yourself an intimate of the younger Altun – why were you Nogai's friend?'

Anglic was the Imperial language. On Tarvaras there were several subject races who spoke a variation of it – perhaps because they were descended from Second Empire colonists – and suddenly Alexei found that there was insufficient subtlety in it to convey precise nuance.

'Expediency is a poor reason for doing anything,' he said in Yek, and saw his father frown.

Horns rang out from the city wall. The parapet which ran behind the wall was wide enough for two carts to be driven side by side along its length. It crossed the face of the house at a level ten or fifteen metres below the supports for the legs on which the floor was braced. Alexei glanced idly down, and he saw that a company of troopers of the guard – C'zaki by their dress, under the command of a Yek officer – were marching up from the direction of the gate, picking up the sentries who had completed their tour of duty, dropping off the night watch. The column passed out of sight below his feet.

'Who am I?'

The abruptness of the question brought Alexei's head round sharply. He hesitated, trying to divine his father's intent in asking it so that he could formulate the appropriate answer. 'You are my father,' he responded at last.

His father nodded. 'But what is my name?'

'Suragai.' Alexei spoke without thinking – without examining the implications of his reply. He understood what he had said, and nodded slowly. 'You are Suragai,' he said, and stopped.

'Suragai who was once Sergei; the counsellor to a Khan who was once a servant of the Empire –' his father pronounced. 'Am I less than I was – or more?'

'I suppose it depends upon who you ask,' Alexei said slowly. 'The Empire would consider it less.'

'But you agree that the value of what I have achieved is relative to my circumstances.'

'Yes. I suppose so.'

'Then you cannot criticise me for making the best of my situation.' His father folded his arms.

They had conducted the same argument, at intervals, since the days after they had realised that they were isolated on an alien world.

'You would have me remain what I was,' Suragai said, 'and alter the rest.'

'If the Yasa permitted the application of our knowledge –' Alexei started.

'But it does not – not enough for us to dictate the nature of our surroundings.'

It was a truth which Alexei had never been able to

105

develop the ability to ignore. Even when he was not thinking about it, it nagged at the edge of his awareness. The Yek who ruled this world lived according to a complex code of law at the very core of which was a presumption which affected every part of their existence – the belief that technological advancement was to a great extent incompatible with the maintenance of civilisation. Thus they treated innovation with extreme caution, and employed advanced technology only when they had satisfied themselves that it could be incorporated without visible effect into their style of living.

'Do you remember when we fought the Alan?' Suragai tucked his hands into the sleeves of his surcoat.

The Alan country was far to the south, beyond the G'bai desert, and its conquest had completed Yek expansion across the continent. Alexei nodded.

'The Alan had guns, but they could not stand against us.'

'Hackbuts.' Alexei recalled the weapons he had seen. 'And muskets – short barrelled, with no range – their powder was badly made too.' He saw his father nod.

'That's true. But do you think they would have beaten us – even if their weapons were better?'

Alexei remembered the sight of the Yek army moving across the plains. The basic unit was the tuman – ten thousand men, mounted on st'lyan, covering two hundred verst a day. The universal weapon was the compound bow, which had a pull of around a hundred and sixty pounds. Against the Alan, as many as twenty tumans had been in operation, their movement co-ordinated with incredible accuracy. Alexei shook his head. 'They don't believe they can be beaten,' he said.

106

Imperial marines could beat the Yek, Alexei supposed. A marine regiment was equipped with plasma cannon, and the marine battle armour was proof against most weapons. But faced with that kind of opposition the Yek would simply re-form and attack again, learning from each engagement until either they discovered how to defeat their adversaries or they were wiped out. It was unlikely that it would ever occur to them to surrender.

'The technology of this world is primitive, I admit,' his father said. 'But consider it in relation to the circumstances. Your complaint has always amounted to the fact that the Yek don't think the way you do – that they don't accept your values.' He paused, and then gestured as if to dismiss the subject. 'How did we get on to this? We will never agree, and so it's pointless.'

Once they would have come to blows. We have progressed that far at least, Alexei thought. 'We were discussing Artai,' he said. He glanced down. The marching men were disappearing around the curve of the wall. 'Do you know he is a mutant?'

'You mean his eyes.' Suragai nodded. 'Yek mutations breed true. If Artai has children, I wonder what they will look like.' He seemed to shiver.

Among humans a mutation could take thousands of generations to become apparent. The same medical technology which improved life expectancy and permitted the surgical replacement of defective organs also obstructed the process of natural selection, so that heightened abilities and levels of perception were still uncommon among ordinary men.

'So many of the Khans fear Artai,' Alexei said. 'I wonder why they elected him.'

His father shrugged. 'It was Nogai's will.'

'And if Nogai was wrong?'

107

Suragai made a face. 'How much harm can he do? He is as much subject to the Yasa as anyone else.'

'You mean the Khans think they can control him,' Alexei said. 'If that is true, then why do they fear him?' He saw his father frown again.

'He is your patron, not mine,' he said. 'You tell me what manner of ruler he will be.'

None of the Khans believed that Artai was so incapable of controlling the violence of his temperament, Alexei thought, or they would not have elected him. 'If he finds that the task of ruling the Khanate is a challenge –' he started.

'The Khanate is settled, and has been for some time,' his father said dismissively. 'Where lies the challenge?'

Alexei had guessed that the path of the conversation would lead eventually to this. '– Which is why I imagine Burun has taken steps to remind Artai that it is the ulus of the Kha-Khan to be the Lord of the Earth,' he said.

Suragai opened his eyes wide. 'Oh, I don't think he required much reminding,' he said.

'Indeed?' Alexei stared disbelievingly. 'In any case I am relieved to find that the embassy to the continents across the Great Sea has, as it seems, your approval.'

'It has, without reservation.'

'You don't think you might have consulted me before you suggested it? – It was your idea, I imagine.'

'The Khans are concerned to keep Artai's energies directed.' Suragai's face was immobile.

Alexei laughed harshly. 'I thought you were going to tell me at least that it was for my own good. Why me?'

'Because Burun will not go – if it was reconnaissance I think he might, but it is not – and so I cannot.'

'So?' The point was lost on Alexei.

Suragai shook his head in apparent irritation. 'I never thought you were stupid. The land across the sea is inhabited – you agree?'

'Yes –'

'And probably the level of civilisation is no greater than it is within the Khanate – otherwise the embassy would be coming the other way.'

The argument appeared to make sense. Alexei nodded.

'Very well then. So there are two unexplored continents – about a third of the land mass of this planet if the maps are to be believed – inhabited by people about whom we know nothing. Do you know of anyone else who is capable of recognising an opportunity if one presents itself?'

'Opportunity?' Alexei's brow creased. 'What kind of –' The direction of the argument struck him suddenly. He stopped, then nodded slowly. 'Cities,' he said. 'Old science.'

'Exactly.'

The lands ruled by the Yek were dotted with the traces of a Second Empire civilisation. There was an abandoned city on the coast to the south of the G'bai, and the G'bai itself was almost certainly the result of either a nuclear war or an accident of such proportions that it had produced large-scale volcanic activity. The black sands were wind-eroded basalt, and where parts of the sheet remained intact – and in basins and wadis – there was still radioactivity so that the desert could be navigated in safety only by the well-tried routes.

'If anything had survived,' Alexei objected, 'there would be another more advanced civilisation. The embassy would be coming, as you say, from the opposite direction.'

Even as he spoke he knew that there were circumstances under which that argument would be invalid. A survival of Second Empire technology could be so small as to be incapable of spreading its influence, or the science could have survived but not the necessary manufacturing techniques for its propagation.

'If you are certain of that, then don't go,' Suragai said.

Alexei considered a retort. 'You didn't convince Burun to let me lead it by telling him that I would be looking for machines,' he said finally. 'Hadn't you better tell me what arguments you used to persuade him?'

The servants were moving around inside the room lighting the lamps now. The sun was a thin red-gold line on a black horizon, and the twin moons were sitting like two silver pock-marked balls in the sky.

'I told him I wanted you out of Kinsai,' Suragai said, and showed his teeth.

It could be the truth, Alexei thought. Even if the means could be found, there were reasons why they might never attempt to beam a distress signal into space. To try to leave the surface of the planet was out of the question.

'You are thinking about how we came here,' his father said sombrely into the silence. 'And why we were forced to remain.'

'Yes.'

It had been no accident, but rather a botched assassination attempt, which had set Alexei's father down on Tarvaras. The two assassins had joined the crew of the navy rescue expedition which had followed the escape pod down from the survey vessel from which it had been ejected, and they had been prevented from finishing off both their intended victim and the accidental witnesses only because of the timely intervention of a Yek patrol. There had been no second rescue attempt – the first vessel had been destroyed by a rigged explosion – and the conclusion the survivors had arrived at had been that they were assumed killed. Tarvaras was a quarantine world, cut off from contact with the rest of the universe by orbiting weapons platforms which were programmed to destroy any craft which did not identify itself with the appropriate recognition codes, and it had seemed unlikely that the civilian survey crew would be tempted to break the stringent regulations which applied to the situation.

'I thought you were content to remain here,' Alexei said.

'I did not say that I intended to leave,' his father responded. 'It is you who are unhappy here.'

Alexei flushed. 'Don't condescend to me.'

Suragai grinned. 'How sensitive you have become. Very well, tell me you will lead this mission, and I will torment you no more.'

'Tell me why you want me to go.'

'I was under the impression that I had explained it to you. We – that is you and I – as well as the Yek, ought to know what lies beyond the Great Sea. You are the best person to go and look.'

'Besides which, it will get me out of Kinsai for a while,' Alexei observed ironically.

'That too.'

He had been herded towards giving his agreement like a p'tar being driven to slaughter, Alexei thought, but even if the latter reason was the real one it was not an opportunity he could afford to pass up. 'Damn you, Father,' he said. 'Of course I'll go.'

'Good,' Suragai said, and smiled.

'Beware Burun,' Siban said. 'You cannot trust him.'

They were both guests at T'zin's house – two

111

among fifty or so of the Khans and Noyons who, apart from Burun, were probably the most powerful and influential men in the Khanate. Alexei leaned a little to one side so that a slave could heap his plate with k'va, the staple grain which was similar to rice. The k'va was the colour of straw because it had been cooked over boiling k'vass, an ale which was made from fermenting the raw grain, and it steamed gently.

'Burun would say the same of you,' Alexei said equably.

Siban's face was seamed like old leather, and his hair was snow white. He examined Alexei haughtily. 'I am a grandson of the Ancestor,' he said, 'whereas Burun is a worthless Merkut chief –'

Alexei grinned. 'Not all that worthless, I think.' A second slave began to ladle stewed meat onto the heaped k'va, and the aroma of the ch'min in which it had been cooked made his nostrils twitch. 'In any case –' He looked back at Siban. 'It is Artai I serve, and not Burun.'

'The whole world knows who pulls Artai's strings,' Siban said sourly. 'There is no one with the power to gainsay him.'

Alexei took out his knife. The Yek served themselves from their plates by extending their talons – in some cases the needle-sharp claws were more than three centimetres long – forking impaled meat into their mouths. He started to eat, aware of Siban's insistent presence by his side.

'Sidacai should be here,' Siban said suddenly.

The comment was meaningless. Siban's son was a prisoner under sentence of death for his conspiracy to seize power. The slaves were bringing cups of chilled wine to the long table. Alexei sipped experimentally, and wondered why some men still preferred k'miss. There were no vegetables – the Yek grew only a limited number – and he selected an apple from a pile in a bowl and started to peel it with his d'jaga. He glanced at Siban out of the corner of his eye, but said nothing.

'Heed me,' Siban said. 'Burun will trap you as he has trapped my son.'

Alexei raised his eyebrows. 'My Lord, if you have proof of that, take it to Artai. Everyone knows that the Merkuts crushed Sidacai's plot to seize power.'

Siban ate sparingly. The meat on his plate had been cut into small segments because his teeth were no longer sharp. 'My son was a fool,' he said. 'And if you cannot see a Merkut hand behind what has happened, so are you.'

It was easiest to shrug, ignoring the offence. Alexei had expected to be seated beside Tulagai and Targoutai, the half-brothers of Nogai and T'zin, but instead he had been led to this place beside Siban. Vaguely he wondered when Siban was going to come to the point. Probably he was going to ask for help in obtaining a pardon for Sidacai, and Alexei thought about telling him that it was Burun's intent that he should be freed.

'Pardon me,' Siban said after a moment. 'You are Artai's good friend, and I have slighted you.'

'What?'

Alexei was unable to hide his astonishment at Siban's subdued tone. He stared. 'My Lord, don't grovel. It doesn't suit you.'

Siban growled angrily. He slashed at Alexei, talons out, but Alexei had anticipated the move. He caught Siban's wrist and held it immobile. Heads turned briefly, and from the far end of the table T'zin was watching, an interested expression on his face.

'Attack me, and you will forfeit my favour,' Alexei said softly to Siban. He saw Siban start.

113

'You are making a mistake –' Siban started.

'Oh?' Alexei felt Siban's wrist bones grate together under his hand, and he eased the pressure he was exerting, ashamed at his use of force against an old man.

Siban's eyes burned angrily, but after a moment he allowed the muscles of his arm to relax. 'You are right, Noyon,' he said at last. 'I had intended to secure your favour, or I would not let you live for this insult.'

Alexei showed his teeth in the grim pretence of a smile. A slash from Siban's talons would have inflicted a wound which would have taken weeks to heal. He released Siban's arm carefully. 'My Lord, you struck first. Do you want to challenge me?' He saw Siban's lips compress.

'You know I do not,' Siban said, 'or you would not dare ask. Remember who I am.'

Only T'zin was still watching the exchange. Alexei looked past Siban towards him, and inclined his head. He saw T'zin react, surprised. After a second T'zin nodded an acknowledgement, then turned ostentatiously to speak to Jehan, Burun's grandson, who was seated on his right.

'My Lord, I am aware of your rank.' Alexei met Siban's outraged stare calmly. 'If you want something of me, then ask me politely. Don't condescend to me, and don't accuse the men who have been my friends in my hearing.'

It was apparent that Siban was torn between his pride and his desire to engage Alexei's interest in his petition to the Kha-Khan. He drew himself up. 'Don't expect me to humble myself, Noyon,' he said coldly. 'I have ruled the armies of the Kha-Khan, and kings have come to petition me on their knees.'

Alexei kept his face expressionless. He waited for Siban to find a way to phrase the request which was so obviously his intent, but instead Siban rose to his feet and stalked away towards the door, his departure so abrupt that Alexei was taken by surprise.

Tulagai slid almost at once into the vacant place. He watched as Siban went out through the door, and then glanced at Alexei. 'Siban does not belong here,' he said. 'T'zin was mistaken to invite him.'

It was difficult to recall at times the fact that Tulagai was Artai's father. Alexei remembered how Tulagai and Targoutai had fawned on Siban before Nogai had been elected Kha-Khan, and how they had voiced their support for Nogai, their own half-brother, as soon as it had become apparent that he had Burun's vote. It seemed improper somehow that someone like Tulagai, his motives suspect, should mock Siban, who had served the Khanate so well, and Alexei thought that he was sorry that he had goaded him into leaving.

The bowmaker was named T'zun-tu, and he was very old. His shop was in the merchants' quarter of the city – a maze of buildings which had been divided and sub-divided, so great was the demand for space, which lay within the strictly enforced boundaries of the streets which radiated from the Golden Yurt like the spokes of a wheel.

'My father has seven of these,' Jehan said, fingering a half-finished bow as it lay in its clamps.

'Your father is Jotan,' Alexei responded, 'and can afford them.'

'Oh.' Jehan smiled engagingly. 'That's true.'

'Bows and women,' Kadan said cheerfully. 'Is there anything else worth spending money on?'

Jehan caught Alexei's eye, and they both smiled. 'Well,' Jehan said, 'a few things maybe.'

Kadan was probably too young to be interested in

women, though he might have been tempted to experiment with one of his mother's serving women if he was offered the opportunity. 'Women spend money, not men,' Alexei said.

'If all that is said about you is true, then you ought to know,' Jehan observed. He avoided Alexei's eyes, and ran his fingers over the grain of the layers of wood and horn which were compressed between the clamps. 'This is very fine,' he said.

Kadan was humming softly. Alexei thought about asking what latest scandal Jehan had heard, and how widely it was being spread abroad. Whatever was being said, probably it did not matter. He took an arrow from the table and sighted along it.

'Not one of those, my Lord.' The bowyer came out of the back of the shop, the bow case which he had been selecting in his hands. 'Those have too little spline for your bow.'

The bow reached to Alexei's mid-chest. The layers of horn and yew had been blended together with such care that it was hard to tell which was set upon which. Alexei set the stock against his instep and nocked the string into place. The great compound curves which swept out from the guard vibrated under his hand, and the bowstring produced a low musical sound.

'Arrows fletched with peacock,' Kadan said. 'They are the best.'

Jehan wrinkled his nose. 'Swan is better.'

Alexei tested the pull of the bow. 'Give me an arrow,' he said.

'Take off your coat,' Jehan protested. 'You will fray the sleeve.'

'He will fray his arm if he shoots without protection,' Kadan observed. 'T'zun-tu, find a wrist guard for my Lord.'

116

The bowyer hastened to comply. Alexei laid the bow aside and took off his coat. Jehan held out his hand for it.

Kadan picked the bow up. He tested the pull, and looked at Jehan. 'You should try this,' he said. 'I think it's too strong for me.'

Alexei took the bow out of Kadan's hands. 'You haven't come into your strength yet,' he said.

T'zun-tu was laying clothyard arrows on the table. The fletchings were dyed in Alexei's colours, and gleamed silver-grey in the shafts of light which penetrated the shop. Alexei took one and nocked it to the bow. He drew and sighted out through the window.

'My Lord –' the bowyer began nervously.

Alexei loosed, and the arrow leapt from the bow and embedded itself in the wooden spike which rose from the dome of a house two streets away.

'Solid hit!' Kadan crowed.

Jehan took the bow out of Alexei's hands. 'Someone give me an arrow.' He drew the string halfway back, then let it out again. 'Name of God.' He looked at Alexei. 'This has a pull like my grandfather's.'

The weight and power of Burun's bows were famous. A normal arrow would shatter if it was fired from one. Alexei opened his eyes wide. 'If it is too strong –'

'If it is too strong, then I must be sickening for something.' Jehan flexed his right arm, then drew the bowstring back to his cheek. He loosed, and his arrow hit the spike a hand's-breadth below Alexei's. 'Here.' Jehan offered the bow to Kadan. 'You try.'

'Oh well –' Kadan took the arrow which the bowyer handed to him, nocked it, drew without apparent effort, and loosed. '– It's powerful, certainly, but I think I could use one of these.'

Jehan shaded his eyes with his hand. Kadan's arrow was stuck in the spike midway between the others. 'I should have made you nominate your point of aim,' he said. 'You're like oxen, the pair of you.'

Alexei knew that he had gained muscle during his years on Tarvaras. Kadan was his half-brother, and even though he was not yet fully grown, he had his father's strength.

In the street below the house with the dome people were pausing to look up at the arrows in the spike. A Yek in the long coat of a merchant came out of the door of the house. Someone pointed out the arrows to him, and he turned and glared in the direction of the bowmaker's window.

'We could send Kadan to get our arrows back,' Jehan said idly.

Kadan glanced out of the window, then drew back again. 'Not likely,' he said.

The bowyer was looking resigned. 'My Lord, that is the house of Yesugai the mercer,' he said. 'I will send to him, though I do not think it will please him.'

Jehan laughed softly. 'If there is a fine, we will pay it,' he said.

'I will pay it,' Alexei corrected him. Men were struggling through the crowd in the street, a ladder between them. The mercer started to direct them as they propped the ladder against the side of the house. The ladder reached the eaves. A man climbed to the top and gazed helplessly at the curved expanse of the copper-sheathed dome. He turned and shouted something to the mercer below.

Kadan picked up the bow case and slid the bow gently into it. The bowyer was hovering expectantly, his hand not quite extended to receive payment.

Alexei took a leather wallet from his belt. He unfolded it, and gold koban slid weightily into his hand, forty of them, yellow as butter, the gold so soft that it deformed if one coin fell against another. He held the money out.

'Lord, thank you.' The bowyer tried to pretend that he was not counting the coins. His fingertips moved as he felt the edge of each gold piece, and then he bowed. 'Lord, you are generous.'

The price of the bow was as much as the income of a common man for a year. Alexei nodded as if it was of no consequence. 'Your work pleases me,' he said. 'Send to me if the mercer asks for compensation.'

The man at the top of the mercer's ladder was clambering awkwardly out onto the roof. He climbed a short distance up the curve of the dome, then his feet lost their purchase and he began to slide back down again. As soon as he was close enough to the head of the ladder to use it as a support, he stood up. He waved and shouted something at the mercer in the street below, then scrambled back onto the ladder again and started to descend.

Jehan watched. He caught Alexei's eye. 'You have left your mark on Kinsai it seems,' he said drily.

'We all have.' Kadan nodded cheerfully.

Alexei said nothing. He was not sure that Jehan had been talking about the arrows, and remembering that Jehan was Burun's grandson he wondered how much he knew, or had been told, about the plan to obtain Sidacai's freedom.

'Siban has spoken with me,' T'zin said.

'Oh?'

They were lounging at their ease in an ante-chamber which was next to the throne room of the Golden Yurt. Now that preparations had been completed for Artai's enthronement there was very little to do, and the normal business of the court –

administration, legislation, taxation – had all but come to a halt.

'He was my guest.' T'zin reached out and took a cup of wine from a tray which was held by a N'pani who stood nearby. 'You offended my hospitality by slighting him.'

Alexei frowned. 'I am sorry for it.' He sipped wine.

T'zin gestured dismissively. 'It is a failing common to those of us who have achieved greatness,' he said, 'that we do not know how to beg for favour.'

'I should have made Siban's task easier.' Alexei nodded. 'Ask on his behalf if you will.'

The cup in T'zin's hand was a sculpted crystal bowl set in a mesh of gold wire. T'zin's gold-sheathed talons were only half retracted, and he held the goblet delicately between them. 'I think you know what Siban wants,' he said.

'Sidacai's freedom?' Alexei suggested lightly.

'Sidacai's pardon,' T'zin said.

Alexei pretended to stare. Sidacai freed might be banished. A pardon implied that he would retain his rank. It would be as if he had never been taken in treason.

'My Lord, I think you over-estimate my influence with Artai.'

T'zin emptied his cup in a single swallow. He held it out in the servant's direction and let it go. The servant got his hand to it just in time to prevent it falling onto the marble floor. T'zin had already turned back to meet Alexei's eyes. 'I think not,' he said.

So many people were interested in Sidacai's fate that Alexei thought it was amazing they had not combined to petition Artai. He noticed that although T'zin was wearing the fancy gold coat of the Altun he had no tunic on beneath it, and his bare chest was visible through the unfastened facings.

120

'Artai trusts me,' Alexei pointed out. 'If I ask him to give Sidacai pardon, I will forfeit his favour.'

'You are an alien,' T'zin said. 'It is well known that you do not reason as other men. Ask Sidacai's absolution and Artai will believe whatever you tell him.'

Alexei snorted softly. 'Artai is not a fool,' he commented. 'He will suspect my motives, no matter what I say.'

T'zin appeared to consider. 'Secure Sidacai's pardon,' he said, 'and you will earn my friendship.'

The servant placed a filled goblet on the table at T'zin's side. Alexei drained his own cup and put it down. 'I will do what I can,' he said finally, as if he doubted his ability to achieve anything worthwhile. He thought about Burun's intent towards Sidacai, and wished he could discuss it with someone.

'Ask Artai tomorrow,' T'zin said. It was advice which appeared to ignore the fact that if Alexei did not, Sidacai's death warrant would be signed and his sentence executed. 'It is the day of enthronement.' T'zin picked up the cup, then gestured with it. 'Artai cannot defy custom – if you ask mercy for Sidacai, he must grant it.'

The women's chambers of the palace opened out onto an arcade which was roofed with trees. The branches with their silver-green leaves spread out to meet one another, intertwined, and cast rows of delicate tendrils around the pillars which were the support for the gallery above. In the centre of the arcade there was a pool in which huge golden carp basked like predatory sharks among the minnows and goldfish.

It was the custom for men to come to the place only by invitation. This was where the Kha-Khan's wives, if he had them, made their entertainment – a space at what was otherwise without question the heart of the government of the Khanate which was occupied with poetry and music, which men were wont to regard as idle pastimes – the place from which rumours were spread, and thus to which every lady of the court assigned an hour, or two, each day.

'Men are fools,' Zurachina said. 'And you are no exception.'

Burun's chief wife was small and slim, handsome in the way that unremarkable women sometimes are when they have matured past the need for beauty, and the red-gold of her hair was as yet unmarred by the silver which would have betrayed her age.

Alexei trailed a hand through the clear water of the pool. The carp feeding around the inlet nudged at his fingers. 'Lady, I know it,' he said.

Half of the women of the court were here – which fact, Alexei thought, should not have surprised him. So long as Artai remained unmarried it was important to the self-esteem of each of them to demonstrate that while neither she nor her family had thus far been favoured with the Kha-Khan's selection, yet she was capable of exercising influence.

'Your name has been connected with ten ladies that I know of,' Zurachina said severely.

Alexei essayed a smile. 'Only ten?'

She frowned at him. 'Noyon, it is no laughing matter. The licence which was permitted under Nogai is a thing of the past now, and while you have not broken the Yasa, there is the matter of custom. The law was not formulated so that men and women could exchange favours promiscuously, but rather that a woman, being unable to decide upon a marriage offered to her, might select for herself without prior commitment from the men available and willing to accept her.'

122

Turakina was her daughter, and must have spoken to her. Alexei had been surprised that the subject of his bachelor status had not been pursued with greater vigour in his step-mother's house. Now he knew why. 'Lady, my conduct is my own affair,' he said.

'Is it?' Zurachina smoothed a finger down one cheek. 'Noyon, your father is a son to me, through his marriage to my daughter. My own son is husband to a lady of Altun blood, and I am Altun. We must be seen to keep the spirit of the law, as well as the letter, or soon there will be no order in the land.'

Jotan's wife Arkhina was reclining on cushions in a nearby alcove, and her mother, a daughter of Arjun the Great, was engaged in conversation with the widow of her cousin, who had been parent to Nogai.

'Tomorrow you will become a Khan,' Zurachina pointed out with calm persistence. 'Your vassals will come to you for justice, and you cannot expect them to accept your judgement if it can be seen that you hold the Yasa in contempt.'

Alexei eyed her. 'Lady, respect for the Yasa is, as we both know, a fiction. It is broken every day.' He glanced pointedly in the direction of the mother of Nogai. Sula was by birth a Manghutt princess, and she had lived under sentence of banishment until her son's accession to the Dragon Throne for her part in her family's attempt to install him as Kha-Khan while his grandfather Arjun yet ruled.

Zurachina followed the direction of Alexei's glance, and she sniffed. 'Noyon your tongue is as agile as your mind,' she said acidly. 'Be careful you do not trip over it.'

Alexei laughed at her, then sobered. He knew that the licence which had pervaded Nogai's court had been its least attractive feature. 'Lady, I accept what you say,' he said. 'But if my name has been so discredited, I do not see a remedy.'

123

A lady of the court, the daughter of a lesser Khan of the Arcutt, moved gracefully along the passageway which bordered the arcade. She saw Alexei, paused and smiled, and then descended the few steps and came towards him. Zurachina turned when she heard the sound of approaching footsteps. She stared coldly, and the lady's smile faltered. She hesitated, then bowed to Zurachina and went away. Alexei grinned.

'Jotan has a daughter yet unmarried,' Zurachina said.

Alexei sat up straight. Jotan's daughter, the sister of Jehan, was the source of as much malicious gossip as he was himself. A year or two younger than her brother she had refused every match offered her, maintaining instead a state of determined independence. She kept, it was said, her own household and ruled her own fiefs, and although her name had never been linked with any man Alexei knew of, marriage to her was not a prospect which he thought he would be able to face with equanimity.

'She is unwomanly,' Zurachina said, as if she anticipated his objections, 'and were it not for her beauty I would wish that she had been born a man.'

'Lady, I do not think –' Alexei hesitated, selecting polite phrases and discarding them again. '– I doubt if your grand-daughter would accept me.' There was no reason why she should after rejecting so many others, he thought, and wondered in the same instant if it would be interesting to court such a woman.

Zurachina's hands lay still in her lap. 'There are reasons why she will accept your suit,' she said.

'Oh?'

The end of the arcade was full of women, all of them whispering and staring towards the place where Zurachina's servants had set down her chair. A pot of

124

ch'ban, a beverage which Alexei thought was quite similar to earth stock coffee, bubbled quietly on a burner which was set in a shallow bowl of sand on the table at her side. She lifted the pot and filled two tiny cups, offering him one.

'Artai's interest has lighted upon her,' she said.

Alexei was pleased to note that the hand with which he raised his cup did not tremble. He sipped the bitter-sweet drink. 'Then surely you consider that an honour which ought not to be declined,' he said gravely.

Zurachina raised her cup between extended talons, but her eyes did not leave Alexei's face. She drank from her cup, then set it on the table. 'Even if Jehana would accept it,' she observed, her tone prosaic, 'it is not a match which her family would consider – appropriate.'

'I would have thought that Burun's influence –' Alexei began.

'My husband's influence does not require to be increased by his grand-daughter's marriage to Artai,' Zurachina said with finality.

Artai could not have declared any public intent to marry Jehana, Alexei realised, or it would have been the talk of Kinsai. Probably there were rumours – nothing was ever entirely a secret at court – and he glanced again at the women who clustered at the other end of the pool.

'If Artai asks for her hand –' he began delicately.

'If he asks for Jehana's hand,' Zurachina said, 'it will be refused.'

Rejection for whatever reason was not a matter which Artai would easily forgive.

'– A response which would damage rather than increase the influence of the Merkuts in the Khanate,' Alexei observed.

125

Zurachina nodded. '– And so it cannot be allowed to occur. I am pleased you follow my reasoning so readily, Noyon. If your betrothal to Jehana is declared quickly, Artai will be unable to demonstrate offence. Has he ever mentioned his interest to you?'

'No.'

'Then he can have no reason to feel that you have acted contrary to his will.'

Her argument was so brutally simple that Alexei was lost for words. He emptied his cup and set it down on the table. The porcelain from which the cup was formed was so translucent that the grain of the wood upon which it sat was faintly visible through it.

I could refuse.

The thought came to Alexei with such force and urgency that he knew that it was not a reasoned reaction.

The expression on Zurachina's face was impossible to read. 'You have nothing to say?' she asked.

Alexei gestured helplessly. '– Only that between you and your husband I see a conspiracy to force me to forfeit Artai's favour.'

Zurachina shrugged.

There was a kind of inevitability about the whole proposal which appalled Alexei. In human terms the reasoning which had been presented to him was filled with flaws and false assumptions. To a Yek accomplished in the ways of the court the whole scheme would make perfect sense however. More than anything else Alexei knew that he was not like his father, and could never belong here.

This is not my world.

It was as if Zurachina had divined what he was thinking. 'As to Artai,' she said calmly, 'he will be reminded that you are an alien. You do not think like a civilised man, although your behaviour has become

126

civilised, and so he cannot ascribe to your actions motives which are suspect – or not according to his understanding.'

The observation contained an insult, but Alexei knew that if he attempted to explain it to her she would be unable to comprehend it. He stared unseeing down the arcade, then looked back at her. 'My courtship of your grand-daughter is then only a matter of form,' he said.

Zurachina looked as if she thought that the observation was unnecessary. 'I have said she will accept you,' she responded. 'She has already agreed.'

The plan was Burun's of course, and Zurachina was doing his will. It occurred to Alexei to wonder how many people were party to the arrangement. Turakina certainly knew – her words to him the previous afternoon had simply been a test of his resistance – and if she had knowledge of it, then so had Suragai. Jotan, as Jehana's father, must have given his consent – and thus probably Jehan.

'Say that you will accept it,' Zurachina prompted.

A bitter reply rose to Alexei's lips, but he suppressed the urge to utter it. Probably Zurachina was aware of his feelings, even though she was incapable of understanding them. 'Lady, I am your servant,' he said.

She sat back, considering him gravely. 'Good,' she said, then smiled. 'Noyon, you shall not regret this, I give you my promise.'

It was clear to Alexei that if the Merkuts did not wish to see Jehana given in marriage to Artai, there were reasons which had nothing to do with the suitability of the match. He recalled how Burun had dissociated himself from acting as Artai's sponsor. Even though it was common knowledge that the Merkuts were the power behind the throne, no one

127

could say that they had ever demanded precedence after Artai. If Artai's reign was marked by disaster or excess they would be able to claim that they were not responsible, and their influence over the affairs of the Khanate would not be diminished.

'You might have warned me.' Alexei watched his father's face for a reaction. He had met him on his way to the stables, and they stood in a yard which was busy with blacksmiths and farriers.

'It might have come to nothing,' Suragai said. The look which Alexei produced was frankly disbelieving, and he smiled. 'Marriage will settle you,' he observed.

Alexei thought that marriage to Jehana was likely to be anything but settling, but he did not argue. 'I have heard betrothal mentioned,' he said. 'Not marriage.'

'I think one follows the other,' his father said mildly. A groom was leading a pair of matched sorrel st'lyan at the trot around the beaten clay of an exercise ring. The gilding on the st'lyan's horns glittered as they tossed their heads. Suragai watched critically, then waved a hand. 'Good, Arvid. Let them be re-shod.'

'I am surprised Burun chose me.' Alexei scuffed his heel through the tan which had been scattered across the clay.

'So am I.' Suragai grinned. 'Maybe he is concerned to improve his bloodline. You know the Altun are becoming inbred.'

The Merkuts were not part of the Golden Clan, but the remark contained a certain amount of truth. The principal families of the Khanate were all inter-related, and so it was not hard to understand why the defective genes which had been responsible for

Nogai's early death recurred in so many of his blood.

The explanation was not a serious one, Alexei thought, or if it was, it was not reassuring. All that was apparent so far was that Burun's intent was to divert Artai's interest away from Jehana. Artai was young, but once he chose a wife – an honour for which there would be contenders enough – reasons for breaking her betrothal might be easy enough to find. Suddenly it occurred to Alexei that in the event that he failed to return from the embassy the question of solemnising the marriage would not arise, and he wondered again how far he could trust Burun.

Arvid was leading the st'lyan across the yard. The smith was a freedman, tall and muscular, a Ch'noze whose facial tattoos indicated that he was of the family of a war-leader.

'Those are nice animals.'

His father's head came round. 'Yes – bred from a mare Burun gave me the year we fought the Alan. Those are the second generation. They're not as heavy, but they're just as strong.'

In appearance st'lyan were not unlike Terran stock horses, though they were much larger and faster. Alexei held to the opinion that they could not be naturally evolved, and thought that the single horn which projected from the forehead of each had been the whim probably of some Second Empire geneticist. Internally the equine similarities ceased. St'lyan had an organ which acted like a supercharger, so that they were capable of long periods of exertion, and like the Yek they were able to endure remarkable extremes of heat and cold.

The smith lifted a hoof onto his thigh, then began to scrape the compacted tan and dung which clogged it with a hoofpick. His apprentices stood in a respectful half-circle to watch, and a crowd of small boys – most of them children of members of the household – loitered in a shy cluster in a nearby doorway.

'Look in the doorway,' Suragai said.

Alexei followed the direction of his father's gaze, and saw that Hulagu and Kaidu were edging gradually to the front of the group watching the smith.

'I see them. Where are they supposed to be?'

'Somewhere. Not here.'

The twins were notorious for their escapades. Kaidu was venturing out of the doorway into the yard now. He glanced towards the place where his father stood, a wary expression on his face. Suragai pretended not to notice. A pair of matched bays were being led into the exercise ring by a groom, and he turned away to watch them.

Kaidu picked up a hoofpick from the smith's bench, and he wrestled the off-hind hoof of the second sorrel up into his lap. The huge animal dwarfed him.

'He'll be trampled,' Alexei said.

'Not by one of my sorrels. Watch.'

The smith was aware of Kaidu's presence now. He glanced in Suragai's direction, his eyebrows raised in enquiry. Alexei saw his father grin and shake his head. The sorrel turned its beautiful head to stare over its shoulder at Kaidu. It snorted, and carefully raised its hind leg and straightened it as if to rid itself of an encumbrance. Kaidu tumbled head over heels. The boys standing in the doorway tittered. The sorrel whickered softly, looking pleased with itself.

Hulagu came out of the clustered spectators. He pulled his twin to his feet. 'Let me try.' He took the hoofpick out of Kaidu's hand, then tried to lift the st'lyan's hoof onto his thigh.

'Here, Noyon,' the smith said. 'It's easier like this.'

He showed both boys how to lift the sorrel's hoof between their knees, and suddenly there was a line of small boys at his side, all waiting hopefully for a turn.

The day of Artai's enthronement was one which Alexei was to remember afterwards as one of the most confusing of his life. From the first it was apparent that it was not destined to be the faultless pageant which the stewards and controllers of the Kha-Khan's household had both intended and arranged. It had rained heavily during the night – a sudden downpour which had filled the gutters and drains which supplied the city's water catchment system – so that when dawn broke it could be seen that many of the drapes and festoons over archways and down the faces of stands and platforms had been torn from the frames by the weight of the water which had soaked them. The forests of banners and guidons which adorned every street corner hung limp and sodden, and where an otherwise laudable economy had resulted in the use of cheap cloth the colours had run so that the insignia upon the panels was streaked and indecipherable.

Alexei had risen before the sun broke the horizon, and because he was engaged to wait upon Jehana at the house of her father – a public display to advertise the fact of their intended betrothal which was designed, he guessed, to make it believable – he was among the first to witness the damage which the teams of wrights and carpenters now laboured to repair.

That much of the decoration was shredded or defaced beyond hope of repair, Alexei thought, was quite clear. Clad in a coat which was so stiff with gold wire and seed pearls that he could scarcely bend his arms he rode with his escort beneath a line of arches which were suspended on ropes between houses on opposite sides of one of the main streets. The material which yesterday had draped them now lay in discarded heaps on the stones of the paving below, and men were hastily tacking new lengths – the mercers and drapers must have ransacked their warehouses to find enough, and the cost would no doubt make the court treasurer blench – to the framework. The troopers of the Kha-Khan's guard who were detailed to line the processional route had been pressed into service to clear away the debris, and their facial expressions reflected their feelings as the dye from the cloth stained their hands and surcoats. The puddles in the hollows of the paving stones shimmered with a wash of colour as booted feet splashed through them, and officials of the court stood with long faces as they counted the extent of the destruction wrought by the rains.

'Bad luck,' Ordai said, riding at Alexei's side. He spat left and right.

Alexei frowned. Some men were already saying that Artai's election was ill-starred. 'Rain at this season is a good omen,' he contradicted. It was the middle of the orange month – almost the hottest time of the year – when the condensation from the mist which clung to the buildings every morning was welcome for the moisture it imparted.

His orderly looked politely doubtful. 'If you say so, Lord,' he said.

Away from the main streets there was less damage. The burghers of Kinsai ranked as lesser Khans, and they had done their best to decorate in suitable style those areas of their city which were not in the path of the official progress. Where cloth had been scarce they had pinned ivy or ch'in-sei, the silver-leafed creeper which grew where nothing else would

132

survive, and Artai's device – an eagle with an arrow in its talons – was painted onto friezes which were roped to gables and lamp cressets. Alexei rode between dragons moulded from paper and paste which were lined up in a side street. The dragons were for the procession, and were designed to be raised upon the shoulders of pairs of bearers. They had been draped with canvas to protect them from the rain, and a watchman in wet buckram saluted civilly, then stepped back in haste to avoid the splashes thrown up by the hooves of the passing st'lyan.

'Bow to your left, Lord. The men in that yard are saluting you.'

'I see them.' Alexei inclined his head as far as the collar of his coat would allow. The result was stiff, distant even, and the three or four burghers bowed even lower. He smiled sourly. He had acknowledged similar courtesies a number of times since riding out, and guessed that it was the sable hat of a Khan which he carried in his hand which was attracting recognition, rather than his actual eminence. The hat and coat had been delivered the previous evening by an officer of the Kha-Khan's guard, and since the news of Jehana's betrothal had been spread through the court hours earlier it had to be assumed that Artai had heard of it, and that either he was inclined to forgive the offence which might be supposed to exist, or else he was pretending that he was aware of none.

Jotan's house was at the end of a street which curved to follow the line of the city wall. The building was constructed from amber-coloured stone, and the roof ridges and gable ends were sheathed with bronze. The sentries had been primed to admit him without challenge, Alexei noted, and as soon as his escort had dismounted a trooper wearing the gorget

133

of a provost came out of the gatehouse and led them away towards the stables.

'Well met.' Jotan detached himself from an alcove beside the main door. Burun's eldest son was a tall rangy man with a lot of muscle and sinew. A famous fighter in his youth, he was now one of the Khanate's foremost statesmen.

'Good morning, Khan.' Alexei bowed politely. He had served under Jotan during the Alan campaign – they had acquaintances in common – but all at once he was unsure what form of address to employ. He saw that he was being appraised, and flushed.

'– Custom dictates that we deal with one another like friends,' Jotan said, but did not smile. '– At least until we start to argue the matter of my daughter's dowry. You could call me Uncle, I suppose, if it pleases you.'

Alexei's father's first wife was Jotan's sister, and so it was possible that the suggestion was a serious one. Alexei made a pretence of considering. '– A term which might be thought by some to overstate our relationship,' he said finally, and was pleased to observe that his tone did not waver.

'As you wish.' Jotan nodded. 'We were both more at ease, I think, when we were not required to hide our mistrust for one another. The Yek offend you because we do not think you are human. You consider the peoples of this world barbarians, uncivilised, and sometimes you do not trouble to conceal your opinion of us. It will be hard for us to pretend friendship.'

Alexei was always taken by surprise by the Yek talent for blunt speaking. 'That being the case,' he said, 'I am surprised you have given your consent to your daughter's betrothal to me.'

Jotan's head went back, and he looked down his

134

nose. 'Your father is my brother,' he replied, as if it explained everything. Suddenly the corner of his mouth twitched. He shook his head and laughed harshly. 'I shall call you comrade, I think,' he said, and laughed again.

It was a term used by common soldiers – men who had shared a tent, a bowl of meat, or the last of the wine. Alexei did not understand why Jotan seemed to be amused by the notion, and so he said nothing.

The inside of Jotan's house was constructed on three levels – galleries off the main building which were buttressed by huge timbers – and the open ends of each living space overlooked the central hall, although the stairways which gave access to them were concealed. Although it was summer a fire burned in the great stone hearth – embers which were all that were left of logs which had been burned during the night to repel the damp which always crept out of the stone walls. The ceiling of the hall was also the roof of the building, and when Alexei looked up he could see the rafters, black with age, the heads of brass nails glittering across them. The hall smelled of cedar wood and sweet wax. The lamps in the cressets gave out the scent of perfumed oil, and somewhere a lutenist was playing quietly.

'Sit.' Jotan gestured towards a chair which was placed upon a circular carpet of Keraistani weave. The colours of the carpet were blends of every shade from oatmeal to deep brown, and the pattern was so intricate that Alexei's eye could not follow it. He sat, and at once a page came out of the shadows with a tray which contained cups and a flask of wine. He went towards Jotan, but Jotan waved him away. 'Serve my guest before you serve me.'

The page was a Y'frike, a boy of ten or eleven years of age, whose skin was the colour of roasted ch'ban grounds. Jotan had spoken Yek to him, for the tongue of the conquerors was employed everywhere, and there were few people in the known world who did not understand it. The page hastened to serve Alexei, his face expressionless. Like Alexei, he had nails on the ends of his fingers instead of talons, and he stared at Alexei's hands as he gave him a filled cup, then raised his eyes and bowed solemnly.

'You were surprised to hear me speak my mind.' Jotan took a cup out of the page's hands, then dismissed him with a flick of his head. 'Does the truth offend you?'

'Truth without malice has an unusual quality,' Alexei said. 'The man who takes offence at it is a fool indeed.'

Jotan was wearing full court dress – a brocaded coat without fastenings, the fabric embroidered with gold wire and decorated with gems and seed pearls, over a high-collared shirt in silk tissue. The shirt was tucked into high-waisted trousers, and the trousers into soft calf-length boots which were embossed with gold. No weapons were visible, although Alexei guessed that a dagger was sheated in Jotan's sleeve. He touched the hilt of the *hiranu* in his waist sash, then stood, smoothing the skirts of his coat.

A door at the end of the hall opened, and Arkhina came in attended by a serving woman. Jotan's wife was tall and slim, and there was a birthmark high on her left cheek. She was Altun, and so her hair was red – a colour like a brightly burning fire. The gold threads and the jewels woven through it sparkled in the light of the lamps.

Alexei bowed to her. 'Khatun.'

It was clear that she had not expected to find him in the room. 'Alexei.' She nodded to him. Her gown had a train which brushed the floor, and she waited

136

while the woman following her looped it up into neat folds and attached them to the fastening at her wrist. 'I was not told you were here.'

There was the sound of movement on one of the galleries above Alexei's head, but he did not look up. It was said that Arkhina was among the most influential women of the Kha-Khan's court, but she was too like her sister-in-law, his father's wife, for him to be on good terms with her.

A door crashed somewhere up beyond a curtain wall, and the voices of women carried like a peal of bells – melodious, chiming upon one another – into the well of the gallery immediately above. Jotan sipped at his wine, and then set his cup in a niche in the wall beside the fireplace. 'Jehana is coming,' he said, and produced an amused smile. 'Try and look like a suitor, will you?' He held out his hand for Alexei's cup.

Alexei drank a little of the sweet wine, then handed his cup to Jotan. The situation had too many of the elements of a farce about it, and he wondered briefly why he had agreed to such a scheme.

The door at the end of the hall opened again. Pages and serving women hastened through it, each of them bearing an item of outdoor clothing. The first, who was a very small page, carried a pair of jewelled gloves. The second had a cap which was sewn with emeralds; the third bore a pair of the high-heeled boots which great ladies wore to walk about the city; and behind them, their faces solemn with barely suppressed mirth, came three women, a high-collared cloak folded lengthwise between them. The white silk tissue of the lining of the cloak was just visible at the hem, and its black brocade gleamed with pearls. Alexei stared frankly at the display.

'My Lord, how prompt you are,' Jotan's daughter

said from the shadow of the doorway.

He had not seen her enter because his attention had been fixed upon the well-ordered panoply of her retinue. Now he knew that it had been a diversion, designed to hold his gaze so that he would be disadvantaged in his dealings with her. He bowed quickly, searching for courtesies to pay her.

Jehana was beautiful – both by Yek and by human standards – and it was remarkable that she had remained thus far unmarried.

Alexei knew that he had always been aware of her – they were not strangers by any means – but now he straightened and stared in open admiration. It was an examination which travelled upwards from the tips of the slippered feet which peeped from beneath the hem of her jewelled and embroidered formal gown to the crown of golden hair which sparkled unadorned like a halo around her head. Her fair skin was covered with sprays of tiny golden-brown freckles, and he could see that she was colouring as she met his eyes.

'Lady, you dazzle me,' he said simply.

Jotan stirred. 'I believe that was the intention,' he observed drily. 'What peacocks we have become, now that we are the masters of this land.'

The kind of wealth which would be displayed in the garments of the Khans and Noyons during the day's ceremonies was usually a product of oppression of the poor, but on Tarvaras there was no one whom Alexei would have cared to class as under-privileged. Even slaves were part of an organised meritocracy, and birth alone was insufficient to assure any man of rank or position.

'It is the role of a suitor to be dazzled,' Arkhina commented, and touched the birthmark on her cheek.

'– And the role of a father to provide the where-withal,' Jotan said.

Jehana still had not spoken. Her maids were unfolding her cloak, and the page who held her boots was kneeling so that she could put her feet into them. Alexei offered a hand to her, and when she took it he stood, meeting her gaze steadily, while she stepped from slipper to boot first with one foot, and then with the other. The neck of her gown was a collar of spun gold, and the front was open, court style, to the level of her breast.

Her touch was cold. Her fingers lay slender and perfect, passive across his outstretched hand. Her sheathed golden talons trembled once, and then they were still.

'Thank you, my Lord.' Her hand withdrew. Wearing the boots she was taller, but still he was looking down on her. Her perfume clouded his breathing, and he stepped back, then bowed again.

It was as if she was unaware of the gesture. She waited while her maids adjusted her cloak around her shoulders, and then took her cap from the page who held it and put it on.

'You ought to discuss your betrothal,' Jotan said. 'But there is no time.'

Arkhina looked amused. 'Lord husband,' she said, 'they are in accord, I think.' She walked past Jotan to the door, and the pages who were stationed there hastened to open it for her.

Jotan looked perplexed by her observation. He glanced from Alexei to Jehana, and then shrugged and strode after his wife.

'My mother is right,' Jehana said. She took her gloves from the page who waited with them. 'There is nothing for us to discuss.'

There was no hint of warmth in her tone, and Alexei could think of nothing appropriate to say. Of all the circumstances which he had envisaged – of all her possible responses to his clearly demonstrated willingness to admire her – that with which he was now faced was the most confusing, the most difficult to comprehend. She walked past him to the door, and though he followed and came quickly up to her side he did not again offer her his hand.

The Dragon Throne rested normally in an audience chamber within the Golden Yurt, the palace of the Kha-Khan. Now it sat upon a plinth of stone the height of two standing men which was at the concourse of the broad principal streets which radiated out from Kinsai like the spokes of a wheel. A canopy had been raised above it, but because the Yasa required the enthronement to be witnessed and acclaimed by people of every degree there was no other obstruction to the public view.

The ceremony of enthronement was simple enough. Men cheered as Artai descended the steps in front of his palace, then walked along a corridor of his guards through the crowd of Khans and other notables who were gathered to witness his accession. The cheers spread to the people who crammed every street which led from the concourse, but Artai did not turn his head or acknowledge them. At the foot of the plinth he stopped and turned. No shaman was present to preside or to ask for God's blessing upon Artai's reign, Alexei saw, for it was a fact that there was no such thing as organised religion on this world, and even casual superstition was not permitted to interfere for long in the affairs of men.

Artai was bowing to left and right now, the last time in his life he would ever be required to offer courtesy to others. Everyone in the crowd was bowing back, and the waves of motion proceeded down each of the streets like ripples out across a pool. At once the officers of the Kha-Khan's guard came through the ranks of the troopers to Artai's side. All of them were big men who had drawn lots for the honour of the occasion, and carefully they lifted Artai and carried him up the short flight of steps to the summit of the plinth. There was a tradition that the Kha-Khan not be required to turn his back upon his people, and so they carried him facing out across the crowd, and placed him directly in front of the seat of the reclining dragon which had been the throne of Tamujin, Ancestor of the Altun, the first Kha-Khan. Then they descended again to the concourse. Artai sat down, and at once the people began to shout his name. The men threw up their arms every time they shouted, and gradually what began as a confusion of noise became a solid roar of acclamation.

'Artai! Artai!'

It was now, at the moment of supreme triumph, that it became apparent once more that the fates were intervening to demonstrate that the day was to be memorable most of all for its disasters. Part of the process of universal involvement in recognition of Artai as Lord of the Earth now necessitated the removal of the Dragon Throne – a solid piece of carving of the weight of seven thousand diram – with its occupant from the top of the plinth down to the concourse from whence it was destined to be borne on a processional route on the shoulders of teams of men of every degree in the Khanate, most of whom had been selected by lot, although there were a few who had paid out considerable sums in gold koban for the privilege of inclusion.

Alexei, Jotan, Jehana and Arkhina were among those of the nobility who had elected to eschew the fervour of the crowd, and watched from a wooden platform which had been constructed across the entry

141

to a side street. Troopers lifted the throne from its staging and passed it to the waiting hands below. It sank for a moment, then rose again, and Alexei saw Jotan raise his eyebrows.

It was the Controller of the Household who later established that no one in authority who was within a reasonable distance of the incident could have realised that the members of the first team of bearers, most of them worthy if nervous burghers of Kinsai, had doctored strung-up nerves with wine and k'miss to such an extent that they were no longer capable of reacting with either fortitude or common sense to the kind of diversions which were now to be expected as part of the rejoicing. The celebration of Artai's Khanate having properly commenced, the common people were anxious to come close to the path of their newly enthroned lord through their city. A press of bodies developed which the guard were unable or unwilling to clear. The cheering throng swayed, and so did the throne on the shoulders of its bearers. A salvo of fireworks lit by a group of well-intentioned N'pani on the outskirts of the crowd exploded overhead. Most of the men carrying the throne had served as army conscripts, and they reacted instinctively to the sound of the explosions. They ducked and flinched, the throne tipped, and Artai fell off into the arms of his officers.

Jotan met Alexei's eyes in a moment of mutual sympathy and understanding, and then ignoring the obvious disapproval of their respective partners they buried their faces in their hands and wept in helpless mirth.

The fireworks were still exploding when the procession came to an end over an hour later.

In fact there had not been one unified element to

the train which followed Artai's progress but several, and those which were the designated efforts of individual districts of the city, or of the guilds, now moved away to become the driving force behind a carnival which ruled every street.

'I have a thirst a C'zak would envy,' Burun said.

He had joined them out of the press in the midst of a guard of taciturn Merkut troopers who were economical in their employment of the brute force necessary to clear their master's path. With Burun were his wives, both of his younger sons, his grandson Jehan, and a small gathering of the senior members of his household.

Jotan looked as though he was considering the alternatives. 'We are summoned to audience with Artai later,' he said, 'but until then we can do as we please.'

Alexei thought that if the phrasing of the observation suggested that Burun was anything other than his own master, it was surely an accident.

Burun gave Jotan a look. 'Your house is closer than mine. We'll go there.'

Which was how the Khan of the Merkuts – along with his escort, his retinue, and the principal members of his family – came to be crossing a bridge which was erected at the height of the second floor across several of the principal buildings in the better part of the merchants' quarter of Kinsai.

Space was at such a premium here that the narrow side streets had long since been filled with structures. No one was permitted to build outside the city wall – indeed it would have been more or less impossible given the sheer drop to the plain – and as a result the ever-industrious Kinsani merchants had expanded in directions which were not forbidden by the law. They had tunnelled down into the plateau, and they had built upwards as far as their materials and construction abilities would allow.

Common thoroughfares ran everywhere and at every level from basement to attic. Passageways were pierced through the walls of houses in some places, and in others they were supported on props along the faces of warehouses and shops, and it was across one of these – a sturdy bridge of timber which was designed to withstand the weight of carts as well as men – that Burun's party moved without very much opposition from the revellers, most of whom clearly preferred the breadth of the main streets.

Matching his pace to that of Jehana at his side, Alexei deduced from the snatches of conversation which carried back to him that Burun was not interested in discussing with Jotan either the agenda or the implications of their programmed audience with Artai. Nor, it became clear, did he wish to talk about the role he intended to play now that Artai was secure upon his throne. For a moment Alexei wondered why Burun did not arrest his eldest son's questions more sharply, and then he realised with admiration how much reassurance the noble hangers-on who had swollen Burun's retinue would draw from what they heard. The Khan of the Merkuts did not fear for his position or for his influence. He was satisfied to allow matters to follow their own course.

They were passing across an open portion of the bridge. Shafts of red sunlight illuminated the timbers as they moved from the support of one building to another across a street filled with people. The faces of the houses gleamed, and crystals in the stone reflected stray sunbeams. Towards the street corner a single papier-maché dragon bobbed in the centre of a circle of dancing men.

A group of children clustered at the place where

144

the bridge forked to provide access to a set of warehouses. There were few adults with them, but those who recognised Burun bowed. A child darted out in front of the striding troopers so that they checked their pace.

An officer to Burun's right stumbled, and he clutched at the handrail at his side. Alexei thought, but did not voice the opinion, that possibly the man was suffering from the effects of too much wine. If that was the case, he would almost certainly be disciplined. More children were crowding into the junction ahead. Some of them waved, and the noise along the thoroughfare increased.

Another trooper fell out of line, and this time when he got a hand to the wooden rail at the side of the bridge he collapsed across it. There was the sound of short swords being drawn, and a controlled explosion of anger and realisation from the officer in charge of the escort. Burun turned his head without interrupting what Jotan was saying to him, and intercepting the look Alexei left Jehana's side and went unobtrusively into the line of Merkuts to the side of a grizzled warrant officer.

'The children. Move them out of the way.' Alexei issued the order incisively.

The warrant officer nodded understanding, and he broke rank and moved quickly forward along the outside of the now almost stationary line of troopers. The bridge though sturdy was not very wide, and one did not desire, on this of all days, an accident in which innocent children might come to harm.

Alexei turned to return to Jehana's side. He had taken a pace or two when something tugged at the shoulder of his coat. A trooper to his left threw up his hands to his face, crying out. He went to his knees, and the men behind him moved aside. Alexei was moving to help when someone gripped his arm, and people closed in around him.

One of them was Burun. He ran his gloved hand up across Alexei's shoulder, and pulled something from the stiff material of the embroidered coat. Alexei jerked, surprised. Then he saw the metal dart in Burun's hand.

'– Blown through a tube,' Burun said. 'The Ch'kasians use them.' He turned and gestured to his officer. 'Take some men. Round up all the children, and tell them that they are to be treated to sweets to celebrate the day. Find an adult with authority in the district and bring him to me –'

A mercer in a fur-trimmed coat was already emerging from a small crowd of bystanders. He bowed to Burun, a worried look on his face. The captain of the escort led him to one side, explaining.

Alexei reached out and took the dart. 'Children?'

Burun glanced back at him. 'Yes. You can tell from the angle, and in any case an adult on his knees blowing through a pipe would have been likely to attract the interest of his neighbours. Anyway I think I saw one of them.'

'Oh?' Alexei raised his eyebrows. 'I did not know you were looking in my direction, Khan.'

'My attention, as becomes my station, is everywhere,' Burun said drily. He turned to address the captain of the guard. 'Is there a place to which the children can be taken?'

'This man has offered his house, Khan.'

'Good.'

The merchant still looked bewildered. 'Lord, do you wish to question the children while they are detained –'

Alexei saw Burun make a face. 'That would antagonise the parents,' Burun said. 'Also the blowpipes will long since have been thrown away. No, I simply wish them to be removed from this place. My officers will conduct their own enquiry, and I will not hold this district to blame unless I am shown evidence of its involvement.'

The clearance of the staging at the end of the bridge took only a short time, and it was not until they were moving once more that Alexei had a sudden thought. 'I thought you said you saw one of the children who attacked us, Khan,' he said.

'I said I thought so,' Burun responded. 'You think I should look for him?'

'It would seem to make sense.'

'So it would,' Burun responded amiably, 'if I expected to know him again.'

They were descending a flight of stairs towards a broad main street, and because of the narrowness of the staircase Alexei was forced to drop back. The impression had been conveyed to him, he noted, that Burun had seen one of their attackers – but not closely enough to identify him. He mistrusted that notion because it was unlike Burun to fail to observe anything accurately. Apart from that, Alexei was almost certain that Burun had lied.

The audience chamber was bigger than the main hall outside. It had a wooden floor which had been brushed with gold leaf so that every knot and line of the grain created a ripple in a seeming golden pool. In the centre of the room there was a raised dais, and it was also roofed with gold. The Dragon Throne had been brought to the dais after the procession, and Artai was sitting upon it.

Alexei stood a little behind and to the right of Burun. He knelt and bowed, and then prostrated himself. The splendour of the room never failed to unsettle him, and the fact that everyone else was going through the same series of salutations did nothing to make him feel more comfortable.

Burun had rocked back onto his heels. The gold on the floor reflected his face, distorting it. Alexei completed his obeisance, then sat up. The people in the room were all members of Burun's family, or served him. His sons Jotan, Orcadai and C'zinsit were in a line to his left, and to Alexei's right knelt Jehan and Suragai, with Suragai's Tarvarian son Kadan at his shoulder.

'Burun Khan, we greet you,' Artai said. His voice was high and clear.

'Lord.' Burun uncoiled himself in a single elastic stretch of his torso, and he stood up. 'I salute you. My family and these here with them who serve me salute you.'

Artai was surveying the men who knelt in line before him. 'Indeed,' he said flatly, 'we see one among them who does not serve you, Khan, or not so far as we are aware. Alexei Khan, how say you?'

Alexei rose to his feet. 'Lord, I am your servant,' he said.

'– And yet we hear that you are now a Merkut also,' Artai observed tartly. He stared at Alexei, and the pupils in his amber eyes seemed to expand, then contract again.

Burun laughed softly, and he gestured apparently without embarrassment. 'Lord Khan, Alexei is betrothed as you have heard to my grand-daughter, and so I consider him a member of my family. He does not serve me.'

'Hunh.' Artai nodded. 'Then we are content.' He did not look at Burun but at Alexei as he spoke. Suddenly he turned. 'Have you told them why they are assembled here in our presence?'

148

Burun pretended to look offended. 'Lord, I would not presume to interpret your will,' he said.

It was clear from Artai's expression that he wished to show that he did not entirely believe Burun's protest. 'Very well,' he said. 'It is our will – the Will of Heaven – that an embassy be sent to the lands across the Great Sea –' He waved a hand. '– Whatever lies to the west, to invite the people there to submit themselves to the protection of our rule.'

Alexei saw that Burun was contemplating the piece of floor between his feet. There was a moment of silence. Alexei took a deep breath. 'Lord Khan,' he said, 'I will go.'

There was another silence. Then Burun raised his head. 'Lord,' he said, 'it is fitting that the ambassador should be your man, and not mine.'

Artai looked down his nose. 'Is not every man in this land our servant?' he demanded.

Burun looked amused. 'Lord, what is the fact, because it is the law, and what is perceived by men, being a matter of their belief, are often different. I meant only that this is a matter of your will, and ought to be seen by men to be carried out in your name and at your direction. You know how I have supported your election. Thus it is that some of the Khans may perceive influence where I have exerted none.'

Alexei mastered a stare of disbelief.

'Then we consent,' Artai said. 'Alexei Khan shall go, in our name. There should be others, however, men of repute in the Khanate, to support him, for he is not of our world.' For a moment it was as if he was casting around for suitable names, and then suddenly he was looking past Alexei towards Jehan. 'You, Noyon, shall be among them,' he said.

Burun's expression did not alter. 'Lord,' he said,

'you honour my house.' He looked once in Jehan's direction, and if there was a warning in his eyes, Alexei was unable to identify it.

Jehan had not risen. Now he bowed from the waist. 'Lord, I obey your will,' he said simply. He sat back on his heels, his face expressionless.

'There will be others.' Artai glanced at Burun. 'We shall send to you, Khan, and you shall advise us – but Alexei shall lead them, and it is to him we shall issue our patent.'

Burun bowed. 'Such details are minor matters,' he said.

Artai sat back. 'Yes.' He stared at Alexei. 'Ask for whom you wish. We shall command them.'

Alexei hesitated. 'Lord, there is one –'

'Oh?' Artai's head came up. 'Name him.'

'Lord, the son of Siban, whose name has been offered to you as one you may see fit to pardon, as is the custom on this day.'

'We have no such intention,' Artai said coldly. 'Sidacai was taken in treason. His death warrant is under our hand.'

Alexei did not look towards Burun. He shrugged as if he had said all that he intended to say, and bowed to Artai.

'Name another,' Artai said. 'Not him.'

Burun stirred. 'Lord Khan,' he said, 'how does it serve you to kill Sidacai?'

'Sidacai has not been condemned in order that we may be served, but to satisfy the Yasa,' Artai responded, bridling.

'– And yet maybe his death should serve you,' Burun said.

No one had ever suggested that Artai was a fool. He gave Burun a look. 'It is not Sidacai's death I am being asked for, but his life,' he said.

150

Burun gestured as if the matter was of little concern. 'What it amounts to is that Sidacai is expendable,' he said. He spread his hands. 'Who knows what may be found when the Great Sea has been crossed? Release Sidacai into Alexei's charge, so that in life or in death he may serve you.'

The argument appeared to provide Artai with a degree of amusement. After a moment he nodded. 'Let it be so.' He looked at Alexei. 'We give you charge of all the matters which may relate to this our command. Serve us well, and you shall receive our favour.'

There was no answer to that, and Alexei bowed. Burun asked, 'Are we dismissed?'

'Oh.' Artai looked as if he was suddenly bored by the whole interlude. 'Yes. Go.'

Alexei followed Burun's example, and knelt once more and prostrated himself. Then he got up and walked out into the antechamber. He heard Burun heave an enormous sigh. 'Name of God, that was tedious,' he said.

Jotan and the others were coming out of the audience chamber now. Alexei laughed. 'It would be simpler if you told Artai what you wanted him to say,' he said.

Burun scowled. 'Everyone thinks that I rule Artai. You saw how he imposed his will upon us.'

'You mean Jehan.' Alexei nodded. It had been clear that Artai's decision to name Jehan as a member of the embassy had come as a complete surprise.

'Artai wants Jehan out of the way,' Burun said austerely. 'I think it would please him if he did not return to Kinsai.'

Lines of servants were filing through the door of the audience chamber. Their hands were empty, and Alexei wondered how many people it took to move Artai from one room of the palace to another. 'All of us seem to have been chosen because we are considered expendable,' he said.

Burun's head came round. 'Everyone is expendable in the Kha-Khan's service,' he said after a moment.

There was no state banquet to mark Artai's enthronement, and so it was without surprise that Alexei observed that everyone who was of importance in the Khanate had been invited to dine at Burun's house. The chimes of bells which stood in every district of the city were being rung as they sat down – both because the ringers had been amply bribed and because they thought it politic to honour Artai and his chief supporter – and a small orchestra of trumpets and tambours had been hired by a steward and was accommodated in the yard, so that Burun's speech of welcome to his guests, as well as their affable replies, were conducted with much opening and shutting of mouths and a deal of dumb show. The lady betrothed to the newly created Khan of the province of Khitai, her face flushed with suppressed laughter, was also trying to make herself heard.

'What?' Alexei shouted.

'I said,' screamed Burun's grand-daughter, 'that I pray that they will cease before the gongs are struck for curfew.'

An officer of Burun's household leaned through the window and bellowed, and the musicians' renderings were suddenly muted.

The bells continued their argument, one of the chimes being now somewhat behind the others and lacking its tenor, but gradually they tailed off into silence. Jehana had completed her remarks while there was still noise to cover her more explicit comments, but other guests had not. There was an explosion of laughter as someone observed with considerable accuracy upon the nature of the disturbance, and then the servants, the offending if well-meaning steward crimson-faced at their head, were entering the room with platters and trays to serve the meal.

It was not the only banquet taking place in Kinsai, but it was clearly the one at which the nobility of the Khanate of even the lowest degree had thought it was incumbent upon them to be seen. Most of the invited guests arrived accompanied by a crowd of hangers-on, and it was already becoming apparent that there was insufficient space at the tables. The gaps between were filled with people looking for seats, with others exchanging seats, and with some who had simply observed friends in other parts of the room and were on their way from one table to another for the purpose of making conversation.

The incomers were all, Alexei saw, minor members of the court who had no invitations. The steward, responding to an icy enquiry from Burun, looked flustered. The servants were being jostled, and one tray of meat had already been spilled. A tripod which supported a lamp burning scented oil swayed alarmingly, and seeing it Alexei climbed to his feet.

'My lords!' His shout cut across every other sound. 'My lords nearest the door! The lamps are about to fall on you!'

There was a hasty exodus by about twenty of those who had not waited to question the accuracy of the statement. A pair of slaves threw themselves against the doors, closing them. Burun stood up to look, glanced once in Alexei's direction, and then he sat down again, laughing.

It was the third hour of the night watch when the banquet ended. Outside a heavy mist obscured everything, and the departing Khans and Noyons went accompanied by lantern bearers and pairs of Merkut guards against the interference of revellers who might forget their manners.

It was apparent that the lack of visibility had altered Jotan's intentions to a quite remarkable degree. Dismissing all but a single guard who was burdened with a lantern on a pole, he began to lead them by the bridges and passageways which cut across the streets in a way which was arguably more direct and certainly less likely to be barred by persistent celebrants.

Both Jehana and Arkhina were shrouded in their cloaks. The loan of similar garments had been offered to both Alexei and Jotan; but Alexei had not felt the need of protection from the elements and neither, apparently, had Jotan, although he had borrowed a sword.

The events of the day had tired Alexei beyond belief. He admired Jotan's detachment, and concluded that it was the lack of direct involvement which made it possible for him to behave as if nothing had occurred which could be the source of concern. The damp darkness of the night seemed to draw the strength from his body. He wanted to sleep, and the prospect of a bed, even one which he would be required to occupy without companionship, was so attractive that he missed at first the signs that all was not well.

They were not to speak, Jotan had instructed, lest they distract the lantern-bearer. Jehana at Alexei's side grasped the sleeve of his coat, and he saw that she carried a *hiranu* which was similar to his own, save that it was encased in a jewelled sheath and was strapped to the girdle which she now wore over her gown.

The mist was so thick that the only colours were

shades of black and white which were smudged and merged together in wisps of vapour. Occasionally a light showed silver, faint in one of the streets below, and but for that, and for the sounds as their feet struck the timbers of a bridge, they might have been walking in some open courtyard instead of in narrow alleys raised between the walls of tall buildings.

They had encountered no one, but suddenly Alexei knew without asking that Jotan's hand rested upon the hilt of his borrowed sword. He loosened his *hiranu* in its scabbard, and concentrated on moving soundlessly.

An open space between two darkened structures – warehouses, Alexei thought, although he was not sure that their route had taken them across that quarter of the city – appeared out of the mist to their left like the mouth of an open tomb, and Jotan caught Alexei's arm and indicated it.

'Put out the lamp and wait here.'

The command was given in a voice which did not rise above a whisper. Alexei nodded. The trooper with the lamp had already stopped, and at Alexei's signal he opened the lamp and pinched the burning wick between his fingers, extinguishing the light. Arkhina had moved calmly into the shelter of the high stone wall. Jehana moved silently to her side, likewise apparently unperturbed by the events which were taking place, and they watched Jotan as he stepped out onto the wooden staging. He faded back the way they had come.

Alexei thought that it was on the whole foolish to remain where he was while there was an armed trooper to guard the two women. Just before Jotan vanished completely into the mist, he walked softly out of the inlet between the buildings and followed him.

155

Jotan walked perhaps thirty paces, and then he halted. Alexei stopped a short distance behind him. The years of his isolation on a world where it was often a good idea to appear without warning had taught him how to move silently.

Carried by some freak of the acoustics of the place or by the mist, Jotan's voice said as it seemed to Alexei in his ear, 'If you move or call out, I shall kill you.'

Where there had been one figure faintly outlined in the frame of the staging there were now two – one large, obviously Jotan, and one much smaller, a child Alexei thought until he saw the muscular build and shortened legs and realised that Jotan had caught a dwarf. The smaller figure twisted and spat in Jotan's impervious grasp, then broke free briefly. He ran in Alexei's direction, saw Alexei in his path, and turned and scuttled back the way he had come. Jotan's hand came out in a roundhouse swing, and the dwarf fell against the wall upon which the staging was supported and slid down, his head lolling.

Before the dwarf had recovered consciousness, Jotan had bound his hands tightly behind his back with a strip of material torn from the hem of his coat. He searched the recumbent form of his captive roughly and, straightening, tossed a slim package to Alexei.

Alexei had been listening for other footsteps coming along the bridge. He caught the packet and unfolded the cloth wrapping. In it were a handful of metal darts and a blowpipe.

'Burun recognised him in the yard during dinner,' Jotan said. 'We were not sure it was you he was trying to kill this morning. You should have stayed with the women.'

Alexei bit back on a retort. 'I thought you might

need assistance,' he said. 'Was that why you dismissed the escort? You wanted to tempt him to follow us.'

'Obviously.' Jotan pulled the now half-conscious dwarf to his feet. 'Now that we have him, maybe we can find out who is paying him. One hopes that it isn't Artai.'

'You're not serious,' Alexei said.

'You think not?' Jotan looked amused. 'You underrate us, Alexei. This morning you thought my father objected to manhandling children.' He shook his captive. 'You! What is your name?'

The dwarf had recovered. He wriggled in Jotan's hands, swearing softly in Yek, and then in Keraistani and C'zak. Jotan slid his borrowed sword out of its sheath, and he laid it with precision against the dwarf's throat. The dwarf fell silent.

'You will walk before me,' Jotan said, 'and you will say nothing. We are not interested in your opinion of us. We wish to know only who paid you to try to kill this gentleman.'

'You will know soon enough,' the dwarf said. He had frozen against the touch of the naked blade, but even so there was a line of broken skin which showed red, then was hidden by a wreath of mist.

'You mean there are others waiting for us,' Jotan said. 'But surely you see now that we were expecting you. My escort is in the street at the end of this staging. Perhaps your friends are all dead, and then who will pay you?'

'Not they,' the dwarf responded calmly, though it was clear that he was nervous of the sword. 'If they are dead, there will be more for me.'

Jotan moved so that the tip of the sword was under the dwarf's chin, forcing it up. 'Say you so? Then your reward must be magnificent indeed, for you to run such risks to gain it. How much have they promised you?'

'Enough,' the dwarf said. Jotan twitched the sword so that it broke the skin again. 'My name is Juba,' the dwarf said quickly. 'They will pay me three koban.'

'So.' Jotan nodded and withdrew the sword, sliding it back into the scabbard. He hustled the dwarf along the bridge until he had reached the place where Arkhina and Jehana waited with their guard. 'Three koban is not much for your life.' Jotan spoke in a conversational tone. 'What would you do for this lady's girdle?' He held out his hand to Jehana. Swiftly she detached the *hiranu*, then unfastened her girdle and handed it to him. It was a minor treasure, a thing of gold wire and seed pearls, and even in the damp darkness it glittered.

The dwarf eyed it. 'They would kill me,' he said at last.

'I shall kill you,' Jotan said, 'or I shall give my sword to this gentleman whom you were hired to kill, and he will do it.'

Alexei saw Jehana's head come up. She stared past her father at him.

'I will tell you,' the dwarf Juba said. He spat to one side to clear the blood from his mouth.

The names were those of two lesser Khans. Jotan raised his eyebrows at Alexei, and Alexei was unable to tell if the answer surprised him.

Jotan released the dwarf into the hands of the trooper. 'What you say may be true.' He addressed the dwarf. 'Now I want proof.'

The dwarf heaved against the restraining grasp of his captor. 'You said –'

'I said I would kill you if you did not tell me,' Jotan said coolly. 'I offered you this –' he allowed the girdle to dangle from his fingers '– if you would speak the names of those who hired you. But how can I be certain that you have kept your part of the bargain?

You will come with us now to my house, and you will remain there until the men you have accused have been taken and questioned. When your story has been proved, I will set you free, and I will pay you as I have undertaken – but not until then.'

It was a sensible precaution. Jehana recovered her girdle from her father's hand and reclasped it without comment. The trooper had the dwarf by a gathered handful of material which was the shoulder of his tunic. He looked helplessly at the lantern pole in his hand, and Alexei took it from him.

'Don't light it,' Jotan said. He was peering into the gloom ahead.

They began to walk along the staging. Alexei was amazed that Jotan had seen fit to risk the lives of both his wife and daughter on an escapade such as this, and he wondered if either of them had been warned about what was to happen.

'Do you think there are others waiting?' he asked Jotan quietly.

'It's possible.' Jotan had one hand on the side rail of the wooden platform, and he was feeling his way forward.

'Then we ought to go back.'

'And if they are behind, and not in front?' Jotan asked. 'We cannot believe what we have been told, and at least I know where my men are waiting. This creature was bound to try to follow, to attempt again what he intended this morning.' He glanced at the dwarf. 'After all, he had three koban to gain by his success. Is that not so?'

The dwarf agreed. He was subdued now, and his feet dragged as they approached the end of the bridge. Confused, Alexei could not understand why Jotan had not sent men ahead along his intended route across the staging to search for ambushers.

Were there so few he felt able to trust?

Suddenly the dwarf was tearing himself wildly out of the trooper's hands, his arms still pinioned, sliding past them towards the darkness behind. Alexei thrust past Jehana and kicked the dwarf's legs from under him, then stood over him, a foot planted on his chest to prevent him from escaping again. He looked at Jotan. 'Was he lying?'

Jotan appeared to consider. 'I don't think so. But he certainly doesn't want to walk with us to the end of the bridge.'

Alexei hauled the dwarf to his feet. 'You were telling the truth?' he demanded. 'Your friends are waiting for us? How did they know what path we would take?'

'They followed the Khan's escort,' the dwarf responded sullenly. 'Let me go. They will kill me.'

It seemed likely.

'How many of them are there?' Alexei shook the dwarf. 'Tell me.'

'Many,' the dwarf said. 'Release me. I want none of your reward.'

'He will need it, however, if he is going to escape,' Jehana said from Alexei's side. She unfastened the girdle again and held it out.

Jotan nodded. He gestured to the trooper, who cut the dwarf's bonds. The dwarf snatched at the girdle, and he bolted.

Alexei peered ahead at the swirling vapour which shrouded the place where the bridge met the face of another building. 'How far are we from a descent to the street?' he asked Jotan.

'Too far. Look. Where the staging touches the wall.'

Within the framework something moved, brushing the mist aside like water. Two men feeling their way out onto the bridge.

160

Jehana had her head cocked to one side, listening. 'There is someone behind us as well,' she observed calmly.

The sound of footsteps on the wooden floor of the staging was faint but distinct. Jotan grimaced, and then he turned to their escort. 'Give the Khan your sword,' he said.

The trooper complied. Alexei unsheathed the short sword and tested the weight.

Jotan went to the edge of the staging and peered over. He gestured to the trooper. 'Get over the rail and wait on the props. When the men who are coming towards us have passed, climb back up and run to the place where the staging descends to the street. You will find your comrades there. Bring them back with you.'

The trooper gazed past Jotan at Arkhina and Jehana. He shook his head stubbornly. 'Khan, my place is here with you –'

'I don't propose to stand and fight,' Jotan said brusquely. 'Do as I tell you.'

The trooper climbed reluctantly over the handrail and then lowered himself onto the supporting props below.

'We could all hide,' Arkhina suggested. There was no hint of apprehension in her tone. She went to Jotan's side and looked over, then stepped back sharply. 'Perhaps not,' she said flatly.

Alexei slid the short sword back into its sheath. 'The alley?' He caught Jotan's eye.

'Yes.' Jotan looked back the way they had come. 'I can't hear anyone coming now.' He began to pace silently along the bridge.

'They have stopped,' Jehana said.

The dark mouth of the alleyway between the high buildings loomed suddenly out of the mist at their side. 'Do you guard your lady,' Jotan said to Alexei, 'and I shall guard mine.'

Alexei glanced at Jehana, and was surprised to see her smile. He closed his hand on her arm and drew her into the gloom of the passage.

The few doors were bolted or barred. They passed along the side of one wall, and at the end were faced with a kind of crossroads in the staging, the mist swirling whitely across it. On the other side, and to left and right, loomed the darkness of fresh tunnels.

Jotan was already turning left. Alexei still had the pole of the lantern in one hand, and now he forced it through the rail at the side of the bridge, then stripped off his coat and draped it artistically, crowning the lantern with his fur hat. 'Follow your father and mother,' he told Jehana. 'I'm going to delay them.' He began to unwrap the package which Jotan had taken from the dwarf.

'I used to puff peas when I was a child,' Jehana said, and took the blowpipe from him. 'Look. They are coming.'

Their pursuers had lit a lantern, the better to see their way, and now two shadowy figures were silhouetted in the alley mouth.

'Then we should move back,' Alexei said. He made her come with him onto the end of the staging down which Jotan and Arkhina had already disappeared. The mist disturbed by their passing closed around the coat which decorated the lantern pole. With the faint light coming from the end of the alley catching the gold of the embroidery, it looked like a man trying to climb into the space between the timbers. Someone stepped on a loose plank in the alley down which they had come from the bridge, and the timber squealed. A man's outline appeared hesitantly out of the mist, and then the first of their pursuers turned

162

and whistled softly. There was an answering whistle, and a second figure came from the alley mouth.

'Ah! They are on me!' Alexei spoke towards the wall, and his voice echoed obligingly across the vault of darkness and rang hollowly off the cornices of the four corners of the buildings which formed the crossroads.

Jehana was fitting a dart into the blowpipe. A man's shout pierced the mist, and the first pursuer rushed out of the end of the alley and cut with his sword at the hatted shape which he saw dimly ahead of him. The sword became embedded in the wood of the handrail, and while his attacker was struggling to free it, Alexei stepped up to him and forced the trooper's sword through the protecting mantle of a leather coat and into the flesh beneath.

The assassin screamed and fell. Alexei pulled the sword out, and he was turning to meet the charge of the second man when Jehana raised the blowpipe to her lips, took a deep breath, and spat.

The second pursuer flung a hand up to his throat. He gurgled unpleasantly, and then knelt awkwardly on the planking. His sword clattered out of his hand. In the mouth of the alley at the end of the tunnel two more shapes starting from the bridge into the darkness hesitated, and then stopped.

Alexei knelt beside the second man, examining him. He looked up. 'Name of God, you've killed him.'

'That was my intention,' Jehana said irritably. She came to his side and stared along the alley at the two men who were standing unwarily outlined in the light of a held lantern. She raised the pipe again and spat hard. A man's voice cried out in pain and anger, and the light was extinguished. 'That will make them pause for a while,' Jehana said, her tone satisfied.

Alexei dragged his coat off what remained of the

lantern pole. The cut of the assassin's sword had split it from below the shoulder to the hem. The top of the pole had been severed, and his hat had fallen out of sight into the space below the staging. He caught Jehana's wrist and dragged her in pursuit of Jotan and Arkhina.

At the end of the tunnel there was another crossroads, and as they entered it Jotan appeared, sword in hand. He took in the blood still dripping from Alexei's sword, and then his eyes went to the blowpipe in Jehana's hand. 'You have made them stop and think,' he said. 'Good. There are some open work-spaces here. See what you can find.'

Arkhina emerged from what appeared to be a dyer's shop. She carried a long pole which was draped with hanks of haigus wool, and she dropped it across the rails of the staging, then turned back into the gloom of the shop again.

Alexei peered into the deep alcove which formed the work-space in the wall opposite. 'A candlemaker,' Jehana said. She went past him gathering up unsevered clusters of candles which had been hung like fruit above a tank. The next shop yielded a heap of half-finished wooden pattens, the footwear used by field workers, along with a satchel full of long nails and several hammers.

Jotan was forcing the lock on a pair of massive double doors set in the gable end of the building which fronted the junction of the alleyways. Inside there was a cart, its body mounted high upon the axle so that it would clear the stagings and pass along the narrow tunnels, and at the back of the enclosure there was a stall in which an aged p'tar browsed at a manger.

'Here's luck.' Jotan picked up harness. He worked the snaffle between the p'tar's huge yellow teeth, then

164

hauled to bring the animal out of the stall. The p'tar sat down indignantly.

Alexei searched for the metal-tipped goad which he knew must be somewhere. It was hanging on the wall, and when he applied it to the p'tar's rump the beast screamed once, as if outraged, and then it trotted sedately out of the stall and allowed itself to be backed between the shafts of the cart. Jotan raced off into the darkness, and Alexei, Jehana and Arkhina busied themselves around the cart, inventive in the face of necessity.

Jotan returned almost at once. 'There are at least two men behind us, and there are more in front,' he said. 'Damn Burun. This was his idea.' He lifted Arkhina into the cart, and then got up beside her. 'We'll go forward. Stay at the cart tail, and when we reach the end of the next tunnel, turn right. There is a stair down to the street there.'

Jehana had thrown off her cloak, and now she took her *hiranu* and cut a wide swathe from her gown.

'What are you doing?' Alexei eyed her long legs without any attempt to disguise his interest.

'I can't run in a gown,' she said. She caught hold of the cart tail as Jotan drove it into the mouth of the tunnel. Across the shafts Alexei had nailed the dyer's spar, and secured to it were the pattens, and clusters of candles.

Jotan glanced back once, and then he applied the goad energetically to the p'tar's hind quarters. It bucked and screamed, then charged head down into the blackness of the space between the high walls. On both sides of the cart the ends of the dyer's spar scraped the stonework. Halfway down the length of the tunnel a patten caught an advancing man under the chin so that his alarmed cry was cut off short as he was lifted and carried for a distance of several

165

paces before he fell away. The wheels of the cart rumbled and crashed over the obstacle, and Alexei jumped smartly to one side to avoid the form which sprawled in his path.

Somewhere ahead a man's voice shouted a question. A figure popped out of a doorway to Alexei's left, and he cut at it with his sword and ran on. Someone grasped at the side of the cart as it went past, and Arkhina smashed his fingers with a hammer. There was a cry, and then the wheels thumped again as they passed across either feet or ankles.

The cart burst out into the open space at the end of the tunnel. There were men clustered in it, and they ducked in a vain attempt to avoid the sweeping mayhem of the laden spar. Someone sailed over the side rail of the staging and disappeared without a sound into the open abyss of the mist which swirled beyond.

'There!' Alexei began to push Jehana towards a space in the handrail which signified, he guessed, a flight of stairs. Two men appeared in front of him, and he caught her wrist and jerked her to one side, raising his sword. Even as he did so, the obstacle was removed because Jotan had dumped the hanks of haigus wool on the men from above so that they became entangled, tripped, and fell cursing.

'Ha!' Jotan said. He jumped out of the cart, lifted Arkhina down, and they ran for the stairway. There was the half stage of a landing a little below, and the stairs diverged. They had reached it before Alexei realised that there were more men running into the street below.

The mist scarcely hid them now. Jotan leaned out over the rail and stared at the movement at the foot of the stairs. 'Not my men,' he said. 'They might be the watch –'

166

'– Or they might not,' Alexei finished for him. 'Can we do anything other than wait to find out?'

Jotan indicated the second staircase, a precipitous exit which turned back from the landing and passed through the wall against which the props for the staging were supported. 'That leads down to the cisterns,' he said.

The cisterns were the huge catchment tanks which held the city's water supply. Jotan was already starting down. Alexei waited while Arkhina and Jehana climbed out past him, and then he followed. Inside the wall there was a new blackness, free of mist, and the most persistent sound was the dripping and trickling of myriad streams into the storage below.

'I hope there is another way out,' Alexei said. His voice rang hollowly in the confines of the tunnel to which they had descended.

'There are several.' Jotan was feeling his way around one wall. The stones overhead gleamed with phosphorescence. Torches were stacked in a niche at the head of the tunnel. Jotan picked up one and ignited it across a striker embedded in the stonework. The impregnated faggots flared. The tunnel sloped downward, and when they emerged from it they halted.

The cisterns stretched away into the distance, a huge lake of fresh water inside a cavern, the roof of which was supported by massive stone pillars in some places and by walls of sheer rock in others. Alexei guessed that where the supports rose there were the foundations of the buildings above ground. He had never entered the caverns and tunnels which ran under parts of Kinsai before. They were the province of the Suristani who maintained the conduits and oversaw the filtration columns. No one else cared for the place.

They were on a promontory which had been built up with blocks of granite. There was a short flight of steps at the end.

'Down there.' Jotan indicated the steps.

Already there were sounds coming from the tunnel behind them. Alexei was surprised that Jotan appeared to know where he was going. Two punts were lashed to rings embedded in the stonework at the foot of the steps. Probably the men who worked in the cisterns used them as a means of travelling from one side of the cavern to the other. Alexei started to pull on one of the ropes.

'There are no paddles,' Jotan said. 'Give me your sword, and take off your coat.'

He took the sword out of Alexei's hand and jabbed it into the planks at the bottom of the punt, then draped Alexei's coat over it. 'It's the best we can do,' he said. 'Get the women behind that wall.'

The end of the promontory was buttressed, and there was room at the base for several people to hide. Alexei climbed across stones slippery with moisture and polished by age. Ahead of him Arkhina gasped as she lost her footing and slid almost to the water's edge. He turned so that his back was to the sloping granite wall and pulled her up.

Jotan had not yet followed them. He was busy in the bottom of the second punt, and when he climbed out of it he cut the rope securing the first punt with his sword, and then used his foot to launch it out across the water. He threw the torch after it, and the faggots hissed as they were extinguished. The punt sailed out across a stretch of the cistern which was as calm as a pond. It found an eddy where the outpouring of a supply conduit splashed steadily, and it swung, steadied, and then moved on into the gloom. Jotan scrambled across the rocks to Alexei's side.

The assassins rushed out of the tunnel, their feet ringing on the stones, emerging onto the promontory in time to catch sight of the punt as it rounded a pillar. Shouts and curses echoed across the vault, and then they were hurling themselves down the steps.

There were five men, and the punt was small. Alexei heard a single splash as a loosened rope fell into the water, and then there came the creak of settling timbers. More splashes followed, and when he peered cautiously around the side of the buttress he saw that the men now occupying the punt were using their hands as paddles to propel themselves away from the promontory wall. The sounds faded away gradually.

There was a narrow stone path, Alexei now saw, around the base of the promontory beyond the buttress. He made out the black shape of another tunnel mouth. Jotan was getting slowly to his feet, offering his hand to Arkhina. Her face was dirty and her gown stained, and like Jehana she had cut the skirt away at thigh level. There were no sounds of pursuit now, and only occasional splashing signified that the would-be assassins were searching the expanse of water somewhere behind the first line of pillars.

'We should be safe enough now,' Jotan said, although he did not raise his voice. He nodded at the second tunnel mouth. 'If I remember correctly, that leads to the square beside the barracks occupied by the Kha-Khan's night guard.'

Alexei glanced across the cistern, but he could see nothing. It was possible that Jotan was being over-confident, he thought, though there was no sign of the punt full of men. All at once, from quite far out on the water, there came an outburst of noise – frightened shouts, and a sound as if someone had fallen in.

Jotan's head came round, and he listened briefly, a

satisfied expression on his face. 'I holed the second punt,' he said. He looked at Arkhina, and suddenly they clung to one another and laughed.

'Such lawlessness cannot be permitted to continue,' Artai said.

They were in a small audience chamber, and they had been excused the customary prostrations.

'I don't think it's likely to become a habit,' Alexei said calmly. 'They relied on the fact that most of the people would be sleeping off the celebrations.'

In fact Kinsai was noted for the peace and order which existed on its streets – there was order everywhere in the land, and very little real law breaking – and it was amazing that his attackers had been able to persist for so long without interference.

'Nevertheless,' Artai said, 'we have issued our order for the watch to be strengthened.'

The principal function of the watch was to deal with outbreaks of fire, and to ensure the security of property. A curfew was imposed after nightfall, but it was ill-observed, and almost anyone who had a reasonable excuse was permitted to walk the streets without hindrance.

'We are particularly concerned with the reasons for the attack upon your person.' Artai inspected Alexei expressionlessly. 'The malefactors named to you have not been taken?'

The men named by the dwarf were being sought by Burun's provost, but it was already apparent that they were no longer in Kinsai. Alexei shook his head. 'No, Magnificence.'

'Then their motives remain a matter for question,' Artai observed.

Jotan stirred at Alexei's side, and he raised his head. 'Both of them have daughters,' he commented flatly.

170

Alexei sat up straight. 'If they have, Khan, they are not known to me.'

'– Their fathers may believe they are however,' Artai said smoothly. 'It is a point worth considering. Think of your reputation, Alexei. You are an alien, and so men may believe they are justified in breaking the Yasa to encompass your death.'

The circumstance which offended most of the Yek who heard of it was not the attempt on Alexei's life, but rather the means which had been employed. A gathering of assassins in a populated area was considered to have endangered life and property. Innocent citizens might have been injured, or lives lost, and it was this above all which was a source of outrage. It troubled Alexei that the failed assassination seemed about to be dismissed as an effort at the removal of some imagined stain on family honour, and he wondered if Jotan truly believed the explanation he had offered, or if he was acting at Burun's direction to distract Artai from the truth.

What is the truth? Why would two men I have never met pay to have me killed?

Burun's analysis of the previous night's events had been scathing, but had provided no answers. The officer in command of Jotan's escort, whose knowledge of the city was apparently imperfect and who had misunderstood the directions he had been given, had been stripped of his rank, flogged, and turned off. None of the attackers, all of whom had been of subject races, had survived to be questioned. A few, it was clear, had made their escape, and two drowned corpses had been recovered from the cisterns.

'Whatever their reasons,' Artai said, 'they shall suffer for it. Who attacks our servant attacks us also. We are pleased, Khan, that you have suffered no injury. Your person is valuable to us, as we have

171

demonstrated by our regard.'

There was more of the same before Alexei and Jotan were allowed to depart, but further enquiry into the matter was not mentioned, and it was as if Artai had lost interest.

If there were absentees from the gathering of Khans and Noyons which waited sycophantically in the antechamber through which they left the palace, Alexei supposed they were the result rather of an excess of celebration than of flight in the face of possible discovery or inquisition. Suddenly he realised the single glaring inconsistency in any line of argument which was designed to point to revenge or the settlement of a grudge as a motive for the attempt. The dwarf had been a mutant, and as such should not have been in Kinsai at all. Moreover the Yek had a horror of the mutations which were still the occasional result of the patches of radiation which were to be found in places around the continent, and they had laws to prevent the proliferation of mutant types through succeeding generations. A mutant who survived to become an adult was permitted to live, but he was forbidden to breed to produce more of his kind.

That was the most puzzling aspect of the whole affair, Alexei thought. No member of the races of the True People would have involved himself in a plan which necessitated the transportation of a mutant into Kinsai. Even the races which lacked talons – whom Alexei considered human in origin – baulked at contact with mutated species, and as a result mutants tended to live in deserted or out-of-the-way parts of the country, effectively quarantined from the rest of civilisation.

'If I have offended you,' Jotan said in a voice which was filled with disarming sincerity, 'I am sorry for it.'

172

Alexei gestured to dismiss the apology. 'You did not speak to give offence, Khan.' It was the conviction that there was more to the affair than was capable of being explained upon the arrest of the fugitive Khans which now governed the tone of his response. Suddenly he was determined to unravel the intrigue which he was certain linked many of the events which had occurred since Nogai's death. He saw that Jotan was watching his expression. 'I cannot take issue with you over the matter of my past character,' he said, and smiled, dissembling the truth of his emotions.

PART TWO

The Sunstealer

The argument had been going on for some time.

'East,' C'zinsit insisted. 'Look at the chart. You can see it's shorter.'

Jehan saw Alexei frown.

'Maybe it is,' Alexei said. His finger traced a narrow band of blue shading on the map which was laid out across the table. 'I'm told it's also the worst stretch of water in the world – storms and an impossible current for more than nine tenths of the year. The N'pani don't like to sail it, and they live there.'

C'zinsit waved dismissively. 'The N'pani are inshore sailors,' he said.

'– And what are we?' Jehan enquired tartly. C'zinsit was an uncle of sorts – the half-brother of his father – but he was several years younger, and Jehan had no hesitation in disputing his point of view. 'You are talking about a sea which has never been crossed in living memory. There are stories, that is all – tales told by fishermen – and half of those talk about reefs and a coastline in which there is no safe haven. We aren't sailors. That's why we crew our ships with Ch'kasians and Suristani.'

C'zinsit glared. 'Arguing on that basis,' he said, 'the whole project is impossible. The Great Sea route means a journey of more than three thousand verst. If we can't cross the Sea of Storms, a tenth of the distance, what chance have we of navigating that far?'

'None, at present,' Alexei said. 'Certainly we'll need a better ship than the kind I've seen in Pantai and Losan.'

Jehan had been wondering when somebody was

177

going to mention that. The ships plying the primary trade routes which joined the known continents and the outlying islands were all variations of a kind of carrack – a two-masted galleon, round-bottomed and broad-beamed, with lateen sails and elementary steering gear. The iron-shod leeboards mounted port and starboard counterbalanced the height of the masts, and provided stability in a following sea. The result was a vessel which was surprisingly fast and manoeuvrable for its size – few were more than twenty drem in length – but they were not designed for an extended sea journey, that was certain.

'The size and number of your ships depends upon how many men you intend to take,' Orcadai observed.

Orcadai was C'zinsit's elder brother, and spent most of his time travelling from fief to fief, overseeing the military training of conscripts and inspecting the condition of arms and equipment.

Jehan saw the look on Alexei's face. In four days of meetings they had managed to decide only the names of the principal members of the embassy. Jehan was used to the kind of council at which nearly everything was decided before the participants sat down to talk, and he wondered why Alexei was allowing so much disruption and argument.

'We should go in force,' C'zinsit said. 'If the inhabitants are like us, they will respect us only if they see that we are strong.'

C'zinsit had presented the same argument every time the topic was mentioned.

'We're supposed to be an embassy,' Jehan pointed out. 'This isn't a reconnaissance.'

'It might as well be,' C'zinsit said. 'We've had to conquer every verst of territory we have ever gained. Why should this be different?'

'The problem is that we know nothing about either

178

the land or the people,' Alexei said. 'If we make assumptions, and they are the wrong assumptions, we will jeopardise the mission.' He glanced past C'zinsit at Jehan as he spoke, and raised his eyebrows as if seeking comment.

C'zinsit sat back in his chair. 'If the embassy fails, the responsibility will be yours,' he said flatly. 'Why are we here, if you don't care for our advice?'

'I thought we ought to be agreed,' Alexei said, and he smiled sourly. 'It's called democracy where I come from. I never thought it would work, but I felt we ought to give it a try.'

Everyone looked at him strangely.

'I heard you speak of democracy to my father once,' Orcadai said. 'Everyone has a voice, no one commands, and decisions are taken by the will of the majority. Even those who dissent are required to act as if they agree once a course of action has been decided upon, and if there is blame, it is shared by all.'

Jehan wrinkled his nose. 'It's a nice idea,' he said. 'But I don't see how anything would ever get done. Anyway, how would people know who to follow? A Khan is served by his vassals because he discharges his responsibility to make decisions which are the best for the majority of his people. If he makes a mistake, he has to rectify it. If decisions are made by a committee, and they are wrong, they can blame one another, and the people suffer just the same.'

Alexei flushed. 'That's an over-simplification,' he said. 'What democracy means –' He saw that Jehan and Orcadai were both grinning, and he stopped, then gestured. 'All right, damn you. I know what you're going to say. If we're going to get anything done, somebody has to be in command. I just wasn't sure that you were ready to follow me, that was all.'

Orcadai spread his hands, and his silver-sheathed talons glittered. 'Our Lord the Kha-Khan has reposed his especial trust and confidence in you, Khan,' he said sweetly. 'Why should we not?'

'Our Lord the Kha-Khan is a wilful child,' C'zinsit said bluntly. He stood up. Like Orcadai, he was more N'pani than Yek, and now he stared inscrutably at Alexei. '– But that's beside the point. Alexei, what my brothers meant to say is that they await your command. As usual they have the right of it, and they shame me. Our father thinks you are the best man to carry out the task which is before us, and so you have our support, whatever you decide.'

'Tell me why you agreed to marry Alexei.'

They were sitting in the garden at the back of Jotan's house. It was early afternoon, and the height of the wall threw the trees into shadow, and brought a welcome coolness to the paths which wound past slopes filled with ornamental fern. A stream trickled artificially, and birds were singing.

Jehana was playing with one of the cats, a Suristani with a prehensile tail. Her fingers running through the ruff of fur around the cat's neck tightened as Jehan spoke, and the cat yowled and it bit playfully at her hand.

'Oh. It's time I was married,' she said at last.

Jehan produced a gasp of laughter. 'I remember what you said last time you were offered that for a reason. Now tell me the truth.'

She released the cat. It sprang down off her lap and prowled off through a flower bed. The singing of the birds stopped for a moment, and then started again.

'The Yasa says that a daughter is required to obey the will of her father,' Jehana said.

'– It also says that a woman may not be given in

marriage without her consent,' Jehan countered. 'Besides, it was not our father's will that you marry Alexei.'

'I am not marrying him. We are betrothed, that is all.'

'Hunh.' Jehan was sitting cross-legged on the grass. He stared at her. 'But one thing generally follows after the other, as I am sure you are aware. The penalty for terminating a betrothal contract without good reason is – I forget what it is –'

'– A heavy fine,' Jehana said steadily. 'I will pay it, if it comes to it. Burun will pay it for me.'

Jehan had been certain before he had asked the question that Jehana did not intend to go through with the match. She had been independent for too long. Now he felt disappointment that she was behaving so predictably. 'Tell me why you agreed to it,' he said.

She eyed him, and he guessed that she was trying to decide what to say. If she told the truth, it would be a miracle.

The birds in the trees stopped singing abruptly. The cat was creeping stealthily through a patch of long grass towards the foot of the largest tree. Every time it moved it froze, one paw outstretched, not quite touching the ground. Suddenly it rushed at the tree, leapt onto a low branch, and ran up the trunk. The birds flew up noisily, circled, and then they came down and settled in another tree not far away. The cat turned and looked at them, and it pawed the air. Then it yawned so that its fangs showed. It stretched out along the branch, its claws out, waiting.

'What do you think of Alexei?' Jehan asked. He watched Jehana's face, trying to gauge her reaction.

She plucked a grass stalk from the ground at her side, then split it lengthwise with her outer talon. She tossed the pieces aside. 'He is a man,' she said.

It was an answer which might mean anything. Jehan showed his teeth. 'Which is to say that the idea of being married to him offends you?'

Her head came round sharply. She examined him, and then shook her head. 'I did not say that.'

Jehan rubbed the back of his neck with his hand. 'I remember once when we were children,' he said, 'you told me you would never marry. I never thought you were serious.' He smiled. 'Not all men cause their wives to submit to their will you know.'

'You are an expert on wives of course,' she responded tartly.

He grinned at her, aware that she was trying to pick a fight so that she could avoid further discussion of the subject. 'Alexei does not offend you –' he mused. '– Or no more than anyone else. In fact you defend him when I suggest it –'

Jehana sniffed. 'If requiring you not to put words into my mouth is defence –'

'Oh, I think it is,' Jehan said gently. He met her stare, and after a moment her eyes dropped. 'You have been offered marriage by every eligible family in the Khanate,' he pointed out. 'Tell me why you consented to be betrothed to Alexei.'

A bird came down in the topmost branches of the tree in which the cat lay in wait. The cat looked up, and then it began to work its way upwards, its eyes fixed on its intended prey. Just as it reached the top of the trunk, the bird flew away. The cat sat up in the branches, and it yowled plaintively.

Jehana looked up. 'Artai intended to offer me marriage,' she said suddenly.

Jehan let out a breath. He nodded understanding. 'That was a match you could not have refused.'

'It would have been difficult,' Jehana agreed austerely.

The understatement was such that Jehan was forced to smile. A Kha-Khan did not ask; he commanded, and it was left simply for everyone else to obey.

'I could not have withstood it,' Jehana said.

'Of course not.' Jehan took her hand and smiled at her sympathetically.

They would not have told Alexei everything, of course. Probably he knew only that Jehana objected to the idea of marrying Artai, and had been told that her family wished to avoid giving offence by rejecting the suit, and so were willing to see her contracted without the preliminary of a courtship. Jehan pondered the circumstances, and he saw how few alternatives there had been. 'We should not have elected Artai,' he said.

Jehana laughed bitterly. 'We did not elect him,' she said. 'It was Nogai's will.'

It was only part of the truth. Jehan knew that many of the Khans had been won over to support of Artai principally by the knowledge that the probable alternative was civil war, and he shook his head angrily. 'And what of the next time Artai expresses desire for some lady of his court?'

The cat ran straight down the trunk of the tree. It sped across the grass and leapt up onto Jehana's lap. She stroked it absently. 'They will put someone suitable in his way, I imagine,' she said.

'Someone barren, you mean,' Jehan said disapprovingly.

Her head came round. 'Of course.'

The point was so obvious that it scarcely needed to be made. Idly Jehan wondered how it was possible to ensure that every woman made available to Artai was incapable of childbirth. Certainly Artai would consider no one who had already been married to another, whether she had children or not. He supposed that the Sechem had the knowledge, and made a face. 'What a mess we have made.'

Jehana shrugged. 'Argue it with Burun; not with me.'

There were several possible replies to that, but Jehan discarded all of them because they were impossible to use without appearing to slight her motives. The dilemma which faced them with regard to Artai was complex – even given the clear direction of the Yasa – and no one who was in possession of all the facts could be blamed for unwillingness to condemn the course which had been decided upon. Although Artai was Altun it was also clear – on the basis of a standard which was applied usually only at birth – that he exhibited a variety of mutant characteristics. Thus his freedom to father children was subject to the law, even though he could not be allowed to know that he was under restriction. All at once Jehan realised that Jehana had not yet given her reasons for consenting to betrothal with Alexei. There was little doubt that there were men who were as eligible, whose names would have aroused less comment. The fact that she had implied that she intended to withdraw from the arrangement as soon as it was convenient did not matter, Jehan thought, unless Alexei's character was to provide the excuse …

Suddenly he understood. 'Alexei is an alien,' he said. 'That is why you accepted him.' He saw Jehana flush.

She gestured. 'The others we thought of are all the sons of influential men,' she said. 'It would have caused offence when I chose to withdraw.'

'– Whereas Alexei can have no recourse.' Jehan nodded. 'I see. And does he know that you are using him?'

Jehana stared. 'He has been told simply that I object to marriage with Artai,' she said. 'If he believes that I have exhibited any preference for his person above that of the others who have offered for my hand, then he is a fool.'

Whatever else the offworlder was, Jehan thought, he was not a fool. Which left him wondering why Alexei had agreed to the proposal at all – for if he knew or even suspected that there was to be no marriage, it was difficult to see where he perceived his advantage to lie. It was on the tip of Jehan's tongue to suggest that Alexei was allowing himself to be used only because it suited him; but it was clear that discussing the subject was making Jehana unhappy, and so he said nothing, sitting quietly beside her until suddenly she got up and went into the house.

Sidacai had been held in chains while he was a prisoner, and the marks of the manacles were plain upon his wrists.

'Don't expect me to fall on your neck in gratitude, Merkut,' he said. He stood in the middle of the room, surveying Jehan, and the guard who was beside the door eyed him nervously.

Jehan grinned. He looked at the trooper. 'Kuchuk, go away.'

The guard opened the door and went outside.

'Kuchuk.' Sidacai looked at the hangings of the ceiling. 'Your grandfather had a standard bearer of that name the year we conquered the Alan.'

'That's his son,' Jehan nodded.

'Hunh.' Sidacai looked at a chair which had been placed by the window, but he made no move to sit down. 'That was a good time. Things were simpler then.'

185

There was a bowl of fruit on the table. Jehan selected an apple. He ran the extended tips of his talons across the golden skin, and the peel fell away. He caught the peel before it hit the floor and threw it out of the window. One of the apes that lived among the rooftops of the city scampered down and picked up the peel, then raced back up to his vantage point beside the eaves.

Sidacai eyed the bowl and licked his lips. 'Am I your prisoner?' he demanded. 'No one has told me.'

'You're in Alexei's charge,' Jehan said. He cut the apple into quarters, then ate one. 'I don't imagine he intends to confine you.'

Sidacai had been delivered to Jotan's house by a small company of the Kha-Khan's guard. If he had been told nothing about the terms of his release, then probably it was Artai's doing. Artai was full of petty cruelties, and it would have amused him to allow Sidacai to wonder if he was being taken to his execution.

The mention of the offworlder's name produced a flush of reaction on Sidacai's cheeks.

'You should not think you have the Merkuts to thank for your freedom,' Jehan said conversationally. He impaled another segment of the apple on his talons, and popped it into his mouth. 'Alexei asked the Kha-Khan for you, otherwise you would be a dead man.'

'Hunh.' Sidacai digested the information. His nose wrinkled. 'And who persuaded Alexei to ask for me, I wonder. So tell me why I am here.'

'Sit down and eat first.' Jehan waved at the table. As well as the fruit there was a tray with cups and flasks of wine and k'miss, and a plate of savoury pastries filled with p'tar meat which steamed with an appetising aroma.

The look in Sidacai's eyes was wary. 'If I accept your hospitality,' he said, 'it will not mean that I forfeit my right to kanly.'

Jehan showed his teeth. 'Declare your feud if it pleases you. I will meet you whenever and wherever you choose.'

Sidacai had never carried any excess weight, and the period of his imprisonment had stripped the flesh from his bones. A new scar ran from the line of his jaw down into the collar of his open tunic, and Jehan guessed that Artai had broken the law which forbade the ill-treatment of captives, and he frowned.

There was a noise in the passageway outside, and Jehan saw that Kuchuk had left the door slightly ajar so that he could hear. He hid a smile. Sidacai looked at the table again, and suddenly he snorted, and then sat down.

Jehan was confident that he could beat Sidacai if it came to a fight. In kanly only the winner survived to walk away. He poured wine into two of the cups and slid one of them across the table so that it was within Sidacai's reach. He was aware that Sidacai's death at this point would be considered a waste, and so it had been a calculated risk to demonstrate readiness to accept a challenge.

Sidacai had already devoured half of the pastries on the plate. He picked up a napkin which lay beside the plate and wiped his hands on it. 'Damn Artai,' he said. 'His jailers were certain he intended to have me killed, or they would not have treated me thus.'

Jehan shrugged. If Sidacai cared to lodge a formal complaint, the jailers would suffer punishment. Probably he would not complain.

Sidacai drank deeply. 'I am released into Alexei's charge, you say. Am I then still under sentence? Tell me.'

Jehan sipped a little of the wine. He sat back, and stretched out his booted feet. 'Alexei demanded your pardon,' he said. 'Artai has agreed, but there are conditions.'

'Hah.' Sidacai laughed harshly. 'Either I am pardoned, or I am not.'

'Oh, well.' Jehan set the cup aside. There was the width of the table between them, but Sidacai's speed and his ferocity in attack were legend. 'Your life is no longer forfeit; but it is upon condition that you serve the Kha-Khan on a venture which Alexei is to command. Your lands and titles will be preserved if you accept.'

'– And if I refuse?'

It was not a serious question, but Jehan lifted a hand and gestured. 'Banishment, of course. And since there is no place in the known world which is not the Kha-Khan's domain, you would be an outlaw.'

Sidacai emptied his cup. He reached out to take the flask, and then suddenly he looked up sharply. 'It's the Unknown Lands of course. An embassy? A reconnaissance?'

'An embassy of sorts.' Jehan lifted his cup and drank, keeping his eyes all the time on Sidacai's face. He had known that Sidacai would work out the nature of the venture before he had to be told. Now that the Khanate was secure, the only challenges lay on the other side of the Great Sea.

'Hah, I thought so.' Sidacai nodded. 'And what do you want with me?'

'Oh.' Jehan smiled candidly. 'You are an available military commander with the right kind of experience. You're used to leading small numbers of men in difficult conditions. We can't take a large force – a company at most probably – and so we think your ability will be useful.'

'I see.' Sidacai poured more wine. 'Now piss down my back and tell me it's raining. I'm considered expendable, naturally, and it would please Artai if I failed to return.'

'Well,' Jehan grinned. 'You always did like strange new places.'

Sidacai pursed his lips. 'You think you need me,' he said. 'Probably you're right. Very well, I'll go. But I pick my own men, and if we ever have to fight, you obey my word.'

Jehan did not think that Sidacai was in any position to impose conditions, but he sat back in his chair, considering. 'You pick the men from a pool which we approve,' he said. 'As to the rest, we would be stupid to appoint you in command if we intended to ignore your direction, however, you must agree to submit to Alexei's will in all things which touch upon the aims of our embassy.'

The frown on Sidacai's face indicated that he was testing the wording of the condition for loopholes. 'I agree,' he said finally, and stood up.

'You're going?' Jehan pretended surprise.

Sidacai looked as if he thought that the question was unnecessary. 'I've agreed to it, haven't I? Am I free or not?'

'Oh, certainly.' Jehan set his cup aside, amused. 'I will send to you as soon as we are ready to receive your advice – tomorrow probably.'

'Good.' Sidacai strode towards the door. Then he halted and turned. 'This does not mean that we are friends,' he said.

Jehan showed his teeth. 'I never imagined it.' He saw Sidacai nod, as if he was satisfied that he had made a point. Sidacai went out through the door, and Jehan speared another segment of apple and ate it while he considered how far the agreement which he

189

had obtained from Sidacai could be trusted. Alexei would think that he had surrendered too many concessions, of course, but he did not understand the Yek mind.

The Sechem was named Parin. He was a slim, spare man in early middle age, and unusually for a member of the races of the True People he had light-coloured hai – the shade of newly sawn wood, Jehan thought. His talons were unadorned, though he had eye tattoos which indicated that he was of the clan of Hanjin.

'Like this,' Alexei said, and sketched rapidly upon the topmost sheet of a folder full of paper. The outline of the keel of a vessel began to takc shape. 'You see? The timbers should be sheathed with copper or tin, to preserve them.'

Parin nodded. He turned to one of his assistants and conferred with him. Each of the assistants was accompanied by a scribe. The scribe indicated a character in the centre of a column of script on the page of an opened book, and the assistant nodded, then stared into the middle distance and began to reel off information. It was by such means that every aspect of knowledge was recorded, stored, and later retrieved. An assistant might serve for years as the keeper of a specific book, being required to follow the paths of investigation which were suggested by the information absorbed, until at last connections were made with other disciplines. Before a youth was apprenticed to the Sechem he was committed to a number of years of study of the Yasa, memorising the codex in its entirety so that he was capable of relating his knowledge of the law to science. There was a constant exchange of information between Sechem, and the implications of every aspect of a science which was likely to be applied practically were studied. The way in which the use of knowledge affected the patterns of life and existence of the people determined whether or not it became adopted. A Sechem's mind was like a sponge, soaking up information until a connection could be made between apparently unrelated areas of scientific fact. Often it turned out that there was no practical purpose to which a discovery so obtained could be put, because of the prohibitions imposed by the Yasa; but that did not matter to the Sechem, for whom the pursuit of information was an end in itself.

The release of information by the assistant was too fast for normal ears to follow, but the Sechem were trained to understand and to interpret for one another. Parin listened for a moment longer, and then he held up a hand. The assistant fell respectfully silent.

'Khan, there is nothing in this which is forbidden,' Parin said, turning. 'A larger vessel, or a smaller, the principles are very much the same. Also the methods which you have suggested are known to us. We do not use them only because those we have employed hitherto have been sufficient for our needs.'

That was the principle of the Yasa so far as the practical application of scientific knowledge was concerned. That which was sufficient for the needs of the people was permitted, but innovation for its own sake, or for the purposes of profit, was contrary to the law. The definition of public necessity was a comprehensive one, and prevented the too casual adoption of what Jehan had learned from Alexei were thought of elsewhere in the universe as simple technological advances.

He grinned. 'Bigger ships mean bigger cargoes,' he said. 'The small traders will have something to say about that.'

It was as if the Sechem were listening to something no one else in the room could hear. Parin's head was cocked to one side. Then he straightened and turned. 'The cost of a vessel such as the Khan has described will be beyond a trader's reach, Noyon, given that men are permitted to make only a profit from an enterprise which may be considered just. Also a cargo of such a size will be costly to store and to dispose of. The ships which the traders employ now are the best size for their needs and purpose. The ship which is built to sail the Great Sea will not upset the balance.'

Jehan had known there would be an answer. The Sechem were seldom if ever wrong when they agreed that a method was to be permitted, for very little of what men considered new science was in fact a matter of recent discovery. All that was important of human knowledge had been handed down – no one knew for certain whence old science had come – and only in interpretation was there ever anything which was novel or innovative.

Sidacai was craning to look over Alexei's shoulder. 'I know nothing of ships,' he said, 'but it seems to me that the vessel that will carry a company of men, and their st'lyan, will be large indeed.'

Alexei nodded. 'It will be three times the size of the largest carrack which sails the Inner Sea,' he said. 'Larger if I can find the wrights with the skills to construct it.'

Jehan grinned at the expressions on the faces of Orcadai and C'zinsit. Few Yek were happy at sea, and a ship-borne invasion of Y'frike years earlier had come close to failure at one point because the reinforcements delivered to its shores had been so weakened by the effects of their voyage.

Alexei was adding details to his sketch. There were no masts, Jehan saw, and he wondered how many would be needed, and how many sails they would carry.

'A ship such as this will require an improved method of steering,' Alexei said. He glanced pointedly in the direction of the Sechem. 'Also I am concerned about the strength of the winds and currents which we may encounter once we have left the shelter of the land.'

'As to the matter of steering,' Parin said prosaically, 'I am content. The Yasa will not be offended against if the ship is steered not by an oar, but by what the Khan has said is called a rudder, being just another kind of oar which is fixed to the stern of the vessel. The question of sailing the ship against winds or currents I submit the Khan ought to leave to sailors. As the Khan knows very well, there are many ways of rigging the sails of a ship.'

The offworlder looked up. 'I was not talking of sails,' he said. 'A sailing ship is at the mercy of the winds, and lacking them goes nowhere. There are other means of driving a vessel through water.'

There was a moment's silence. The youngest assistant raised his head, and he looked down his nose at Alexei. 'The Yasa says –' he began.

Parin glared, and the assistant went crimson and stopped. 'The Khan is talking about machines, of course,' Parin said. He did not appear to be disturbed by the notion.

'Of course.' Alexei sat back in his chair. He crossed one booted foot over the other, his manner relaxed. 'You agree that a ship of the size I have indicated is necessary,' he said. 'Ships such as the traders use might make such a journey given that the conditions are not adverse. We do not know what we may encounter, however, and thus our duty requires us to ensure our success by using our knowledge to build a better ship. If a ship of an improved design is not a contravention of the Yasa, then surely a means of propulsion which will drive it so that it can overcome the winds and currents is also permissible.'

The Sechem smiled tight little smiles of appreciation at the logic of the argument. Jehan watched Parin's face, and he wondered what he was going to say. It was impossible to conduct a real argument with the Sechem because they were above all the interpreters and arbiters of the Yasa, the authority on the law to whom men turned when they were in dispute.

'It is true that there is no law against machines,' Parin said at last. 'Just as there is no law against knowledge. It is the use to which men put both which sometimes breaks the Yasa.'

Jehan nodded, and he saw that others in the room were doing the same.

Alexei appeared untroubled by the rebuff. 'Tell me the law,' he said.

Parin stirred as if he did not understand the request. 'Khan, there is a world of law,' he said.

'– And the first law of all?' The offworlder looked at his hands, and then he raised his eyes. 'Speak it – for I would hear it from your lips.'

Jehan saw where this was leading, and he knew that Parin also saw the path down which he was being led.

The Sechem seemed to draw a breath. '– There shall be but one Lord upon the Earth,' he said.

'– For thus it is in Heaven.'

Jehan was scarcely aware that he had spoken the words aloud. The lips of the others had moved also, repeating the litany. It was the reason behind every effort at conquest, and the justification, if one was required, for their embassy.

'So.' Alexei stared at Parin and showed his teeth.

It was the first time that Jehan had ever seen a Sechem at a loss for words.

Orcadai opened his mouth to speak, and then closed it again. He looked around for support, and then gestured. 'Khan, you argue that unless you are permitted to build the kind of ship you require, the embassy will fail –' He broke off, shaking his head as if he was at a loss to know how to deal with the notion.

'I argue that unless such a ship is built, the Yek can never cross the Great Sea or circumnavigate the world,' Alexei responded. 'And thus the Will of Heaven will be denied.' He stared around the room. 'Come, dispute it with me. Can you tell me of your knowledge that it is not so?'

The Khanate was encompassed about, as all men knew, by the limitations of the ability of its people to sail the seas. Yek Khans ruled N'pan to the east, and as far as Suristan and Ch'kasia to the west. To the south their influence controlled Y'frike and Dr'gasia, though far away N'czuan was ruled by default for part of every year because it was hidden across the Gulf of Mists, which only the men of the islands knew how to sail safely.

Parin's hand lay on an open book – one of the *suras* of the Yasa – and it was as if he drew re-assurance and strength from it. When he spoke again his tone was dry and unemotional. 'Khan, your proposition is clever, and your argument is difficult to counter. How if we draw from the records of our knowledge to find a way to drive this ship of yours without the use of machines?'

It seemed to Jehan as he watched Alexei's face that the offworlder was reflecting inwardly upon the sum of his own knowledge, testing it against his belief in what was recorded in the books controlled by the Sechem. Suddenly he opened his eyes wide and he smiled. 'In such a case I must be satisfied,' he said blandly. 'For I am concerned only for the success of our embassy, that the Will of Heaven be served.'

If Parin doubted the truth of the offworlder's statement, he was too polite to show it. 'We will examine the extent of our knowledge,' he said. 'And if we fail –'

'Steam,' Alexei said decisively. 'Engines driven by steam will propel a ship such as I have described, and they are within the ability of the men of this world to build.'

Jehan could not imagine how steam could be used to drive machines, although it was clear that the notion was not new to the Sechem. Parin nodded, and he signed to his assistants to roll up the books so that they could be packed away in the boxes and chests in which they were stored.

He opened his eyes in darkness. It was the third hour of the night watch. Somewhere outside the house a sentry's feet crunched on pebbles. The familiar sounds brought Jehan to a sense of the place and the time. His father's house in Kinsai. Now that he knew where he was the details of the room became familiar, and he knew at once what had wakened him, and strained his ears to hear it again. Obligingly it came, a long low cry like the call of an animal, or maybe a lost soul howling in the wind. It was somewhere outside, and Jehan sat up in bed. He had heard it the first time as a child, in his grandfather's yurt on the Khirgiz, and going to Burun's quarters had found him awake also. Then Burun had told him that no one other than the true Lord of the Merkuts ever heard the sound.

Jehan knew that he would be unable to go back to

sleep again. He rose and went next door to find the girl he knew would be sleeping there.

The girl was Alan – slim and dark, with long legs and small breasts. Probably her family had been taken as captives when she was a child, for the conquest of the Alan country had taken place when Jehan was a youth. The girl herself was free, and had come to the house through the offices of a steward. Jehan shook her awake.

'Get up.'

She sat up, rubbing the sleep from her eyes, and then she looked at him archly. It had not occurred to him that he was naked, but it did not matter in any case what she thought. He drew her by the wrist off the bed, and went back into his own chamber. She was wearing a simple shift, and he pulled it up around her waist. She gave a small shiver, and started to cover herself, but did not.

'Take it off,' Jehan said. He pulled the top of the shift over her head. She grabbed for it.

'I don't like to sleep without –'

'That's too bad,' he said. He got onto the bed, holding her, and lay on his side facing her.

'You see?' Alexei dusted his hands together, and the dirt rose in tiny clouds. 'I told you it would work.'

The steam boiler had been set up in a shed at the back of the offworlder's house. The Sechem were nowhere to be seen, and Jehan wondered if they knew what was going on. There was no law, strictly speaking, against experimenting, although considering the stage which Alexei's trials had reached, it was clear that he must have been working on this for some time.

The two men who were tending the fire under the boiler were Dr'gasians – squat and bald, with decorative tattoos which ran across their shoulders and down inside their tunics. Not a drem of their skin between neck and waist was uncoloured, and the variety of the designs fascinated Jehan every time he looked at them.

'So you can boil water to make steam,' he said. He shrugged. 'Now show me your miracle.'

Alexei laughed as if he knew that Jehan was being deliberately discouraging. He gestured to the elder of the two fire tenders, and the man pushed a lever at the side of the boiler away from him, and then pulled it back again. The boiler was like an upright wooden barrel banded with copper. On top of it there was a copper funnel, and there were rods coming out of the end of the funnel attached to a wheel. The rod on the side nearest Jehan rose with a jerk, turning the wheel. When it had almost reached its zenith, the second rod also moved, so that the motion of the wheel was continued. The Dr'gasian adjusted another lever delicately, and the motion of the shafts increased in speed. An opening in a small pipe near the end of the funnel chuffed steam in bursts.

Moving closer, Jehan saw that the ends of the rods were not attached directly to the wheel, but rather to the shaft upon which it was mounted. The shaft itself was not straight. Instead there were kinks in it where the rods joined it, and the ends of the rods were attached to collars which were secured around the kinks. The second Dr'gasian was applying oil and grease with abandon to the shaft and the collars.

'The more rods attached to the shaft, the more smoothly the wheel turns,' Alexei said. 'Two engines are better than one, of course.'

'Of course,' Jehan said, amused.

The offworlder produced a hostile stare, and then suddenly he laughed. 'I show you something which could change the face of your world,' he said, 'but it does not impress you.'

Jehan made a face. A machine worked, or it did not. If it was necessary for some purpose proper to the existence of the people, then there were engineers whose task it was to build and operate it. Such matters were not the concern of a Khan. 'It makes a lot of steam,' he observed critically, 'and the fire smokes.'

Alexei picked up a cloth from a bench which was laid across a pair of trestles. He scrubbed energetically at his hands. Some of the grime had transferred to the front of his tunic, and there was a streak of oil on his face. 'There are a few disadvantages,' he said, nodding. 'The water boils away eventually, and has to be replaced. It has to be fresh water, which would be a problem at sea.'

Sawn logs had been piled beside the boiler. One of the machine tenders used a piece of wood to knock down a catch on a door in the base of the copper sheathing around the bottom of the barrel. A fire burned brightly inside. The man threw several logs onto it, and then tapped the door shut, shielding his face from the heat of the flames.

'It eats a lot of fuel,' Jehan said.

'Yes. Coal burns longer than wood, but coal is scarce.'

A chimney led from the side of the boiler away to the end of the shed. It was belching smoke, and a downdraught caught some of it and blew it back towards them. Jehan took several paces back and he screwed up his eyes. 'Name of God,' Jehan said. He coughed to clear his throat of the taste of the smoke.

Alexei signalled to one of the engine tenders, and the man fiddled with the levers so that the rods rising and falling at the top of the funnel slowed jerkily and then stopped. A cloud of steam shot out of the tube, and the man who was in its path skipped nimbly to one side.

'It works, at least,' Alexei said cheerfully.

Jehan rubbed the back of his neck with one hand. The Yek used wind and water power, but this was clearly independent of both. He had a sudden vision of the looms which were used to weave cloth being powered by such machines. One engine would do the work of ten water wheels. Then he thought of a line of chimneys belching smoke across the country, and of the fuel they would require, and he grimaced.

The offworlder seemed to sense his disapproval. He glanced back at the boiler. The Dr'gasians were damping down the fire amid clouds of smoke and steam. Alexei threw the cloth onto the bench. He took a pace or two. 'It's not a very clean form of energy, I agree,' he said, and he pursed his lips. 'The problem is that clean power other than from wind or water usually requires the application of the kind of technology which is prohibited by the Yasa. I can make this engine more efficient – there is a method of recondensing the steam so that it can be re-used – and I can design a firebox which will burn the fuel down to ash. A flue in the chimney will increase the draught and reduce the smoke. But I can't think of a way to power an engine aboard ship which doesn't require fire and water. Fire means heat and smoke, and water gives off steam.'

It sounded too much like an apology. Jehan stared at the boiler. 'And yet you say that this is the method which is common on other worlds?' Now that the smoke and steam had cleared, he could see how much soot and dirt had accumulated. And yet the thing had been in place for probably no more than a matter of weeks.

Alexei was looking down at the skirts of his coat. He frowned and brushed at them, but the stains marking them did not disappear. He looked up. 'There are stages to technology,' he said. 'Primitive machines are followed by others which are more sophisticated; but always there is a progression which starts with steam.'

'Machines to make machines,' Jehan observed. 'I heard your father explain it once. Maybe that's why our law prevents us from adopting methods more than are sufficient for our needs.'

He saw Alexei frown again.

The Dr'gasians pushed a door at the end of the shed back on its runners. Now that they stood in the light, Jehan could see that both of them were blackened by grime and oil. He saw where the smoke had discoloured the facings of his coat, and wrinkled his nose.

'When I said that this was necessary to allow us to cross the Great Sea,' Alexei said, 'I spoke no more than the truth. If there was a better way, I swear to you I would employ it.'

Jehan shrugged. Vaguely he wished that he had taken more interest in old science. The knowledge which was held in trust by the Sechem was available to all. One had but to ask for the information. 'Maybe a better way can be found,' he said.

The offworlder looked doubtful. 'Maybe,' he said. 'But if it cannot, then this is the method we will have to use.'

'I hear stories of machines which smoke like the dragons in the tales,' Jotan said.

It was quiet in the courtyard. Grey stone walls rose about them, and winged roofs surfaced with rose-red tiles caught the sun so that they seemed to be on fire.

Jehan pulled his tunic over his head, and he laid it on the empty stool to his right. He ran a forefinger across the line of the moustache which he was growing, brushing the hairs horizontally across his lip. When they were long enough, he intended to curl them and allow them to extend down at the sides of his mouth. It was an old style – one which men like his grandfather had adopted – but fashions were always changing. He smiled. 'Alexei is experimenting,' he said.

He saw his father frown. 'Artai has given him too much authority,' Jotan said.

'Have there been complaints?'

'Not yet.' Jotan's expression suggested that he thought that it was only a matter of time.

'Tell the Sechem to read a little faster,' suggested Jehan. It had been four days since the offworlder had said what he thought would be required, and still Parin had not provided his answer.

'One does not hasten such matters,' Jotan responded frostily. He was wearing a variation of court dress – a coat of midnight blue which had no fastenings but which was secured by a sash of the same colour – which indicated that he had spent the morning in council with the civil servants who were charged with overseeing the administration of some aspect of the government. 'The cost of the venture is set to be high enough, and I can envisage no return which will provide the treasury with recompense.'

Jehan laughed disbelief. To imply that the Kha-Khan's exchequer was likely to be burdened beyond its ability to support the embassy was nonsense, as they both knew. The economy of the Khanate was not subject to shortages or even temporary deficiencies, for its operation was controlled by the law.

'Eventually I suppose the Unknown Lands will

become Khanates,' Jotan said. He glanced sideways at Jehan as if he expected a comment.

'Probably.'

It might be years before the lands on the other side of the Great Sea were secured. If they were un-inhabited, they would be settled of course, but it would be some time before the Kha-Khan's tenth was repaid.

A slave came out into the yard, a broom in his hand. He stopped when he saw Jotan and Jehan sitting there, and then bowed hastily.

'Your inclusion as a member of the embassy surprised us all,' Jotan said. He ignored the slave.

Jehan stroked his moustache again, and he saw his father's jaw tighten in irritation. The slave was backing out of the gate let into the high wall which separated the courtyard from the barracks of the Kha-Khan's guard. Orcadai was conducting an inspection in the barracks, and Jehan had come here to wait upon him.

'Pay attention to me, damn you,' Jotan said. 'I am trying to suggest that since it is clear that Artai wants you out of Kinsai, you ought to think about asking him to award you one of the new Khanates. If you are far enough away, maybe he will leave you alone.'

Jehan looked back over his shoulder. 'I would have to conquer it first.'

'So you would.' Jotan returned his stare. 'I don't doubt that it is within your ability.'

The sun had moved so that it was setting on the roof of the building on the western side of the yard. It looked like a red dome on top of the tiles, and the air around it seemed to waver in a haze of heat. Jehan closed his eyes against the glare. In his belt he had a horn container which held a mixture which was supposed to be smeared upon the eyelids under such conditions to increase the density of the clan tattoo. He felt lethargic, unable for the moment to move, and turned his head slowly.

'Is this your idea?' He looked at his father. 'Or has my grandfather had second thoughts?'

'Burun does not understand Artai,' Jotan said. He waved a hand. 'A Kha-Khan is not to be haltered like an unruly st'lyan. Sooner or later it will occur to him that he has only to command to overthrow us. He will never be content, so long as he knows that he is in our debt.'

'Oh, well. I think he would require more justification than that,' Jehan said mildly.

Jotan raised his eyebrows in an expression of amazement. 'You think Artai cares for the law?' he demanded. 'Artai cares for the will of Artai, and for little else.'

Jehan said nothing. He could not remember if his father had always been so wary, but he thought not. It is rising so high that makes us afraid, he thought, lest we fall or are cast down.

The stool upon which Jotan sat put his back to the sun, and his face was deep in shadow. 'The provost took Yusagai, you know,' he said.

'Oh?' Jehan looked up in interest. Yusagai was one of the men named in the attempt to kill Alexei. He examined the expression on his father's face. 'Let me guess. He died, or he was killed.'

Jotan nodded soberly. 'He was at Pesth. The men who arrested him were our own, all Merkuts. They confined him, and in the morning when they went to release him they found him dead.'

'Killed?'

'There was no mark on him.' Jotan turned his head, and he stared away blindly at the wall. 'I fear it was Artai's doing,' he said. 'Who else could have arranged it?'

Jehan did not think that the subterfuge required in order to arrange an assassination was quite Artai's style, but he did not say so. 'Why should he seek to kill Alexei?' he asked. 'It makes no sense.'

'Alexei is betrothed to Jehana. Artai desires her,' Jotan said.

It was true that men had been killed for less reason. 'If Alexei is killed, the embassy may fail,' Jehan said, and stared at his father. 'Maybe you should tell that to Artai.'

They had descended the causeway which wound around the plug of rock upon which Kinsai was built, and now they were close to a stream which ran as a tributary into the D'neistr, the river which flowed north to the Sea of Tears. The grass was a dense carpet of short green spikes, and the slaves had spread carpets on it. Burun was sitting on a chest which had been used to carry the food, and his second wife, Kiku, whom men called the Regal Lily, was standing behind him dressing his hair while he admired himself in a hand-held mirror.

Kiku saw that Jehan was staring at her, and she glared at him. Jehan grinned back. Kiku was always pretending that she hated the stares of men, but in reality she was the vainest person alive.

A long Ch'kassian rug was stretched out beneath Jehan's feet. He sat down on it, staring around. His mother and father were walking beside the bank of the stream, talking. Alexei was under a tree with Kadan and his father, and on a carpet which had been spread with great care on a level piece of grass sat Jehana, ignoring everyone.

Jehan grinned. Jehana was trying so hard to demonstrate that she did not care for Alexei's attentions that he was sure that she felt attracted to him.

For his part, Alexei treated Jehana with the kind of respect a man might give to an aged relative, polite and always attentive, but there was a careful absence of warmth every time he spoke to her.

'When Alexei marries Jehana, will she be my sister?' Kaidu had popped up out of nowhere. He bounced into Jehan's lap, working his head in under Jehan's arm.

'– A kind of sister,' Jehan said. He glanced sideways to see if Jehana had heard Kaidu's question, and saw from her expression that she had. 'Where is your brother?' He looked around.

'Which brother?' Kaidu craned past Jehan's arm to look at Jehana. He extended his talons experimentally into the grass, and then withdrew them again. 'I have several.'

'Hulagu.'

'Oh.' Kaidu wriggled out of Jehan's arms. He stood up. 'He is in the water on the other side of the stream, building a dam, but I'm not supposed to tell anyone.'

Jehan grinned. 'That doesn't surprise me. Go and tell him to come out, before your mother arrives. Tell him it is my command, or he won't come.'

The carts in which the other members of the three households were riding had been forced to take a longer route to the spot. Jehan doubted if Mei Ling would be disturbed by her son's descent into the water, but he thought it well to have attempted to do something, however belated.

Kaidu dashed away. A slave was serving Jehana with sweet cakes on a tray. Jehan uncoiled himself and went over. He scooped up a handful of the cakes, and popped one into his mouth. The slave was young, female, and pretty, and he smiled at her.

Jehana frowned. 'Brother, go away. Your presence offends me.'

The first cart was coming around a bend in the road. Kadan pointed, and then he started to walk up onto the road with his father. They strode to meet the carts, and Alexei came out from under the tree. He walked over to where Jehan stood. Jehan offered him a cake.

'Thank you.' Alexei bit into the cake. He swallowed the first mouthful, and then examined what was left as if he was not sure what it contained. Finally he put it in his mouth.

The slave was hovering behind Jehana, unsure whether to go or to stay. Jehan took the tray of cakes out of her hands, and then he grinned ferociously at her so that she backed hastily away. Jehan heard Alexei laugh. Jehana glared at them both. 'This is unbearable,' she said.

Burun was combing his moustaches now. One side was always thinner than the other because he chewed them when he was angry. Jehan stroked his own moustache with a finger. He knew that Alexei was staring at Jehana, willing her to deal with him.

'Lady,' Alexei said, 'is my presence such a trial to you?'

Jehana was wearing a long gown of cream-coloured cloth. There were raw unspun fibres of a darker shade running through the material, and it clung to her. Her steward walked from the place where the pack animals were tethered, a paper parasol in one hand. He raised it and stood, trying to place himself so that he could offer Jehana shade from the sun. Jehan knew that he was in the steward's way, but he saw no good reason to move. He gave the steward a warning stare. The steward hesitated, and the parasol in his hand wavered. Jehana gave a gasp of exasperation, and she stood up. At once Alexei took her hand. 'Lady,' he said. 'Walk with me.'

She wrenched her hand away. 'Name of God,' she said. 'You are a sorry suitor.'

Jehan chuckled. 'Alexei has been diverting all his energy towards our venture. He is out of practice with other pastimes.'

The carts were turning off the road now, and people were climbing down from them. Jehan saw that Kadan's sister Irina was coming across the grass, and he bowed to her.

Irina inspected him. Then she gazed past him at Alexei. 'My brother looks angry,' she said.

'He has just been rejected,' Jehan said.

She looked disbelieving. 'When I have suitors,' she said, 'I will allow no one to remain in my presence who does not please me.'

'Oh?' Jehan juggled sweet cakes. 'Tell me how to please you so that I can court you.'

Irina took one of the cakes out of mid-air. 'You are too old,' she said. 'And in any case we are related.'

'Only in the second degree,' Jehan said cheerfully.

She looked down her nose at him. 'Maybe I shall consider you,' she said. 'But it isn't interesting to be courted by someone you know.'

'Someone you know can't pretend to be other than he is,' Jehan suggested. 'Surely that's an advantage?'

Jehana stirred. 'Men always make up fantasies to tell women when they court them,' she said. 'It is only after you are married that you discover their true nature.'

Irina eyed her sagely, and then she glanced at Alexei. 'If my brother displeases you,' she said, 'you should send him away.'

Suragai and Kadan were walking their st'lyan on the grass where the stream curved away out of sight, each of them with one of the twins in the saddle. The sun was large in the sky because it was the hottest time of the year, and there were no clouds. A light wind ruffled the leaves of the trees, but it was warm, not cold like the winds of winter. Jehan glanced at Jehana to see why she had not answered, and he saw that her face was crimson with embarrassment. He hummed softly to himself, and then winked at Irina.

'A woman does not marry a man simply because he pleases her,' Jehana said at last. She gave Irina a superior smile. 'When you are older you will understand.'

Irina gazed from Alexei to Jehana, and then back again. Alexei's expression was anguished, and it was clear that he wished himself elsewhere. Irina moved between them, taking both their arms. 'Walk with me,' she said.

They stared at one another unwillingly above her head, and then Alexei shrugged. They fell into step together, and went down onto the path which followed the bank of the stream. Jehan laughed softly, and then he sat down in the middle of the carpet to eat the last of the sweet cakes.

They rode back to Kinsai late in the afternoon. Because Irina did not want to travel in one of the carts, Jehan had taken her up in front of him. Beside him Jehana rode a mare which had a yellow coat through which fine white hairs ran. The st'lyan's mane was so white it looked as if it had been bleached. Even the horn was of a much lighter colour than usual, although it had been gilded with silver. Wherever Jehana rode, Alexei kept pace with her. The offworlder's st'lyan was a bay with brilliant black points, and Jehan saw that he had his bow case strapped to his saddle.

'Why does she behave that way?' Irina asked. She was sitting turned in against his chest, and he rode with one arm around her, supporting her.

'Who?' Jehan stared about, pretending he did not know who she meant.

'Your sister, of course.' Irina glanced around the curve of his arm. 'She pretends to pay Alexei no heed; but whenever he is not watching her, she looks to make sure that he will follow when she rides away.'

Jehan grinned. If Irina had observed Jehana's behaviour, then so had everyone else in the party. 'Maybe she does not want him to think that she is surrendering herself too easily,' he suggested.

Irina wrinkled her nose. 'When I decide to marry a man,' she said, 'I will make him attend me everywhere.'

The road wound past fields and passed through a thicket of young trees. In the undergrowth at the side of the road something moved – a wild pig maybe, Jehan thought, although game this close to the city was unusual. He saw Jehana ride in after it. She was a little way from Alexei, and when he saw her riding off the offworlder reined around after her. The st'lyan crashed through the dried-out ferns, and Jehana yelled jubilantly. Jehan reined in. Because of the passage of the st'lyan along the road there was a cloud of dust and it was hard to see anything in the failing red light. He caught a glimpse of Jehana's mare between the trunks of larger trees, and riding behind her, hard in pursuit, Alexei's bay. Jehana shouted again, but this time there was a note of alarm in her voice. Jehan suddenly thought about the possibilities of ambush, and he wheeled around to look for the trooper who was riding escort on this side. The man was at the far end of a line of slowly moving pack animals, and he had not noticed anything. Jehan swore softly.

He gathered his reins. 'Hold on.' Irina clung to his

210

neck as Jehan spurred his st'lyan into the patch of low brush. The animal was a grey, sturdy and broad-chested, stable under almost any conditions, and it did not even check pace as it charged through the young trees which obstructed its path.

Beyond the brush there was a clearing between taller trees. Jehana's mare was stopped at the far end of it, and Alexei was at her side. Jehan saw him reach across to catch hold of her reins. Jehan fumbled for the short sword which he kept tucked between the straps behind his saddle. He kicked the grey into a gallop, and it thundered across the grass, throwing up torn lichen and humus.

Two figures were crouched at the base of a tree in front of Jehana's mare. She must have disturbed them, Jehan thought, or they would have lain in the bushes until we passed.

The larger had only one arm, and a head which was the wrong size and shape. It had an old wound on one exposed shoulder, and the lenses of its eyes showed milky white. The smaller had legs like long sticks, and where one of the eyes should have been there was nothing – smooth skin without even an indentation. The good eye glittered with fear and hatred.

'It is hurt,' Jehana said. She was attempting to pull her reins out of Alexei's hands.

Jehan looked past her at Alexei. The offworlder shrugged, and he made a face.

She knows the law, Jehan thought sadly. She had come to no harm, but that was beside the point. A child wandering in the wood might come upon them, and anything might happen.

'Jehana, ride off,' he said.

'We cannot –'

'I said ride off.' Jehan rode up beside her, and he leaned out of the saddle and took her reins out of

Alexei's hands, then led her mare in a circle back round towards the road. When he looked back he saw that Alexei was uncasing his bow. The hum of the bowstring when it came was like the sound of a harp being tuned, and when Jehan glanced back again Alexei was getting down from his bay to recover his arrows.

'Send to the farmer who occupies the land to have the bodies burned,' Burun said later when Jehan told him. He eyed Jehan keenly. 'Why are you so troubled? The Yasa is clear. They interfered with the progress of the Altun, and in the circumstances you found them some other person could easily have come to harm.'

Jehan shrugged. 'They hid because they were afraid,' he said. 'If they had been ordinary men –'

Burun snorted. 'If they had been ordinary men,' he said, 'they need not have hidden.'

Everyone had been bidden for the evening meal to Burun's house. The yard was busy as Jehan rode into it, and slaves and servants rushed to and fro between the bakehouse and the kitchens, and the scent of food on the air made his mouth water. He thought again about the incident in the wood, trying to dismiss it from his mind. As Burun had said, there was nothing to be done. The law was clear.

In one corner of the yard there was what had been at one time an underground cellar. Now the wooden cover had been replaced with iron bars, and pacing within the space was a p'ntar – a kind of hunting cat which some misguided Ch'noze baron had sent Burun as a gift to secure his interest in some lawsuit or other. The Yek did not keep animals save as pets, and Burun had the beast confined only until he could find a way to release it safely back into the wild.

Jehan dismounted. Suragai's twin sons were

212

kneeling at the edge of the pit. The p'ntar snarled and bounded up against the bars. Kaidu recoiled, but then he picked up a stick and poked it between the bars. The stick struck the p'ntar across the face, and it snarled again. Jehan walked up behind them.

'Both of you ought to be spanked,' he said severely. 'Come away.'

Kaidu's head came round first. He nudged his twin, and both boys tittered.

'We are in no danger,' Hulagu said cheerfully. He made no move to draw back from the edge of the pit.

'It's not you I am concerned about,' Jehan said. 'That beast has a sorry enough time of it, confined as it must be until a way can be found to release it. It is not yours to poke and tease.'

Hulagu said something in an undertone to Kaidu, and they stared insolently at Jehan, their shoulders shaking with suppressed laughter. Jehan glared at them. Kaidu dropped the stick down through the bars, and then both of them got up and walked away.

The yard was full of people now. Jehan stared down into the pit. The p'ntar was tawny, with a short mane which was darker in colour – all black and brown. It prowled around the floor of the cellar and then set its forepaws on a stone lintel which had once been the base of a set of stairs. Staring up at Jehan it snarled again.

They were midway through dinner when the dogs began to bark hysterically.

Burun stood up at once. 'What's that?'

A voice shouted in panic outside. Then Jehan heard the roar of the p'ntar, deep-throated, defiant, and he glanced in sudden intuition down the length of the table. 'Kaidu and Hulagu are gone.'

Burun went towards the door, Jotan and Suragai

213

following him. Jehan got up, and then he glanced at Alexei, and after a moment the offworlder and all the other men in the room stood and moved to follow Burun. The p'ntar roared again.

A flock of servants came bursting through the door just as Burun reached it. They started to babble incoherently, but Burun shouldered his way through them, ignoring them. He started across the antechamber towards the outer door, the others following him in a crowd. Jehan stopped and took the lance out of the hand of the sentry who still stood guard there. Alexei came last out of the room, and they met one another's eyes.

'The p'ntar is out.' Jehan hefted the lance.

'I can hear.' Alexei looked at the lance, and he made a face. 'You'll need a bow if you intend to kill it.' He lifted a lantern down off the wall.

'Maybe we won't have to.'

They went out into the yard, pushing past the men who were crowded in the doorway. The p'ntar was running back and forth across the flagstones, unable to go anywhere because the walls round the yard were too high and the outer gate was closed. Cooks and scullions were packed frightened into the doorway of one of the bakehouses, and every time the p'ntar sensed their movement it stopped and roared. A pack of dogs clustered in one corner of the yard, all climbing over one another in their frenzy, their barking constant. The grille which had been across the mouth of the cellar had been prised up and was propped open with a baulk of timber. Jehan was surprised that the twins had been capable of lifting it without assistance. He looked around for them, and saw that they had climbed up the face of the gate and were clinging to the crossbar.

Burun pulled at one of his moustaches, and then he

said something to Suragai, and both of them laughed. The laughter spread gradually to all the other watching men. Somebody pointed at Kaidu, hanging by his hands from the timber above the gate. Hulagu had his feet braced on one of the iron bolts, and it was clear that neither of them were in much danger.

The p'ntar made a short rush towards the corner full of dogs, and the dogs hurled themselves back on top of one another, yelping. The p'ntar paced majestically back into the centre of the ward.

A movement at the edge of Jehan's field of vision made him turn. Suragai's wives were at the head of a group of women who were coming out of the door. Jehana and Irina were immediately behind them. The men fell to one side to allow them to pass.

Suragai took a pace or two out into the courtyard. He watched the p'ntar for a moment, and then glanced at the twins hanging from the top of the gate. 'Name of God,' he said, his tone relieved, 'let them spend the night up there.'

Burun laughed again.

Turakina went up to her husband's side. 'I don't think it's funny,' she said.

Burun glanced down over his shoulder at her. 'Daughter, you would not,' he said.

Jehana stirred. Her arm was around Mei Ling's shoulders. 'Consider their mother if you will consider nothing else,' she said, and stared austerely.

Jehan saw his grandfather grin. 'It would be a pity for the animal to suffer,' Burun said. 'Where is its offence?'

Alexei strolled out into the ward. The p'ntar eyed him. The offworlder looked back at Jehan. 'We will need a net,' he said. 'Or a rope will do maybe.'

Jehan joined him, the lance held horizontally in his two hands. The p'ntar's amber eyes followed them. It started suddenly towards them, and Jehan lunged out at it with the lance, shouting, so that it retreated. The people watching cried out, but Alexei walked calmly off in the direction of the stables.

The Alan captain of one of Burun's tumans came up to Jehan's side. In his own land the Alan was duke of a large province. He was small, but he was muscled like an ox. His fair hair gleamed in the lamplight, and in his two hands he held a long straight sword, the fingers of his left hand cradling the blade. He watched the p'ntar steadily.

Jehan turned his head. 'Grandfather, get everyone back into the doorway.' While Burun ushered the women back so that they were behind the men, he stood watching the p'ntar as it prowled up and down. After a while it lay down near the mouth of the pit, its long tail drooping over the edge. Every time it sensed some movement, the tail flicked up again.

Alexei was coming back from the stables. He had a rope coiled over one shoulder, and there was a long drover's whip in his hand.

'Brother!' Kaidu called from on top of the gate. He said something about falling, and Alexei looked up and answered shortly. At the sound of his voice the dogs began to bark again. The p'ntar got up. Jehan took a fresh grip on his lance.

The offworlder walked quietly out into the centre of the ward. He shook out the whip and then glanced over at the door and called out several names. Four of Burun's officers came at once out onto the flagstones, Kadan following them. The p'ntar eyed them, its posture alert, its ears pricked up.

Burun said, 'Kill it if you have to.'

Alexei shook his head.

They formed up in a line which stretched from one side of the yard to the other, and started to walk

216

forward. Apart from Jehan's lance, none of them had anything more than a sword. The p'ntar came up towards them, stopped, and then trotted back the way it had come. Suddenly the dogs seemed to run out of breath. Their tongues lolled, and they lay on top of one another in the corner watching.

The p'ntar was on the move again. Alexei walked steadily towards it, Jehan on one side of him, with D'mitri, the Alan captain, on the other. The p'ntar ran along the line as if seeking a way past, and when it was level with D'mitri it lashed out, snarling. D'mitri stood his ground. He waved his sword, although now his left arm hung at his side and streamed blood from the cuts inflicted by the p'ntar's claws. The p'ntar snarled again, and it raced away and bounded down into the pit. Jehan licked his lips and wondered if they could bolt the grille fast to the ground so that it could not be raised again.

Kaidu and Hulagu dropped down off the gate. Alexei was only a few drem away from them, but he ignored them as they sidled past him. He coiled the whip carefully, then took a strip of rawhide out of his sash and tied it. Kaidu and Hulagu were approaching Suragai by tentative steps. Jehan went to look at the cuts on D'mitri's arm. The Alan was already wrapping his sash around them. He grimaced. 'I should have ducked, Noyon,' he said.

Burun gestured at the officers, and they kicked away the baulk which propped open the grille and it crashed back into place. Burun glanced back at Suragai, then eyed the twins. 'Suragai, shall I hold them for you?' he enquired.

Kaidu was slightly ahead of Hulagu. He came up in front of Suragai. 'Father,' he said in a brave voice, 'I can explain –'

Suragai grabbed him by the nape of the neck,

whirled him across his knee, and then held out his hand. 'Somebody give me a sword.'

D'mitri laughed shortly. He reversed his sword and passed it across, hilt first. Suragai's arm went up, and he began to spank Kaidu with the flat of the blade. Kaidu yelped. 'Father – no – please – not here –'

Hulagu was edging past, but there was nowhere for him to run. All the doors were filled with people laughing. Suragai lowered the sword and released Kaidu. He turned Kaidu around to face him. 'Stand there.'

Kaidu was holding his backside with both hands. He stared at the ground in front of his father's feet. Hulagu started off towards the kitchen door.

'The other villain is getting away,' Burun said.

'Hulagu!' Suragai turned.

Hulagu stopped in his tracks. He turned, and then marched back to face Suragai. 'Father,' he said, 'I am sorry.'

Suragai showed his teeth. Looking at Burun he said, 'I think he believes that if he does not show fear, I will be easier on him.'

'Let him hang from the gate a while,' Burun said. 'I liked that.'

'Father?' Hulagu looked alarmed.

'It was my p'ntar after all,' Burun observed reasonably. 'I ought to have some right of recourse, don't you think?'

It was as if Suragai was considering the point. He looked back over his shoulder at Mei Ling, raising an eyebrow in an unspoken question, and hesitantly she nodded. Suragai spun the sword and offered it to Burun, who took it.

Burun crooked a finger at Hulagu. 'Come here, boy.'

Hulagu took a reluctant pace in Burun's direction,

218

and then another. He eyed the sword in Burun's hand, then stared back at his father, his expression appealing.

Suragai said, 'My son, if you are big enough to commit the crime, you are big enough to pay the penalty. It was the Khan you offended most by your conduct.'

Hulagu's face fell. He sidled up in front of Burun, and then bent over. His beating was no harsher than that which had been administered to Kaidu. Most people were already moving back into the house before it had ended. Irina had rushed, however, to tend the cuts on D'mitri's arm, her face shining with adoration every time she looked up at him. Alexei came past them towards the door. He stopped at Jehan's side, and nodded in their direction. 'Now we know how to please a woman,' he said, and smiled crookedly. 'A little blood spilled.'

Jehan was not sure whether the offworlder's tone indicated amusement or derision. 'They are her brothers after all,' he said, producing a tentative smile.

Alexei gave the whip to a passing servant. 'Mine too, I believe,' he said. 'And you are her cousin. Do you think she will look at us like that?'

Jehana was still waiting beside the door with Mei Ling. In the centre of the ward Suragai was lecturing the twins with short harsh sentences. Jehan saw them flinch. He glanced at Jehana's face and saw that she was watching Alexei. 'My sister already knows you are courageous,' he said. 'You did not have to attempt this to impress her.'

'Oh.' Alexei laughed. 'That wasn't why I did it.' He went past Jehana without looking at her into the house, and Jehan stared after him, puzzled.

*

'How much of it have you worked out now?'

Burun moved his elephant down the board in a straight line to threaten Jehan's overlord. Looking towards the men who were watching, he raised four fingers to indicate that he was increasing his wager. Markers changed hands.

Jehan saw that Joden was holding at least five of the ivory spills which indicated a commitment of ten koban, and he smiled grimly, studying the board. There was a diagonal line of Burun's warriors screening his fortress from attack. Jehan moved his overlord a square to the left. 'You have brought Artai to power as you intended, and your influence is stronger than ever.'

'Oh.' Burun showed his teeth. 'That's true enough. Although if you are trying to tell me that you can discern no more of my intent than that, then either you are a fool or else you think I am.' He moved his elephant three squares to the right, taking one of Jehan's warriors. The watching men murmured respectfully.

The officers were out of earshot, but even so Jehan was surprised that Burun had raised the subject. He rested one hand on his knee, the knuckles curled, and teased at the wisps of his moustaches with the other. 'What will you do if Artai names a successor?' he asked.

Burun sat up straight. He studied Jehan for a moment. 'Artai is not yet a man,' he said at last. 'It will be years before anyone is called upon to succeed him.'

Jehan grinned. He had not expected a straight answer. Of the grandsons of Arjun, the third Kha-Khan, only T'zin was in direct descent, for the others were the sons of a second marriage on the part of either Arjun himself or his son Khotan. Even Artai was the son of a son of this last line. The whole world knew that T'zin would never lay claim to the throne, and he had no offspring. Thus if Artai died childless the issue of the other lines of descent from the Ancestor would have to be examined to locate a suitable heir.

'The Khans could find no one better than Artai when Arjun was alive,' Burun said. 'Tell me who they will choose now, if you will. The sons of Siban maybe?'

Siban had two sons – Sidacai, whom no one in the Khanate would trust now that he had been taken in treason, and Berke, a mystic who followed the cult of Sufi.

'There are others,' Jehan observed mildly. 'There are the descendants of Batu for instance –'

Burun frowned. 'Haratai's sons have never been legitimised,' he said, 'and there has been blood shed over it from here to the Inner Sea. As for the others, it is true that they are soldiers; but a man has to be something more than that before he can be judged worthy to sit on the Dragon Throne.'

Jehan moved his overlord another square to the left. 'The Yasa says only that the candidate must be of Altun blood,' he pointed out, and thought at once of his own case. Burun had married into the Altun line by taking as his wife a daughter of Vortai the Black, who was a son of Daijin. Then he had married his son, Jehan's father Jotan, to a grand-daughter of Arjun.

The succession had not been in existence long enough for the question to have arisen of descent through the females, but there was nothing in the law which ruled it out. Jehan saw that Burun was watching his expression, and he pretended to study the board again. If they had to discuss Burun's intent at all, then it was as well for it to be like this, obliquely.

221

Burun took another of Jehan's warriors. More markers changed hands as side bets were covered. Joden's face displayed a hint of concern now, although it was Jehan's money he was holding.

'Check.' Jehan slid his elephant up the side of the board, bypassing the fence of warriors, capturing Burun's fortress. A smile of relief lit Joden's features, and he waved the ivory counters in his hand at the officers sitting at the next table, mocking them.

Burun stared at the board. He brought his head down so that it was level with the table and looked along the ranked pieces. Then he sat up again, chewing at his moustaches, and growled something wordlessly deep in his throat.

Jehan grinned and leaned back. 'You should not have taken that last warrior, or supported Artai,' he said. 'It is likely that both will see you undone.'

It was true that a civil war had been averted by electing Artai, for there had been no other candidate. The problem lay in the fact that the Khans had since agreed that Artai could not be permitted to father an heir, and that thus no lasting settlement of the affairs of the Khanate had been achieved.

Burun glowered. 'I see no problem,' he said. 'I shall take your elephant with my overlord, and with the aid of the Khans I shall secure the succession according to the precepts which are contained in the Yasa, and thus there will be order. Also I shall be no longer in check.' He reached across the board, exchanging the pieces one-handed.

'– And thus mate,' Jehan said. He moved the fourth warrior down behind Burun's overlord, isolating it. 'To win this one, Grandfather, you needed an extra piece.'

'Why so I did.' Burun surveyed the board. 'Very well, you have won the game. But that does not mean you are right about Artai.' He tipped his overlord onto its side, and a small sigh ran round the room. The officers holding Burun's wagers began to pay off the others, and Joden smiling stacked heaps of gold koban on the low table in front of him.

To anyone who had overheard them, Jehan thought, their conversation had touched on Artai's intent rather than Burun's. In truth what Artai did probably mattered very little, except to those who were directly affected by his commands.

Suddenly Jehan was certain that whatever was at the root of Burun's intrigues, it was concerned with the succession only by some kind of association of events. If Burun's sole intent was to place a Merkut on the Dragon Throne, he would be unwilling to discuss the possible candidates to follow Artai so openly. Thus there was something else – a matter of greater import which Jehan was unable for the moment to guess at, since it was hard to imagine anything more important than securing the succession.

He raised his eyes and saw that Burun was watching intently. 'Whatever it is,' Jehan said, 'it has to do with the aliens.'

Burun looked startled. 'That's a remarkable deduction,' he said, 'given that there is almost no evidence to support it.'

Jehan narrowed his eyes, and then he realised that what Burun had said was not actually a denial. The involvement of the offworlders ran through every series of events like a thread, and joined them. If there was a pattern however, Jehan could not discern it. He saw that Joden and the others were getting to their feet. At any moment they would be surrounded by Burun's officers, and they would be unable to speak further. Jehan smiled cheerfully at Burun. 'Whatever it is,' he said, 'it is as well that it is not easy to comprehend.

223

If it is too obvious, probably it will fail.'

The stare which Burun returned was expressionless, almost hostile, and he said nothing by way of a reply.

What the Sechem offered Alexei in the end was compromise, and it was the surprise with which the offworlder received it that demonstrated once again to Jehan how different the Yek mind was from the alien's.

'It's a steam engine,' Alexei said as soon as he saw the sketch.

'A kind of steam engine,' Parin said.

The fact that the Sechem were agreeing to the construction of a powered vessel did not signify a change in attitude, Jehan realised as soon as the method was unfolded. If Alexei hoped by this means to see the introduction of steam power throughout the Khanate, he was doomed to disappointment. If they managed to power a ship it would be a major achievement, given what was involved, and the possibility that the method would be capable of reproduction did not exist.

'Steam provides the power to turn the shaft.' Parin traced a line with one finger nail.

'I can see that.' Alexei squinted at the drawing which was unrolled across the table. 'What I don't understand is how you intend to produce the steam. Where is the heat source? And what is this? I've never seen anything like it.'

'It is a reflector,' Parin said.

'Powered by what?' Alexei looked amused. 'Sunlight?' He gestured. 'Solar cells can be produced only if you have the technology to support the introduction of electric power. In any case I doubt if we can build anything efficient enough to heat a boiler.

It's pointless anyway. If you can produce solar power, you can run an electric motor.'

'I assure you, Khan, there is a method.' Parin did not appear to be put out by the objections being offered. 'Our science tells us that a reflector lined with sunstones will provide a heat source which will be effective even at night.'

Sunstones. Jehan blenched. Sunstones were so rare that they were valued as jewels, and he knew of no one who possessed more than one of them. The largest in the world was worn on state occasions by the widow of Arjun, being of the size of a koban piece mounted in gold in a diadem. Cut properly a sunstone picked up every glimmer of available light. Even in a room which appeared dark it found light and reflected it. The facets of every jewel were carefully calculated so that all the light was not reflected out of a single face, otherwise whatever that light struck would be burned.

The offworlder was gaping disbelief. 'I have heard of sunstones of course,' he said. He smiled. 'Now tell me you have a cache of them.'

There were two other Sechem with Parin. Because of their snow-white hair Jehan guessed they were librarians. None of them had come accompanied by their assistants, which was unusual. Maybe they did not expect to gain knowledge from the encounter. Jehan opened his mouth to enquire how they expected to gather sufficient sunstones to line a reflector – from the drawing it would be about the size of a horse trooper's shield – and then he closed it again. The Sechem never did anything lightly. If they were proposing such a method, then they were certain that both the materials and the expertise to employ them were available.

'The Kha-Khan is to issue a command for every

225

stone in the land to be surrendered,' the taller of the two said. His tone was prosaic. 'Their use in a reflector will necessitate some re-cutting of course. The owners need not, however, suffer any permanent loss – not, that is, provided the embassy returns,' he finished drily.

It was already mid-afternoon. The sun sat redly on the gold-clad roofs which Jehan could see through the open window. Every building more than fifty drem distant wavered in the heat haze which rose off the ground. The heat was so intense that it seemed to deaden even sound. Carts moved in the street, but although Jehan strained his ears to hear it, he was unable to distinguish the noise of wheels passing across paving stones. All that he was aware of was a kind of hum, as if the whole city vibrated with the heat. He shook his head to clear the sound, knowing that it was not real.

'It would be simpler surely to build an engine such as I have described,' Alexei said. 'What you propose is a machine. What I propose is a machine. Where is the difference?'

The Sechem stared at one another as if they were at a loss to answer in terms which would be understood. It is because he is a non-human that he does not comprehend, Jehan thought.

'The difference lies in the Yasa,' Parin said at last. 'Khan, what you propose would require us to accept the principle of a method which is adaptable to many purposes. The argument for employing a machine at all is based on the necessity of the mission – of crossing the Great Sea – and we accept it. You should consider our function thus therefore. The Yasa is eroded as we know in small ways, and our task is to minimise the effect of that erosion so that its fabric, which we call order, may be maintained. By our proposal there will exist one event – one remission of that part of the law which we interpret to discourage the use of machines. The method we propose is incapable of repetition, however, and so the Yasa will be maintained.'

Alexei seemed to consider. All at once he looked up and encountered Jehan's interested stare. 'Damage limitation,' the offworlder said, and smiled sourly. 'I never thought of it thus.'

The yard was full of carts, and so was the street outside. Because the project to build the ship was something new there were Sechem in profusion. They accepted little discipline and Sidacai, whose responsibility it was to order the train and its escort, had been reduced to employing very short sentences every other word of which was an obscenity.

'This is like a state occasion,' Kadan said. He stood in his stirrups and stared around. Burun had come out to watch of course, and there were Khans gathered around him.

'They are saying farewell to their jewels,' Jehan said.

The chest full of sunstones was in one of the green carts. Because of its value they had decided to take a few precautions, and so five identical carts had been driven into the yard where they had been loaded by servants of the Sechem. Now they were dispersed along the column, and no one was quite sure which contained the treasure.

'Here comes my father.' Kadan pointed.

'I see him.'

Suragai was riding out of a side street. Turakina was on a chestnut mare at his side, and behind them jogged a dozen men bearing a bright blue litter. 'That's my step-mother,' Kadan said.

Burun's second wife came out of a crowd of women beside the gate. The litter stopped, and a slave held the curtain aside so that the woman inside could get down. The second wives of both Suragai and Burun were N'pani, and they bowed to one another, and then embraced. Jehan stared. He had not known that they were friends.

Sidacai came striding up the side of a line of carts. 'We are ready now, I think,' he said. Suddenly he caught sight of Mei Ling. He drew his breath in harshly. 'Ah now. There's a sweet little thing for a man to play with.'

Kadan edged his st'lyan up to Jehan's side. 'I wouldn't advise it. That's my father's second wife.'

Sidacai was watching Mei Ling with bright eyes. He turned. 'Damn,' he said. 'Everything good I see, I find belongs to Burun Khan or to one of his creatures. I thought she was a concubine.'

Jehan eyed him. 'She was, once.'

Sidacai had turned to watch Mei Ling again. Burun's wife said something to her in a low voice, and she turned and gave Sidacai back a look which was as cold as solid rock.

Alexei came up the other side of the leading cart. He saw the look on Sidacai's face, and followed the direction of his eyes. 'Stay away from her, Sidacai,' he said. 'I've only seen my father kill a man in single combat twice, and both times it was over her. Don't think that because we aren't human by your standards we won't fight for what we own.'

'I can imagine.' Sidacai relaxed suddenly. 'There are thousands of beautiful women, and anyway we are leaving Kinsai.'

Alexei glanced up at Jehan, and they both grinned. Jehan kicked his st'lyan into a walk, and he rode off towards the place where his escort was assembling. It amused him to think that Sidacai was afraid to cross an alien, and he wondered if there was a way he could use the knowledge to advantage.

On the third day of the journey to Pantai they rode south of the foothills of the ranges of mountains which formed the boundary of the province of Ch'nozia. The train of carts and wagons stretched out for more than a verst across the grass-covered plain, and groups of armed troopers rode at intervals on both sides. There was at least one trooper on every vehicle, usually seated beside the driver.

It was close to midday. The grass of the plain was thigh high in places, for the herds of st'lyan which were bred in Alexei's province of Khitai had not yet been moved north to graze. The snow had vanished now from the peaks of the tall mountains, and only in the few streams which flowed down onto the meadows was there a sign that the weather was ever anything but hot.

'We would do better in Losan,' Sidacai said for the third time. 'It's Alexei's city. How can we not be well provided for?'

Jehan shrugged. 'It has to do with the harbour, and the depth of the water off the land.' Losan was a fishing and trading port. If they built ships at all, they were the high-prowed sloops which were used by fishermen. 'Pantai has shipyards and men.' Pantai was also surrounded by forests of tall trees. Sidacai knew all that of course, but he had been niggling at Alexei's organisation of the mission since they had left Kinsai. Alexei's temper was still intact, but there were signs that it was shortening rapidly where Sidacai was concerned.

A lone trooper came spurring over a low rise a little way ahead. He veered towards the tight escort which marked the place where Jehan rode, and when he came up to them he reined his st'lyan in so hard that it sat down on its haunches.

'Lord, I bear a message from Kadan Noyon.' The man threw out a salute which might have been interpreted to recognise either Jehan or Sidacai.

Sidacai reined across. 'Speak,' he said.

'Lord, I am to say that the advance guard has seen traces of a body of mounted men, a hundred or so from their sign. They are riding parallel with our track to the north of us.'

'Very well.' Sidacai nodded. 'Find refreshment. I will send you back with my word in a while.'

The man saluted again, and then he rode at the trot down the column towards the wagons occupied by the provisioners and sutlers.

Jehan raised himself in the stirrups and looked about for Alexei. The totem which signified the presence of the offworlder's guard was about halfway down the right-hand side of the column, beside a cart which had been pulled out of line. Men were wrestling with one of the wheels. Jehan glanced back at Sidacai.

'Could it be some Khan – or a Ch'noze baron with his escort?' he suggested.

Sidacai made a face. 'Why should they ride parallel with us? They must have seen our dust. A child would know we are here.'

Alexei had seen the messenger. He rode his st'lyan across to intercept the man and spoke to him. Then he reined around and kicked his animal into a trot, coming up the line. Jehan frowned. He met Sidacai's stare. 'Bandits then.'

'I imagine so.' Sidacai did not appear troubled by the knowledge.

'Trouble?' Alexei rode up at Sidacai's side.

'Bandits we believe – Ch'noze probably – to our north,' Sidacai said economically.

'I see.' The offworlder digested the information. 'And what are we doing about them.'

Sidacai showed his teeth. 'Why Khan, since I am subject to your command in all things, I was awaiting your will. I thought we might hold council about it. You are fond of that, it seems. Then maybe after that, if it is not too late, I can go and deal with them.'

Jehan stirred, displaying his irritation. 'Name of God, Sidacai.'

Sidacai's head came round, and he stared coldly. 'What's the matter, Noyon? Am I too blunt for your taste?'

Alexei laughed harshly. 'Jehan, let it be,' he said. He returned Sidacai's stare with interest. 'As for you, if you don't want the authority to command the military escort of this train it suits me just as well. Shall I send you back to Kinsai? How long do you think Artai would leave you alive?'

Jehan saw Sidacai go a shade pale. Then his head came forward. 'Would you do that, Khan? I think you're bluffing.'

Alexei looked away down the column of carts and wagons. Then he turned back, smiling grimly. 'Try me and see, Sidacai. You're the last person who can afford to test my good will.'

It was not the way Jehan thought he would have handled the situation, but it was effective all the same. Sidacai reddened. 'Khan, I swore to serve you,' he said. 'If I am uncomfortable with this, it is because I am master and servant both.'

The offworlder raised his eyebrows. 'Have you never shared a command? Don't try my patience, Sidacai. If you are going to give orders, then do so. If you are wrong, I will hold you accountable. If you act in good faith, then I will support you in the face of other men even though you are wrong, and the accounting shall be between us. What more do you want me to say to you?'

Sidacai looked irritated, as if he knew that he had lost countenance. 'Nothing.' He shook his head. 'Khan, you shame me. I never expected an alien to show me my duty.'

It was a kind of apology, but Jehan saw that Alexei was not entirely pleased by the way it had been phrased. The offworlder's jaw tightened, then relaxed again. 'You have a task to perform, I think,' he said. 'Send to me when you have made your dispositions.'

There was a look on Sidacai's face which suggested that he had not expected to be dismissed so soon. He inspected the expression on the offworlder's face, and then he nodded and rode off down the line.

'He expected you to fight him,' Jehan observed.

Alexei was watching Sidacai's departure. There was a thoughtful look on his face. 'I know,' he said. 'But it is easier to deal with him this way. If I fight him and lose, he will continue to cause trouble.' He reined over so that he was riding at Jehan's side. 'Will he respect me if I beat him?'

'Maybe.' Jehan considered the question. Alexei's method of dealing with the situation amused him. Sidacai was expendable, as Burun had said, and so he could be replaced if he became too troublesome, or he could simply be killed.

The groups of mounted troopers who were riding at intervals along the train were moving now so that they formed a single unbroken line down both sides of the column. Two groups with about a hundred men in each galloped away to the north-east. Sidacai is sending them to circle round, Jehan thought, and he wondered if the advance guard would also be re-

232

inforced, or if it would be left vulnerable to attack, bait to tempt the bandits in case they feared to try for the train. The advance guard was a small force – less than fifty men, and they were under the command of Alexei's half-brother Kadan, who was inexperienced.

Bandits. Probably Sidacai was right, Jehan thought, and they were Ch'noze. It was not unusual to find them raiding in the foothills, and no doubt they felt safe in such strength. An ordinary caravan would have difficulty withstanding them, although most of the trains travelling these parts went well guarded. Jehan had spent two periods as a garrison officer, keeping order among the Ch'noze strongholds in the north-west of the continent, and the experience had taught him a degree of respect for the courage and fighting ability of the tribesmen who lived in the hill country which was common there. Like the Yek and the N'pani, the Ch'noze were of the races of True People. They possessed talons. The resemblance ended there however. The Ch'noze did not adhere to the Yasa – indeed they had no sense of order of any kind, and behaved as barbarians. Each tribe was controlled by a warlord, a military leader who held power for only so long as he could fight off younger contenders. The warlords paid occasional tribute to barons – who were simply more powerful warlords themselves – and as a result the various bands had to be subjugated separately, a process which usually involved installing a permanent garrison, because the Ch'noze tended to rise in revolt the moment they sensed that the occupying power had relaxed control.

Thus there were always bandits.

Another band of men, fifty or so strong, came riding up the column. They spurred ahead, and out of their dust came Sidacai, a satisfied expression on his face.

'Even if they do not attack us, we will deal with them,' he said. 'I have sent to Kadan to keep riding, and I have given him more men, although he's a good boy. He won't panic if he's faced with numbers greater than his own.'

It was hard to remember that by Yek standards Kadan was only thirteen. Jehan chided himself for the thought, and remembered that at much the same age he had been riding to war. It was a demonstration of how much attitudes had changed in the intervening years of peace. *We used to be a race of warriors. Have we become weak, that these small engagements find us so unprepared?*

'If they try for the train, we are strong enough to send them packing,' Jehan said.

'We are if Kadan is right, and there are no more than a hundred,' Sidacai said shortly.

Alexei's head came up sharply. 'You think there may be more?'

'It's possible.' Sidacai shrugged. 'If I wanted to attack a train this size, I would send men to ride with it for a day or so, and I would place an ambush ahead of its path.'

'That would require a lot of men,' Jehan objected. 'If they are bandits, they will not be riding in a band so large.'

The whole train was closing up now, and the shouts of the carters and wagon masters echoed up and down the line, and whips cracked over the heads of the oxen.

'I'm only taking precautions, Noyon,' Sidacai said. He glanced at Alexei and showed his teeth. 'That's what I am here for.'

It would be a remarkable coincidence for the strongest train of wagons and carts to cross this part of the country since the wars to be attacked, Jehan thought. Bandits might raid at night, stealing a few st'lyan or pack beasts, but it did not make sense for them to try for a prize which any scout must see was so well guarded. It was apparent that both Alexei and Sidacai were thinking the same. Alexei turned in the saddle and looked back along the line of wagons. 'Put extra men on the green carts,' he said.

Sidacai nodded. 'And I'll double the night guard.' He wheeled his st'lyan around and rode back the way he had come.

The offworlder was wearing a cloak which had been treated with reflective material so that it shielded the wearer from the worst of the sun. He pushed it back from his shoulders so that it fell across the crupper.

'You think they are after the sunstones,' Jehan said.

Alexei put one hand up to look at the sun. At this time of year the days were long and the nights were short and light, because both moons were usually in the sky. He glanced back at Jehan. 'The edict which caused them to be gathered was published in every part of the Khanate,' he said. 'Even if they can't be stolen to be sold, they could be ransomed.'

Jehan nodded. 'At the very least, it would delay our embassy.'

Alexei took one foot out of the stirrups, and he crossed the free leg over the pommel of his saddle, riding at his ease. 'Either that, or the Sechem would be forced to agree to a vessel with the kind of propulsion I had in mind when I first discussed the matter with them,' he said cheerfully.

Jehan looked at him sharply. If the offworlder was determined to impose his ideas about the use of technology on the Khanate, he could do no better than to ensure that steam power – based on the burning of wood or coal – received general acceptance. It occurred to Jehan that they were riding close to the northern border of Alexei's own province of Khitai. If the bandits had come from the south, instead of from the north ...

'You are thinking that I am pleased by this development.' The offworlder was watching Jehan as he spoke.

'You noticed,' Jehan responded drily.

Alexei took his other foot out of the stirrups, and he worked at the muscles of his legs to ease them. 'I won't deny that it would give me satisfaction to see this world enter the steam age,' he said. 'The Sechem can't hold back time forever, you know.'

'I don't think that's exactly what they intend,' Jehan said mildly. He readied himself for another attempt to deal with the offworlder's simplistic approach to the employment of science. Travelling with the train to Pantai there were a number of Sechem, all of them capable of relating the Yasa to the store of knowledge which had been accumulated over the years. Every one of them would use the same forms of words to respond to Alexei's arguments were he to broach them. None of them would comprehend his concern.

I barely comprehend it myself, Jehan thought, and yet if Burun seeks to use the aliens for his purpose, I must try.

The offworlder did not press the point however, but instead produced a snort of laughter. 'In our attitude to such matters we are too different, Noyon,' he said. 'I should know not to raise them, though they irk me.'

Jehan considered him. 'It never struck me before that your interest is well-intentioned.' He allowed his reins to fall loose across his st'lyan's neck so that he could pursue the notion. 'I always thought you wished to see us use technology because you

236

imagined your knowledge would make you great.'

Alexei looked embarrassed. 'I thought that way once,' he admitted. 'But what I hold in here –' He tapped his forehead. '– Is not new to the Yek.'

'Then surely you must allow us to decide for ourselves what serves us,' Jehan suggested gently. 'You have lived long among us, Alexei, but still you have not absorbed our ways.'

They camped that night on the crest of a brief escarpment, and Sidacai threw sentries and patrols in arcs around the slope which was accessible. Both of the moons shone in the sky, one large, the other small, and elsewhere above them the stars glittered against a background which was scarcely darker blue than might have been expected during daylight.

Few men slept. Instead they clustered round campfires, the drovers and wagon masters mixing with the troopers who were off watch, and the night air was heavy with the scent of the wood gathered along the way from copses of aromatic s'dar, the fuel preferred by the cooks because it burned with only a little smoke.

The advance guard had ridden in about nightfall, the men had eaten, and then they had ridden out again quietly. When Jehan questioned it Sidacai gave no explanation, only a look which suggested that he knew his own business best and damned Jehan for his interference.

'Your brother is with them,' Jehan said to Alexei.

The offworlder shrugged. 'As I judge it,' he observed, 'he is old enough. He is your vassal in any case, not mine.'

It was a sensible observation, but it irritated Jehan. 'If I recall him he will be disgraced,' he said.

Alexei was drinking wine from a flask. The liquid

237

gurgled as he raised it. He wiped his mouth with his hand. 'And so you think I should use the excuse of kinship?' He corked the flask and threw it one-handed to Joden, who was on the other side of the fire. 'Kadan has been looking after himself since he was old enough to draw a bow. Sidacai trusts him, and that is enough for me.'

Jehan thought of pointing out that Sidacai might consider placing Kadan in danger a suitable method of repaying the grudge which no doubt he bore following the words exchanged that day. He compressed his lips and stared across the fire.

Sidacai came from a row of parked wagons. He squatted on his heels and held his hands to the fire. An orderly who was working at one of the cook fires looked up, saw him, and ran across, a bowl of stewed meat in his hand. Sidacai took it. He speared the larger chunks of meat with his talons, and then upended the bowl and poured the contents into his mouth. He dropped the bowl, wiped his moustaches, and then raised his eyes to meet Jehan's stare and smiled.

'How long are we going to camp here?' Alexei rested his wrists across his knees.

'Until it's light enough to see where we are going.' Sidacai did not turn his head, but continued to watch Jehan.

'It's light now,' Jehan said.

Sidacai wrinkled his nose. 'We're coming to a row of hills,' he said. 'You can hide a lot of men in a fold in the ground, especially at night, and I don't intend to be ambushed.'

'Is that why you sent Kadan back out?' Jehan demanded. He saw Sidacai grin, and clenched his teeth. Sidacai was being secretive only because Alexei had told him to use his authority. If Sidacai believed that he might be reinstated in the Kha-Khan's favour, Jehan thought, he might behave. As it was, however, he probably guessed that he was not expected to survive for too long, and so he thought he had nothing to lose by crossing anyone who annoyed him.

A st'lyan screamed shrilly somewhere beyond the first line of carts. Sidacai looked up sharply. Men were running in twos and threes at the outer edge of the light thrown by the fires near the slope from the escarpment to the level of the plain. Joden stood up. 'Damn,' he said. He peered at the movement. 'Some of the animals are loose. Ah, it's all right. The guards have them.'

'If they have,' Sidacai said calmly, 'they must have left their posts.' He stood up, following the direction of Joden's gaze. 'If you wanted to attack a camp at night, how would you arrange it?' He turned and looked down at Alexei as he spoke.

Alexei rose in a single sinuous movement. 'A diversion – confusion.'

'Exactly,' Sidacai nodded. 'We're being raided, I think. Come on.' He strode to the end of the first wagon and pulled himself up onto the side of it. Jehan scrambled up beside him.

The slope to the plain was illuminated so that the men and animals moving across it were touched with silver. Dark colours looked black, but except where there were shadows Jehan was able to see clearly.

'There.' Sidacai pointed.

The troopers were a line of identifiable figures moving across in front of the loose herd of st'lyan spilling from the enclosure which was one end of the lines. Behind them alone in the grass there were the men who had stayed at the posts, their heads turned to watch what was happening, and beyond them were others, most kneeling, facing upslope. Jehan saw the

239

glitter of arrow heads as bows were raised.

'Troopers!' Sidacai's voice carried along the line of wagons, and men checked and turned. 'Gather your weapons. Form a line.'

Some men were already armed – the experienced men who had known that a disturbance in the night did not always signify simply the loss of sleep. Arrows were coming into the camp, a few shafts arching down out of the sky, the marksmanship a matter of chance more than anything. Someone in front of the st'lyan had thought to use a rope to prevent them from breaking out of the enclosing line of troopers. An arrow or two fell in the midst of the milling animals, and a st'lyan screamed.

'If it's a raid, it's not a very effective one,' Alexei observed. He was standing with his feet resting upon the horizontally placed spokes of a wheel of the cart. His bow was in his hand, and there was an arrow nocked to the string.

'It's not.' Sidacai nodded appraisingly. 'Which suggests that either this is not a serious attempt –'

'– Or it's a diversion,' the offworlder finished flatly.

Jehan stared around. Troopers were moving into orderly lines under the command of their officers. A company of about a hundred volleyed in a single instant their reply to the desultory fire which was still coming from the men kneeling in the grass downslope, and a hail of arrows passed across the face of the larger moon and sleeted down on their target.

'The Ch'noze have little skill as archers,' Sidacai said in a conversational tone. 'They are on the other hand quite excellent in close combat.'

Jehan saw that not all the troopers were moving into the line which ran from one end of the wagon park to the other. Some were drawn up in vee-shaped wedges facing back towards the edge of the escarpment. He turned. 'You expected this,' he accused Sidacai.

Sidacai looked complacent. 'I thought they might try something,' he said. 'Once I had worked out what, it was simply a matter of when and where.'

'To which end you decided to make it easy for them,' Alexei said. 'You might have told us.'

'I don't think it's over yet,' Jehan said. He looked for his orderly, and saw that the man was waiting with Joden. The guard captain was fully armed, and he took Jehan's sword out of the orderly's hand and passed it up.

'Someone ought to get the drovers and wagon masters out of the way,' Alexei said. He too was watching not the action beyond the carts but the darkness where the edge of the escarpment fell away sharply towards the plain.

'I'll do it.' Jehan jumped down. He gestured to Joden. 'Bring some men. Tell anyone who is still beyond the fires to move into the wagons.'

'Yes, Noyon.'

Jehan trotted across the short grass. Most of the men who had been engaged to drive the vehicles which made up the train were professional carters, and not the servants of either his house or Alexei's. The few who had not gone to watch the fire being exchanged between the escort troopers and the raiders were round the fires near the escarpment edge. They were of various races – C'zaki, Ch'kasian, and even Y'rabe – but they all stood respectfully to greet Jehan as he came towards them.

'You are not safe here,' Jehan said. 'Go join the others by the wagons.'

A tall Y'rabe opened his mouth to argue, and was shushed to silence by those about him.

'Go.' Jehan waved. He looked past them and saw

that Joden was marshalling a small crowd of others away from a brightly burning fire. One man turned to protest, and was bundled on his way by a trooper.

One moment the place where the escarpment fell away was a line which was drawn sharply across the vague shadow down on the plain, and then suddenly it was moving with the shrouded figures who swarmed up off the rock. Jehan's heart thumped in his chest. He stared around to see how far he had come from the safety of the wagons, and decided that there was too much ground to cover. He shook the scabbard from the sword he carried in his hand. The first raiders were already bounding across the short grass. A trooper at a fire near to one end of the escarpment gave a cry of alarm.

'Heads up there!' Joden's voice rang out crisply. 'Form line. Protect your Lord.'

There were eight or ten troopers, all fully armed. They moved into line on either side of Jehan. A man offered his shield, and Jehan shook his head. His sword was a *jusei*, the two-handed weapon of the Manchu, a gift of the alien swordmaker who had been Suragai's officer. He brought it into the guard position. A rush of dark-clad attackers engulfed them, and all at once there was no time for thought. Jehan cut, reversed, cut again, and yanked his sword blade free of a falling Ch'noze. A lance head thrust at his throat, and it was beaten down by Joden's sword. A trooper went in at the side. He stabbed Jehan's assailant, using the body as a shield. Everyone moved back a pace, and Jehan readied himself to receive another assault.

'Hot work.' Joden grinned. He pulled Jehan to one side as a Ch'noze hurled himself out of what appeared to be a mass of raiders coming up over the escarpment edge. A trooper with a lance caught the rushing man under the breastbone, and he heaved. The Ch'noze cried out once, and then it was as if the force of his rush carried him through the air past their heads. The trooper jerked his lance free with a grunt of satisfaction, and he swung round to face the front again.

Arrows began to whip steadily across the space between the wagon line and the fires.

'Someone has noticed that we need help,' Joden said calmly. 'About time.'

Jehan had no breath to laugh, but suddenly he was cheered by the coolness of the men around him. The Yek did not fight at close quarters if they could help it, and then only provided the odds were in their favour.

Wedges of troopers were moving up, beating opposition aside, crushing the raiders in the path of their advance. The base of each wedge opened out steadily, overlapping with the next to create a solid line so that the Ch'noze were forced back. The raiders who were not killed jumped over the edge of the escarpment. Jehan drew breath, and he wiped the sweat from his eyes.

Alexei came trotting along the rear of the line. 'You aren't hurt,' he said. 'Good. Next time pull back a little, will you? We couldn't shoot for fear of hitting your men.'

'I thought you were giving me a chance to distinguish myself.' Jehan pulled a tuft of grass from the ground at his feet, and he wiped the blade of his sword. 'Is it over?'

There were still men at the base of the escarpment. Some who had climbed part of the way up the face were lowering themselves back down now. On the level ground there were others holding the head-ropes of groups of animals. Troopers were kneeling along the edge of the escarpment to shoot, selecting their targets, but it was clear that some of the raiders were going to escape.

A wave of mounted troopers swept suddenly out of the area of shadow where the ground folded beyond the line of the rocks. They roared as they smashed into the milling men coming away from the escarpment, and where they passed there remained only a litter of the fallen. St'lyan ran free across the plain, and the Yek troopers near Jehan cheered.

'Kadan,' Alexei said. 'I wondered where Sidacai had sent him.'

Sidacai came striding across the grass past the fires. He craned to look at the plain below. 'It worked then.'

Jehan stared down his nose. 'Did you have any doubts?' His face still felt wet, and when he wiped it his hand came away with blood on it. He felt along his hair line and winced. The tip of an assailant's sword had sliced a shallow groove in his scalp, and although he had felt nothing at the time, he remembered the face of his adversary. He had ducked, amazed that he had not been decapitated, and then he had thrust upward –

Sidacai stepped away from the edge. 'If I doubted my ability, I would not be here,' he said. He inspected Jehan's wound. 'Did you bump into something in the dark, Noyon?'

Already Jehan felt the tightness which signified that the cut was closing. 'Yes. But whatever caused it will suffer for it.' He showed his teeth.

He was certain that Sidacai had held back the wedges of troopers until the very last moment. What Alexei had said about the inability of the archers to fire upon the raiders in front of the line, Jehan thought, had been the truth. He remembered that most of them had been placed in the centre.

A trooper brought the scabbard of his sword from where he had discarded it. Jehan slid the empty scabbard into his sash, and then sheathed the blade, careful to allow the circle of the reverse to part the air in front of Sidacai's face. He saw Sidacai flinch. Jehan smiled, making it clear that he had noticed, and then he turned and walked away.

'If you are going to fight Sidacai, don't involve me,' Alexei said.

They were riding through a series of narrow valleys, the slopes of which were lined with tall straight trees. The road ran in an almost straight line out of one into the next, always climbing.

Jehan was concentrating on guiding his st'lyan past a line of wagons stopped on a steep part of the road. Double teams of oxen were being harnessed to each. He glanced round, a hand on one thigh. 'I didn't know I was.' Alexei stared in polite disbelief, and Jehan reflected on the denial he had made. It was almost the truth. 'Sidacai's dangerous,' he said. 'He could kill any of us for spite, or simply because it pleases him.'

'You're only annoyed because he left you exposed during the fighting,' Alexei said.

Three troopers were sitting on the open tail of a cart on the road ahead. They were all drinking, and Jehan frowned, troubled by the obvious lack of discipline. The troopers saw him staring, and they laid their cups aside quickly and jumped down onto the hard-packed stones. Jehan turned. 'He hates us all. I don't know why you asked for him.'

'Your grandfather requested it.'

Jehan jerked in the saddle, appalled. 'I don't believe you.'

Alexei shrugged. 'You saw how he supported me when we were in front of Artai.'

'It's contrary to reason,' Jehan started. He stopped. There were several sets of circumstances which would explain why Burun might seek to preserve Sidacai. He considered each in turn.

Alexei's st'lyan was a chestnut, one of a string he had been riding during the journey to test them. It nipped at Jehan's sorrel, and the sorrel kicked out to the side. Jehan tightened his grip on the reins. The cart in front was green. He urged the sorrel past it. There was a ditch down the side of the road. The sorrel missed its footing on the soft verge, stumbled, and then recovered again. Jehan turned around in the saddle. 'If the sunstones were in that cart, you would tell me.'

The offworlder opened his eyes wide. 'If I knew, Noyon, of course.'

'Just as if I knew, I would tell you.'

'Of course.'

They met one another's eyes. Jehan suspected that the offworlder knew which cart carried the stones, and he wondered again if the bandit attack had been coincidence. 'We will be in Pantai soon,' he said.

There was a tiny plateau of level ground to one side of the road. Jehan reined across onto it, and he dismounted. A few stones piled on top of one another indicated that there had been a building here. It was a strange place for a house, and Jehan guessed it had been a guard post or a way-station maybe. He struggled to remember the name of the people who had occupied this part of the land – not the Ch'noze – some other – but he could not. They had taken Pantai during the Khanate of Daijin, he thought. The Yek had conquered the territories north and south of Kinsai, and they had spread westward until they had encountered the sea. 'The sea is a boundary to be crossed just like any other,' he said aloud.

246

Alexei was getting down out of the saddle. The chestnut nuzzled at the fresh green grass growing through the stones. 'And after you cross the seas,' Alexei said. 'What then?'

'You mean what will we do when there is nothing more to conquer?' Jehan said. 'We will stop, I suppose. We don't do it because we enjoy conquest, but to create order in the world.'

It was said that Daijin had hungered after the power which came from conquest; but Daijin had been mad. Jehan thought about the different natures of the men who had ruled the Khanate, and he shivered. Burun had served Daijin, whom men called the Terrible, and whenever he talked about him it was apparent that he had feared him.

A cart rolled past, hauled by bellowing oxen who dug their hooves into the stones while the drover's whip cracked over their heads. Two men came behind with a log suspended between two ropes, ready to slide it under the rear wheels so that if the team was forced to stop the cart would not run back. Jehan walked over to a bush, unfastened the front of his breeches, and made water. When he looked down he saw that the bush was growing up out of a matrix of dry bones.

Pantai was a city full of yellow stone houses. The houses ran in rows along both sides of an inlet from the sea. The roofs were of red tile for the most part – a sign, Jehan thought, of the prosperity which had accompanied the trade with Suristan. Along the mouth of the inlet lay the wharves and shipyards which were at the heart of that trade. Vessels were crowded into the roads, carracks, brigantines, and a single barque, probably from Ch'kasia – and a port-master's barge ran busily across the mouth of the

247

anchorage to intercept a sloop inbound.

The guildmasters of the shipyards had given up their houses to Alexei and Jehan. Both of the houses were behind the yards, facing onto a paved square. The contents of the carts had been dispersed into warehouses, but the chest containing the sunstones was locked in a room in Alexei's house, and it was guarded night and day. In the first light of the morning the crystals embedded in the yellow stone of the walls glowed with luminescence. In the square shipwrights and carpenters were already gathering in crowds, for word of the project to build the ship had been spread abroad as soon as it had become known that the embassy would depart from Pantai. A maniple of sentries attempted to maintain order, but Jehan thought that probably the best way to disperse the anxiously waiting men was to tell the guilds what would be required, allowing them to select the workmen with skills which were appropriate to the task.

Rolls of drawings were laid out across a table in the first-floor room of the house occupied by Alexei, and it was these the guildmasters were studying, their brows furrowed, their expressions doubtful.

There were three of them, broad muscular men with curled beards. Their heads were shaved but for the long scalp locks which had been plaited and bound with cord. Their dark-blue gowns were embroidered with the insignia which proclaimed them the masters of their respective crafts. The tallest of them muttered something in a low tone to the others, and they nodded sagely. Every time they shuffled the topmost drawing aside to examine the next they glanced almost instinctively at Parin, who stood calmly at Alexei's side. The presence of the Sechem is to reassure them that the task is possible,

Jehan thought, otherwise they would have voiced their objections long since.

The offworlder sat in a carved chair, an elbow on one knee, his officers and the stewards of his household attending him. He wore a coat which was a copy of the one he had received from Artai to celebrate his ennoblement, and a *jusei* in an enamelled scabbard rested between his legs, the tip against one instep, the hilt supported across the opposite thigh.

Jehan hid a smile. The display was nicely calculated to ensure that the chief men of the city understood that while Alexei was not in truth their direct overlord – Pantai was part of a Kerait fief – yet he had at his disposal the authority of an officer of the Kha-Khan, and as such superseded all but the most high.

In fact the burghers of the city were falling over themselves to offer the Kha-Khan's alien ambassador their co-operation. For building the ship they were to be paid – a sum which was yet to be assessed, although there was little doubt that payment would be generous – and for the provision of materials there was to be remitted such a portion of their tithe to their feudal overlord which might be deemed appropriate. Jehan had already decided that the avaricious looks on the faces of certain of the suppliers of timber and iron suggested that the numbers of clerks and assessors would require to be doubled. The Yasa prevented men from making more than a just profit from their enterprise – or at least it was the basis upon which such a judgement might be made – but that was hardly likely to stop the men involved from trying. The kind of opportunity which was presented by the embassy came most men's way but once, and so they could scarcely be blamed for seeking to benefit.

If the offworlder was impatient at the length of

time it was taking the three men to inspect the drawings laid out before them, he was taking care not to show it. Jehan was sitting in the angle of the window, one booted foot across the sill. He altered his position, and saw Alexei's glance shift briefly before it returned to apparently interested contemplation of the guildmasters. The door at one side of the room opened, and Sidacai's head appeared round it. A steward hurried towards him, and there was a curt exchange, then Sidacai withdrew. The taller of the guildsmen glanced round, and then he said something to the others, and they straightened and turned. They bowed to Alexei.

'Lord, this is not the kind of vessel we have ever built before,' one said, 'but we will do it.'

There had never been any doubt of that, but no one seemed to feel that it was necessary to observe upon the fact.

'You will have the assistance of the Sechem,' Alexei said. 'Techniques such as will be required may be new to you.'

Parin said nothing, but the guildmasters brightened visibly.

'Order the construction as you see fit,' Alexei continued. 'Engage what men you require, and you shall be recompensed. You should understand however that it is not my will you serve, but the Kha-Khan's. And since no man's patience is infinite, it seems to be proper to observe that there shall be a time limit upon your activities.' He broke off and seemed to stare past them for a moment. Then suddenly his full attention was concentrated upon them again. 'A space of two months was mentioned, I think.'

The guildsmen went pale. The man who had spoken first was olive-skinned, although the hair of his topknot was pure white. He took an agitated pace forward. 'Lord, we are not magicians. A ship such as the traders sail upon the Inner Sea takes such a time to build –' He looked around at the others, seeking support, and they nodded vigorously.

The tallest man ducked his head respectfully. 'Lord Khan, for this task we must needs construct longer slipways, and if there exist the timbers of a size to provide such a keel, I have not seen them.'

Parin stirred. 'Timbers can be joined,' he said, then turned and bowed to Alexei. 'However, my Lord, I am of the opinion that we ought to heed the objections of these men to the limit you seek to impose. An additional month might not be unreasonable.'

It was clear that the guildmasters expected Alexei to haggle. They watched his expression with the demeanour of a group of traders prepared to bargain to the last.

'So be it.' The offworlder waved a condescending hand. He turned his head and spoke in a low voice to a secretary. Then he turned back. 'I myself shall direct you,' he said.

They looked surprised. 'Khan, we were not told you had knowledge of our craft,' the third man said.

'The Khan has knowledge of many things,' Parin said tranquilly. 'The vessel you will construct is his design.'

The statement was not a complete exaggeration, Jehan thought. The Sechem's expression betrayed no hint of awareness that he had spoken anything but the truth, and the bows offered by the guildmasters to Alexei as they left the room were almost reverent.

Jehan stood up. 'Clever. I especially liked the way you made them believe that Parin had persuaded you to a concession. Didn't we estimate that construction would take four months at least?'

Alexei stripped off his coat. He was bare-chested

251

below it, but when a servant offered him a tunic he waved it aside. 'How wet is next month's rain? Not even Parin can tell us for sure how long our ship will take to build. Our best estimate is little more than guesswork.'

The men crowded into the square outside began to separate into orderly queues. The officers of the guilds were conferring noisily on the front steps of Alexei's house. One of them glanced up and saw Jehan standing with Alexei in the window, and he said something to the others. They turned and bowed, then shook hands with one another and went off in different directions. The queues of wrights and smiths and carpenters filed after them, and soon the square was empty except for the troopers of the guard.

The keel was laid a scant three days later. It stretched from the tidemark at the base of the slipway as far as the wall at the head of the yard. As the hull was raised the wall would have to be demolished, for the stern would overhang the street which ran beyond it. Jehan paced the distance and thought that the shipwrights had probably reduced Alexei's dimensions somewhat. From the upsweep of the stem to the sternpost the ship would measure nearly forty-four drem. The prow would extend some way beyond that, Jehan knew, although there would be no need, strictly speaking, for a bowsprit. The ship would be fitted with only one mast upon which the lookout post would be mounted, and thus there would be only a limited amount of stays and rigging.

Forests of props were being erected – a framework which was intended to provide support for the futtocks, curved wooden ribs which would sweep out and up from the keel. The planks for use as strakes – the timbers which would be fastened lengthwise over

252

the frames – were being hauled into the yard on wagons. One of a multitude of carpenters' apprentices staggered past Jehan burdened down with a tub of copper-headed nails. He ducked his head in a travesty of a bow, and continued on his way.

The commander of Jehan's guard was standing at his shoulder. He laughed softly. 'They're seeing more nobility in a day than most of them ever expected to encounter in a lifetime,' he observed. 'The wrights laying the keel spent so much time bowing to the Khan that he had to order them to stop.' Joden grinned reminiscently. 'I thought the overseer was going to faint.'

Sawdust and shavings covered the surface of the yard like a carpet. Jehan scuffed a heel through them, feeling out of place. 'We should have left all this to the Sechem.'

One of the things which sometimes made Jehan feel uncomfortable in the presence of the aliens was their easy familiarity with the trappings of technology. Jehan supposed he knew as much as most men about the application of science to the fabric of human existence. One could not rule a fief without understanding the processes involved in the production of goods as diverse as pottery and cloth. A Khan ought to be aware of technology; but surely it was unnecessary for him to concern himself directly with it. A Khan's place was to rule – to command and to be obeyed. How far he was required to exercise personal supervision over the activities of those of his vassals who were craftsmen or engineers was, in Jehan's opinion, a matter for dispute.

A crowd of blue-coated guildsmen near the head of the slip indicated the place where the offworlder was still supervising the insertion of the last of the bolts which secured the enormous timbers of the keel.

Alexei was like his father in that respect, Jehan thought. He was to be seen more often in the company of Sechem, or of the engineers who worked at their direction, than he was with common soldiers. Even in a culture dominated by prohibitions against the too liberal employment of technology there seemed to be a place for someone who thought in almost every situation about the application of technique.

None of the shipyard workers had talons, Jehan realised. It was not that there were no Yek craftsmen in the land, simply that none were employed here. The thought troubled him. The presence of the Sechem provided reassurance, and he wondered why the law did not require their supervision of such a place on a permanent basis.

'What are you thinking about?' Joden asked.

They had been standing in the one spot for some time. Jehan mumbled something noncommittal, and he walked off along the length of the keel towards the head of the yard. The offworlder was moving more slowly in the same direction. The hem of his coat was dusted with shavings of fresh wood, and his face was flushed, his expression animated.

'Artai should have given you a guild to master, and not a Khanate,' Jehan said as he drew level. He did not mean to sound so sour, but Alexei's head came round sharply.

'I might have done more good,' he commented. 'You're bored. You should have stayed in Kinsai.'

'I may go back there.' Jehan matched his pace to Alexei's. 'What am I going to do here for three months?'

'Well.' The offworlder smiled. 'There are things to prepare.'

Jehan knew he was being treated with condescension. He gritted his teeth. 'We can provision the ship in a week, and as for the men, they're Sidacai's problem.'

'Then you can hunt, or ride. Haven't you a fief near here?'

'You know I have. It's up the coast towards N'tan.'

'Then surely you can find employment there,' Alexei suggested.

Jehan thought that the offworlder was becoming more ambassadorial with the passing of each new day. 'You aren't going to occupy every day like this?' he said.

Alexei shrugged. 'Why not? It's important enough, God knows.'

The masters of the guilds were waiting respectfully near the gate. They doffed their caps and bowed. 'We trust you are pleased, Khan,' the tallest of them said.

The offworlder nodded. 'Brise. Yes, I am.'

From the insignia on his coat the man was the officer of a guild which incorporated woodworkers and carpenters. It was apparent that he was flattered that Alexei had remembered his name.

The master of the shipwrights was the olive-skinned man whom Jehan remembered from the audience chamber. 'Lord,' he said hesitantly, 'it is the custom among us for the timbers of a ship to be stamped with a sign – that being equivalent to the name the ship will bear. Does it please you to impart to us your will regarding this?'

The Sechem were coming through the props which had been raised to support the frames for the stern. They stopped to listen. Alexei's expression was perplexed. 'I had not thought about a name,' he said. He looked at Parin, seeking assistance.

'The vessel is to be powered by the sun,' Parin offered. 'It might be fitting, Khan, for the name to be chosen to signify that.'

'Yes.' Alexei nodded, pleased with the notion. He thought for a moment, and then looked at the guild-master who had posed the question. 'There is a creature of the desert, like a mouse, which adjusts its form to suit the conditions in which it finds itself. When the sun is large, its coat stands erect, catching the rays; and at night it uses the energy it has stored so that it withstands the cold. How is it called?'

All three men grinned. 'Lord, you mean the *shoutap*, which men call the sunstealer,' the master of the shipwrights answered.

'Then put its sign upon the timbers,' Alexei said. He glanced at the Sechem, who nodded agreement. 'And as for the name of our vessel, *Sunstealer* it shall be.'

PART THREE

A Few Harsh Words

Burun had brought his wives, and as a result there were so many servants in his entourage that there was insufficient room to accommodate them in the house which had been prepared for him.

'Is Kinsai so free of intrigue against us that you can afford to absent yourself?' Jehan enquired. A pair of servants struggled through the door, an enormous chest between them, and he stepped to one side to allow them to pass. They set the chest down in the centre of the room and then stood back, breathing heavily.

Zurachina came out of the next chamber. She saw the chest. 'Not here,' she said. 'The room on the other side of the hall.' She ignored Burun and Jehan, but she smiled at Alexei.

The servants stared at her mutely. Then they lifted the chest and staggered out through the door again. Zurachina went after them.

Alexei was leaning against the wall beside the door. There was no furniture in the room yet, and so there was nowhere to sit down. Burun was still clad in riding clothes – a loose tunic and black breeches tucked into calf-length boots. A coat with a fur collar was draped across his shoulders, but he had not bothered to put his arms into the sleeves. He stood in front of the open window staring out at the view. Then he turned.

'I am here at Artai's request,' he said. 'And as for Kinsai, your father is there.'

Alexei pushed himself away from the wall. 'Then this is an inspection?'

'Not exactly.' Burun spread his hands. 'Although of course, the court is interested in what is happening here.'

'I thought you were getting reports from C'zinsit,' Jehan remarked acidly.

C'zinsit's function was supposed to be unofficial. Burun grinned, unembarrassed. 'I am. Noyon, why are you so hostile? I'm not here to find fault, and even if I were, it is Alexei who is the ambassador, not you.'

A new string of carts rolled into the courtyard below. Burun's house was on the hill overlooking the shipyards and the inlet beyond. The incomplete hull of the ship rose stark above the roofs of the houses below, overshadowing them. The timbers had been coated with a preservative – a substance made from distilled pitch – and in the late afternoon sun the half-finished vessel was a dull red structure looming above everything, the detail around it blurred by the reflections of shafts of light from the crystalline content of the stone of the walls.

Jehan paced the floor, the iron heels of his boots ringing on the planks. He gave Burun a look. 'Then by your leave, I'll go.'

'Oh, by all means.' Burun waited until Jehan had left the room, and then he gave Alexei a perplexed stare. 'What was all that about?'

Alexei made a face. 'He is unhappy here. There isn't enough for him to do – or at least that's what he feels. And apart from that he is fighting Sidacai.'

Surprise showed on Burun's face. 'Indeed? I wouldn't have thought Sidacai would feel secure enough to set himself up against any of you. Have they come to blows?'

'It might be better if they had.' Alexei thought about the number of times he had seen Jehan stride away from a confrontation with Sidacai, and he grinned. 'I think it worries him because he knows you want Sidacai preserved.'

Burun made a face. 'Sidacai is useful because he is expendable,' he said.

Alexei opened his eyes wide. Burun was pretending that he did not care what happened between Jehan and Sidacai. The fact was that if he did not care, Sidacai would not be here.

'So tell me why you are here,' he said.

A horde of servants emerged from the doors of the house into the yard, and they began to unload the carts. 'Kinsai is uncomfortable at this time of year,' Burun said. He did not meet Alexei's eyes.

'Oh?' Alexei loosened the fastenings of his coat. At the front gate the troopers of his escort were squatting on their heels in a circle, a dice cup passing between them. The reins of their st'lyan were draped across their shoulders.

'Have you heard from your father?' Burun asked suddenly.

The question took Alexei by surprise. 'Should I have?'

A servant came into the room carrying a low table. He put it down, then bowed in Burun's direction. At once the chamber was filled with slaves, all bearing carpets or items of furniture. There was an interlude of chaos, and then they organised themselves. The two men who were carrying the carpets unrolled them so that they were spread diagonally in a line across the floor. The others put a long table and several chests and stools against one wall. They all bowed to Burun and filed out through the door. Not a word had been spoken.

'I asked him to negotiate with Jotan on your behalf,' Burun said.

Alexei raised his eyebrows. Little had been said

about the matter of his betrothal to Jehana since it had been announced, and he had not expected the matter to be pursued. 'My father has told me nothing,' he said. 'Is it a device to satisfy Artai?'

Tarvarian marriage settlements were often complicated affairs, and negotiations were sometimes protracted almost indefinitely.

Burun produced a look which suggested polite surprise. 'Why should you think that? The Kha-Khan has expressed an interest, it is true – but the terms of the contract are a matter for our respective families.'

There was a sound at Alexei's back, and he turned. Two of the household serving women came into the room. They knelt down at opposite ends of one of the carpets and started to tease out the fringes. The scent of the perfumed oils which they used on their bodies filled the air. Alexei's nose twitched.

'I only thought your father might have written to you to ask your will in the matter,' Burun observed innocently. He watched Alexei, his eyes bright as a bird's.

'No, he has not.'

'Hunh.' Burun shrugged and gestured. 'Probably it does not matter. We are Khans after all, and Jotan will be disposed to be generous, I have no doubt.'

If there were negotiations at all, then they were to convince Artai that the marriage was going ahead. Alexei wondered again why Burun had left Kinsai, and thought that whatever his reasons, Burun would conceal them.

More women came into the room. They ran hangings along the rails which were attached around the walls, draping them. The hangings were silks and damasks in colours which varied from purple to violet, and the shades seemed to alter subtly as they were adjusted.

'Don't worry about Jehan,' Burun said. 'I will find him employment.'

Jehan was like many of the men who had been brought up to follow the tumans. He had been bred for war, and he was uncomfortable with anything else. Alexei thought that Nogai had been right. The conquest of the continent was easy in comparison to the task of ruling it in peace. He gestured idly. 'He doesn't trouble me.'

'Oh.' Burun grinned. 'I don't imagine he does. I was right to choose you for this, Alexei. Power suits you.'

If it was a reminder of the fact that the whole project had been Burun's idea, then it was one which Alexei thought he preferred to ignore. He gave Burun a sideways look, saying nothing, but Burun only smiled and turned away to look out of the window again.

'My grand-daughter sends you her duty,' Zurachina said.

'Oh?' Alexei hid an expression of disbelief. He had parted from Jehana on terms of such strained politeness that he had been convinced that he was right in his assumption that she intended to wait only until she could find a suitable excuse so that she could withdraw from the arrangement.

'She has not written to you, I know.' Zurachina poured ch'ban into two tiny cups and offered him one. 'It would not be proper at this stage.'

Alexei emptied the cup. The liquid was hot enough to blister his tongue, but he ignored it. Unsweetened, ch'ban was a strong stimulant. He strained to remember the taste of Terran stock coffee, but could not.

'If you have a message for her,' Zurachina continued persistently, 'I am sure that I could find a way

263

to send it to her. Perhaps when I send news to her mother.'

The cup was so fine that if he compressed his fingers it would shatter. Alexei resisted the impulse. He laid the cup gently on the table. 'Lady, I can think of nothing I ought to say,' he said.

If Zurachina was irritated by the lack of interest in his tone, she did not show it. 'You do not believe she intends to marry you.'

'I can think of no reason why she should.' Alexei wanted to rise and walk away, but it would have been impolite. The chamber in which Zurachina had received him was floored on two levels. The table which had been placed on the upper part was so low that it was possible to use it only when kneeling on one of the cushions which had been set on opposite sides of it. Alexei shifted slightly, moving so that his weight was no longer resting entirely on his heels.

Zurachina lifted the ch'ban pot from its burner. She refilled his cup, pouring one-handed from a distance three or four hand's-breadths above the cup. The thin stream of liquid which issued from the spout flowed directly into the cup, and not a drop was spilled. 'Men are all the same,' Zurachina said. 'Do you think that if Jehana wanted to be your wife, she would tell you?'

Alexei allowed himself the luxury of an acid smile. If it was Zurachina's intent to convince him that Jehana had sufficient regard for the betrothal agreement to honour it, she was wasting her time. 'If Jehana wants to marry me,' he said, 'she will have to wait until I return to Kinsai.' He emptied the cup again, and turned it upside down on the surface of the table so that it could not be refilled.

Burun dealt with the feud between Jehan and Sidacai by separating them. Jehan he sent up the coast to visit his fief at Kaiden, and Sidacai he ordered south to Losan where a caravan waited for escort. For several days there was peace.

There were now almost as many visitors in Pantai as there were inhabitants. Given that part of the population depended upon the migration of shipyard workers from Suristan and Ch'kasia, there was in any case considerable fluctuation during the course of a year. Now the inns were crammed, and additional barracks had been built to house the troopers who rode escort to each of the principal members of the embassy. The fact that only a small proportion of them would be included in the company which Sidacai was responsible for recruiting to travel aboard ship did not appear to matter. Alexei dealt harshly with the troopers who were brought before him for judgement following the outbreak of a series of disputes concerning the use by different clans of the various taverns around the waterfront. He had already had occasion to direct that a provost patrol the city streets after nightfall, and while the citizens of Pantai did not appear to be distressed by the influx of men – indeed it was clear that they welcomed the trade which was the result – he saw no reason to allow discipline to slacken further.

Burun showed no immediate desire to come to grips with the activity which was taking place in the shipyard. Apart from a brief audience during which the Sechem were invited to explain the nature of the developments which were being permitted, he did not interfere. The guildmasters who attended on him the day following his arrival were treated courteously, but with little interest. It was as if Burun intended to make it clear that the project was Alexei's to command, and that beyond him there was only the direction of the Kha-Khan. Alexei noted the fact, and it increased his certainty that Burun had left Kinsai so that it would appear that he was dissociating himself from active involvement in Artai's rule.

Sidacai came back after three days. Bandits had attempted to raid the caravan the night before it had reached Pantai, and they had been beaten off in a brief but bloody engagement. Summoned to Burun's presence, Alexei listened to an account of what had taken place, and he nodded.

'Every brigand and thief in the Khanate has heard about the embassy,' he observed. 'Are you surprised we're being raided?'

Most of the bandits were Ch'noze, of course, but there were Ch'kassy pirates, and maybe odd Alan who had refused to surrender after the war.

'We could deal with them if we had the men,' Sidacai said.

Burun stared at him. 'Name of God, how many do you need?' A map of the region was laid out across the table at his side. He gestured at it. 'I could keep order here with a thousand, or less. You have your escort –'

'– A thousand men or thereabouts.' Sidacai nodded. 'Is it your will that we strip Pantai? Khan, to protect the roads properly we ought to have a full tuman at least. We need guard posts along the foothills, scouts, and regular patrols.'

'And if we bring that many men into the area, we will need to supply them,' Alexei commented. 'Which means more trains.'

The Khan within whose fief Pantai lay was elderly, and he satisfied himself with providing guards for the caravans which passed between the cities and which carried the annual tribute to Kinsai. There was farming down on the plain of course, but in every case the granary lay within or near a keep which was occupied by an officer who was the Khan's vassal in the area. In any case grain held little attraction for thieves. Grain was bulky and required to be hauled away on wagons. The small bands of brigands who had operated successfully hitherto had relied upon speed to evade pursuit. It was only now that there were increased numbers that the problem was a matter for concern.

Alexei thought that it was not like Burun to make an error concerning logistics. He watched as Burun's extended talon traced the map, following the road north from Losan.

'Very well.' Burun looked up suddenly. 'I have three tumans in summer quarters near Pesth. You may have one of them detached to your command. Directing their activities will give Orcadai and C'zinsit something to do.' He gestured aside to a secretary, and before Alexei had risen he was dictating an order.

Sidacai followed Alexei outside. 'I am a fool,' Sidacai said. 'I did not realise what he was about.'

Alexei nodded. With ten thousand men Burun would be able to seal off Pantai from contact with the rest of the country if he chose. 'Do you think Burun has quarrelled with Artai?' he asked.

'If he had,' Sidacai responded, 'I would have heard it. Do you think C'zinsit is the only person with access to couriers?'

Siban and Sidacai were in communication of course. It was a realisation which Alexei found did not cause him undue surprise. 'Then what is Burun's object?' he asked.

'How should I know?' Sidacai threw up his hands. Then he turned. 'Whatever it is, you should take heart,' he said. 'For it is clear that he wants the success of your embassy.'

The road which ran north from Pantai along the coast

was laid upon a shelf which had been cut from the rock. Several small landslides which appeared to have occurred during heavy rains had not been cleared completely – a fact which indicated that carts seldom travelled it, Alexei thought – and there were dried-up outpourings of clay and stones at places where the bank reared up vertically from the roadside.

Because it was morning the light was coming from the east, and the shadows of the tall trees which grew on the slopes above the road darkened their path. Alexei guided his st'lyan around a windfall which projected out from the bank, and then he turned to watch Burun. Burun was riding a chestnut mare which had the worst manners of any animal Alexei had ever encountered. When it came up to the fallen tree it stopped, backed, and then screamed and shook its head. Burun tapped it in the barrel with the toe of his boot, and after a moment it started forward again.

'Lead it around,' Alexei said.

There was only a narrow space between the end of the tree and the outer edge of the road. Beyond, the hillside dropped away precipitously down to the shore.

'There's no need.' Burun urged the st'lyan up towards the gap. The chestnut backed again, its hooves rattling on the stones of the road. 'Hah,' Burun said. 'Make a liar of me, would you?' He lashed the st'lyan with the ends of his reins, and it bolted through the space. A shower of small stones fell out of the side of the road and tumbled down the hillside, but Burun did not even look back.

Some way before the road wound down to Kaiden there was a place where a river ran out through a cleft in the hills and fell by a series of cataracts to the sea. The rocks were very old and hard here, and they had not been much worn away by the passage of the

268

years. On the upper reaches of the watercourse at the point where the road crossed there was a mill, and there was a ford across the river on top of a weir. Roads came down both banks of the river towards it, and tracks ran away at all sorts of angles.

'This land is good for farming when the timber is cleared,' Burun said.

Around one side of the mill there was the cleared ground of a meadow inside a split rail fence. When Alexei and Burun rode up to it they saw a cart with three men in it blocking the way. Beyond them were Yek troopers, some mounted and some watering their animals at the place where the ground shelved down to the ford. The captain of Jehan's guard was sitting on top of the fence, one leg swinging. He nodded to Burun, but did not get down. Instead he jerked his thumb towards the mill. 'Khan, you should stay to watch this,' he said. 'The miller has been giving short weight.'

'And where is my grandson?' Burun shaded his eyes with his hand, looking up at the towering structure of the mill.

'Drowning the miller maybe,' Alexei said.

Joden laughed. 'Not yet, Khan. We just took the stones inside. Nothing has happened so far.'

Alexei stepped off the back of his st'lyan onto the fence, and with Burun he walked across the meadow to the steps which led up to the door of the mill. He pushed the door open.

Inside there was a circular room which resounded with the howl of grindstones. The floor and every other surface was caked with mouldy flour. Wooden gears and shafts turned inside a mass of it, yellowed and evil-smelling. Burun circled around the hole in the floor, staring down.

The scales were at the far end of the catch room

below. The miller was watching as two boys piled stone weights onto them, his features slack with apprehension. 'Lord,' he said to Jehan, 'my father had those weights.'

Jehan was pacing up and down in front of the scales. His eyes never left the miller's face.

Burun moved a stacked sack of flour and stood so that he could see the scale. 'He cheated on his weights when I had this fief,' he said to Alexei.

The miller's face was dripping with sweat. The boys heaved a checkweight with the Kha-Khan's seal on it up onto the balance side of the scale, and they kicked away the chock. The scale rocked and settled, balancing evenly. Burun shook his head, his expression disbelieving. Jehan waved at the boys. They removed all the stones from the scale, and then went through into a recess at the back of the room and brought out another set of weights.

'Lord,' the miller shouted, protesting, 'I never use those. I never even knew they were there. I use only the good weights. You saw they balanced –'

The boys hoisted the second set up onto the left-hand side of the scale, then placed the checkweight on the right-hand side again. The scale crashed down heavily onto the checkweight side.

'In the Name of God,' the miller shouted, 'I swear to you, Lord –'

Jehan seemed not to hear. He gestured to the boys, and they gathered the false weights up from the scale. Jehan went out onto the staging through the open side of the mill, and the boys followed him and threw the weights into the mill pond. The three men with the cart jeered at the miller and shouted curses at him. Jehan called to them to bring their flour back into the mill to be weighed again. On the floor above the staging Burun smiled.

'Lord –' The miller still protested. '– I have never cheated anyone – I never knew those other weights were there – I never used them –'

Jehan stared at him coldly. He said, 'Henceforth you shall give my bailiff one koban every quarterday.'

The miller's voice gave out suddenly. His shoulders slumped and his face went grey.

'If he cannot steal,' Burun said in Alexei's ear, 'that fine will beggar him.' He banged his heel on the wooden floor, and both Jehan and the miller looked up. The miller climbed hastily up the stairs from the catch room. He came towards Burun, his hands held out in appeal. 'Khan,' he said, 'have mercy on me.'

Burun grinned, showing his teeth. 'If I judged it, you'd be in the pond along with your weights,' he said.

Jehan came up the steps. 'Have you been here long?'

'Long enough.' Burun turned his back on the miller.

The miller turned to repeat his plea to Jehan. Jehan said, 'If you do not offend again, I will consider a remission.' He walked past them out of the door. The cart was coming through the gate into the meadow, the men in it looking pleased.

Alexei followed Jehan outside. Jehan's dun st'lyan was being held by a trooper. Jehan took the reins. 'It is said that only God can make something out of nothing,' he observed, then grinned at Alexei. 'I just made four koban a year out of twenty diram that don't exist. Justice is profitable.'

Burun came out of the mill and down the flight of stairs into the yard. The miller followed at his back, still protesting. Burun gestured, silencing him. 'I am not your Lord,' he said.

Joden came down off the top of the fence. He

glanced at the miller. 'Maybe he'll stay honest now,' he said.

Burun snorted. 'Have you ever seen a snake fly?' He scowled at the miller, and the miller quailed. 'He was giving false weight when I got this fief of Arjun.'

Jehan looked back over his shoulder. 'And how did you deal with it?'

Burun frowned. 'It was never proved,' he said. 'How did you know where to find the other weights?'

'Oh.' Jehan stared away at the rushing water beyond the weir, then turned back to look at Burun again. 'I simply asked myself where I would hide them were I the miller. He is lazy as well as a thief. I knew they would not be far from the scales.'

Burun laughed. They mounted and rode down the winding road to Kaiden. The keep was on a rocky promontory which projected out into a sheltered bay, and there were houses and a narrow wharf beyond. A few fishing boats were drawn up onto a strand of fine golden shingle.

'How old were you when you got this fief, Khan?' Alexei reined over at Burun's side.

'Oh.' Burun shook his head at a memory. 'I was a young man, still unmarried. It was in the days when Zurachina's father had Pantai. I saw her in the market there, and vowed to have her.'

The road widened out beyond a low stone bridge. Wagons full of grain were coming the other way, and the men driving them waved to Jehan, then saw Burun and bowed.

Alexei said, 'If you keep talking like that, Khan, I will forget what a spider you are.' It was easy to forget that the lands which had been Vortai's belonged mostly to Burun now. Alexei saw Burun glare, and he chuckled. The short causeway up to the gate of the keep was neat, and it had been swept free of dung and loose stones. In the bailey Jehan's bailiff was waiting at the head of a line of liveried servants.

Burun stared around, his expression impressed. 'You may not care for feudal responsibilities,' he said to Jehan, 'but you show a remarkable talent for them just the same.'

It was a compliment, but Jehan did not look as if he appreciated it. He dismounted, throwing his reins to a groom. 'Did you come here to assure yourself that I was still capable?' he asked. 'Or are you already tired of Pantai?'

Burun showed his teeth. 'I thought you might care for something more onerous.'

Jehan's head came up. 'Meaning what, exactly?'

'Oh.' Burun got slowly down out of the saddle. 'We are having some problems with bandits.'

'Really?' Jehan grinned derisively. 'Bandits are giving you problems? They must be remarkable men indeed.'

Burun threw up his arms. 'If that's your attitude, you can stay here until you rot. Alexei will ask the Kha-Khan to have you replaced.'

Jehan flushed. He stared past Burun at Alexei. Alexei shrugged, as if dissociating himself from the whole matter. Jehan took a deep breath, and let it out again slowly. He looked at Burun. 'What do you want of me?'

'I want you to come back to Pantai,' Burun said. He gave Jehan a level stare. 'I want you to do your part.'

'And Sidacai?' Jehan returned the stare.

Burun made an impatient sound. 'If you have a quarrel with Sidacai, then settle it.'

'You don't care how.'

'Exactly.' Burun stalked past the waiting bailiff and went into the keep.

Jehan watched him go, and then he turned and

looked at Alexei. 'Even when he is wrong, he manages to be right,' he said.

Alexei dismounted. A groom led his st'lyan away towards a line of stables. 'I used to feel like that about my father,' he said.

'Used to?'

'– Until I learned to ignore what he was,' Alexei said. He watched Jehan's expression. 'We are much the same in that, you and I. When our actions are under the control of others, we are unhappy.'

Jehan nodded slowly. 'You mean I should forget about being his grandson and concentrate on being myself.'

It was not quite what Alexei had meant. He wrinkled his nose. 'Something like that,' he said.

Jehan looked thoughtful. After a moment he nodded again, and then he walked to the door of the keep and went inside.

Jehan took half a tuman and cleared not only the road which ran between Pesth and Pantai but also the countryside for over two hundred verst on either side of the road. In three weeks he caught or killed over a hundred bandits or casual thieves. Their severed heads decorated posts at regular intervals along the approaches to the roads from the north, and raids against the caravans and supply trains using the route ceased abruptly.

Orcadai and C'zinsit took three thousand men. They patrolled the land between Pantai and Losan – a strip of coastline about three hundred verst wide which was mostly rolling plain – but met with rather less success until they started to employ Jehan's methods. As soon as it became apparent that anyone who was caught would be beheaded, the attacks on the caravans stopped.

Alexei used the interlude to visit his keep at the heart of his province of Khitai, and found it peaceful. Khitai was mostly steppe and farmland, and it had been settled for over a hundred years. He spent two days talking to stewards and administering justice – there were a number of cases awaiting disposal which might otherwise have been heard by one of his bailiffs, but the plaintiffs in every instance had reckoned that their newly ennobled lord might be disposed to be more generous in awarding damages than the local officers who knew without question what was proper – and then he rode back to Pantai.

The construction of the *Sunstealer* was moving apace. Alexei had delegated to the guildmasters the tasks involving day-to-day supervision, although there was little question that his habit of appearing without warning in the yards had the effect of ensuring that both the quality and the quantity of the work were maintained.

'They have never known a Khan with such an understanding of their mysteries,' Parin said, when he was asked to comment.

In fact Alexei was finding that he was at times stretched to remember important elements of the processes which were being employed. His awareness of technology was limited for the most part to the kind of exposure which all well-born young men in the Empire underwent. Just as officers of the Imperial forces learned their battle skills from machines, so he had spent weeks of his late youth with every hair shaved from his body, immersed in a tank of oxygen- ated fluorocarbon, hooked up by electrodes to the civil version of an Accelerated Life Situation Computer. By this process he had learned his advanced mathematics, and the application of science involving everything from the use of force to the re-action of elements. He had never been required to exert his strength upon the end of a lever, or to mix the chemicals to create reactions, but the sequences which he had absorbed in the tanks were indelibly stamped upon his memory as if he had. All the same he was discovering gaps. Either Imperial scientific knowledge was incomplete – a possibility which he was only now beginning to come to terms with – or his recollection had been dimmed somehow by the years spent on Tarvaras.

It was now nine weeks since the laying of the keel. The ship was a massive structure which loomed above the shipyards and the warehouses around them, and worried shipwrights were already pressing the Sechem to calculate the additional weight of chain which would be required to be attached to the hull to prevent it from running up on the opposite bank of the inlet on launching. The inlet it was clear was barely wide enough for the task, and a few of the fainter hearts had begun to talk about alternative methods of getting the vessel into the water.

It was late in the afternoon of a particularly hot and airless day when Alexei left the yard after a tour of inspection and walked not in the direction of his house but instead towards the centre of Pantai.

A trooper waiting with the reins of his st'lyan was ignored, and Alexei heard the rattle as the reins were secured with haste to a metal ring set in the wall beside the gate, before the man trotted to catch up.

'I want a bath.' Alexei did not turn.

'Yes, Lord.' The trooper was doubling to keep pace with Alexei's long stride. 'There is a bath house next to the White Goat Inn, Lord.'

Further east the larger houses had their own baths. A bath house was either an adjunct to the main

276

building, or else it was constructed entirely separately – often in the garden. Alexei had seen swimming pools on other worlds which were smaller, and it was only the fact that he was hot and tired, and felt the sweat which had soaked the back and waistband of his tunic, that had persuaded him to discard his reservations about the practice. A Yek bath house was used communally – customers scrubbed themselves before immersion – and the water was normally hot enough to strip the flesh from a man who did not lower himself into it by stages. It was not in other words a place for anyone with the kind of regard for sexual taboos which was common elsewhere in the Empire. In fact the Yek did not trouble themselves about nakedness, except under certain very specific circumstances relating to the veiling of women where required by their husbands, and their peculiar approach was one of the many aspects of their way of life which Alexei found it hard to grow used to.

The citizens who recognised Alexei stopped, stared, and then bowed hastily. Alexei smiled grimly. Provincial cities were not used to such informality. A Khan rode or was carried in a litter if he was aged. If he walked at all, it was only for a short distance under circumstances in which it was impractical to use st'lyan.

The bath house was a long low building constructed out of the same yellow stone which was common elsewhere in Pantai. The roof was of black tile, and overhung the side walls by over a drem so that there was an area of deep shadow on the side away from the sun. The sign which decorated the lintel announced that the establishment was named 'The House of Supreme Pleasure'.

Alexei sniffed. 'The House of Supreme Embarrassment, more like,' he muttered.

'What did you say, Lord?' The trooper's head came round.

'Nothing. It doesn't matter.' Alexei took another hard look at the bath house. 'Is this the best house in Pantai?'

'Oh yes, Lord.' The trooper nodded vigorously. 'The girls who work here are all very pretty, very clean.'

It was not what Alexei had wanted to know. A gowned N'pani whose girth was almost as great as his height was emerging from the door. He bowed to Alexei, his moon face wreathed in a huge smile. 'Lord Khan, you honour my humble establishment,' he said. He bowed again. 'Enter, Lord, I pray you. Name your pleasure, and I undertake to provide it. Rest here an hour, or a day, it is all the same. However long you remain under my roof, you are welcome.'

The speech was well rehearsed, and had no doubt been employed before. Alexei thought that he had encountered less flowery salutations outside the houses of joy which were to be found in the pleasure streets of the Imperial capital Knossos.

'And I did not go into those,' he muttered aloud.

'Pardon, Lord, I did not hear what you said.' The N'pani was looking worried. He glanced an enquiry at the trooper, and the trooper shrugged.

Alexei ignored the byplay. Probably they thought he was mad. If he turned and walked away, they would think he was madder still. He went through the door.

Inside was not what he had feared. It never was. In spite of the grandiose claims made by their proprietors, the bath houses were required to cater principally to families or to whole households, and as such the facilities they offered were more functional than sybaritic. There was a neat antechamber which was floored in varnished timber. A low laquered table

278

had been placed in the centre of the floor, and behind it knelt a smiling if somewhat plain young woman. She was fully clothed.

'Lord Khan, welcome.' She bowed so that her forehead touched the surface of the table.

Alexei grunted noncommittally. The trooper was fidgeting at his shoulder. 'Khan, I am supposed to stay with you –' he began nervously.

It was the sole precaution Alexei had agreed to following the attempt upon his life. He shrugged. 'Come if you wish,' he said.

The trooper brightened. The N'pani clapped his hands, and several more young women issued from an open doorway. There was a scent of warm sweet oil on the air, and Alexei thought he could almost smell the steam.

'This way, Lord.'

The N'pani trotted in apparent agitation ahead of them into the next chamber. Here it seemed Alexei was expected to disrobe. He pulled his tunic over his head. Normally the women assisted their male customers to undress. In his case, however, they would have required to stand on stools to reach above his head. He dropped the tunic carelessly. An older woman appeared from nowhere and gathered it up. Provided he remained in the bath house long enough, his clothes would be returned washed and ready for wear. Alexei slipped the scabbards of his two swords out of his waist sash, and stood holding them while the sash was unwound. One of the women held out her hand to take the swords. Alexei hesitated, and he glanced over to the place where the trooper was receiving similar treatment. The trooper was in the act of resisting the attempts of a diminutive N'pani woman to take his short sword. Alexei grinned. He surrendered his *jusei*, but retained the *hiranu*. It was scarcely longer than a dagger, small enough not to attract attention if he carried it into the bathing area.

Naked, Alexei kept his eyes firmly to the front. He strode into the next chamber, a bare room floored with stone slabs between which ran gutters for the spilled water. Here the women were unclothed. Alexei did his best to ignore the fact. He lowered himself onto a tiny wooden stool. There was one other man in the chamber – a squat Dr'gasian with tattoos which covered his skin in one continuous design from his neck down past his waist and across one thigh. He nodded shortly to Alexei while two women scrubbed at his back. Alexei felt the heat of the water which was being poured from the dipper held by the girl whose responsibility it was to sluice away the soap after he had been washed. He winced as a stream was emptied down his back. On the other side of the room the trooper was surrounded by girls, most of them laughing at his jokes. The trooper's hands moved familiarly to encircle the girls' waists. He saw Alexei looking in his direction, blushed, and took his hands away. A moment later they were back again.

The N'pani was moving in nervous little paces back and forward in the doorway, apparently anxious for the comfort of his noble visitor. Both the women and Alexei ignored him. As soon as the last of the soap had been rinsed from his shoulders, Alexei rose and walked swiftly into the steam which was coming from the bathing area. Inside he made out the stone pillars which supported the roof above a pool which was perhaps fifty metres the side. The water in the pool steamed. Alexei walked around the side of the pool looking for the place where the movement of the water told him the fire was located beneath, and then he made his way to the far side of the bath. There were stone ledges at various heights descending into the water. He sat down on the first, and put his feet into the water, then took them out again. Gradually he was able to keep them in, and he slid down onto the next ledge to begin the process of immersing his legs.

A Yek would walk into the pool down the ledges, immersing himself without hesitation up to the neck. The races of the True People were practically immune to extremes of heat and cold, which was one of the reasons why bath houses were more common as one travelled east.

The Dr'gasian was entering the bath chamber now. His feet pattered on the flagstones which surrounded the sides of the pool and he passed out of Alexei's sight into a wall of steam. A muted splashing sound indicated that he had entered the water.

Alexei frowned. Probably the man was a shipyard worker. The Dr'gasians were a strange people who came from a large island which lay to the west of Y'frike. By Alexei's standards they were human – they had no talons. They were almost uniformly small and broad in stature, the men were hairless, and even the women smelled strongly of the garlic which they appeared to consider an essential part of their diet.

The trooper had persuaded two of the wash house girls to accompany him into the pool. Either the N'pani had not objected for fear of offending Alexei, or else some financial arrangement had been arrived at. The trooper came through the steam, an arm around both girls. They gave a yell, and jumped off the side of the bath into the water. The girls were N'pani, and of course they possessed the same ability as the trooper to endure the almost boiling water. A wave washed up against Alexei's chest, and he gasped. The part of his body which was not immersed was soaking with perspiration from the heat. He lowered himself gingerly another centimetre or so.

One of the girls detached herself from the trooper, and she walked through the water to a ledge near Alexei and settled herself, smiling at him. He returned the smile guardedly, wary of encouraging her. She put her head back against the side of the bath, closed her eyes, and appeared to go to sleep. Alexei tried to relax. The temperature of the water was not completely unbearable at this end of the pool. Eventually he would accustom himself to it, but by then it would be time to leave. He looked down at himself. His body was still lightly tanned, a combination of the residual effects of Longivex and exposure to the planet's red sun. Skin cancers should have been the norm, he thought, on a world exposed to what amounted to a red giant. In fact cancer of any kind was unknown on Tarvaras. Either carcinogens could not survive in the atmosphere, or there was something in the soil perhaps, and thus in the diet of living creatures, which prevented their development.

A movement in the water caught Alexei's eye. Suddenly he discerned the shape of a man swimming below the surface. Why anyone should want to do such a thing was beyond Alexei – he thought at first that it was the trooper, but then the trooper's voice echoed across the pool from the far side, and the girl with him laughed and answered.

The Dr'gasian then. That was even stranger. All at once Alexei felt exposed. He was on a ledge which permitted him to sit with most of his body immersed in the water. Even standing up, he was in the bath to his waist.

A swirl in the water at the Dr'gasian's heels was the only indication that he had kicked hard, propelling himself in Alexei's direction. Alexei reached for the *hiranu* which lay sheathed on the topmost ledge. He unlocked the blade, and parried as the Dr'gasian surged out of the water, a Yek d'jaga sweeping upward in the stroke which would have gutted Alexei if he had not intercepted it.

His assailant grunted in surprise. Neither weapon had more than a rudimentary guard. The blades slid together, and then the Dr'gasian grasped Alexei by one ankle and jerked him off the ledge into the water. They rolled, trying to find their feet, grappling desperately.

For Alexei it was the sudden shock of the hot water which was the most distracting element. The Dr'gasian did not seem to notice any discomfort, and he was powerfully built. Alexei's head went under, and he closed his eyes instinctively to protect them. The Dr'gasian's left arm was around his waist, preventing him from finding his feet. The other ...

Alexei sensed the sweep of the arm as it came round, and he forced his own left arm free and blocked the stroke. His own right was trapped inside the encircling band which was his attacker's left arm. His feet touched the bottom of the pool, and he kicked wildly. They surged to the surface, and the Dr'gasian lost his hold. Alexei threw himself back, away from his assailant. He felt one of the stone shelves at the side of the bath against his shoulders. The Dr'gasian had taken a single deep breath, and then he had submerged. He came through the water towards Alexei, knife hand outstretched, probing. Alexei hurled himself desperately to one side. He was outmatched in such intolerable conditions, and it was only a matter of time before the assassin's d'jaga found its mark.

The trooper came off the side of the bath in a headlong dive. He came to his feet at Alexei's side, and the

Dr'gasian, turning below the surface, found himself faced with not one pair of legs but two. He kicked off the bottom and surfaced, his head and shoulders popping up out of the water in front of them. The trooper brought his hand with the short sword in it round in a swing which almost decapitated the Dr'gasian. He gurgled, and slid beneath the surface. The blood pouring from the wound in his neck stained the water crimson. On the side of the bath one of the N'pani women saw it, and she screamed.

'This cannot be allowed to occur again,' Burun said.

Apart from the fact that his face felt as if it had been scalded, Alexei was unharmed. Sooner or later he knew reaction would set in, and at that point he thought he would like to be sitting down. He lowered himself slowly into the chair.

'My men are questioning the N'pani.' Burun took a pace around the table. 'But if they learn anything from him I'll be surprised.'

The proprietor of the bath house had raised the alarm in fact, but that had not saved him from arrest.

'Had you used the place before?' Burun turned suddenly.

'Never.'

The Dr'gasian had entered the bath house ahead of him. Alexei considered the fact, and he wondered if someone might have overheard in the street when he had announced that he wanted a bath. He strained to remember if he had seen the Dr'gasian among the passers-by outside the shipyard, and thought not.

'It was chance then.' Burun threw himself into the other chair. 'That means we do not know if he was alone, or if he was one of many.'

It was not a comforting thought. There might be twenty more assassins, each with instructions to wait

284

until an opportunity like the visit to the bath house presented itself. Alexei eyed Burun's troubled expression, and then he looked away.

Jehan was leaning against the wall beside the window. He used the thrust of one foot to push himself upright, and then he came across and perched on the edge of the table. 'Of the Khans who were named the last time,' he said, 'one is dead, and the other cannot be found.'

Burun looked up. 'The implication being that we are supposed to believe that he who remains in theory alive is still trying,' he said. 'I don't believe it.'

Alexei did not believe it either. He caught Jehan's eye. 'Have they traced the place where the Dr'gasian was staying?' he asked.

Jehan shook his head. 'I have a provost of fifty men out questioning innkeepers,' he said.

If the Dr'gasian had slept at an inn – and if he had taken a room, and had not chosen to sleep in one of the communal public rooms – it might be possible to establish whether or not he had met with others. It was a slim chance, and Alexei guessed that if there were others involved, they were even now covering their tracks.

'As for Orta,' Burun said, 'I don't know whether to reward him or flog him.'

Alexei smiled painfully. The man he had thought was a common soldier had turned out to be an under-officer, a member of Burun's personal guard. 'If you don't reward him, Khan,' he said, 'I will.'

Burun frowned. 'I told him I wanted the next assassin alive,' he growled.

The fact that Burun had anticipated a further attempt was not lost on Alexei. The basis for the objection was so ridiculous, however, that he was unable to stifle a laugh. The result was painful, and he pressed one arm against his chest. Some of the hot water in the bath had entered his lungs. 'It would have been a neat trick if he could have managed it,' he said. 'But I really don't think he had any choice, do you?'

'Hunh.' Burun produced a crooked smile. 'Probably not.'

Jehan was teasing his moustaches. After a moment he raised his head. 'If we knew why the attempts were being made,' he said, 'probably we would be able to work out who is responsible.'

'A marvellous conclusion.' Burun snorted derisively. 'Do you think that hadn't occurred to me?'

A slave came into the room with a flask of wine. He bowed and placed it on the table close to Alexei's hand. It was beaded with moisture. Jehan leaned across the table and took a cup from a pile. He offered it. 'Drink some of the wine,' he said. 'I had it brought specially.'

Alexei poured from the flask into the cup. He sipped experimentally. The wine had been chilled, and it went down into his stomach like a river of ice extinguishing the fire. He gasped.

'A bath house.' Burun shook his head angrily. 'I still don't believe it. What were you doing there?'

The coldness of the wine was expanding, easing the pain in his chest. Alexei ignored the question.

'I think even offworlders bathe now and again,' Jehan said. He sounded amused.

Burun gestured rudely. Then he looked at Alexei. 'From now on you go nowhere unescorted.'

Outside the sun was setting, a red semi-circle sitting on the water across which threads of black clouds passed. Alexei watched them, and then he turned back again. 'As to the person responsible,' he said, 'your son once suggested that I had offended the relatives of some lady of the court.'

'Indeed?' Burun's head came up sharply.

Alexei remembered that at the time he had suspected that the suggestion had originated with Burun. Now he knew that he had been mistaken. It was clear that the notion had been put forward by Jotan alone, and that he had mentioned it to no one else, because the expression on the faces of both Burun and Jehan was one of complete surprise.

There had been no room for the Merkut tuman inside Pantai, and so they were camped on a plain which lay about a verst to the south. Burun was in the course of attempting to mount each tuman on st'lyan of one colour. Most of the animals grazing the short grass were piebald, and because it was the height of summer there were breeding mares among them.

The st'lyan which were cavalry mounts were uniformly strong, deep-chested, and were about twenty-four or five hands tall. The single spike of horn which projected from the forehead of each was undecorated. The Khans and their officers sometimes gilded the horns of their favourite animals, even though the projection was not regarded as a weapon. In battle a st'lyan reared and lashed out with its hooves. It seldom attempted to gore an adversary, although contact with a sweep of the tusk was usually lethal.

The troopers serving with this tuman had spent the previous winter and spring putting down a rebellion among the northern Ch'noze, and they were fit and disciplined. The majority of them were Merkuts or members of Merkut sub-clans, and there were as a result few conscripts in the ranks. Volunteers who had served for five years were easily distinguished by their long moustaches, and by their plaited, gold-banded top-knots. The officers dressed their hair in the Yek formal style which was not unlike that which was to be found among men of the Manchu worlds. Alexei had often marked the similarity, and suspected that there was a Second Empire connection somewhere, maybe as the result of a landing or attempted colonisation. No one knew how many worlds the Second Empire of Man had contained before its collapse.

An ordinary trooper shaved the forepart of his scalp, drawing the rest of his hair together and enclosing it inside a corded slide which was usually about a handspan in length. The loose hair hung down from the end of the slide in a kind of ponytail, and a trooper who wished to wear a helmet had to pull the slide loose in order to be able to put the helmet on.

Uniform was unknown except in the case of escorts or personal guards; however, because the Khans who raised the tumans provided tunics and breeches, men tended to wear clothing which was at least generally similar. A trooper possessed a cloak which might be fur-lined if he had the wherewithal, and he wrapped himself in it as protection against the elements or to sleep. Most carried the d'jaga, although talons were considered an excellent substitute. The lance was a popular weapon, but every trooper carried at least one compound bow, cased and strapped to his saddle.

On a level stretch of ground an archery range had been set up. The targets were posts which were situated at intervals of about ten lengths down the side of the range. Troopers were required to ride past them at the gallop, firing from the saddle. A miss under such conditions was fairly unusual. The Merkuts were supreme equestrians – Alexei still held that the st'lyan had been bred from the Terran stock horse – and they were trained to ride with their reins lying loose across their st'lyan's necks, their hands occupied between bow and cased arrows.

The competition which was in progress had commenced as a straightforward practice for the men of the third tenth of the tuman. Very soon it had come down to a matter of wagers between officers encouraged by the members of the embassy who had ridden up to watch, and support for the contestants who had survived the early rounds was hotly partisan.

The commander of the third tenth was named Jenjin. He was a burly broad-chested Merkut with greying hair who had risen through the ranks, and as such he was the popular favourite of most of the common soldiers. He took the course at a flat gallop, standing in his stirrups, firing as fast as his right hand found the next arrow. Because the difference in skill between the competitors who remained was now so slight, thin clay discs had been affixed to the tops of the posts. Jenjin shattered the first five while his st'lyan was reaching the peak of its stride. The next three he took as he rode past them, and the last two he broke with shots which he fired while turned in the saddle to face back downrange. The men packed on the grass along the side of the range cheered wildly.

'We should mark a line between which all arrows must be fired,' Orcadai said. 'That last one was struck when he was out of the range.'

'He hit all ten, didn't he?' C'zinsit turned. 'Anyway, you can't change the rules at this stage.'

'If they all complete the course, we will have to,' Jehan observed, shading his eyes with his hand. A lean under-officer was flying down the range, shattering targets with calm accuracy.

Alexei had not been invited to compete, and privately he was glad. On foot or with the time to select a point of aim he was as able an archer as anyone could be who had not been raised with a bow in his hand. Merkuts were riding almost as soon as they could walk, and even the smallest boy possessed a toy bow which fired child's arrows.

'It's your turn.' Jehan prodded Orcadai between the shoulder blades.

Orcadai spun round, and he glared. 'Don't push me, damn you. Have you no respect?'

Jehan raised his eyebrows. He put both hands into his belt and stood, feet apart, staring insolently. Beyond Orcadai the officer who was acting as range-master hesitated nervously. 'Go and shoot, or I'll tell everyone you forfeit,' Jehan said. He grinned at Orcadai.

'Aah.' Orcadai spat in the dust at Jehan's feet, and he turned and tramped away towards the place where a trooper was walking his st'lyan in a circle.

There had been a handful of similar incidents since Jehan's return from Kaiden. It was as if he was practis-ing for a fight with Sidacai by picking arguments with the others, Alexei thought. Thus far Burun had taken care to ensure that Jehan and Sidacai were not free in Pantai at the same time. When one was in the city, the other was leading a patrol or escorting a caravan. Suddenly Alexei remembered that the supply train which Sidacai was escorting from Pesth was due to arrive, and he wondered if Jehan was aware of it.

Orcadai negotiated the course without a miss, and he rode back up the side of the range, his st'lyan high-stepping, its neck arched.

'That's everyone,' C'zinsit said. 'I still think I can win it.' He glanced at Alexei. 'Will you double the stakes?'

Alexei laughed and shook his head. 'Not I, Noyon.' Burun's sons were all noted marksmen, and at this stage of the contest it was anyone's guess who was going to win.

C'zinsit looked disappointed. 'You have no sporting instinct,' he said.

Alexei ignored the jibe. He stared along the range. The surface had been pounded to dust by the passage of the st'lyan's hooves, and where Orcadai had ridden the haze still hung on the air.

'I said we would have to make it harder,' Jehan said. He pushed past C'zinsit and strode over to talk to the rangemaster. They began to mark a line across the start of the course with their boot heels. A trooper came up from the lines with a bucket full of sawdust, and he filled the furrow so that it stood out clearly. Jehan shouted at the troopers nearest to him in the crowd, and several of them ran out and picked up a coil of rope. They unwound it, stretching it so that it ran parallel to the line of posts at a distance from them of about ten lengths.

C'zinsit cocked an eye at Alexei. 'I wish Sidacai would return,' he said. He glanced up the range at Jehan. 'He's been insufferable these last few days.'

Alexei grinned, but he said nothing. He was one of the few people Jehan was troubling to be polite to, and in any case he had no desire to become involved in what was turning out to be more of a family squabble than anything else.

Jehan came back. 'That should make it more interesting.' He gestured downrange. A second furrow was being drawn about a length past the end of the course. 'No shot to count which is fired outside those lines, and all courses to be ridden this side of the rope.'

There were seven officers left in the contest

including Jenjin. They clustered round him, eyeing the activity on the range. One shook his head.

The first to ride was a young hundred commander who had only just survived the previous course, one of his discs having fallen to the ground while he was riding. His st'lyan was crossing the line which marked the end of the course while he still had two arrows left to fire. Three more officers were knocked out by similar problems, and there was a stir of interest among the troopers in the crowd.

Jehan was the next to ride. His st'lyan was a bay with a gilded horn, and after he had mounted he walked it around in a great circle so that when he reined in he was facing down the range at a distance of nearly thirty lengths from the start. He uncased his bow and nocked an arrow. The rangemaster dropped his arm, and the bay leapt forward. Jehan was at the aim when he crossed the start line, and loosed at once. His last arrow left his bow a stride before the bay crossed the finish.

'Ah.' C'zinsit nodded. 'I knew there had to be a way.' He signalled to the trooper who was holding his st'lyan.

Now that Jehan had demonstrated how the course had to be ridden, the remaining contestants were quick to follow his example. Of the three officers left, only one failed to strike all his targets while he was still between the start and finish lines. Jenjin and the lean under-officer both survived, as did both Orcadai and C'zinsit. The rope which marked the distance to the targets was moved out a further three lengths.

This time both Orcadai and the under-officer were knocked out. The officer was judged to have fired an instant after his st'lyan had crossed the finish line, and Orcadai missed his next-to-last disc.

'There is too much dust,' he complained when he

rode back. 'You can hardly see the posts, let alone the discs.'

C'zinsit jeered at him. He swung into the saddle, rode around behind the crowd, and charged down the range, whooping as he fired.

'Name of God, we could go on like this all day,' Jehan said at Alexei's side. He walked across to talk to the officer in charge of the range again. Jenjin strolled over, and they conferred, heads together.

'What are they cooking up?' C'zinsit demanded. He rode up in front of Alexei and reined in.

Alexei shrugged. 'I don't know, Noyon. Why not ask?'

C'zinsit grunted. He walked his st'lyan over to where Jehan was arguing with the others and spoke, his tone enquiring. Jehan turned and he replied tersely. C'zinsit laughed, and he nodded and reined around. The rangemaster threw up his hands, and he went over to the trooper who was holding the rope near the start point, turned, and began to pace. At a distance which Alexei estimated was a further seven lengths from the original target line he stopped and waved. The troopers with the rope moved out across the field until they were level with him.

'Twenty lengths,' C'zinsit said. He dismounted beside Alexei. 'I hope you are ready to pay me.'

At twenty lengths the discs would be little more than white dots on top of the posts. Alexei did not see how anyone could hit such a target under the conditions which now prevailed along the range. At least the sun was now in the west, and the contestants would be firing with it over one shoulder.

Jehan rode up. 'Whoever strikes the most discs is the winner,' he said. He stared at C'zinsit. 'Is that clear?'

'Oh, perfectly.' C'zinsit gave a saturnine smile. 'You

don't really think you can beat me, do you?'

The spectators clearly did not think that the chances for accuracy were improved. The troopers who had been crowding the grass only a short distance beyond the posts were moving back.

Jehan grinned. 'We'll see,' he said. He rode away.

Jenjin rode first, and broke eight of the discs. The arrows which missed the discs struck the posts upon which they were mounted, but the watching troopers showed no inclination to move forward again.

'My turn,' C'zinsit said. He mounted and rode up around the crowd again before running the course, and Alexei realised that he was giving the dust time to settle.

The ninth disc failed to break, although C'zinsit's arrow struck it squarely. C'zinsit rode back to the start. 'I claim full hit,' he said to Jehan.

They were both mounted. Jehan gigged his st'lyan round. 'If I fail to break all ten, I will forfeit to you,' he said equably. He walked his st'lyan up past the watching troopers.

C'zinsit dismounted, scowling. 'Even if Jehan breaks all ten,' he said, 'we ought to run another course. He said the winner was to be whoever struck the most discs, not whoever broke them.'

Orcadai was standing at Alexei's side. They met one another's eyes, and Orcadai made a face. 'Whatever Jehan said, we all know what he meant,' he observed.

Sidacai came suddenly up through the crowd to join them. Kadan was with him, and he grinned past the others at Alexei.

'Who is winning?' Sidacai asked.

'I am, so far,' C'zinsit said. 'But Jehan is still to ride.'

Jehan was walking the bay in a circle out beyond the crowd. He had uncased his bow, and now he was knotting his reins so that they would lie short across the st'lyan's neck. Sidacai put one hand up, palm out, blotting out the sun so that he could see. 'Then he has bested you all,' he said, sounding amused.

C'zinsit started to turn, an angry flush mounting out of his collar. 'Jehan's started his run,' Kadan said, as if he was observing upon the weather. C'zinsit swung back again.

The bay was galloping flat out before it hit the start line. Jehan's first arrow left his bow in almost the same instant, and the crack of the shattering disc was followed by a roar from the crowd which seemed to roll down the length of the range with the sequence of shots. A trooper at the end of the range threw up a scarf to indicate that the last arrow had been fired before the line had been crossed, and C'zinsit spat into the dust.

'Damn him,' he said. He shook his head.

A haze of sun-reddened dust hung across the course. There was no need to look to see if all the discs had been broken, Alexei knew. The cheers of the troopers down the line of posts announced the result.

Jehan rode up the side of the range. He reined in, and then saw Sidacai. His mouth closed in a thin line, and then his stare moved on and landed on C'zinsit. 'You owe me money,' he said.

It was apparent that it was on the tip of C'zinsit's tongue to dispute the matter. A moment passed, and then he shrugged. He pulled a purse from his sash and tossed it up to Jehan.

Sidacai stirred. 'Greedy child,' he said. 'Is that why you tried so hard?'

Jehan stared at him. 'Among friends it is usual to wager,' he said. 'You would not know about that, since you have none.'

'Indeed.' Sidacai showed his teeth. He glanced

295

around. 'Somebody lend me a mount and a bow.' He turned back to address Jehan. 'Since I am too late to wager, I will compete with you for honour, Noyon.'

Jenjin was signalling one of his officers. A fresh st'lyan, a skewbald with a pure white mane was led up. Sidacai mounted, and he uncased the bow which was strapped to the saddle, examining it.

'You can only equal my score,' Jehan said. 'You cannot beat me.'

'Oh.' Sidacai laughed harshly. 'I can think of a way.' He urged the st'lyan into a canter past the crowd of troopers, and when he flung up his arm they cheered him.

'Is he any good?' Kadan came up to Alexei's shoulder and spoke.

'He's very good. Watch.'

The dust along the range had almost settled, but the light was poorer. Sidacai was knotting his reins off short. He pulled an open case of arrows up so that it was high on his saddlebow, and tied the leather thong which secured it. The skewbald pranced a pace or two to the side, then settled. The rangemaster raised his arm.

'Now,' Kadan said softly.

Sidacai backed the st'lyan up a pace and let her go just as the rangemaster's arm swept down. The skewbald hit a gallop after about ten strides. Sidacai was standing in the stirrups, and he loosed his first arrow on the start line, his second two lengths before he drew level with the next post, and his third while he was still halfway between the second and third targets.

'Name of God,' Kadan said, awed.

'Close your mouth.' Alexei did not even glance round. 'The wind might change, and you'll stay that way.'

Kadan chuckled.

Sidacai fired his tenth arrow while he was passing the ninth post in line. It shattered the disc, and at once Sidacai turned in the saddle. There was another arrow nocked to his bow. He let fly, and it zipped through the air past Jehan's head.

'He meant to miss,' C'zinsit said. He reached for Jehan's bridle.

If Jehan heard, he paid no attention. He pulled the bay into a curvet and let her go. The st'lyan charged up the range.

Sidacai was reining in, turning the skewbald. Unhurriedly he took another arrow out of the case at his saddlebow and nocked it. Again the shot flew past Jehan's head, making him duck.

Orcadai swore in a high clear voice. He ran to his st'lyan and wrenched his bow out of its case, then reached for an arrow. C'zinsit took three or four quick paces and caught his arm. 'He isn't trying to kill him,' he said. 'If he was, Jehan would be dead by now.'

The distance between Sidacai and Jehan was closing rapidly. Still Sidacai seemed unconcerned. He jammed the bow back into its case, and then kicked the skewbald into a canter. They closed on one another.

Jehan was setting himself to ram Sidacai. Smoothly Sidacai switched leads. The skewbald altered direction without a falter. The st'lyan ran past one another. Jehan reached out to grasp Sidacai's arm, and he missed.

Sidacai's animal was moving easily, and it was not hard for him to rein around. He spurred directly at Jehan as he pulled the bay around, and Jehan was thrown out of the saddle. He rolled in the dust, and then got to his feet.

Orcadai pushed the end of his bow back into the

mouth of its case. 'If they don't kill one another,' he observed, 'it won't be for want of trying.'

'We can stop it if we have to,' C'zinsit said. He let go of Orcadai's arm and they stood together, watching.

Alexei thought that C'zinsit was being a shade optimistic. Sidacai was riding a tight circle around Jehan, taunting him. 'Are you hurt, Merkut?' he shouted. 'I said I could find a way to beat you.' He veered in suddenly and charged Jehan down, knocking him off his feet. Jehan rolled away from the skewbald's hooves, and he got to one knee. Sidacai hauled the st'lyan's head round, preparing to charge again. At once Jehan came up off the ground. He took two running paces and flung himself at Sidacai, catching him around the waist, hauling him out of the saddle.

Sidacai landed on one shoulder. There was a surprised look on his face.

Jehan pulled himself into the saddle of the skewbald. He reined around. 'Are you hurt, Sidacai?' he jeered. 'Tell me about it.'

'Now he'll kill him,' C'zinsit said.

'Who?' Orcadai's head came round. 'Sidacai? Jehan?'

C'zinsit spat to one side. 'Either,' he said, and gave a harsh laugh.

Alexei expected Jehan to ride Sidacai down, but instead Jehan rode off a little way. Then he uncased the bow which was strapped to the skewbald's saddle and nocked an arrow. He loosed without seeming to take aim, and the shaft whipped past Sidacai's head.

Sidacai got slowly to his feet. There was an odd look on his face, as if he did not care now what happened.

Jehan loosed another arrow. It plucked at the sleeve of Sidacai's tunic. Orcadai swore. 'He'll use

Sidacai for target practice if we let him continue,' he said.

C'zinsit compressed his lips. 'A moment ago you were ready to kill him yourself,' he pointed out. 'Let them settle it, and then we can have peace for a while.'

The troopers crowding the sidelines were quiet now, watching to see what Jehan intended to do. Jehan took an arrow out of the open case. He nocked it but did not draw the bow. Instead he kicked his feet out of the stirrups, and then sat gazing at Sidacai. Sidacai stared back, his arms hanging loose at his sides.

There was a moment when Alexei was sure that Jehan meant to end it by killing Sidacai. Then Jehan slid suddenly out of the saddle. He shot the arrow into the ground at Sidacai's feet, and then he turned, raising his arms. 'I call you all to witness,' he shouted. 'This man owes me his life.'

A murmur of comment ran round the crowd.

'Can he do that?' C'zinsit turned.

Kadan moved from one foot to the other, and then back again. He looked up. 'It's according to the law,' he said. 'You know Sidacai fired first.'

Jehan dropped the bow on the ground, and then he turned his back on Sidacai and walked to the place where the bay was cropping the grass at the end of the range. When he had mounted again, he rode away.

Sidacai got drunk, and stayed drunk for three days. On the third day Alexei rode up to Sidacai's house, knowing that something would have to be done. The house was in a narrow street away from the centre of the city. The stonework was grimy and uncared for, and there were pigs rooting in the garbage which was heaped in places along the street. All Sidacai's servants except one woman had deserted him. In his drunken anger he had raged and thrown furniture. Pieces of a smashed chair lay in the yard outside the door, and there was a broken bow lying in the hallway. Sidacai was sprawled on his back across a couch in a room on the ground floor. The carpet and all the hangings stank of wine and k'miss and vomit. Sidacai slept with his mouth open, snoring. His clothes were greasy and stained with sweat and spilled wine.

'Name of God.' Alexei wrinkled his nose in disgust. He turned and stared at the woman. 'How long has he been like this?'

The woman was slim and had long dark hair. She gave Alexei a look. 'Since yesterday. Before that he was able to walk.'

'He should be in bed.'

She shrugged. 'The bedrooms are all up there.' She gestured in the direction of the upper floor of the house. 'He fell downstairs, and I could not carry him.'

The servants who had run off had taken refuge with Burun. Alexei looked at the woman, wondering why she had stayed. She was an eastern Alan, he thought, with a brown skin and shining dark eyes. She returned his stare boldly.

Sidacai thrashed and muttered unintelligibly in his sleep. Alexei rolled Sidacai onto his side, moving his arm so that he could not turn onto his back again. The carpet under the couch was cheap stuff. The woman saw him staring at it. 'When it is too dirty, I take it out and burn it,' she said. 'He gets drunk. Then he gets sick, and after that he wakes up again for a while – long enough to get drunk again.'

The smell in the room was enough to make Alexei want to hold his breath. 'I'll send you some slaves. Take it up and get rid of it. Get rid of everything. Burn it all.' He gestured at Sidacai. 'When you have help, get him upstairs. Don't give him anything more to drink.'

She raised her eyebrows. 'He'll beat me.'

'No he won't. Tell him it's my order. Heat some food and make him eat it.'

Probably she shared Sidacai's bed, and that was why she had stayed. Alexei looked out through the open window. The troopers of his escort were loitering beside the gate, and serving women from the house next door had come out to flirt with them.

The smell in the room was unbearable. Alexei lifted a hand to his nose, and he gagged at the stale odour which had come from touching Sidacai in order to move him onto his side. He turned. 'I'll come again tomorrow. Clean up this mess. Send to me if you need more help, or if Sidacai gives you any trouble.'

The woman smiled knowingly. 'I can manage him.'

Alexei frowned. He brushed past the woman out of the door.

In the yard there was a well. He stopped and washed his hands at it. Every time he took a breath he could smell the vomit and filth in which Sidacai had lain. It was in his hair, Alexei thought, and clung to his clothes, and he knew he would have to wash and change to rid himself of it.

The area which Alexei supposed ought to be termed the *Sunstealer*'s machine space was in the process of being decked over so that the arrangement for the power source could be installed. The problem so far as Alexei was concerned was that he was not sure how a space-age steam engine should look. Certainly what was now sitting on the lower deck of the vessel was nothing like the primitive affair which Alexei

301

himself had designed and built several months earlier. He had seen steam in use only on New Georgia, a world of the Empire which had an agricultural economy, and which could afford as a result little in the way of advanced technology. New Georgia was a curiosity – the kind of place the Imperial nobility visited because its people were quaint, and maintained outmoded traditions and customs. They used steam to power farm machinery, and steam engines were to be found in the cloth mills. The machines were crude and cumbersome, and what lay in the *Sunstealer*'s engine space bore no similarity to them.

Alexei was sure that the moving parts of the layout worked, because he had insisted that the shafts and linkages be dry tested prior to installation. There was a single propeller shaft to which two engines were connected through camshafts and wheels moved by pistons. The pistons, provided that steam could be generated to operate them, would turn the shaft. If one set of pistons was disengaged the remaining set would still provide sufficient power to propel the vessel, although at a much reduced speed.

Generating the steam, that was the problem, Alexei thought. The boilers on the deck below were only vaguely similar to those he had seen on New Georgia – upon which he had based his own design. Essentially a boiler consisted of a tank divided into two chambers. Water was contained in one, and steam was built up under pressure in the other, and was released by valves to power the pistons. The *Sunstealer*'s boilers were rather more advanced, having a set of recirculation chambers – basically a system of tubing wound around the tank inside a metal skin to provide for the re-use of steam and to minimise water loss.

The thermal efficiency of the design was probably

quite high, Alexei thought. His principal doubt lay in the fact that where there should have been a firebox he could see only the bulbous projection which was the base of the tank. This was being surrounded by what to Alexei's eye appeared to be porous cladding – a mixture of clay and some kind of fibre. The whole affair had been moulded, and lay at present in an insulated cupula which had been lowered to the deck below the boilers. Further sections of insulated casing lay stacked in rows against a bulkhead awaiting completion of the work. A long copper tube lined with a hard ceramic substance led from the centre of each casing, and Alexei knew that it was through these that the heat from the reflectors was to be projected.

The reflectors remained to be constructed. Perhaps it was this more than anything – and the resulting lack of evidence that the system would produce an effective and controllable heat source – which was at the root of Alexei's continuing scepticism. His only experience with the conversion of light energy to heat related to lasers. The properties and uses of sunstones seemed to be totally unconnected. According to the Sechem the ability of a sunstone to produce a single emission depended upon precise calculation of the internal angles of the facets cut on it, and was governed by its unique reflective and refractive indices. The confidence with which the explanation was provided was not reassuring. It was hard for Alexei to accept that a culture which was capable of being considered otherwise quite primitive had mastered scientific knowledge which far exceeded that owned by the Empire.

The carpenters were securing the last of the deck timbers in place. There was only an open hatchway left. Alexei stared down into it.

The shafts and the other moving parts of the vessel's system of propulsion had been milled, and they gleamed. The Yek capability for producing high-quality steel for military purposes had been turned effortlessly to the manufacture of machine parts. The milling had been achieved by a process so archaic that Alexei would not have believed the results had he not seen them. Lathes turned by water power – or when that was unavailable by treadmills moved by oxen – were such a ridiculous notion that they defied belief. In fact all the work was of a high standard – nothing like Imperial technology of course – but the fact did not please Alexei. Instead it made him uncomfortable. He had anticipated technology which would be crude and unsophisticated. The Yek, however, had applied machine principles with the same lack of fuss with which they did nearly everything else. From Alexei's point of view the vessel's engines would be a techno-logical leap forward – provided they worked. So far as the Sechem were concerned, the application of their knowledge was nothing out of the ordinary.

Alexei frowned. Either the system of propulsion designed by the Sechem would work, or it would not. In the meantime he had other things to worry about. He strode along the deck to the bow and looked over.

The strakes had been nailed down and coated with sealant now, and an outer covering of copper sheeting had been fastened into place. The copper covered the timbers to a height of more than three-quarters of the way up the hull, and a staging had been erected round the bow to allow men to scribe lines onto the copper prior to filling them with paint. Alexei would have hesitated to admit that the weight of the ship and its contents had been something which had occurred to him only after the keel had been laid. The shipwrights of course were confident that the vessel would float. For his part Alexei had not been satisfied until he had completed the calculations which had also provided the height from the base of the keel to the lines now being marked on both sides of the bow. The lines served to indicate what amounted to the vessel's seaworthiness. When it was overloaded, water would cover the uppermost line. In a heavy sea there would be a risk that the ship would sink or capsize.

The shipwrights were unimpressed by the precaution, but Alexei was proud of his idea. All that was necessary now was for everything taken aboard the ship to be weighed. It was a practice which had met with a degree of opposition – probably only the Sechem had understood the reasoning behind the concept – but because Alexei's authority came from the Kha-Khan there were now scales at the foot of every gangway.

The gem cutter was a thin, hook-nosed Keraistani with a fringe of greasy black beard which ran under his chin and up across his cheeks. Neither the condition of his gown nor the state of his workshop suggested that he might be accustomed to dealing with articles of value. The sunstone in the stand in front of him was a honey-gold piece of luminescence, completely unfaceted, and Alexei guessed that the gem had been found on the bed of a river.

Most sunstones were dug from limestone. At some time in the history of Tarvaras – several million years ago so far as Alexei could make out – there had existed a freshwater lifeform not unlike a small jellyfish. As these had died they had sunk into the ooze of pools and riverbeds. Erosion and alteration in the paths of watercourses had resulted in the deposition of other material on top of the ooze. Eventually the pools had dried out and the layers had been

305

compressed tighter and tighter until the ooze had become limestone, and the entombed creature a lump of dense golden-coloured crystal the size of a ch'ban bean. A sunstone started life smooth, but many became chipped or faceted by nature before they were found, either as a result of exposure to the elements or because of the movement of the parent rock. They were not particularly hard – not as hard as diamond certainly – but their colour and rarity were enough to make them valuable. A sunstone attracted even the smallest amount of light, and glowed except in total darkness.

The cutter blew fine chalk onto the surface of the stone to reveal the presence of flaws and striations. At his side there was a diagram showing the precise angle to which the facets on the stone were to be cut. A three-dimensional grid of wires inside a metal frame lay on top of the diagram, and matched it perfectly. Alexei had already seen one stone cut, and he had noted how as each sliver was shaved from the stone the result was compared with the grid. The cutter's only aid to close vision appeared to be an arrangement like a pair of telescopes mounted on a headband. Thus far four stones had been lost – shattered by badly positioned strokes of the cutting tool. A hundred more lay in a wooden tray on the bench. A covering of heavy cloth had been arranged across the tray.

So far as Alexei could see the precaution was unnecessary. The cut stones glittered visibly when they were exposed to the light, but they did not appear dangerous. He glanced at Parin. 'Can a stone create so much heat?'

The cutter's head came up. He looked round.

The Sechem seemed to sense the movement. He said, 'Juba, show the Khan.'

It was clear that the cutter disapproved. He sniffed audibly. 'As you wish.' He picked up a pair of tongs from the bench, and then extracted a single stone from beneath the cover. It gleamed brightly, but the result was otherwise disappointing. Alexei gave Parin a look.

There was a candle in a holder on the wall. The cutter crossed to it, and he brought the tongs up towards the flame, turning his head away as he did so. A beam of light seemed to shoot from the stone. It struck the wall beside the door. The cutter was already lowering the tongs. He put the stone back in the tray and covered it again.

Alexei examined the wall where the light had struck. There was a burnmark at shoulder height. He touched it, and took his hand away quickly. The stonework was hot enough to raise a blister. A rash of similar spots on the wall showed where the cutter had tested other stones. Alexei raised his eyebrows, impressed.

The cutter was already concentrating once more on the stone in the holder on the bench. The holder was a tripod of hardwood, and the stone had been cemented into it with a mixture of gum and resin. The cutter seemed to glance for only a moment at the diagram, and then he lifted the cutting tool – an instrument like a cleaver – placed it on top of the stone, and struck it sharply with a wooden mallet.

Crack!

A shaving slid down the face of the sunstone onto the bench.

Crack! Crack! Crack!

The Keraistani was working swiftly. The base of the tripod was fastened to a turntable set in the bench, and with each stroke the cutter kicked a release beside his foot, freeing the cam which turned the table so that it moved round by a tenth of a revolution. The cutter's shoulders were hunched, his expression intent, and he was breathing shallowly. A drop of perspiration had formed on the end of his nose, but he made no attempt to brush it away.

Crack!

Another shaving slid off the face of the stone. There was a pile of them heaped around the base of the stand – tiny slivers which gleamed and glittered in the light thrown by the candle on the wall, each of them worth a fortune.

The workshop was dim – the shutters had been drawn, and only candles and shaded lamps provided illumination. Alexei frowned. He had been impatient with the cutter's progress – fifty or more stones remained uncut. Now the brief demonstration of sunstone power had provided an inkling of the risks the man was running while he worked. A stray shaft of light striking the cut face of the stone in the holder might be thrown in any direction – the cutter for instance could lose an eye.

Alexei reflected that it was often the case that the extraction of power from the forces of nature was accompanied by danger to those who worked to harness it. It had been thus with nuclear energy, and it was still the case now that plasma fusion was the most common power source. Alexei made a face. The danger was the price man paid for his mastery of the universe. Power was necessary to conquest. Without it space could not be travelled, or the peoples of the inhabited worlds governed.

Suddenly Alexei became aware that he himself was vulnerable should a beam be emitted from the stone. He moved back, and on an instinct glanced round. Parin was standing in a corner of the workshop – that corner to which he had walked on entering the room.

308

Apparently the Sechem had known of the risk, but he had chosen to say nothing.

'You keep few women in your house.' Burun stretched across the table for the k'miss flask.

Alexei was cleaning a sword. He ran a soft cloth along the blade, taking care not to touch the honed edge. Then he turned. 'They distract me.'

Burun grinned. 'I think that's why most men keep them,' he said.

'– And you thought, considering my reputation, that I would have a house filled with them,' Alexei continued equably. He slid the sword back into its scabbard. 'Khan, I'm too busy. In any case, if someone wants to kill me, that would be the most obvious way.'

'Hunh.' Burun nodded. 'The thought had occurred to me likewise. And so you will take none with you when you sail?'

It was customary for serving women, usually slaves, to accompany the baggage trains of land expeditions. Women served as cooks to the army and occasionally they became soldiers' companions, although they were not camp followers in any true sense of the word. Alexei shook his head. 'I can't think of any reason why I should.'

Burun had arrived halfway through the afternoon, and he had been talking about nothing in particular ever since. He had already emptied one flask of k'miss, and now he was starting on another. Alexei watched his eyes, but he could see no sign that the amount Burun had had to drink was affecting him. There was wine on the table, and Alexei poured a little into a cup. He drank, wondering when Burun was going to come to the point of his visit.

Hooves clattered suddenly in the square in front of

the house. Alexei got to his feet and looked out of the window. Sidacai was just dismounting. He let his reins trail loose, and stamped past the sentry through the front door. He pounded up the stairs and came into the room.

Burun turned at the sound.

'Sidacai.'

Sidacai stopped in his tracks. He stared at Burun, and then looked past him at Alexei.

A trooper was catching Sidacai's st'lyan. Alexei turned away from the window, leaving the shutter open. He met Sidacai's stare.

Sidacai threw himself into a chair. He said, 'Khan, your grandson has offended me.'

'Really?' Burun looked amused. 'What is it this time?'

The front of Sidacai's tunic was wet. He crossed his legs, then uncrossed them. Suddenly he leapt up. 'He drank before me. He's always been careful before this, but today it was as if he paid me no heed. I am the grandson of a Kha-Khan – what is he compared to that?'

Alexei sat down carefully. 'The great-grandson of one?' he suggested.

Burun emptied his cup.

'My honour is in this.' Sidacai walked around the room, one hand in his belt. He turned. 'You see?'

Alexei met Burun's eyes for a moment, and then he turned and nodded gravely.

Sidacai stopped beside the window. He stared out. 'He did it in front of everyone,' he said. 'I can't let him get away with it. Before I could have dealt with it, but I have been humiliated. Now no one supports me.' He looked at Burun. 'I see your hand in this, Khan. It's your fault I had to run.'

The cup in Burun's hand was a chalice with a wide

310

bowl and tiny sculpted feet. He rolled it between his palms and then set it aside. Then he looked up. 'If Jehan has humiliated you, you have no one to blame but yourself. As for your rank, both you and he are descendants of the Ancestor.'

Sidacai glared. Then his head came round. He looked at Alexei. 'Let me stay here,' he said. 'Jehan will have me chained if he can get hold of me. You brought me here. You owe me this.'

The reasoning amused Alexei, and he showed his teeth. 'I do not.'

Sidacai's shoulders sagged. Before he could speak again more st'lyan galloped into the square. When Alexei looked out he saw Orcadai and C'zinsit getting down out of the saddle. He went out of the room and down the stairs.

Orcadai said, 'Has Sidacai come here?'

'A few moments ago.' Alexei nodded.

The part of the square which was visible through the open door was filling with mounted troopers of Jehan's personal guard. Orcadai gave C'zinsit a meaningful glance.

C'zinsit said, 'Did Sidacai tell you –'

'He told me. Sidacai is a guest in my house.'

Orcadai looked nonplussed. 'He cursed Jehan to his face, and knocked his cup from his hand. Jehan was at his own fire, and he has ordered him taken.'

Alexei put his hands in his belt. He stared at the floor between Orcadai's feet, and then looked up. 'What, will you use force? I will not permit it.' He pushed past C'zinsit and slammed the door in the faces of the troopers who were coming up the front steps. Then he turned and set his back against it. 'Well?'

C'zinsit glanced back up the stairway. 'Let us tell Jehan that Sidacai is in your custody,' he appealed. 'That will satisfy him.'

311

'Sidacai can come and go as he pleases,' Alexei replied. 'He is my guest for so long as he chooses to accept my hospitality, but he is not my prisoner.'

Burun was coming out onto the head of the stairs. Orcadai said, 'Jehan has sent to my father. Let me tell him that you are holding Sidacai for him. It will all be forgotten as soon as we sail.'

Alexei looked past Orcadai at Burun. He gave Orcadai a hard stare. 'Tell him now,' he said.

Orcadai spun round. He saw Burun, and his mouth opened, then closed again.

'Go and tell Jehan that Sidacai is staying here as my guest,' Alexei said. He went past them up the stairs, then stopped and looked back. 'Tell him your father was my guest when Sidacai arrived.'

C'zinsit put a foot on the bottom step. 'You can't –' he started.

Alexei looked pointedly at C'zinsit's foot. 'Did I invite you into my house? Get out of here.'

Orcadai took C'zinsit by the arm, and they went outside. The men of Jehan's escort were crowded around the door. They shouted questions, and Alexei heard C'zinsit answer in a high, offended voice.

Burun waited until Alexei had reached the top of the stairs. He glanced at the door of the room. 'Sidacai was sure you were going to surrender him,' he said.

'Are you going to tell me I should?' Alexei readied himself for an argument.

'Oh.' Burun smiled, and he held up his hands. 'This isn't my quarrel.' He went downstairs. At the bottom he turned. 'If Jehan has sent to me to judge it,' he said, 'I will do so fairly.'

Alexei shrugged. He waited until Burun had gone outside, and then re-entered the room. Sidacai was standing beside the open window. He turned. 'Khan, I will cause you no trouble,' he said.

'That's very kind of you.' Alexei picked up his wine cup. He drank and set it down again. 'Don't mistreat my servants, and you will retain my good will. If you want a woman, send for your own.'

Sidacai's head went back. After a moment he nodded. 'You are going to enjoy this.'

'I'm going to try,' Alexei said.

Jehan was sitting on a stool a few places down the table from Burun when they entered the room. He gave Sidacai a long look, and then he stood up. 'This is an insult,' he said.

Sidacai was starting forward. Alexei put one hand on his arm, restraining him. He gave Burun a look.

Burun said, 'Sit down, Noyon.'

'No. This man has abused me to my face.'

Burun had already lowered his head again. There was a letter in his hand, its fastenings dripping with seals. He glanced up. 'This is a kuriltai,' he said, 'and I summoned everyone to attend it. If you want me to judge a complaint, then send to me with your case. This is not the time. Now sit down.'

Jehan subsided, crimson. The officers to left and right of him sat silent, open-mouthed at the brusqueness of Burun's tone. Beyond them sat Orcadai and C'zinsit. They stared at Burun, and then met one another's eyes and shrugged.

Alexei had assumed that the meeting would be an artifice to allow Jehan's grievance against Sidacai to be aired. Now that he knew that it was not, he felt able to relax. He shoved Sidacai into a vacant chair, and then sat down himself.

Sidacai glared across the table at Jehan. He growled deep in his throat.

Burun glanced up. 'Stop fighting,' he said. 'We have too much to do. Sidacai, behave yourself.'

Jehan was leaning forward, tensed. He sat back slowly. Orcadai was summoning a servant to serve wine. He glanced past Jehan at Alexei and grinned. The tension seemed to ease. Burun cleared his throat and said, 'I have a letter from Kinsai which you should all know about.'

One of the seals on the letter was Artai's. Alexei stared at it. Burun was rolling and unrolling the parchment between his hands. He raised his eyes.

'I hope the construction of your vessel is well advanced,' he said, and looked in Alexei's direction. 'Artai is coming here to see it launched.'

Orcadai's hand with a full cup of wine in it was halfway to his mouth. He jerked, and the wine spilled. 'The Kha-Khan is leaving Kinsai?' He shook his head. 'It's unheard of.'

Burun glanced towards the disturbance. Orcadai sat back in his chair. 'It's not unknown for the Kha-Khan to make the progress of his domain,' Burun said prosaically. 'And of course Daijin was more at home in a yurt than he was in his palace. Even Arjun commanded his own early campaigns.'

The commander of Jehan's guard leaned forward. 'That was before we ruled the world, Khan,' he objected. 'Nogai never moved out of Kinsai after he was enthroned.'

'Maybe he never felt the need,' Sidacai observed cheerfully. He picked up a pear from a bowl on the table in front of him, extended his talons and ran them around it, peeling it.

'It's not for us to question the motives of the Kha-Khan,' Burun said shortly. He laid the letter aside. 'What is necessary is that we make suitable preparations, and to that end I am sending orders for the second of the tumans camped at Pesth to be detached to Pantai. The roads along Artai's path will require to be guarded. This city is not Kinsai, but it must be made to appear that it is for the length of the Kha-Khan's visit.'

That the news of Artai's intentions was as much of a surprise to Burun as it was to his audience was already clear. Alexei caught Burun's eye. 'How much time have we?'

'About ten days,' Burun said. 'The Kha-Khan's letter says that he does not intend to travel in state. That means, I suspect, simply that he will not bring the whole court. A mounted party would arrive in a much shorter time of course. I think the Kha-Khan's escort will have litters and carts to contend with.'

'You're saying that they were about to leave when the letter was despatched.' Jehan raised his head. 'Why weren't we warned sooner?'

Burun shrugged. 'As to that, Noyon, I have no information. Maybe the decision was taken upon an instant.'

'Or maybe Artai hoped to take us by surprise,' Orcadai said sourly.

'Hardly that.' Burun produced a grim smile.

Jotan was in Kinsai and should have sent warning, Alexei thought. There was the possibility that Jotan himself had not known of course. Artai was wilful, and a sudden whim would not be uncharacteristic. Alexei considered the question, and he wondered how crucial it would be to Burun's power if Jotan were to be displaced from Artai's confidence.

C'zinsit stood. He came round the end of the table and bent down beside Alexei. 'Will the ship be ready in time?'

Alexei took a breath. 'Probably.' He met Burun's eyes across the table as he spoke, and Burun nodded expressionlessly.

*

315

'You look as if you are weighed down by the cares of the world,' Burun said. 'Is it Artai's visit which concerns you?'

Alexei thought that the question was unnecessary, and he allowed his expression to reflect his feelings. Burun's mouth twitched, and he looked away.

The reflectors were encased in containers which looked like inverted clam shells. Teams of wrights were lowering them into position on top of a framework which already supported the heat tubes leading down to the boilers. Parin was directing the operation, and his robes were grimy with dust. Wood shavings clung to the hem of his gown, and there was paint in his hair. The Sechem checked the alignment of the holes for the bolts which were to be used to connect the tubes to the casings, then slid them into place. He stepped back and nodded. A pair of brawny engineers strained on the bolts to tighten them.

'If you had to, you could launch today.' Burun rested one hand on the bulwark at his side. He did not look at Alexei as he spoke.

Alexei sniffed. 'That's true,' he said. 'Launching the ship is not the problem. Raising steam is what concerns me.'

Burun's expression did not alter. He turned his head slowly. 'Surely you don't question the Sechem's designs?'

The bolts had been tightened. Parin was walking around the assembly, examining it.

'The whole matter is outside my competence, Khan,' Alexei said. 'I can confirm that sunstones which have been cut in a certain way reflect a single beam of light, and that the beam gives out heat. As for this –' He gestured at the reflector mounting. '– We shall see.'

Parin turned. 'Khan, we're ready,' he called.

The open hatchway which gave access to the *Sunstealer*'s engine space was at Alexei's feet. Alexei looked down. The engineers were Suristani, slim fair-haired men with pale blue eyes. They stood in a circle around the foot of the companionway. Alexei waved to them. 'Ready.'

The Suristani were as far from the boilers and heat tubes as the confines of the compartment would allow. Alexei smiled grimly. The only people who were completely confident about the performance of the reflectors were the Sechem. Of the rest, the spectators down on the slipway and festooning the framework which was still erected around the vessel were those who suspected that the power of the sunstones would set the ship on fire. Those on deck probably thought that nothing very special was about to happen. The presence of the Suristani was essential, and so they had no choice about where they stood.

Alexei looked for the engineer whose task it was to be to operate the reflectors. He nodded to him. 'Very well.'

The reflector controls were handwheels connected to the gearing on the hinged side of each casing. The engineer was a small dark man who wore a heavy leather coat and a pair of padded gauntlets. He cranked the wheel mounted on the side of the star-board casing, averting his eyes. The two halves of the casing cracked open, then began to move steadily apart. Nothing else happened.

A few of the men in the crowd on the deck were already displaying expressions which suggested that they had known all along that the demonstration would be a failure. Someone made an amused comment, and several of those standing near him laughed.

317

There was a gap about a hand's-breadth wide in the mouth of the casing now. Suddenly the centre of the reflector was exposed, and a beam of light the thickness of a man's arm sprang into being. It entered the mouth of the open heat tube.

Alexei had not realised that there would be any sound. He guessed that some freak of the reflective effect of the sunstones was causing the emitted wave to vibrate, because the beam was accompanied by a faint but persistent noise similar to high-frequency radio transmission. He swallowed to relieve the pressure on his ears, but the sound continued.

It hurt his eyes to look at the short span of the beam which was visible between the open casing and the mouth of the heat tube. Parin had his hand up to block the light. After a moment he turned. 'Khan, we ought to open the reflector fully to complete the test, but the light and the noise will both be unpleasant I think.'

Alexei thought of suggesting that the most important element of the test would be the production of steam in the boiler. He glanced down through the hatchway. The gauges mounted on the boiler tubes were primitive – floats moving up and down in graded tubes – and one of the Suristani was examining them. It was too soon of course. Raising steam New Georgian style usually took several hours, and even with a heat source which seemed to be so immediately effective, there would be nothing for some time. A Suristani boilerman put a hand casually on the boiler casing, yelped, and snatched it away again.

Obviously heat was reaching the boiler. Alexei was glad that he had insisted on insulation and metal shielding on the deck and across the bulkheads around the boiler space. He looked up at the Sechem.

'I agree that there ought to be a complete test,' he said. 'But first you must do something about that noise, and there should be screens on both sides of the reflectors to protect men's eyes.'

Parin appeared to consider the point. 'If we do that, Khan,' he objected, 'less light will enter the reflectors.' He looked unhappy about the prospect.

Alexei estimated that normal steaming would require the kind of heat to the boilers which could be generated by reflectors no more than a quarter open. The temperature being produced by the sunstones was impossible to measure of course, but it was greater by far than he had anticipated. 'In that case the strength of the beam will be less,' he observed calmly. He gave Parin a look. 'It is enough, I think, for our purpose.'

Parin opened his mouth as if to argue, and then closed it again. He bowed. 'The Khan wishes,' he said.

Alexei nodded and turned away, hiding his satisfaction. In one sense the words were little more than a formula commonly used to acknowledge a command. In another however they signified Parin's submission – his acceptance of the fact that it was for Alexei to direct, and for others, the Sechem included, to obey.

Burun rubbed his ears. 'Name of God,' he said. 'I should not like to endure that for too long.'

Other spectators were showing signs of a reaction to the sound now. Alexei nodded. 'I hope we can muffle it somehow. The mouth of each reflector has to be open to admit the light, and so it may be difficult.'

The engineer beside the reflector was cranking the control wheel. As the mouth of the casing closed the beam vanished and the noise ceased.

'You must be relieved that it works,' Burun said. He turned and walked slowly down the length of the

319

deck, and the men crowded there moved hastily out of the way. 'How much remains to be done?'

There was very little in fact. Alexei summoned up a mental review of the progress which had been reported to him up to that morning. He gestured at a mess of sawdust and wood shavings which obscured part of the planking. 'Some cleaning. The carpenters have finished fitting stalls in the hold. We tried lifting one of Orcadai's st'lyan yesterday, and the hoist and its slings worked perfectly. The crew and escort quarters have to be finished still. As for the rest –' He wrinkled his nose. 'There are bound to be small problems we won't discover until after launching, but the rest is a matter of provisioning and moving gear aboard. If Artai was not coming, I would launch tomorrow, and we would be ready to leave in two or three days.'

'Somewhat in advance of Artai's arrival,' Burun remarked.

Alexei gave him a sharp look. 'Maybe we should just go,' he said after a moment.

There was no one within earshot. Burun took another pace, then met Alexei's stare. His expression was placid. 'Maybe you should,' he said. 'Will you?'

Alexei snorted softly. 'No.'

Burun laughed. 'I didn't think so,' he said.

Artai's advance baggage train was over a verst in length. It emerged out of the tree-lined fold in the hills onto the coastal plain, dust hanging in the air above it like the cloud of a summer storm.

Alexei released his reins and let them hang loose across his st'lyan's neck. The st'lyan was a light chestnut with a blond mane. It shook its head from side to side, and then began to crop at the tufts of short grass on the crest of the knoll upon which they had halted. Troopers from one of Burun's tumans were spurring across the flat to intercept the head of the train. There was no room for such a great assembly anywhere close to the outskirts of Pantai, and so it had been decided to camp them on level ground to the east, a space which lay between the city and the surrounding hills. A full tuman had worked for two days and a night to clear the low scrub from the ground, and they had already marked out sites for wagon parks and tethering lines.

Jehan walked his bay forward. He raised himself in the stirrups, and then sat down in the saddle again. 'It will be near nightfall before they are camped,' he said. 'Damn Artai. He should have stayed in his palace.'

The rumble of cart wheels was still just a murmur in the distance. Alexei stripped off his gauntlets. 'I thought it was an offence to curse the name of the Kha-Khan,' he observed mildly.

'Hah.' Jehan spat into the dirt. 'Then it is an offence which every man under arms in Pantai has been committing for some days past.'

The men who had been engaged in brush clearing in particular had been quite vocal. Alexei grinned and said nothing. The first of the guides riding down on the column of carts were wheeling to pair off with the foreriders of the train's escort. Gradually the head of the column began to turn to follow the tree line north.

Jehan sidestepped his st'lyan until he was at Alexei's side. 'Tell me why you sided with Sidacai against me,' he said.

Alexei raised a hand to block out the sun, peering to make out the detail on the banners ahead of the carts. He heard Jehan move impatiently at his side, and turned his head and smiled. 'Noyon, I did no such thing,' he said.

321

'Call it what you will.' Jehan gestured angrily. 'When I would have taken him, you gave him shelter. When I sent to you to demand his arrest, you refused me.'

'Oh.' Alexei grinned. 'You know very well your request was not lawful. Would you have me break the Yasa for love of you?' He saw Jehan scowl.

A herd of pure white mares ran out onto the plain, their herders splashes of darker colour among them.

'Sidacai dishonoured me.' Jehan gathered his reins as if to ride off. 'He deserves to be punished.'

'You want to humiliate him to make a point,' Alexei said. 'He will be useless to me after that.'

Jehan compressed his lips. He looked away, and then back again. 'Tell me what use he is now. I have told you that you cannot trust him. He hates us all.'

Alexei suppressed the urge to display his irritation. 'You know that Sidacai is detailed to command of the embassy's escort,' he said patiently. 'True, it is a task which could be carried out as well perhaps by another; however, it was the will of your grandfather that Sidacai be given it. Have you asked him why he wanted Sidacai freed?'

If Jehan asked Burun for an explanation, it would be the same as admitting that he was unable to work out the answer for himself. Burun's interest in Sidacai was no whim, that was certain. Burun never did anything without a good reason.

'You know I have not.' Jehan shook his head.

A stir of movement to the right caught Alexei's eye. The grass of the plain was as high as a st'lyan's shoulder in places, and through a sea of it came Orcadai and C'zinsit. Orcadai had a buck draped across the front of his saddle. He waved to Jehan and rode on.

Jehan's expression was a study in disquiet. 'I would

I were like my uncles,' he said, low-voiced. 'Their concerns are all hounds and hunting. How easily they pass the days.'

He does not trust Burun's motives, as I do not, Alexei thought. He laid a hand on Jehan's arm. 'Forget your quarrel with Sidacai,' he said. 'Heed me, and don't fight with him.'

'As well tell me not to breathe.' Jehan drew his arm away.

'Don't breathe.'

Jehan was silent for a moment. Then he gathered up his reins once more. 'Artai was right to make you a Khan.' He twitched the reins straightening them. 'Power becomes you. You use it well.'

It was not the answer Alexei had expected. He waited for Jehan to speak again.

A horn was sounding clear across the plain. A company of men on dun-coloured st'lyan trotted out of the tree line, then adjusted themselves until they were riding in a screen parallel to the carts.

'Artai might be persuaded to change his mind about freeing Sidacai,' Jehan said suddenly, his tone neutral.

Alexei frowned. 'I would take that ill, I think,' he responded.

'Oh.' Jehan's head came round, and he showed his teeth. 'I know.' He tapped his st'lyan with the toe of his boot, and moved sedately down off the knoll into the waving grass. The seed heads of the grasses were all shades of red and orange, and riding through them Jehan looked as if he was walking the bay through a sea of flame.

The pavilion at the centre of the temporary camp was far larger than any yurt Alexei had ever seen before. The framework alone was the height of four standing men, and in circumference it measured almost five hundred drem.

'I didn't know Artai had decided to move Kinsai,' C'zinsit observed sourly.

'Oh, well.' Burun produced an amused smile. 'It isn't quite the Golden Yurt. Just be thankful we weren't asked to provide the timbers.'

The floor which was being laid was of tongued and grooved ch'press planks, each marked with a number so that it could be placed correctly. Carpenters tapped each plank with wooden mallets until the markings matched, then pinned it to the cross struts of the underframe. The whole structure was complex, a masterpiece of design, and it occurred to Alexei to wonder if it had come out of store, or if it had been built specially for Artai's progress. He glanced at Burun.

'If this was made at Artai's command, then we should have received much more warning of his intent to visit us.'

Burun nodded thoughtfully. 'That's true.'

The fact that there were two pavilions rather than one added weight to the argument. As Artai moved from one camp to the next, the prefabricated palace which he left behind was torn apart and rushed ahead to a site which it was judged he would reach on the day following. In such a way he never arrived at a camp which was not prepared to receive him. It was a provision which had amazed and amused Burun's entourage when they had heard of it, and it further lowered Artai in their estimation. A Yek camp was always orderly and well-organised; however on the march everyone, Khans included, slept in the carts or in the open under the stars. Even the dignity of the Kha-Khan did not merit such care – for he was a man like other men, and expected to show at times an example.

Long strips of felt were being laced to the uprights now to provide the walls of inner chambers, and already the awnings of heavy treated linen were being swayed up above the whole area. The great panelled constructions of material were remarkable, and reminded Alexei of the kind of tents used by the Imperial circus. They were supported from thirty to forty metres off the ground by an intricate network of stays and cables, so that beneath them the occupants of the camp would be able to move and work in comfort through the hottest part of each day. Alexei remembered that parts of Imperial Knossos were covered by huge permaglass canopies floating on contragrav. The awnings above Artai's camp were held up only by strategically placed poles, but otherwise the similarity was amazing.

An officer on a piebald st'lyan came galloping in past the tent lines. He saw the guidon which denoted Burun's escort as he rode in under the shade of the main awning. At once he wrenched at his reins, bringing his mount to a shuddering halt. The st'lyan screamed and arched its neck. Its coat was caked with sweat. The officer was a Sihani, a clan which was a sept of the Darjin. He threw up one hand in salute.

'Lord, the Kha-Khan approaches!' he shouted dramatically.

'Oh?' Burun put one hand on his thigh. 'The last I heard it, Artai was half a day hence. Truly he must be coming like the wind for you to have ridden in such haste, and yet I hear no sound of horns or the cheers of men signifying his arrival.' He leaned forward, a patient smile on his face. 'Tell me,' he enquired, 'are you the Kha-Khan's own messenger, or some other man's dog?'

The officer flushed crimson. 'Lord, I serve Jotan Khan,' he said. 'The Kha-Khan is in the pass between

325

the hills which leads to this plain. I am to tell you that, also that he knows that you will wish to meet him.'

Burun showed his teeth. 'Why so I will.' He turned his head as if looking for someone, then swung round again. 'When he enters his camp.'

The Sihani looked outraged. He opened his mouth, then closed it again. Finally he saluted again, hauled his st'lyan's head round, and rode back the way he had come.

Alexei walked his st'lyan up to Burun's side. 'Was that wise?' he asked.

'Hah.' Burun tugged at one of his moustaches. 'If Artai wanted me to attend him, he should have said so. Probably he does not, but other men think I should.'

It was a neat point. Alexei drew his reins together between his fingers. 'The messenger was Jotan's,' he said.

'– And my son thinks there is something to be gained by flattering Artai,' Burun said. 'I know that.' He made a face. 'Maybe he is right. If you wish it, we will ride out to meet Artai.'

Alexei allowed the surprise to show on his face. 'Khan, don't lay it at my door. The message was not to me.'

'I see what you mean,' Burun said, as if the objection had not occurred to him before. 'In that case give me your counsel. Do you think I should go?'

Alexei pursed his lips. 'Khan,' he observed tartly, 'in this as in everything else, you will do whatever serves your interests best. What I think has nothing to do with it.'

Genuine amusement appeared in Burun's eyes, and after a moment he chuckled. 'How well you have come to know me,' he said. Then he reined around and rode off through the camp, his back to the direction from which Artai was approaching.

'It's like a festival,' Kadan said. A serving woman was passing, a basket full of freshly baked loaves balanced on one shoulder. Kadan reached out and plucked one, then rode on, chewing happily.

'I can think of better ways for the Kha-Khan to spend his tithes,' Jehan said. He eyed a line of petty officials, each of them gorgeously gowned in ivory silks, and frowned.

Whatever the exchequer spent, it was always replenished, Alexei thought. The economy of the Khanate was controlled by the law, and forbade profit in excess of an amount considered to be reasonable by the Khans, who did not themselves engage in trade and therefore had no vested interest. Every man was taxed a tenth of his assets in tribute, but since the tithes were spent back into the system, there was no imbalance.

The column which had wound its way into the camp an hour earlier had consisted principally of domestic servants and minor functionaries. Most of them had travelled either on carts or in litters supported between pairs of p'tar, and while the cooks and others had dispersed to their duties without incident, the chaos of the pecking order was only now being established. A secretary with a pill-box hat which bore the red button of his rank upon it was busily berating two clerks whose hats bore only a piping of blue. Sensing the st'lyan at his shoulder the secretary paused in mid-flow. He turned and bowed to Jehan, and then again to Alexei. Alexei nodded acknowledgement, but Jehan made a noise which was midway between disgust and exasperation.

'The best thing Arjun ever did was to limit the size

327

of the secretariat,' Jehan said loudly. 'Civil servants don't make anything – not even decisions. All they do is record what is said or done by others.'

Alexei edged the chestnut past a pile of tables which were being transferred into a long commissary tent. 'Surely some records are necessary?' he suggested gently.

Jehan made a face. 'Maybe,' he conceded. 'Although between men of good faith, a word should be enough.'

'I see.' Alexei met Jehan's stare innocently. '– And when men break faith with one another?'

'A man who breaks faith offends the Yasa,' Kadan quoted, 'and must be punished according to the magnitude of his crime.'

It was characteristic of Yek attitudes that contracts and agreements were more often verbal than written. 'On other worlds, everything is recorded,' Alexei said, and knew at once how Jehan would respond.

'What unhappy people they must be,' Jehan said, 'that cannot trust one another to keep their word. How can they expect to gain the trust of others, if they cannot trust themselves?'

In the space outside the great yurt were crowded the lesser Khans who had journeyed from places near Pantai. Behind them were guildsmen, and beyond them the troopers of the tuman which was not providing escort to Artai. Kadan stood in the stirrups and stared about. 'I don't see my father,' he said.

'Our father,' Alexei corrected. 'If he wrote to you that he was coming, then he will come. He will be with Jotan, I expect.'

'– Who will be with Artai,' Jehan said. He reined to the side to avoid a flat cart laden with strips of treated linen. 'In this press it will be a wonder if anyone can find anyone else.'

328

'It will sort itself out, I expect.' Kadan dusted crumbs from the front of his embroidered coat. His red hair had been freshly dressed that day, and the minor nobility who observed the Altun colouring bowed respectfully.

Alexei's escort was forcing a space in the crowd which now surrounded the spread awnings in front of the main tents. Alexei wheeled his st'lyan into it, debating. The choice was to remain for the moment mounted – giving an advantage of view over the heads of the other spectators which would be nullified as soon as Artai rode up because they would have to get down to bow to him – or to dismount, disposing themselves in comfort. In the latter case the slaves would be able to lay mats and carpets as soon as the st'lyan had been led away. Alexei glanced down at the already well-trampled grass and thought that he was not overjoyed by the prospect of performing the required prostration on such a surface. He kicked his feet free of the stirrups and slid from the saddle. A groom ran up. He took the chestnut's bridle, and began backing her up under the rear part of the awning. A group of minor court officials who had thought to obtain a privileged view of the Kha-Khan's arrival by coming through from the back of the tent were forced to scatter out of the way. The st'lyan screamed shrilly, tossed her head, then settled, nosing at the sack of oats which was held up by a sweating slave.

Jehan dismounted. He threw his reins to a trooper of his escort and then looked up at Kadan. 'If you would get down off that beast,' he said mildly, 'we might be able to arrange ourselves before Artai comes.'

Kadan's head came round. 'Cousin, how impatient you are.' He stepped out of the saddle onto a trestle

329

table. The table tilted, and Kadan jumped down.

'You forget you're my vassal,' Jehan said, eyeing Kadan ungraciously. 'You're supposed to obey me.'

Slaves were bringing carpets from the back of the tent. They unrolled them across the grass, crossing them in layers on top of stretchers of timber, and the troopers of Alexei's escort arranged themselves so that their lances formed a fence around the space so defined. Kadan stared away across the heads of the men who separated him from the main passage towards the great yurt, and then he turned. 'You don't keep me for my willingness to obey,' he said, and gave Jehan a grin. 'Here is your grandfather coming.'

Whatever retort Jehan was going to make, he seemed to change his mind. He looked where Kadan pointed and nodded. 'I see.'

Burun was riding a bay st'lyan, and was clad in a flowing black coat which had gold embroidery down each of the facing panels. His moustaches had been combed and oiled so that they gleamed, and for once one side did not look more sparse than the other. Behind Burun were the officers of his household, followed by a guard of troopers in black livery. Guidons and banners waved above their heads. Everyone bowed as they rode up through the crowd, and the off-duty troopers at the rear of the throng cheered and waved their arms.

'The show can begin now,' Jehan observed drily. 'The main attraction has arrived.'

Alexei chuckled. 'If your grandfather is here, Artai will not be far behind,' he said.

Jehan snorted softly. He gestured to a servant who stood with a tray on which were cups and flasks of wine and k'miss. 'Give me something to drink.'

The servant ducked his head. 'Yes, Noyon. Do you want wine or k'miss?'

Jehan glared. 'I'm a Merkut, not one of the effeminates of the Kha-Khan's court. Give me k'miss!'

The exchange was so uncharacteristic that Alexei laughed. Jehan was taking a cup from the servant's hand, and he turned, his expression frigid. 'Your pardon, Noyon,' Alexei said. 'But you reminded me there of your grandfather. I never knew you drink k'miss before.'

Jehan glowered for a moment, and then the harsh lines on his face softened, and he laughed and shook his head. 'You're right,' he said. He drank from the cup in his hand and made a face. 'I never had a taste for it until now.'

Burun walked his st'lyan into the space in the crowd in front of them. He stared at them for a moment, and then swung down out of the saddle. 'Grandfather, good afternoon,' Kadan said, his voice loud and clear across the tumult.

The bay had a horn which was gilded for about two-thirds of its length. At the sound of Kadan's voice it tossed its head, and the gilding caught the sunlight and glittered. Burun was adjusting the hang of his coat, a servant kneeling at his feet to remove his spurs. He raised his head, examining Kadan. Kadan looked back steadily.

The form of address had been correct, Alexei thought, for Burun was the father of Kadan's mother. It was not a title, however, which had been used publicly before.

Burun appeared to consider, and then at last he smiled. 'Good afternoon, Noyon,' he said.

He prefers men about him who are not afraid, Alexei thought, and wondered if Kadan had chosen the moment deliberately, or if it had been impulse which had caused him to speak.

A murmur of noise beyond the crowd increased

331

gradually so that it became identifiable as the echoes of cheers repeated upon one another.

'Artai,' Jehan said softly. He looked at the cup in his hand, and emptied it.

Burun glanced back over his shoulder, and then he turned and nodded. 'He would have been here sooner,' he said. 'But he wished to ride the last verst of the way.'

Someone made a rude noise, but Alexei could not tell if it was Jehan or Kadan, or maybe one of the young officers in the press behind them. Alexei maintained a neutral expression. Artai's progress from Kinsai had taken in all an extent of fifteen days, for Artai had travelled the greater part of the journey by litter.

The cheers were increasing steadily in volume. An officer of Burun's personal guard came across the carpets, Burun's lined cloak in his hands. A fresh wave of noise made him turn back for a moment. Then he held out the cloak, bowing. 'The Kha-Khan is coming, Lord. Hear how the people adore him.' The officer shook his head as if he was not certain that he approved.

Jehan stirred at Alexei's side. 'They would cheer as loud for a trained bear, did it but sit on the Dragon Throne,' he said softly.

Only Kadan and Burun were close enough to Alexei to hear. Kadan said nothing, and he did not look round. Burun took his cloak. He adjusted it, dismissing the officer, and then his head turned.

'Who men cheer is never what matters, Noyon,' he said. 'It is who they follow, who they obey at the end, that makes all this possible.'

Artai's st'lyan was pure white. It was caparisoned in gold, and gold threads had been woven through its

332

mane, decorating the length of it. Artai wore a long variation of the fancy gold coat of the Altun, collared and piped with gold wire, the panels faced with his arms, the sleeves slashed and inset with gold tissue. It was apparent at once that it was so stiff that it was going to be impossible for its wearer to dismount by normal means.

'They'll have to lift him down,' Kadan observed. He sounded amused.

The Kha-Khan looked in any case like a golden doll on the st'lyan's back. Although reins were attached to the bridle, and lay across the animal's neck, Artai was not guiding it. Instead leading ropes had been attached to a halter, and officers of his household walked ahead on foot with them in their hands. No one else was mounted, and it was not clear how far the Kha-Khan's entourage had been forced to walk. There must have been other riders in the party at some point, Alexei reasoned, and he guessed that the company had got down from their st'lyan on the outskirts of the camp. He grinned.

'There's my father,' Kadan said suddenly.

'And mine.' Jehan's tone was cool.

Alexei saw that his father was among a small group of Khans who were following immediately behind Artai's st'lyan. Jotan was wearing a court dress of midnight blue, but Suragai was clad in pastel shades. There was a lot of gold adorning the facings of his coat, and in his hand he carried the fur hat of a Khan.

Alexei caught Burun's eye. 'Suragai Khan?' he enquired.

Burun managed to pretend a measure of discomfort. 'I should have told you,' he said. 'Artai wrote to me that it was his wish to reward your father as he had rewarded you, for his service to the Khanate. I think it was in his mind to secure his loyalty, knowing

333

that he is my counsellor.' The likelihood did not seem to perturb Burun at all.

Alexei nodded slowly. 'It is because we are aliens,' he said. 'Artai thinks that our motivations are less suspect, for he believes that we do not reason as other men.'

'In that case you are fortunate,' Burun said equably. 'Trust is a valuable commerce, but few men are there who profit from it.' He turned away.

The sections of the crowd nearest the Kha-Khan were making their obeisance now, prostrating themselves in waves which progressed back past the tents to include the troopers beyond.

'I don't see Sidacai,' Jehan murmured.

Alexei did not turn. 'He isn't here. I sent him out on patrol duty this morning.'

'Ah.' Jehan sounded pleased. 'How convenient.'

Alexei gave him a sharp look. 'Noyon, don't set yourself to oppose your grandfather's will and mine. If you must make life unbearable for Sidacai, then at least let it wait until our embassy has been completed. You're not strong enough to fight all of us you know.'

'Oh.' Jehan looked swiftly round. 'I'm aware of that. I just wasn't sure if you were.' He grinned amiably at Alexei, and there was mockery in his eyes.

Artai! Artai!

The procession was moving up to the front of the great yurt. Alexei frowned at Jehan, and then knelt and prostrated himself in a series of economical movements. When he stood up four officers of the Kha-Khan's personal guard were positioning themselves beside the white st'lyan. They held up their arms to Artai, preparing to lift him down from the saddle, but Artai gestured them away. He turned stiffly in the saddle, staring about.

334

'My Lords,' Artai said, 'we bid you welcome to this our encampment of Pantai.'

The response was unrehearsed, and therefore it was confused. Artai waited for the murmur of voices to die, and when it did not he raised one hand. At once there was silence.

'Sensible,' Kadan said softly. 'So long as he remains mounted, everyone will be able to see him.'

'Quiet!' Jehan hissed. He did not look round.

Artai seemed to scan the crowd. 'Burun Khan, are you there?' he called.

The screen of troopers in front of Burun opened, folding back upon itself so that there was a clear space which extended almost to the white st'lyan's side. Burun walked into it. 'Lord Khan, here I am,' he said placidly.

Artai's head swivelled. He eyed Burun, and then nodded. 'Burun Khan, we greet you. Where is Alexei Khan?'

It was going to be a piece of theatre, Alexei realised. He swept back one side of his coat, and resting his hand upon the hilt of his sword he stepped forward. 'Magnificence, I am happy to see you.'

'As we are,' Artai said, 'to greet our faithful servants. Are the preparations now advanced for the embassy for which we issued our patent?'

Burun was bowing, and Alexei followed suit. 'Lord, they are,' he said.

'It is well.' Artai was looking more at Alexei than at Burun as he spoke. 'Although in truth there was no doubt in our mind that you would have done as we commanded.'

A smile creased Burun's features. 'Lord,' he said, 'if we had not we would be many verst hence, hiding from your anger.'

There was a titter of appreciation from the crowd.

335

Artai smiled frostily. 'We have heard much of a certain ship,' he said. 'And tomorrow it will please us to see it launched.'

The *Sunstealer* had been ready for launching for almost a week now, but probably that was beside the point. It was the tradition for absolute rule, Alexei reflected, that it was for a monarch to pronounce and for his subjects to ensure that whatever was pronounced was so. How Artai would have reacted to news that the vessel either was not fit to be launched or was already in the water was not something which needed to be contemplated.

He bowed. 'Magnificence, it shall be as you command.'

The expression on Artai's face suggested that any other response would have been inappropriate. He nodded, contemplating Alexei, and then he turned in the saddle to look around again. 'Be it known that we recognise the efforts of these our servants,' Artai said grandly. 'Burun Khan we have rewarded hitherto, and he knows how high in our esteem he stands. Alexei Khan likewise has been accorded our favour, but it pleases us that we find that we are able to exert our interest in a matter which touches him, and so to reward his service to us.'

A reward of any kind was not something which Alexei had anticipated. He did not understand what Artai meant about exerting his interest, but he bowed. 'Lord, I thank you.'

Artai's head went up. 'Indeed you will thank us,' he commented serenely. 'For we render unto you your heart's desire.'

Comprehension began to dawn. There were women with the Kha-Khan's party, Alexei knew, but they were in the heavily guarded tail portion of the caravan which had followed Artai's progress into

336

Pantai. Jotan's wife was among them, also his father's. Alexei stared past the shoulder of the white st'lyan towards Jotan, seeking confirmation of his suspicion, and Jotan gazed stonily back.

Alexei looked up at Artai. 'Magnificence —' he began, and then stopped, unsure how to continue.

'You are not certain that you understand our meaning,' Artai observed tranquilly. 'Are there then so many rewards which would so please you? Your betrothal, it seemed to us, is that which would be most happily resolved, and it has lasted in our opinion long enough.'

If Burun had received warning of Artai's intentions, there was no suggestion of it in his manner. 'Lord,' he said in a tone of pleased surprise, 'you honour both our houses.'

'— And will honour them further,' Artai responded swiftly. He gestured to one of his household officers, and the man extracted a sheet of parchment from the wallet in his hand. He gave it to Artai, bowing.

'The matter of a marriage settlement is often protracted, we are aware,' Artai observed prosaically. He did not even glance at the paper. 'To provide our servant with the reward which we have determined is most fitting, we therefore endower the lady, the daughter of Jotan and the grand-daughter of Burun Khan, and provide for her marriage settlement from our exchequer. To that end we have given an order under our seal. Thus the period of betrothal need last no longer. Alexei Khan's chief desire, we feel sure, is marriage to this lady, and this it will be our pleasure to see enacted before he departs our shores.'

That it was a command was apparent to everyone who mattered. The nobility, those who did not understand the implications of the affair, applauded and exclaimed at the extent of Artai's generosity. Burun

337

glanced once towards Jotan. He raised an eyebrow, the only indication so far as Alexei could see that he was out of countenance, and then he bowed low to Artai.

'Lord, on behalf of my son and our house, I thank you,' he said. 'For your favour to Alexei advantages us also.'

Jotan did not stir, and he said nothing, even though Artai glanced back at him.

'The fact had not escaped us,' Artai said. He produced a thin smile. 'Alexei Khan, we feel sure, will also thank us when he has had time to compose himself.'

Alexei had been watching Jotan. He looked up at Artai. 'Lord,' he said, 'you know I will.'

Artai nodded, composed. 'In such a case, noble Lords, we give you leave. Attend us at our pleasure.' He waved to the officers of his guard, and they led his st'lyan under the awning in front of the great yurt. A screen of lances moved across the opening, shielding Artai from the view of everyone outside as he was lifted down from the saddle.

Burun still stood a little way in front of Alexei in the space which had been created by the movement of his escort. He was staring thoughtfully towards Jotan. Suddenly he turned and faced Alexei, his brow furrowed.

Beyond Jotan, Alexei saw his father following Artai into the entrance of the yurt. He did not even glance in Alexei's direction.

Alexei met Burun's eyes. 'You did not know the Kha-Khan intended to interfere. You had word of none of this.'

Jotan was striding off through the crowd. Burun made a face which might have indicated discomfiture. 'None,' he said. 'As for Artai, it was always possible that he would choose to interest himself.' He made to walk past Alexei, and then suddenly he stopped. 'Whatever you may think,' he said, 'this has very little to do with you. Artai is demonstrating how well he can control our lives. What he decided could as easily have disadvantaged you.'

What troubled Alexei most was his inability to see how Artai gained by promoting Jehana's marriage. It might be a whim of course, or pique because she had chosen an alien rather than be betrothed to the Lord of the Earth. Alexei thought that he mistrusted both alternatives. He stared at Burun, willing him to supply a motive for Artai's generosity which made sense.

Burun pursed his lips. 'Well,' he said. 'It's done now.' He went past Alexei through the screen of his guard, and they moved with orderly precision to make way for him through the crowd.

Jotan's yurt was ringed by sentries. The antechamber inside was hung with silks, long swathes of fabric draped across screen poles suspended above the wall frames, the ends of the silks lapping over the felt laced to the panels. A fire of bright coals burned in a copper dish which was set inside a tray filled with brushed golden sand. A herb of some kind was being burned with the coals, and a scent like incense hung on the warm air. Female slaves with shyly lowered heads brought wine and sweetmeats on trays, and then departed silently. A whisper of conversation carried past the screens from some other chamber in the yurt. Alexei considered the stools arranged around the low table, and decided that it would be safer to stand. If Jotan used this room, there was no sign of it. It was a woman's place, full of women's things. Outside he could hear vaguely the murmur of the still settling camp. Within the yurt was another world.

The hangings at the end of the chamber swished abruptly, and Jotan came through them. He was still dressed as he had been when he had walked with Artai. He saw Alexei and stopped, and Alexei wondered what kind of greeting to expect.

'I will not say you are welcome, Khan.' Jotan went past the table. He paced to the wall and turned. The restrained violence of his movements made Alexei flinch. Jotan said, 'You know that what Artai proposes is none of my intending.'

That much had been clear from the moment Alexei had observed Jotan's expression after Artai had spoken. He tried to think of a suitable reply, then realised that Jotan did not expect a response. Jotan paced past the table again, rounding suddenly to stand feet apart.

'Speak to Artai,' he said. 'Persuade him that this wedding should not take place – that it should be delayed until your return.'

Alexei opened his eyes wide. 'Khan, I would, if I could provide the Kha-Khan with a reason I thought he would believe.'

Jotan pushed back the facings of his coat and set his hands in his sash. 'Tell him anything. You see how he favours you and your father both. Only tell him that you do not care to leave a new wife for so long and he will believe you.'

If Jotan had been speaking for Burun, he would have made his entreaty less strong. The thought came out of nowhere into Alexei's mind.

'Khan, it seems to me that Artai has already spoken to counter such an argument,' Alexei said. He brushed a hand down the facing of his coat, smoothing it. 'Your father says that the Kha-Khan is proving that he has the ability to control our lives.'

Jotan was staring at the floor. He looked up sharply.

340

'If he is, then there will be no gainsaying him.'

The hangings moved as if stirred by a wind, and Jehana came into the room. Jotan stared at her. 'Daughter, you should not be here,' he said.

Jehana was dressed in a flowing gown of azure silk. The dye had been treated in the vat with aloe and turpentine so that the effect had been to swirl it upon the fibres of the material, and fantastic shapes could be discerned. No two parts of the gown seemed to be of quite the same shade, and the colour shimmered in the light of the lamps suspended above them.

Alexei bowed. 'Lady, I am pleased to see you again,' he said.

She gave him a smile which held a hint of polite enquiry. 'Are you, my Lord? And yet I know that you did not seek to bring me here.'

Jotan produced a snort of exasperation. He gave Alexei a look. 'Mark what I asked of you,' he said. He went past Jehana through the hangings, leaving them tangled.

'Your father wants me to persuade the Kha-Khan to postpone our wedding.' Alexei offered the explanation flatly.

She went to the table, folding herself gracefully onto a stool. 'Will you take wine, my Lord?'

'Thank you.'

Her hands were slender, and she was wearing no rings. Whatever he said now, Alexei thought, it would not be what was truly in his mind. The circumstances did not allow for that. There was no place for it here. He took the filled cup when she handed it to him and drank.

'As to my father's wishes in this,' Jehana said. 'He acts, as he believes, in my interest. For my part I am content.' She glanced up. 'Approach Artai if you wish.'

'– And if I do not wish?'

341

She shrugged. 'I had not thought you so keen a suitor,' she said.

Alexei felt confused. He had assumed that she did not want the match – had been certain that she would use the first opportunity to withdraw from it. Certainly it would explain her behaviour, and much of what she had said. Now it seemed that she would offer no opposition if he wished to continue. He eyed her.

'Is your aversion to Artai so strong?'

Jehana frowned. 'It is not that which is at issue,' she said at last. 'The Kha-Khan has expressed his will. It is for those of us who are concerned to comply.'

There was no hint of emotion in her tone, and Alexei was unable to tell how she felt about the turn of events. He drank more of the wine, then laid the cup on the table. He took a breath.

'Lady, if you wish it, I will speak to Artai. If your desire is to consider no man, then maybe I can persuade him to that.'

Jehana was reaching out to lift the cup. Her hand stilled. At last she looked up. 'If anyone could persuade the Kha-Khan, my Lord, it is you,' she observed. She seemed to stare for a moment at her hands, and Alexei saw her talons extend and then retract again. Finally she met his eyes. 'Would that you were a Yek, or a Merkut, Alexei,' she said. 'For then you would understand why I cannot express my will.'

There was a message in the words, did he but know how to decipher it. Alexei had expected her to add her request to Jotan's. The fact that she had not seemed to make no sense, but it was pointless to question. Alexei bowed. 'Let us obey the will of the Kha-Khan then,' he said. He turned without waiting for her to reply and went outside into the bustle of the encampment.

Because of the width of the inlet, the launching of the *Sunstealer* was timed to coincide with the afternoon high tide. As a precaution the shore line on the opposite bank had been excavated so that an indentation almost twenty drem in length now existed at the furthest extent of the launching path. It was Alexei's private opinion that if the vessel had not slowed sufficiently by the time it reached the main depth of the channel, then probably it was destined to run fully up onto the bank. Like the shipwrights, he was putting his faith in the ten additional lengths of chain which were now attached to the *Sunstealer*'s stern. The wrights were demonstrating their trust by volunteering to be on board the vessel now that the crucial moment had arrived. Alexei had little choice in the matter, but he was relatively unconcerned.

The Kha-Khan had been dissuaded from being present on deck during launching only with difficulty. The yards, it was true, had not been designed to accommodate the Khanate's overlord, his guard, his household, and the major proportion of the court and its attendant hangers-on. A system of passwords had been introduced in an attempt to exclude from the immediate vicinity all but a manageable number. The platforms erected for the purpose of viewing had been something of an afterthought, and they were neither large nor strong. An hour prior to the event the price of the principal password had risen from one koban to five. In spite of this the stagings were overcrowded, and swayed alarmingly every time a new influx of spectators arrived on them. The silks worn by the Khans were brushed at every turn by sweating humanity, and obtained in the process both moisture and the quality of disarray. The guildsmen who were not involved in the launching were dressed in padded brocades which would have been more suitable for a winter audience, and perspired from their positions high on the stagings onto liveried guards and royal retainers alike. Jehan, who had elected at the last minute to come on board, leaned on the bulwark and smiled.

'Are we launching the ship or the platforms?' he enquired, and turned to look at Alexei. He nodded at the staging which ran parallel to one side of the hull. 'Another man on that, and it will enter the water before we do.'

The staging was leaning considerably to one side, and a team of carpenters was engaged hastily inserting props to prevent it from collapsing and depositing its load into the oily water which sloshed along the bottom of the slipway.

'Here's Artai,' Kadan said, and pointed.

The announcement was unnecessary. The height of the deck above its surroundings was such that everyone on board had been provided with an excellent view of the Kha-Khan's progress from the moment it had started through the outskirts of Pantai.

There was so little room in the streets that those who had not gained access to the shipyard had taken to the roofs. Men and boys sat on cornices, and clung to chimneys and waved and cheered as the cavalcade moved past below them. Every window was packed, and there seemed to be no space which was not occupied by people.

Alexei glanced at the sun, and then eyed the water mark at the end of the slip. Already a line showed where the tide was receding gradually. He made a face. A master of shipwrights was craning over the side near the bow, and when he leaned back inboard he came along the deck, his expression worried.

'Khan, we will have to launch soon, or we will lose the best water.'

'Thank you. I know.' Alexei looked back over the stern to see what point the procession had reached. It was coming along the street which led to the yard gate. 'Ready your men.'

'Yes, Khan.'

'Pray Artai doesn't decide to make a speech,' Jehan remarked. He glanced down the length of the deck towards the bow. 'Are the boats waiting?'

It had been decided that it might be foolhardy to launch the *Sunstealer* with fully charged boilers, and so there were galleys in the inlet to take the vessel in tow once she was safely in the water.

'They'd better be,' Alexei said shortly.

The litter which contained Artai was being carried up to the platform which faced the stern now. Some people were prostrating themselves – an exercise which was hazardous in the extreme in view of the fact that most of them were occupying plank benches on stepped stagings. A knot of banners and guidons indicated where Burun and his retainers had stopped clear of the worst of the press. Alexei saw his father at Burun's shoulder. He waved, but could not tell if anyone saw. Certainly there was no response.

Artai walked the three steps from his litter to the centre of the platform. He turned and raised his hands.

'I knew he would make a speech,' Jehan said.

'Lord –'

It was the shipwright, urgent at Alexei's side. Alexei saw Artai's mouth opening and closing, but he could hear nothing. Even the people on the other platforms did not appear to know what was going on, for they were still moving about and conversing with one another.

If they waited, they would lose the benefit of the tide. Alexei glanced over the side once more, then nodded decisively.

'All hands, launching stations.'

'Aye, aye.'

The shipwright looked relieved. He picked up a pole which had a bright red streamer attached to it, leaned over the side, and waved the pole energetically. At once the afternoon resounded with the noise of hammers and mallets striking timbers. The *Sunstealer* shook perceptibly, then started to slide towards the water.

Whatever Artai was saying was lost in the rattle of chains and the creak of greased timber. There were floats on either side of the bow to keep the vessel upright as it left the support of the slipway and entered the water. Alexei leaned out across the bulwark, and saw them disappear in the curtain of spray. He waved and yelled, and the men at the ropes which secured the floats severed them.

Jehan was hanging onto Alexei's arm. The ship swayed, and Kadan reached out and caught both of them as they lost their balance.

They were in the water. 'Are we afloat?' Kadan enquired cheerfully.

Alexei straightened, adjusting his stance. 'We seem to be.'

The bow of the *Sunstealer* was still travelling towards the opposite bank. Alexei glanced quickly back over the stern and saw the dust rising where the chains were unfolding, whipping down the slipway, knocking aside loose timbers.

'Aren't we moving a little fast?' Jehan put one hand on the varnished rail at his side.

The men in the bow were throwing ropes to a pair of advancing biremes. One rope fell short, and was

346

hauled back. They were more than halfway across the inlet, still heading for the bank.

Another bireme was sliding in under the port side. Ropes arched out, and were secured. The head of the ship was coming round slowly, the short bowsprit moving like a pointer along the shore line. A rope parted, and men on either side of it ducked as it whipped past their heads. Suddenly the forward motion had ceased. Jehan took his hand away from the rail. He walked nonchalantly to the side and looked over, then turned, grinning. Behind them in the yard people were cheering and waving. Alexei nodded to the two helmsmen who had been putting their weight on the wheel. It had been a calculated risk to attempt to stop the ship in such a way. He tried to remember if he had heard anything coming loose, and thought not. A wright popped out of a forecastle hatchway. He trotted over to the master of the wrights, reported briefly, and slipped out of sight again.

'Khan, everything below is secure, and the seams are tight.' The shipwright bowed.

'Very well.'

Already the biremes were pulling the vessel along the inlet towards a vacant wharf.

'Does anyone know what Artai was saying as we went into the water?' Kadan was watching the shore. A movement of banners showed where the Kha-Khan was being escorted from the yard.

Jehan looked round. 'Does it matter?'

They held Artai in so little esteem, Alexei thought, it was a wonder they had elected him. He remembered the incidents, and the pointed remarks, and knew that what young men like Jehan and Kadan said was only a reflection of what the Khans, who held the real power, thought of their overlord.

347

Some of the people were trying to leave the yard by making their way along the shore. The deposit of years of shipbuilding lay in the form of caked wood pulp and shavings, and places which looked solid were not. A man fell into the water, followed by another, and wherries plied industriously along the shelving bank, rescuing those who were prepared to pay.

Alexei caught Jehan's eye. 'You don't respect Artai,' he said. 'Why did you vote for him?'

'I didn't.' Jehan stared back levelly.

'You know what I mean.' Alexei saw that Kadan was turning, ready to add his opinion, and he pressed on. 'Your grandfather supported him, even though he knew Artai would use his power to satisfy his own desires once he had been elected. Now Artai amuses himself scoring points off the men who have best served the Khanate. Even if he is a better ruler than most men expected, he is still wilful as a child.'

The wharf towards which they were being pulled was packed with people. A man fell off into the water, and troopers started to force those who were obstructing the longshoremen back through a warehouse.

Jehan's expression reflected his surprise. 'You don't understand us, Khan,' he said after a moment. 'My grandfather loves order above all things, which is why he supported Artai. As for the other Khans, you seem to forget that they knew that Artai's election was Nogai's will.'

It was clear that Jehan expected the answer to be sufficient. Alexei knew that it was not, but after a moment he nodded, and turned away.

The need for further negotiation relating to dowry having been removed, the preparations for Jehana's marriage to Alexei were pressed ahead with a degree of haste which was matched only by the speed with which the *Sunstealer* was being readied for sea. A brief propulsion trial was sufficient to demonstrate both that the ship's engines worked and that the vessel itself was seaworthy in excess of expectations. The absence of much superstructure provided for somewhat more stability than had been anticipated. Likewise it was apparent that although the crew of Ch'kasians and Suristani were unaccustomed to the duties which related to such a vessel, yet they knew in general terms what they were about. Their captain was a native Losani named Ch'un Chu who was reputed by some to have sailed with pirates in his youth. He was small and sturdy, scarred where he was not tattooed, and he reminded Alexei vaguely of the starship officers who sometimes served with commercial lines. His clothing was of finer material than was usually seen on seamen, and everything he wore was always neat and clean.

About the crew he was perfectly frank. 'Lord, they are the best you will find, but not the best on the coast,' he said, and accepted a cup of wine when Alexei offered it. 'The word is that we are going where no living man has ever gone –' Ch'un Chu nodded towards the setting sun. '– The other side of Heaven, some men call it.'

It was the first time Alexei had heard interest expressed in their destination. 'You have heard of the Unknown Lands?' he enquired.

Ch'un Chu nodded. 'Aye, Lord.' He drank. 'Far travel's not a prospect that troubles me greatly, or I'd not be a sailor. Don't concern yourself about the crew, Lord. I'll answer for them.'

Alexei sat back, satisfied. Among other things, Ch'un Chu was said to be lucky, and men sailed with him because he always returned eventually to port. If he was confident about the prospects for the voyage, then the fact would be communicated to the crew and they would remain calm in the face of adversity.

Arrangements for the wedding were fully completed only the day before the embassy's departure from Pantai. It was the custom for the ceremony of marriage to take place in the early evening, before the setting of the sun. There was no room inside the city for everyone who wished to attend, and so one of the huge canopies was moved out from the camp onto open ground, and its perimeter was lit by torches and cressets. The grass beneath it was surfaced with shredded bark, and this was floored where it mattered with timber planking and covered with the carpets and rugs which were borrowed from every yurt and tent in the encampment.

It was nearly nightfall when Alexei stood up in front of Jotan to vow to take Jehana as his wife. At his side Jehana was shrouded in golden veils, and it occurred to him to wonder if a last-minute substitution had been made, and if in fact it was she who stood with him. He took her hand to make the formal vow, and was reassured by the slender fingers which rested upon his.

The custom did not require a woman who was being married to speak. Jotan followed the ritual of asking Jehana if she assented, and she nodded silently.

Burun was at Jotan's shoulder the whole time. It was as if he expected Jotan to falter in his conduct of the ceremony. After the last words had been spoken it was Burun who came around and walked with them to the place of honour at the long table which ran the length of the canopy side. Alexei's father walked at Jehana's side, and her other hand rested on his arm.

Jehana sat down, and her maids lifted back her

350

veils. She was wearing a gown in traditional style, sewn with pearls and gold droplets which were spread out from the neckline in layers like the ripples which move outward when a stone is dropped in the centre of a pool. Her hair had been combed out so that it covered her shoulders, and it was woven with golden threads which were decorated with tiny seed pearls. She kept her eyes lowered demurely. Alexei stared at her, willing her to look up, but she did not.

The servants had been borrowed from the households of many different Khans. They filed in rows along the rear of the table, bearing in their arms trays of meats and pastries. Artai had been given a special place which was separated from the chair of honour only by the members of the immediate family of the bride and groom. Representatives of every house had brought gifts to the ceremony, and they laid them in front of Alexei and Jehana as they moved to sit. Soon there was a pile higher than a standing man and twice as broad.

It should have been Jotan who made the opening speech, but at the appointed time it was Burun who stood. His toast to the wedded couple was interrupted constantly by the jokes which were shouted by the guests. Alexei ate and drank sparingly, and saw that Jehana scarcely touched what was served to her. The members of the embassy stood up in turn to drink Alexei's health. Alexei mixed water with his wine, knowing that it made sense to keep a clear head.

Women were already drawing Jehana away from the table. A Seljuk Arcutt said something to Jotan, and he replied easily, and then raised his cup to Alexei. Whatever animosity he had felt before, it was not to be displayed here. Alexei nodded politely, but he did not raise his cup.

351

Jehana was being pulled towards the yurt which had been raised according to tradition on previously unbroken ground. Alexei rose and strode after her, and at once there was a yell from the guests. Jehan and Kadan raced up. They lifted Alexei bodily, and ran with him past the women on the path. Orcadai and C'zinsit charged up. They wrenched off Alexei's coat, and tore off his boots and tossed them aside as they ran. Hustling him through the door of the yurt they dumped him on the floor and tried to strip him. He fought them off, and they went outside, laughing. Alexei could hear the high voices of the women coming from the next room. Jehana's mother came through the hangings with her maids. They bore Jehana's gown between them. They stared at him standing half-dressed in the middle of the floor, laughed, and went out through the door.

Alexei brushed the hangings aside. The women still in the bedchamber screamed when they saw him and ran out. Jehana was kneeling naked in the middle of the bed. A nightgown of almost transparent white silk lay draped across the foot of the bed. Alexei lifted it and laid it across a chair, and Jehana looked up at him for a moment. She moved her head from side to side, parting the tresses of hair which had been combed down to cover her breasts. Alexei eyed her, but she made no attempt to cover herself.

He pulled his shirt over his head, then unwound his sash and dropped it. He sat down with his back to her and drew off his hose, then stood again to take off his breeches and undergarments. He climbed onto the bed and knelt facing her.

'My Lord.'

She did not move as she spoke. Alexei took her hands in his. He raised one open palm against his cheek, watching her eyes.

'Lady, I do not know how to come to terms with you,' he said.

Her lips parted in the hint of a smile. 'My Lord, I think you want me to tell you how to rule me,' she said.

'Do you?' He held her eyes. 'It was not my intention.'

They were married. Suddenly there were no rituals of words which they could use to ease the awkward moment. Words in fact were the problem.

It would have been different if he had courted her, Alexei thought. Instead they had moved without any transition from one state – the formal relationship between men and women who were protected by the expectation of courtship – to another, of marriage, in which the only barriers between them would be those which they would erect for themselves. The sense of helplessness surprised him the more because he was unprepared for it. He saw that she was waiting for him to speak again, and searched for phrases which would be appropriate, then discarded them. Finally he said, 'Lady, I do not know what to say to you.'

She seemed to consider. Then she smiled tentatively. 'My Lord, maybe one of us should admit that this marriage was not altogether contrary to our will,' she suggested.

It had never occurred to him that she might desire him, or that she could be a willing party to the match for no other reason than a wish to be his wife. Still he could not find words to break the silence.

'Shall I speak it first?' she asked, low-voiced.

The fact that they were of different species was not even an issue. He shook his head. 'No.'

She had expected more from him. He cursed the reputation which had preceded him. 'Lady, if you wish to be here now, it is enough. For myself, I would be nowhere else.'

'Then we are agreed,' she said. She smiled, and her eyes lit for the first time.

'Yes,' Alexei said. 'We are.'

He reached for her, and she came into his arms.

PART FOUR

A Long Way to Travel

'If Alexei doesn't come soon,' C'zinsit said, 'we'll miss the tide.'

With water lapping only a drem or so below the head of the wharf, the remark was clearly nonsense. Orcadai was leaning on the bulwark beside the gangway. The sleeves of his tunic were turned back, and his shirt was open to the waist. He turned. 'Would you be in a hurry if last night was your wedding night?' he enquired. 'He'll come.'

'He has delayed this long –'

'He'll come.'

The dockside was lined with troopers from Burun's personal guard, and Burun himself was standing under the shade of an awning which had been erected at the end of the warehouses. There were casual onlookers of course, but they were not as numerous as had been expected. If the Kha-Khan intended to be present at the embassy's departure, few of the citizens of Pantai were aware of it.

Probably Artai would appear, Jehan thought. A constant flow of couriers and officers of the household was moving in from the street, and parties escorted by mounted troopers were arriving all the time to swell the crowd.

Jehan glanced towards the stern. A wisp of steam was escaping from a pipe which emerged from the open hatchway. The screens around the reflectors now hid the beam being projected into the heat tubes. They also damped the sound so that the hint of it touched the very edge of Jehan's perception. Ch'un Chu was surveying the deck from a position beside the wheel, and Parin was standing behind him. The

357

captain's feet were set apart, and his hands were tucked into his belt. He caught Jehan's look, but did not alter his easy posture. Jehan raised an eyebrow and looked away.

Sidacai was inspecting a case of boarding pikes on the foredeck. He glanced up and their eyes met. Jehan stared, determined not to be the first to look away.

The problem in continuing the feud with Sidacai was the limiting size of the vessel. They were going to be thrown into one another's company on a daily basis, and there was nowhere for either of them to go to avoid confrontation.

Kadan came up to Jehan's side. Sidacai was gazing back, his face expressionless. Kadan said, 'Everyone wonders why you did not kill him.'

Jehan did not turn. 'It was not the right time.'

He heard Kadan laugh softly.

'Will it ever be?' Kadan asked.

It was not a question Jehan felt capable of answering. He had been sure that he was right to mistrust Sidacai. He had also known instinctively that it was not the time to kill him.

Horns were sounding on the outskirts of the city, a sign that someone important was approaching.

'If that is Artai, Alexei will be with him,' Kadan said.

Sidacai was looking away towards the direction of the sound. Jehan turned. He walked to the head of the gangway. 'All this ceremony is pointless,' he said. 'Artai should have stayed in Kinsai. What has his presence achieved?'

Kadan grinned. 'Alexei might not agree with you.'

Jehan was unable to suppress a smile. 'That's true.' He glanced at the awning under which Burun stood. Suragai was at Burun's shoulder. 'Have you said goodbye to your father?'

358

'Twice at least,' Kadan said, amused.

Where the Kha-Khan was, Jotan would be also. Jehan thought about the steadily widening rift between his father and grandfather, a separation which was demonstrated by the fact that they had exchanged little more than formal politenesses since Artai's arrival in Pantai, and he frowned, troubled.

A small cavalcade of guards and standard-bearers was coming down the street which led directly to the wharf. Artai was at its centre, his white st'lyan standing out clearly among the bays and chestnuts which surrounded it. Jehan looked for Alexei, and saw him riding a few lengths behind Artai, Jehana at his side.

Jehan strode down the gangway. Kadan followed. They arrived on the wharfside just as Artai's escort began to wheel in at the end of the warehouse. A cheer rose up from some of the spectators – townspeople and the like – but the files of Burun's guard did not stir, and the troopers continued to face the vessel.

Artai was reining around in the middle of a screen of his officers. He was dressed as if for a hunt, and handled his st'lyan with easy grace.

'He rides well,' Kadan said, sounding surprised.

'He's Altun isn't he?' Jehan snorted impatiently. 'Of course he rides well.'

Jehan looked for his father among the men who were with Artai, but he could not see him. The Kha-Khan was dismounting now, and Burun and the others under the awning were bowing. The customary prostrations were being omitted, but if Artai noticed, he did not seem to care. He sprang to the ground and threw his reins to an attendant guardsman. His golden hair had been dressed so that it looked as if there was a snake poised above his

359

forehead, ready to strike. The afternoon sunlight was deep red, and Artai's skin looked like burnished copper. When he turned to look in Jehan's direction the amber irises of his eyes looked huge, and Jehan was reminded of a cat examining its prey. He swallowed, then bowed quickly.

Alexei had dismounted, and he was turning to lift Jehana down out of the saddle. She slipped to the ground inside his arms, and the look of contentment on their faces made Jehan momentarily envious. Jehana said something, and Alexei replied softly and nodded. Then he looked past Jehana and saw that Jehan was watching.

'Brother, good afternoon,' Jehan said.

Jehana turned and she smiled prettily.

Jehan watched Alexei's expression. The offworlder seemed to consider. Then he nodded. 'Yes,' he said. 'It is a good afternoon.'

They were happy then. Jehan had not been sure they would be. He opened his mouth to comment, but could think of nothing appropriate which did not sound superior. Finally he said, 'Everything is ready for you.'

Alexei nodded. 'Thank you. I expected it would be.'

Artai appeared to be in no haste to take part in any ceremony of farewell. He spoke briefly to Burun – a pleasantry it seemed, because Burun smiled and replied, and the men around laughed politely. Alexei took Jehana's hands in his. 'Lady,' he said, 'this is where we must part.' He drew her aside, and Jehan could not hear what else was said. He glanced away, and saw that Artai was watching intently.

He intends something, Jehan thought, but could not imagine what.

The whole group of people around and under the awning began to move forward, the Kha-Khan at the

360

front accompanied by Burun. Alexei was turning. He bowed to Artai. 'Lord, I take my leave of you.'

Artai gestured languidly. 'Alexei Khan, we wish you well. Return successful and you will repose in our favour.'

Success, Jehan supposed, implied some indication of willingness on the part of the peoples of the Unknown Lands to submit themselves to the rule of the Universal Khan. The likelihood that anyone would be prepared to surrender sovereignty on demand had not been taken into account. Nor had it ever been.

Burun said, 'Lord, it will be sufficient, I think, if they return to tell us what they have found.'

The Kha-Khan looked down his nose. 'It is for us to determine what is sufficient,' he said, 'and not for our servants.'

Burun's face assumed a patient expression. He returned Artai's stare placidly.

'Do you dispute us?' Artai demanded. 'We are Lord of the Earth. It matters not if the lands across the Great Sea are unknown; they are subject to our will.'

There was no one present who was likely to take such a claim seriously, but it was likewise clear that it was neither the place nor the time to offer a contradiction.

Jehan saw several men smile covertly. Burun only raised his eyebrows. He said, 'Lord, saying it does not make it so.'

The Kha-Khan frowned at him. Jehan moved to Alexei's side. 'We should go.'

'Yes.' Alexei nodded. He bowed to the Kha-Khan again. 'By your leave, Lord.'

'Oh. Yes.' Artai waved absently.

Jehan nudged Kadan, and they bowed. A wind whipped suddenly across the wharf, stirring the banners. The people crowded to watch beyond the soldiers were indistinguishable from one another, and Jehan was able to pick out no one he wished to acknowledge. Alexei was taking a pace backward. Burun said, 'Have no fear for your lady. We shall care for her lovingly.'

Artai's head came round abruptly. He said, 'As we have endowered her, so shall we keep her in our care.' He made the statement flatly.

Jehana's expression was frozen in surprise. Alexei was straightening, digesting Artai's words. Burun said, 'Lord, that would be contrary to the custom.'

'Nevertheless,' Artai said, 'it is our will.' His tone suggested that he intended to brook no argument.

Jehana was to be a hostage for Merkut loyalty, Jehan thought. He saw that the Kha-Khan had promoted her marriage to Alexei as a means of placing her in his power. Her husband's absence from the Khanate was a convenient excuse.

Only the expression in Burun's eyes showed that he understood Artai's intent. The men around him were watching to see how he would respond. The Kha-Khan glanced from Burun to Alexei and back again. His eyes were bright with malice.

Alexei seemed to glance once in Jehana's direction, and then his hand moved naturally to rest upon the hilt of his sword.

There were too many witnesses, Jehan thought, which was probably why Artai had chosen to speak now rather than later. Whatever Alexei said or did, he would place himself at the Kha-Khan's mercy.

It was Kadan who moved first. He put a hand on Alexei's shoulder. 'Accept it,' he said softly. 'There is nothing you can do here.'

Alexei's head went round. He twisted his shoulder out of Kadan's grasp.

Suddenly Jehan knew that Kadan was right. Artai

would have to be opposed, but not now. He had stated his intent to offend against a custom which amounted to law, but he could not be challenged here, under these circumstances. Artai did not appear to have noticed the byplay. His attention was concentrated upon Burun, waiting for his reaction.

Burun could only stand there, Jehan realised. Whatever he might be able to do to counter this act of Artai's, it would be later, when Artai thought that all resistance to his will had been overcome.

Jehan touched Alexei's arm. 'Bow,' he hissed.

'But –'

'Bow!'

Alexei bowed falteringly.

'Now step back ... turn.' Jehan pressed in at Alexei's side. They had taken ten steps towards the wharfside when the offworlder turned, his expression outraged. 'My wife –'

'– Will be perfectly safe. Artai is using her, that is all.'

They were at the foot of the gangway. Jehan forced the offworlder onto it. The group around the Kha-Khan had fragmented. Jehan could not see Jehana, and he forced himself to concentrate on getting Alexei on board ship without incident. Artai was staring after them, his expression thoughtful.

Four paces up the gangway ... five. Jehan gestured at Ch'un Chu. 'Get under way.'

Ch'un Chu gave Jehan a sharp look. He glanced at the offworlder, seeming to sense that something was wrong, and then he nodded.

'All hands to stations.'

Ch'un Chu's command carried crisply across the deck. The lines which tethered the vessel to the land were hauled in. The gangway was lowered to the wharfside. Jehan eyed Alexei. He does not believe that he walked away, he thought. Jehan wondered what he would have done in similar circumstances, and he was glad that he had not been faced with such a decision.

Orcadai and C'zinsit came from the bow. C'zinsit stopped to look over the side, and he caught Jehan's eye. 'What happened there?'

'Ask me again later.' Jehan did not turn.

A bireme was already pulling the *Sunstealer* out from the wharf. The line splashed into the water and was pulled in. The offworlder seemed to be recovering from his daze. He shook his head. 'Damn you all,' he said.

It was too late to deny the substance of what had occurred. Artai did not even need to keep Jehana a prisoner. The implied threat was enough. Probably she would be commanded to attend the court, Jehan supposed. Leave to absent herself would be refused, of course. Suddenly he knew that the Yasa provided for one way to deal with the Kha-Khan's betrayal of trust, and he wondered if Artai knew that he had exposed himself. When we return, Jehan thought, there will be a reckoning. Then he dismissed the matter from his mind.

The engines were throbbing, their beat muffled by the planking beneath Jehan's feet. It was not a sensation Jehan yet felt comfortable with. He looked at Alexei. 'Don't curse us,' he said, and knew in the instant he spoke that what the offworlder hated was his helplessness in the middle of so much intrigue. How alike we are, Jehan thought, and yet how different.

The vessel was gathering way, moving under its own power out into the estuary. People on the shore began to cheer, hesitantly at first, and then with abandon. Jehan looked back at the wharf and saw that Artai was already turning away.

Alexei unfastened his coat and took it off. Jehan gestured to an orderly, and the man came and took the garment out of the offworlder's hands. Alexei seemed not to notice. He rested his hands on the bulwark and stared at the shore. 'I should have done something,' he said.

'Can you think of anything, even now, which would have made a difference?' Jehan asked.

The offworlder shook his head slowly.

They were leaving the wharves and shipyards behind now. The cheers of the people were fainter, and almost no one among the crew was paying attention.

Suddenly a wherry shot out from below the headland. The two oarsmen were straining to move the tiny craft along a heading which would intercept the *Sunstealer* as it moved out to sea. A single cloaked passenger was waving to attract the notice of the starboard lookout.

Jehan stared, and then he turned and gestured to Ch'un Chu. 'Slow down!'

Ch'un Chu spoke a single word to the mate, who shouted down the open hatchway at his feet. The engine noise decreased. There were rope ladders at several points along the side. Jehan bundled one of them over, craning to see. The wherry was coming in under the bow. Its passenger stood, and caught one of the ropes of the ladder as it swung past. Alexei seemed to wake up to the fact that something was happening. He took one look at the wherry's passenger, then exclaimed and went in haste over the rail and down the ladder. He caught Jehana's arm and drew her up, hoisting her bodily over the side onto the deck. She began to unfasten her cloak, smiling. Alexei clambered over the rail behind her. He seemed to be having trouble adjusting to Jehana's presence.

365

'Husband, aren't you pleased to see me?' Jehana was still clad in the riding dress which she had worn on the wharfside.

Jehan glanced over the side, and he saw that the wherry was pulling swiftly away.

Alexei was staring at Jehana. 'Of course I'm pleased.' His eyes devoured her.

Jehan saw his sister blush. He smiled and turned away, knowing that they would not speak what was in their eyes in his presence.

It was Burun's doing that Jehana was on board the ship of course. Jehan saw how it must have been arranged, and he gave a laugh, imagining the Kha-Khan's fury when he discovered how he had been thwarted. He signalled to Ch'un Chu. 'Take us out of here.'

'Yes, Lord.'

The *Sunstealer* began to pick up speed again. It moved past the headland into the light swell outside the inlet. The red sun was directly in the west, and it was reflected off the water so that there seemed to be gold gleaming somewhere in the depths. A land mass on the horizon to the north-east was the island of Suristan. Beyond it lay the Great Sea.

'Lord, they are signalling us from the land.' Ch'un Chu pointed.

A heliograph on the headland was flashing a message. Jehan did not even attempt to interpret what was being said. 'Ignore it.'

Probably Artai had discovered Jehana's absence, and he was attempting some ruse to bring them back to port. Not even the Kha-Khan could lawfully command Jehana to return, because under the Yasa her first duty was to her husband.

The heliograph flashed again. 'Lord, they'll think we're blind,' Ch'un Chu said unhappily.

'Let them.'

Just as Artai had been unable to declare publicly that Jehana was a hostage, so he could not now object because she had chosen to join Alexei on the ship. It was the perfect solution.

Orcadai and C'zinsit and the others were greeting Jehana now. She had no baggage, but none of them seemed to be surprised to see her.

Jehan guessed that Burun had divined Artai's intent in advance, and had planned everything. Jehan's immediate instinct was to be angry because he had not been told. He thought about asking Jehana how much warning she had received about what had happened, and knew at once that she would deny that it had been anything other than a surprise. Probably she had known, but would now insist that it had been her own idea to join the ship. That way Burun would be protected.

It was amusing to picture Burun explaining to Artai about Jehana's sudden impulse to go with her husband. Jehan imagined Burun's innocent expression, and Artai's disbelief, and he laughed again and shook his head.

Even at night the sunstones provided sufficient heat to power the engines. Jehan asked Parin for an explanation, and did not completely understand the reply he got. He could see that the beam shining from the reflector at night was a different colour from that which shone by day – it was whiter and the sound which accompanied it was different. Otherwise it appeared to be as effective, for both moons were in the sky.

The sea beyond Suristan was a deeper green, but it was still calm, and the weather remained fair. The wind blew from the south-west, and would have troubled them if the *Sunstealer* had possessed sails. Jehan found that he preferred to be on deck whenever possible – the cabins which he and Kadan and the others shared were cramped – and he guessed that an extended period of heavier seas would be an uncomfortable experience. The crew occupied hammocks in the forecastle, and seemed not to notice the lack of space. The troopers were billeted in the hold along with the st'lyan, and most of them like Jehan slept on deck when the weather permitted. A few had been sea-sick the first night out, but they had recovered.

Navigation was a task which was shared between Parin and Ch'un Chu. The Losani appeared to carry a map of the night sky in his head, and steered always towards one bright star. Parin for his part used instruments and a set of tables which provided the position of the sun relative to the earth at all times of the year. According to the Sechem, they were being carried somewhat to the north, possibly by a strong current, and there were daily discussions which had to be mediated either by Alexei or by Jehan. Sometimes they decided on a course adjustment, but since they were travelling all the time approximately west, a variation of a point to the north was felt to be of no great consequence.

'One day we will be able to fix our position both east to west and south to north,' Parin observed. 'We could do so now, Noyon, did we but measure time accurately enough.'

They were five days out from land. Jehan squinted at the tables in the Sechem's hands, and he shrugged. The offworlder seemed to know what Parin was talking about. The words 'latitude' and 'longitude' had been mentioned, both men shaking their heads. Jehan stared around the horizon. He could see nothing but

368

sea. 'Do we know where we are?'

'More or less,' Alexei said. Ch'un Chu at the offworlder's shoulder looked moderately offended. 'At the very worst we are a hundred verst further north than we believe,' the offworlder continued, 'and maybe a hundred verst or less further east.'

Jehan frowned. He stared at the main chart. 'The Unknown Lands are large,' he said. 'It will be hard to miss them.'

Ch'un Chu had been keeping a log of each day's journey, recording the condition of the sea, the current, the strength and direction of the wind. A daily attempt to find bottom had been thus far unsuccessful, but the Losani did not appear to be troubled by the fact. Long thin fish kept pace with the ship. The *Sunstealer*'s speed was measured using a log line, and Ch'un Chu examined the results, eyed the fish, and then declared that they were covering close to three hundred verst in a day's sailing. Jehan raised an eyebrow at Parin, who looked nonplussed. 'Noyon,' he said, 'it is possible.'

Men who used science were often unwilling to admit that they were unable to provide exact answers. Jehan looked at Alexei, and they both smiled.

They had been sailing for another hour when the crewman who was occupying the cage at the mast head called down. 'Land! Land two points to starboard!'

Parin examined the map. His finger tapped a marked cluster of islands. 'It's Surasai, Noyon,' he said. 'It can't be anything else.'

Whether or not the Sechem was correct, it made sense to turn north. The *Sunstealer*'s head moved round onto the new course.

The morning passed. Lookout reports confirmed that what lay ahead was not a continent.

369

'At least we know where we are,' Parin said. He sounded pleased.

Alexei and Jehan climbed together to the masthead to examine the landfall. Jehan thought that he was glad that the lookout station was enclosed. The deck below looked uncomfortably narrow, and when the ship rolled they seemed to be poised for a moment over the water first to port, and then to starboard. He took the glass from Alexei's hands and gazed through it, ignoring his fluttering stomach.

The islands were quite large, and mostly low-lying. A line of white water off the nearest indicated reefs. A few houses were dotted on the headland above, and there was no sign of a landing place.

Ch'un Chu made a face when he saw it. 'Best we don't go too close, Lord,' he said to Alexei.

Orcadai was in the middle of a group of men who were studying the chart. He looked round. 'There are several islands,' he observed. 'We should sail round them at least.'

Alexei seemed to consider, and then he nodded.

'We're an embassy after all,' Orcadai said.

The Losani grimaced. His index finger traced what appeared to be a channel which ran due west between the two largest islands.

'As the Khan wishes,' he said. 'But Lord, you made me captain. If you won't take my advice, I might as well not be here.'

The offworlder showed his teeth. 'I'm always prepared to listen to advice.'

Ch'un Chu's expression reflected a measure of polite disbelief. 'In that case, Lord, I say we should proceed slowly. I'll put two hands in the bow to swing the leadlines.'

They nosed the vessel cautiously past a long shoreline which seemed to consist entirely of grey cliffs topped with windswept grassland. More houses became visible – farms Jehan thought, for they were not grouped together. A passage between two smaller islands to starboard appeared too narrow for ships. The troopers lining the deck had hoped to stretch their legs ashore, and they looked disappointed.

'We could heave to,' Alexei said. 'A small boat might find a landing place.' He did not sound enthusiastic.

'If there are people here, they are not numerous.' Jehan saw something move in the passage between the islands as he spoke. He put up a hand to shade his eyes from the sun. 'There must be a harbour somewhere. There's a boat coming out to meet us.'

In fact there were several – broad-beamed craft with lateen sails and banks of oars. Ch'un Chu gave them a single troubled look, and then he turned. 'Lord,' he said to Alexei, 'don't ask me how I know, but those are pirates. They mean to board us if they can.'

Five ships had now emerged into the main channel. They bore down on the *Sunstealer*, and Jehan saw the beak of a ram beneath the prow of each.

Jehana had been taking the air on the afterdeck. 'Idlers below,' Ch'un Chu said. 'Sechem, my Lady – stay in your cabins until you're called.' He glanced at Alexei for confirmation.

Alexei was peering at the approaching ships. He turned. 'Yes. Although I doubt if we will have to fight. We can outrun them easily.'

The approaching ships had their oars out. The sweeps worked smoothly, rippling down the sides of each vessel. Jehan heard the faint beat of drums, and he guessed that they were being used by the galley masters to keep time.

The throb of the *Sunstealer*'s engines increased in

371

volume, and the gap which separated their stern from the prow of the nearest enemy ship began to widen.

They were drawing clear. Jehan waited for the pursuit to fall off, but it did not. He caught Alexei's attention. 'They're still following us.'

Men were busy in the bow of the leading pirate ship. Jehan saw smoke, and suspected a catapult.

'They can't believe they have a hope of catching us.' Alexei looked back, and then he turned and stared up the channel ahead. A sail came into view around a headland which led to the open sea. It was followed by two more. The offworlder shook his head. 'They were ready for us,' he said. 'We're going to have to fight after all.'

Sidacai was marshalling men across the foredeck. An orderly brought Jehan his bow. He uncased it, watching the ships which were closing to intercept.

The three ships which were cutting across their path were running in staggered formation. Jehan made out the detail of the design painted on the sails. The ships were packed with men.

'We can't let them ram,' Alexei said, his tone casual.

Ch'un Chu was concentrating on the vessels ahead, and he did not turn. He said, 'Your pardon, Lord, but I've done this before.' He laid a hand on the helmsman's shoulder. 'A point to port,' he said calmly.

The ship was surging through the water. It heeled as the helm came down. The catapult on the intercepting pirate ship fired in almost the same instant. A missile of some kind went over their heads and splashed into the water. Sidacai was calling ranges to the troopers standing in the waist. Jehan heard a command, and then the space between the *Sunstealer* and the leading enemy vessel was black with arrows. It turned into the wind, and the next ship in line was forced to veer to avoid a collision.

'That's discouraged them.' Sidacai grinned at Jehan, and then he turned back to watch the pirates.

The third vessel was still bearing down on the *Sunstealer*. It had an iron ram which protruded slightly out of the water. A bow wave curled away on either side of it, and it had closed to within thirty drem when Ch'un Chu gave another quiet helm order. The *Sunstealer* heeled to starboard.

The pirate ship came on. Jehan eyed the ram, and thought that the gap between them was closing. The ram seemed to grow larger, and then suddenly it was no longer aimed amidships, but into their wake.

'Hold your course,' Ch'un Chu spoke calmly.

The pirate fell further and further behind. Its bow swung to follow the *Sunstealer*, and it was taken aback by the wind. The sails flapped, and Jehan heard the angry shouts of the men on the deck.

'They'll have to get that sail down and row to wind-ward,' Ch'un Chu said, sounding satisfied. 'Never catch us now.'

The other ships were turning away, or were coming about to run parallel with the shore of the larger island. The oars of the first two vessels which had tried to intercept had become jammed together. The troopers on the *Sunstealer*'s deck cheered and gestured rudely.

Alexei stared back at the chaos, unsmiling. 'May they rot,' he said. 'One day we will come back and kill them all.'

'We will find land in five days,' Parin said confidently.

They had turned south-west. Finding Surasai had allowed the Sechem to confirm certain of his calculations, and he seemed to be certain that he could steer them to precise landfall on the more easterly of the two large land masses which made up the bulk of the Unknown Lands.

There was nothing on any of the maps to indicate where a harbour might be found. Lakes joined by a river appeared to cut the northern part of the continent almost in two, but the mouth of the river was on the western coast, entering a gulf where the depth of the water was unmarked.

It was nothing like a reconnaissance, Jehan thought. The sea voyage itself had been fairly uneventful thus far, but he could imagine how difficult it would be to keep a large number of ships together, all following the same course towards an invasion landfall.

'I wonder what else we'll find,' Kadan said softly.

They were sitting astride the portside rail, the green water rushing past below them. Fish with grey skins and great dorsal fins kept pace alongside, leaping out of the water every so often, then diving again.

The serious business of the embassy would commence only when they found a centre of population. A land mass the size of the one they were approaching had to be inhabited. If it was not, then it could be claimed for the Kha-Khan. Jehan considered the possibility that so much territory remained unoccupied, and thought that it was unlikely.

'It's a long way to travel, just to prove that it can be done,' Jehan said. Parin was rolling up his charts. The Sechem had shed the gown of his office, and was dressed as they all were in serviceable breeches topped by a stiffened tunic of buckram. Jehan stared at the surface of the water. There were trails of bubbles inside every wave, and he wondered how they were created.

The remark seemed to amuse Kadan. 'Other people

might not understand,' he said.

Jehan shrugged. 'We can always go back.'

Whether or not they continued past the first land-fall, it would prove nothing. One day there would be nothing left to explore. Then they would be forced to stop.

Parin descended out of sight through the hatchway which led down to the cabins.

'If there were no seas to cross, our task would be easy,' Kadan commented.

'Maybe it would.' Jehan looked up at the sky. It was late in the afternoon, and thin lines of clouds were following the prevailing wind, streaming across the face of the sun like smoke from a dying fire. 'We will have to learn to master the sea, just as we have mastered the land.'

Jehana and Alexei were standing together under an awning which was spread across the afterdeck. The offworlder looked relaxed, and Jehan remembered how resistant both of them had been to the whole idea of marriage, and he smiled.

Kadan followed the direction of Jehan's gaze. He said, 'Have you noticed how differently we behave, now that we are not in our fathers' shadows?'

The observation took Jehan by surprise. He reviewed the words, and knew that Kadan was not really talking about parental influence. Kadan had not been discussing the progress of the embassy either. Jehan frowned at the thought. 'You mean we will behave differently when we return to Kinsai,' he said. He was aware that Kadan meant nothing of the kind.

'Do I?' Kadan swung both feet down onto the deck.

Sidacai emerged suddenly from the companionway which led to the hold. He stopped when he saw Jehan, and then seemed to make up his mind about something. He walked steadily towards them, stopping beside the rail, balancing easily against the pitch and roll of the ship. Kadan was staring at his feet. He looked up slowly. Then he glanced from Sidacai to Jehan and back again. He started to hum softly.

'I think we ought to declare a truce until the embassy is over.' Sidacai caught Jehan's eye. 'There is no room on a ship for us to fight.'

Jehan gave Sidacai a hard stare. 'You know I can beat you if I choose, he said.

'Oh.' Sidacai grinned. 'I think that's what we're fighting about. You know I'm not afraid of you.'

They could fight here and now, and no one would interfere. Jehan tensed, anticipating an attack. Sidacai's talons were half extended. He seemed to take a deep breath, and shoved both his hands into his belt.

Jehan let out the breath he had been holding. 'Very well. Truce.'

Sidacai took a pace back. 'You agree?' He sounded surprised.

'Haven't I just said so?' Now that it was done, Jehan was impatient with even the suggestion of further discussion. 'We don't fear one another, and there is no trust between us, but we won't fight – not until the embassy is ended.'

'God's Name, you're blunt.' Sidacai took one hand out of his belt. He ran it up across his scalp.

'What did you expect?' Jehan saw that Kadan was enjoying the exchange. He glared.

'Oh, nothing whatever.' Sidacai gave a harsh laugh. He turned and walked away.

The move was so sudden that Jehan was left gaping. He thought about what had been said, wondering if he had agreed too easily. It made sense for them to declare a truce, and Jehan was pleased

376

that he had not been the one who had proposed it. Coming from Sidacai it was like an admission of defeat, and Jehan suspected that although Sidacai was not afraid, he knew when he was beaten.

'What are you going to do about Artai?'

Jehana was working on one of Alexei's dress coats, altering it so that it would fit her slender figure. Like everyone else on board she wore tunic and breeches, and the fact that she had no gowns or women to attend her seemed not to be an inconvenience. The problem of what she would wear when the embassy went ashore was another matter entirely, and it was against such an occasion that the alterations to Alexei's coat were being made, in case nothing more suitable could be found.

Jehan watched his sister's hands. She forced a needle into the stiff backing of the coat. He did not attempt to meet her eyes. 'What makes you think I intend to do anything?'

Her hands stilled. 'Alexei cannot,' she observed in a matter-of-fact tone. 'He is my husband, but he is not human and he has no recourse under the law.'

The gold facings of the coat caught the light as Jehana turned the garment in her hands. Jehan stirred uncomfortably. 'There are others,' he suggested.

'Are there?' Jehana looked up quickly. 'Our father will not, as we are both aware. And as to Burun, it would not be fitting. Only you are of the rank. You are Altun, as Artai is, and you are more Yek than Merkut –'

'Oh, thank you.'

She gave him a look. 'Don't pretend offence.' She laid the coat aside. 'Artai offended custom by his attempt to use me as a hostage. Now he is vulnerable. Did you think I would not work it out?'

377

Her face was a finer version of his own. Jehan looked away, incapable of dissembling sufficiently to lie to her. They were seated in the *Sunstealer*'s aft cabin, the only large room below deck. Beyond Jehana the windows were open along the stern. A sea bird swooped past, calling raucously. Finally Jehan said, 'I will tell you what I intend if you tell me why you married Alexei.'

He did not expect her to answer. She produced a snort of laughter. 'You want to understand why we are what we are,' she said, 'so that you can use us.'

It was too close to the truth for comfort. Jehan spread his fingers. The gold sheathing of his talons glittered. He looked up. 'I will never marry,' he said.

Jehana wrinkled her nose. 'I said that once.'

It was the obvious reply. Jehan frowned. 'You don't like men.'

She made a face at him. 'Tell that to my husband.'

Jehan ignored the riposte. 'Marriage means sharing a part of oneself. I don't trust other people's motives enough for that.'

Women's intrigues were always far more complicated than those which were practised by men, Jehan reflected. He watched Jehana's expression, and guessed that she found his reasoning simplistic.

Jehana began to tease a length of silk from a twist of many coloured strands. 'I have gained as much from my marriage as I have surrendered, I think,' she observed primly.

She was pretending to be diverted away from the subject of Artai. Jehan grinned, applauding the skill with which she had avoided answering the essential question about her relationship with Alexei. 'I don't doubt it.'

A bell was being rung to indicate the change of the watches. Jehan felt the throb of the engines coming

378

up through the deck planks under his feet. He stood. Jehana had picked up the coat again. She ran her fingers down a seam, flattening the fabric.

Jehan hesitated, unsure how much to tell her. He saw her glance up, and flushed. 'Don't ask me about Artai,' he said. 'I will deal with him when it is time.'

The shore line was an almost unbroken stretch of silver sand. It ran north and south as far as the eye could see. Behind it there were occasional dunes. A few fishing boats were drawn up above a high water mark, and there was no sign of a harbour.

'We could continue south,' Alexei said. 'Maybe there is a port.'

'– And maybe there isn't,' C'zinsit said. 'We have been in sight of land for half a day. Surely the best way to find a city is to ask.'

It was the moment arrived at by every embassy, when somebody had to make the first contact with the native inhabitants. Jehan gazed towards the roofs of buildings which were partially hidden from view by a long sand dune. There were men working at a boat on the beach below the dune, but if they had observed the *Sunstealer*'s approach, the sighting had aroused neither interest nor the least sign of consternation.

'They don't look very hostile,' Jehan said. 'I'll go.'

'They may not be all that friendly once they find out what we want,' Orcadai remarked. 'You ought to have an escort.'

Everyone looked at Sidacai.

Sidacai said, 'If the people along this coast were hostile, we would know it by now. I'll go with you, Noyon, of course. But too many of us will make it look like an invasion.'

Alexei frowned. 'I'm the ambassador. I should go.'

Orcadai looked irritated. 'You can't all go,' he said. 'What if none of you come back?'

Sidacai laughed softly. 'Ambassadors are expendable.'

A muscle rippled along the line of Alexei's jaw. 'Are we?' He examined Sidacai coolly.

Jehan stared out to sea. A light wind had sprung up, and it was stirring the wave crests and whipping white spray up over the side of the ship. Orcadai and C'zinsit were not the oldest members of the embassy, but they seemed to spend much of their time acting to dampen the more exuberant spirits of the others. Burun had justified their inclusion by saying that their presence would provide balance. At moments like this, however, they seemed to be able to contribute nothing useful. Jehan turned. 'We all know the risks we face,' he said flatly. 'We'll go ashore because that's why we're here. We would be fools if we didn't expect the worst – and bigger fools if we let it deter us.'

Orcadai sniffed. 'A fine speech. It doesn't answer my question. What are we to do if none of you return?'

It was a pointless question. Sidacai snorted. 'Do what you like,' he said. 'It won't matter to us.'

The boat which was lowered from the *Sunstealer* a short time later was large enough to hold twice the number of people who finally occupied it. Apart from the crew of oarsmen, the landing party which was settled upon consisted of Jehan, Alexei, Sidacai, and Kadan. Orcadai and C'zinsit watched disapprovingly from the side of the ship as the boat pulled away. Jehana was in the open window of the aft cabin. If she had any feelings about the nature of the expedition, she had not made them public.

The keel of the boat grounded only drem from the shore. Jehan splashed through ankle-deep water,

380

unwilling to wait for the oarsmen to pull them up onto the sand. Away from the water's edge the beach was gritty, and crunched beneath his boots. He lurched, unaccustomed to a surface underfoot which did not pitch and roll.

A handful of men working at a high-prowed boat paused, looked round, and then went on with what they were doing. Jehan eyed them, thinking that they were as disparate a group as he had seen anywhere in the Khanate. For a start they were of no identifiable physical type – they were tall, short, fat, thin, and their skin colours varied from pale white to deep ch'ban brown. Clothing varied as much as appearance. A tall fellow with a black beard and hair knotted in pigtails was clad in trousers which had one blue and one red leg. He was bare-chested, but wore boots. The little man at his side had no hair at all, and wore a rusty black coat which descended to his calves. His feet were bare. The next man in line had hair which was dyed green, and it had been cut so that there was a comb a hand's-breadth in height running back across his scalp. The hair at the back hung down to his waist, and his only articles of clothing were a hide waistcoat and a breechclout. He wore sandals. None of the men had talons.

Kadan was staring openly. 'They don't look mad,' he said.

Of the ten men who were scraping the hull of the nearest boat, there were no two whom Jehan would have identified as being of the same ethnic origin. He had to assume that they were either fishermen or ship labourers, but was able to pick out no one who seemed to be in charge.

'They certainly aren't hostile,' Alexei observed.

Jehan looked up the gentle slope of the beach and saw that there was a wooden staging which appeared

381

to lead in the direction of the cluster of buildings. He said, 'Let's see if we can make ourselves understood.'

They walked towards the boat. Tiny particles of sand were kicked up by their progress. They glittered in the sun. Jehan stopped in the shade provided by the tilt of the vessel. A man who was seated on a plank propped across two stones looked round slowly, then spat into the sand.

'Greetings,' Jehan said.

He had used the Yek word. There was no reaction. The man sitting on the plank wore a brown jerkin over a yellow shirt. He was grey-haired, and there were tufts of beard growth on his cheeks, although his chin was clean shaven.

Jehan tried N'pani, then Ch'noze, and finally C'zak. At the last the grey-haired man's expression altered. He said something in an undertone to the man at his side, and they both laughed.

Alexei started. 'Anglic,' he said. 'It's similar to C'zak.' He looked at Jehan. 'You wouldn't remember, Noyon, but it's the language my father and I spoke when we came to this world.'

Burun had mentioned it. Jehan nodded. 'You'd better do the talking then. They think my accent is strange.'

'Yes.' Alexei gave the grey-haired man a courteous nod. 'Good day,' he said.

There was a moment's silence. Then Grey Hair made a sound which might have been amusement. 'Good for you, maybe,' he responded.

Alexei produced a polite smile. He said, 'I'm sorry to trouble you –'

'Are you?' Grey Hair looked disbelieving.

'– But we need to speak to the leader of your community,' Alexei continued, pretending that he had not heard the interruption.

Jehan eyed the scales adhering to Grey Hair's coat, and thought that he was probably a fisherman. Grey Hair moved round so that he was facing them. He had a broad-bladed chisel in his hand – he had been using it as a scraper – and now he laid it aside. He gave Alexei a stare. 'Nobody's leading me anywhere,' he said levelly.

The language was very like C'zak, but the vowels were different. Jehan found that he could understand quite easily. One had to concentrate, that was all.

The offworlder's smile was a little strained. 'You don't understand me,' he said.

'Can any man understand another?' the fisherman asked philosophically.

Jehan saw Alexei take a deep breath. He hid a smile.

'There must be a man among you who is of greater importance than any other,' Alexei attempted. 'That is the person we seek.'

Grey Hair rubbed his hands together to clean them. 'Of greater importance,' he echoed. He ran one hand across his chin. 'You're not from these parts, I reckon.'

'We are from across the sea.' Alexei gestured. 'That is our ship.'

'Ah.' The fisherman glanced briefly at the *Sunstealer*. 'Foreigners. I thought so. And does the kind of man you are looking for exist where you come from?'

'Of course.'

They seemed to be getting nowhere. Jehan nudged Alexei. 'Ask him again –' he started.

Grey Hair seemed to be unaware that Jehan had even spoken. He eyed Alexei speculatively. 'And this person of importance – what will happen to your land when he dies? Will it cease to exist?'

'No,' the offworlder admitted.

'The lives of other men will go on as before?'

'Yes.'

'Then he cannot be of importance,' the fisherman declared. He picked up his scraper and resumed work.

Jehan saw that both Sidacai and Kadan had followed the gist of the conversation. Kadan was looking amused, but Sidacai put a hand on his sword hilt. 'Let me take his head,' he said in Yek. 'The others will answer soon enough.'

It was not a serious suggestion, Jehan thought. He shook his head. 'That won't achieve anything.'

Sidacai stared at Grey Hair's broad back. 'It might teach them some respect,' he commented.

The tone of the fisherman's voice had lacked any hint of a suspicion that he might be dealing with persons of rank. Jehan teased at his moustaches. 'We've run up against the local character, that's all. There's someone like him in every small settlement.'

'Not on any of my fiefs,' Alexei said. 'All the same, I think you're probably right. If we're going to learn anything of value we ought to move on.'

There were nine other men working on the boat, but none of them appeared to be even remotely interested in the presence of the strangers who were so clearly discussing them. Jehan eyed them irresolutely. 'I hate to walk away.'

Alexei gestured. 'So do I. But do you have a better idea?'

It wasn't how an embassy was supposed to proceed, Jehan reflected. Usually they knew something about the people of the land in which they were travelling. He shook his head.

They climbed onto the staging and walked along it through the dune. Sidacai glanced back. 'One day they will respect us,' he said.

Now that his view was less obstructed, Jehan saw that the few buildings he had observed before were part of what was clearly a village of some size. None of the houses conformed to any kind of pattern. Several were tall and narrow with more than one floor. Others were low, and sprawled off in odd directions as if the rooms had been tacked on when they were needed. A diversity of building materials had been used, and no two roofs were of the same colour.

'Unusual,' Kadan remarked.

The houses were like the people who lived in them, Jehan realised. He supposed that there was no reason why a man should not express his personality in his appearance, his dress, or in the style of his abode. It indicated an absence of order however, and Jehan wondered if they ought not to sail on and try elsewhere.

A man was cutting wood in an enclosure at the side of an open barn. He looked round at the sound of their footsteps echoing off the boards of the staging. Alexei gave a nod. 'Greetings, friend.'

The woodcutter was wearing nothing apart from a pair of bright blue tights. His hair was pure white, and it was fastened in a top-knot which was bound with ribbons. He swung his axe at a billet of wood, splitting it, and then turned. 'What gives you the idea I'm a friend of yours?' he enquired. 'I don't know you.'

Jehan saw Alexei's lips compress for a moment. The offworlder seemed to bite down on a retort. He said, 'It was a figure of speech. I was trying to be polite.'

Blue Tights' eyes opened wide. He eyed Jehan and the others, and then looked back at Alexei. 'I suppose that's worth trying for,' he remarked. He hefted his axe once more.

They were speaking the same language, Jehan

realised suddenly, but their understanding of meaning was quite different. He said, 'Pardon my accent, sir, but I'm not used to your tongue. May I have speech with you?'

The woodcutter lowered the axe, resting his hand on the haft. He tugged at his top-knot. 'I can make out what you're saying,' he said. 'Speak your piece if you want. It's your privilege.'

It was the first sign of a co-operative response. Alexei said, 'Can you tell us the name of this place?'

Blue Tights gave him a look. 'Yes.' The single word was uttered with careful precision. The axe came up again.

'– What my companion means is will you tell us,' Jehan said quickly. He saw comprehension begin to dawn on Alexei's face.

'Foreigners,' Blue Tights said. He swung the axe overarm so that the head bit into the solid block which was braced against the foot of the woodpile. He turned. 'I should have known. The way you're dressed, you're not from around here.'

Jehan showed his teeth. 'Is there something wrong with the way I'm dressed?'

A frown appeared on the woodcutter's face. It was as if he was struggling to deal with some alien concept. 'As to that, I couldn't say,' he said finally. 'And as to the name of this place, it's Patris.' He gave Jehan a curt nod, and then bent down and lifted a billet of wood onto the block. He jerked the axe free with an easy twist of his arm.

Jehan opened his mouth to speak, and then closed it again.

'This is ridiculous.' Alexei caught hold of the wood-cutter's arm. He pulled him round. 'There must be a headman in this village. Tell us his name and where we can find him.'

Blue Tights looked down at Alexei's hand on his arm. There was surprise on his face. He raised his eyebrows at Jehan. 'Is this necessary? I am busy.'

'Answer my question,' Alexei said.

The woodcutter ignored him. He stared steadily at Jehan.

Jehan drew a breath. He gave Alexei a look. 'Let him go,' he said in Yek.

'He hasn't told us –'

'He isn't going to. What are we going to do about it – kill him? That won't unstop his tongue.'

The offworlder's eyes flickered. He let go of the woodcutter's arm. The woodcutter gave Jehan another nod. 'That makes us even,' he said. He turned away, lifting his axe. It was as if they no longer existed.

'I hope you didn't expect thanks,' Kadan murmured. He grinned.

'It isn't funny.' Jehan was unable to keep the irritation out of his voice. 'Do you understand what it will mean if everyone in this land behaves the same way?' He strode to the end of the staging. A flight of wooden steps led down to what appeared to be the main street. Alexei and the others had to quicken their pace to keep up with him.

The Anglic and C'zak words for a village elder were the same. '*Hetman*,' Alexai had said, and the look in the woodcutter's eyes had shown that he did not comprehend the term.

No one in the village street gave them more than a second glance.

'No weapons,' Sidacai observed. 'Whoever rules this land, there has been peace for years.'

The few men Jehan saw with knives were using them as tools. There was a blacksmith's shop at one end of the street. Jehan peered inside, but saw no sign that the smith was also an armourer.

They were not customers, and so at first they were ignored. Alexei attempted a brief conversation with the smith, and received answers in monosyllables.

'Headman?' The blacksmith was a head taller than Alexei, with a physique to match. He repeated the word, brow furrowed, and shook his head. 'Means nothing.'

He was telling the truth, Jehan thought. 'We're going to find that they settle disputes among themselves,' he said as they walked away from the smithy.

'– You mean once we can persuade them to talk to us,' Kadan said.

Jehan ignored him. 'Everyone deals with everyone else as an equal,' he pointed out. 'Even in dealings with their overlord, there probably isn't any one person who speaks for all.'

'If they have an overlord.' Alexei made a face.

It was inconceivable that the land had not been claimed by someone. Jehan thought that the offworlder was allowing himself to be too easily discouraged. He said, 'Maybe this place is too far from anywhere for them to be much concerned about who holds the power.'

Even as he said it, Jehan knew that it could not be the explanation. If a feudal overlord did not claim tribute – maybe because an area was too isolated for him to exercise control – then someone else moved in and established himself as master.

The houses were neat but strange. Jehan recognised a few tools and other items, but there was nothing which appeared to be made to a pattern. Everything was individually designed.

Sidacai indicated a low grey stone building with a thatched roof. 'That looks like a tavern.' The stones from which the front wall was constructed were shiny with age. Three men sitting on a bench outside were drinking from earthenware mugs, and kegs and barrels were stacked in an enclosure.

Alexei paused in mid-step. He looked at Jehan. 'I think we've been going about this the wrong way,' he said. 'When you want to know something, you don't interrupt a man who is working, you –'

'– Talk to a man in his cups,' Jehan finished. 'I should have thought of that.'

There were tables of some grey-coloured wood along the front of the tavern. They sat down at one of them. The tavern keeper came out of the front door. He eyed them suspiciously. 'Do I know you?'

'I doubt it.' Jehan fitted his tongue around the unfamiliar Anglic vowels.

'Foreigners.' The tavern keeper looked disappointed. 'I thought you might be customers.'

Alexei's head went round. 'Why can't we be both?'

The tavern keeper was a small man with a nose which suggested that he regularly sampled whatever it was he sold. He was wearing an orange coat which had seen better days. He said, 'I serve ale. I don't give it away.'

Jehan caught Alexei's eye. 'He thinks we can't pay. Do you have koban?'

The offworlder nodded. He extracted a wallet from his tunic and unfolded it. The gold koban gleamed yellow as butter in the sunlight. Alexei held one out to the tavern keeper. 'We don't have any of your money, but if you value gold, then maybe we can agree a rate of exchange for this.'

The entire stock of the tavern was probably worth less than the value of the coin. The tavern keeper did not look impressed. 'Gold, you say?' He weighed the koban piece in his hand, and then tested it between his teeth. 'I have never seen it in this form. But what use is it to me?'

'It's of no value?' Jehan was unable to conceal his surprise.

'To someone who makes trinkets for women maybe,' the tavern keeper conceded. 'But there are none such in Patris.'

Alexei frowned. 'What do you use for money?'

The word appeared to puzzle their host. 'What is money?' He turned the gold coin over in his fingers.

'It's –' Jehan paused, struggling to find words to describe an idea which he had never imagined would require description. '– It's a medium of exchange. Say we give you that gold piece to pay for our ale. Then later you use it to pay the farmer who supplies your hops, or maybe you give it to the man who makes your barrels. The value of the coin is determined by the amount of work or the quantity of goods which can be exchanged for it.'

The tavern keeper looked superior. 'Like a token, you mean.' He shook his head. 'That may be the practice where you come from, but we have no need of that here, for we are men of trust. I get my hops from Yevgeni Preeyev. In return I serve him and his hired men for a season. I serve his friends too, or those who are in his debt, so that he owes me, and he brings my wife meat and cheese until we are even.'

It was the phrase which had been used by the fisherman, Jehan recalled.

'A barter system.' Alexei nodded. 'I understand.' He gave the tavern keeper an interested stare. 'But tell me how you deal with matters which involve settlement with many rather than with one. Say there is a fire in your tavern.'

The landlord laughed harshly. 'In such a case I would have to beat the men of Patris from my door, such would be their haste to come to my aid. If they can place me in their debt, I will be required to serve them until we are even again. To that end I give every man in the village free ale one day a year, so that they owe me. Thus if there is a fire, or if I call on them for help, they remember that they are in my debt. The carpenter, the mason, the cooper, all owe me service, such is the strength of my ale.'

Jehan pondered the tavern keeper's explanation. Its simplicity was appalling.

'All this doesn't settle our thirst,' Sidacai said in bad Anglic. 'Will you accept our gold?'

The tavern keeper scratched his head. 'I must be getting soft,' he said. 'Very well, your gold for ale today, tomorrow, and the next day. Also I'll give you my note to Ivan Orlov who keeps the eating house. He will feed you for the same number of days.'

'Ivan Orlov owes you,' Alexei observed drily.

'He likes my ale.' The landlord grinned.

Tomorrow or the next day they would move on. In the meantime it was worth being swindled – the tavern keeper's offer was much to his advantage – to maintain a contact who might be prepared to provide information.

'Then probably so shall we,' Jehan said, smiling.

The owner of the eating house was a tall man with an enormous belly. He had slanting eyes like a N'pani, and wore a long flame-coloured gown. He read the tavern keeper's note, looking pleased. 'Food for three days. You have cleared my debt to Vasily Ilich.' He held the note to a cresset and watched as the paper was consumed. 'Order what you will.'

The meat dish came in a large bowl, and the only eating implements were wooden spoons. Jehan ladled a portion onto the trencher of bread which served as a plate, and he started to eat. The first time he used his talons the heads of the men seated at the next table came round, and they stared.

'They've never seen talons before,' Kadan commented. He speared a chunk of meat and transferred it to his mouth.

'But they're too polite to remark on it,' Jehan said. He remembered how the fisherman had refused the opportunity to offer criticism about their style of dress.

'I don't think it's politeness.' Alexei broke some bread from his trencher. 'They just don't think it's any of their business.'

It would explain a lot, Jehan thought. 'Dress how you like, build how you like, live how you like, so long as you don't interfere with the right of others to do the same,' he said.

'Exactly.' The offworlder nodded. 'It's how they show that they are free.'

'It probably means that they don't fight much,' Sidacai observed. He gazed thoughtfully around the room.

'Not among themselves at least,' Jehan said.

There was no way to tell how people with such peculiar ideas would behave in the face of an invasion.

The eating house was a big round building with a cone-shaped roof. The cooking fires and ovens were all in the centre, and there were flues and chimneys leading up through the rafters. Joints of meat and lengths of several kinds of sausage were hanging from smoke-blackened beams. The servers were male, but all the cooks were women. Their customers were mostly tradesmen, although there were a few who were either fishermen or farm workers.

Strangers would be few, Jehan realised. Possibly Patris saw occasional travellers – members of pack trains exchanging cloth or wine for dried fish – but the barter system would tend to ensure that trade remained a local affair. The attitude of the inhabitants to contact with others had the effect of isolating them. Probably that was why they did not bother with weapons.

'We still don't know who is lord of this land,' Alexei observed.

It was some time before their host returned to the table. The offworlder phrased his enquiry carefully, doing his best to avoid the possibility of misunderstanding.

The owner of the eating house looked amused. 'I have heard about your questions,' he said. 'Why should any of us submit to the rule of another?'

Alexei looked as if he thought the answer ought to be obvious. 'Because he provides leadership and protection.'

'Protection from what?'

'From others who seek to impose their will –' Alexei stopped, and Jehan guessed that he had worked out where the polite inquisition was leading.

'You are saying that we should give one man the right to tell us what to do, and render service unto him, and in return he will prevent others from doing the same.' The landlord summed up. 'That doesn't make sense.'

'Aah.' The offworlder threw up his hands in a gesture of exasperation. He appealed to Jehan. 'You explain it.'

Their host was signalling to a server to bring wine. The wine was tart, and there was only a hint of sweetness which lingered on the palate after it had been swallowed. Jehan sipped at his cup. Then he looked up. The thing had to be taken in stages. 'Landlord, tell me how you would deal with a man who drank your wine and then refused to discharge his debt.'

The landlord made a face. 'The next time he came

into my house I would refuse to serve him,' he said. 'Also I would post his name in the village square so that he would not get service from another.'

It made sense. Jehan nodded. 'But how if he comes in the night and steals from you?'

'Then I must needs fit stronger locks,' the owner of the eating house responded. He frowned. 'And if that fails, I must engage men to protect my goods. Everyone else will do the same, and after a time the thief will be able to get nothing, not even by stealth. No one will give him shelter, and he will starve.'

It was brutally simple. Alexei said, 'But say that a man steals, and carries on stealing until everything is shut against him. All he needs to do is to move to a new village and start again.'

'Not in this land.' Their host shook his head. 'A man such as you describe might survive for a month in one place, and for two weeks in the next. But remember that he must be a Taker from the start. Wherever he goes, men will suspect him, for they will not know him. Soon the word will spread from place to place. In the third village he will survive for a day. The fourth he will find barred against him.'

'You could take him prisoner, and punish him for his misdeeds,' Jehan suggested.

Their host looked puzzled. 'How would that restore the balance?' he asked. 'In any case freedom belongs to each man and cannot be bartered. And as to punishment, a man's suffering is his alone. How can it be given to another to pay what is owed?'

They would not understand the function of bailiffs or stewards, Jehan thought. He guessed that disputes were settled by a process of negotiation, and that order was kept by mutual agreement, because it served the interests of the community to combine against the wrongdoer. He said, 'Suppose that instead of one man there were many. They would be strong, and so they would be able to take whatever they wished. How would you stand against them?'

The landlord's expression indicated a firm belief that the case could only be imaginary. He shrugged. 'In this village they would take everything,' he said. 'How would we prevent it? But no man would render them service, even on pain of death. Soon there would be nothing left for them to steal, and they would be forced to move on. By that time the word would have been spread. Corn would have been hidden. Animals would have been driven from the fields.'

'Enough men might gain control of the land,' Jehan pointed out.

Their host pondered. 'True,' he said. 'But how would they get service? Men such as you describe must apply themselves to every task. They must mill the corn they steal to make flour, and bake the flour into bread. Not a thread will be woven or a stitch sewn except by their own hands.'

'A lord would protect you,' Jehan said.

'– And would demand goods and service for his protection,' the landlord countered, 'and we would no longer be free.'

Jehan saw that Sidacai and Kadan were listening intently, and he guessed that they thought as he did that it would be remarkable if no one in the whole land lived by making others submit to his will. He smiled at the owner of the eating house. 'You argue conclusively. But tell me truly, will all the men of Patris die before they bend?'

'Enough will,' their host said succinctly.

'The whole country cannot be ordered by such principles,' Orcadai said.

It was the morning of the next day. Most of the fishing boats which had lain on the beach had put out to sea the previous evening, and they had not yet returned. One of the *Sunstealer*'s boats had gone for fresh water, and another was drawn up on the sand awaiting the return from Patris of Kadan, who had taken two casks of wine to barter for fresh meat.

'It's not impossible,' Alexei said mildly.

'But how do they agree laws?' Orcadai stared towards the beach.

'They don't need many,' Jehan pointed out. 'They're brought up to do as they please so long as they don't offend the rights of others. Everyone respects the beliefs and attitudes of everyone else. So long as no one tries to force others to think or act according to his interpretation there is no conflict.'

'– And if someone does, he becomes an outcast,' Alexei said. 'Apart from that they have a system of exchange which involves both goods and services. It even affects the way they behave. You can't divert a man from something he has decided to do unless he can see it's going to be worth his while. Ask a question, and you'll get back the minimum response required to avoid giving offence. Beyond that it depends on how a man feels – if he's amused or curious, or bored maybe, you can get him to talk to you. If he's busy he'll tell you so, and expect you to respect the fact.'

'I don't believe they won't fight if they are attacked,' Orcadai said.

'I didn't say they would refuse to fight.' Jehan raised his eyebrows. 'It's the attitude of the people to force, and to the threat of force, which is unusual.'

Kadan was coming down the beach towards the waiting boat. The men accompanying him were struggling beneath the weight of four animal carcases.

Alexei followed the direction of Jehan's gaze. Then he turned.

'Civil disobedience,' the offworlder said. 'It's an old Terran concept. Say someone decides to make himself lord of the land hereabouts. He can call himself lord and no one will argue. It's when he tries to exercise control that his problems will start.'

It was a considerable understatement. Jehan snorted softly. He saw Alexei's head come round. The offworlder's face was expressionless, and there was no way to tell what he was thinking.

Alexei looked back at Orcadai. He said, 'The new lord waits until the harvest is in, and then he demands tribute. His men take the corn by force – they have to, because no one will render goods willingly.' He paused, allowing the picture to register in their minds. 'The corn has to be milled of course. However, the miller refuses to work the mill. He is thrown into prison. His assistant won't do the job, and the same applies to the men who are finally brought to the mill in chains. Soon the would-be lord has a jail full of millers, and the corn still hasn't been ground. Maybe he kills one or two as an example to the others, but it does no good. Meanwhile his men are ready to revolt because they are starving. They can't get animals fed, ale brewed, walls built, roofs thatched, or even a load moved from one place to another. Anything they aren't prepared to do themselves doesn't get done. They have a population in chains, or dead, but in the end the man who took the power is lord of nothing but wilderness.'

The idea that men would die before they would submit was so alien that Jehan shivered. To die fighting was one thing, but to die slaughtered like cattle seemed to make no sense. Orcadai looked disbelieving. 'Who decides who owns a piece of land?'

Jehan looked up. 'I asked about that. Here a plot of ground belongs to the person who is in possession of it – the one who is making use of it. Nobody disputes a man's claim so long as he continues to occupy the land and is putting it to use. The moment he ceases, however, it's anyone's for the taking.'

'But surely the new occupant owes the previous user for any buildings he leaves,' Orcadai said.

'Not at all.' It was Alexei who spoke. 'The first occupier gives up of his own free will, probably for the sake of something which is more attractive to him. Probably the land he moves onto is free, and he can't expect to gain from what he leaves behind.'

C'zinsit had been sitting all the time at Orcadai's shoulder. He looked bemused. 'There has to be a catch.'

Jehan smiled. 'There is a kind of catch. The man who starts a farm – or any other enterprise for that matter – has debts from the first. He has to commit himself to supplying the carpenter who built his barn with meat and cheese, corn and eggs. He gives produce to the tinsmith who makes the churns for his milk. Maybe the mason doesn't want farm produce – it could be that he gets his meat from somebody else – but he owes the smith for his tools, and passes on the debt by having the farmer supply the smith with whatever he desires.'

'How complicated.' C'zinsit ran a hand across the back of his neck. 'It must be hard for them to keep track of who owes what.'

It was a valid point. Jehan pursed his lips. 'Maybe it is. But they make a great to-do about being men of trust. And the system seems to work.'

Kadan's boat was heading back towards the ship now. The troopers of the guard were lined up along the side of the ship, watching enviously because no decision had yet been made about letting them go ashore.

It was not that the land beyond the beach was any different from land in the more fertile parts of the Khanate. The trees and plants were of similar species. There were no st'lyan of course, and no p'tar. Instead there were animals which were rather like small st'lyan, called equines, which lacked a horn.

The land did not represent the danger, Jehan thought. It was the people who were strange.

'This is one small part of the country.' Orcadai ran his index finger across his eyelids, wiping away the grease paint with which he had darkened his clan tattoo against the intensity of the early sun. He stared at the black stain on his fingertip. 'We don't know that everywhere is the same.'

'That's true.' Alexei nodded. 'There may be cities in the interior, and for that reason I think we ought to agree that some of us should ride across the land to the west coast. We already know that the old maps are accurate. We can designate a meeting place, and the ship can sail around to it.'

Orcadai looked unhappy. 'And if we miss one another? The land party could be here forever.'

Jehan wrinkled his nose. 'The men on the land will build a signal fire. That way the ship will find them – or if it does not, it can be sailed up and down the coast, searching.'

C'zinsit looked from Alexei to Jehan and back again. 'You have already decided,' he said, looking annoyed.

'I am the ambassador,' Alexai said.

Jehan hid a smile. It did not really matter what Orcadai and C'zinsit thought. Alexei was the only one among them who knew anything about making contact with alien species.

And they are alien; even though they look like us.
Jehan frowned at the thought.

Kadan came up the ladder onto the deck. He said, 'I
got the meat we wanted for only one cask of wine.
The people in the village are fools.'

If the meat was good, then probably Kadan had got
the best of the bargain.

Alexei looked round. 'Did you find out how scarce
wine was?' he asked. 'In the Khanate there is wine in
plenty. Here they don't even stock it in the taverns.
It's a luxury, only available when you go to an eating
house.'

Kadan's face fell. 'I didn't think of that.'

That was their problem, Jehan reflected. They were
attempting to judge what they found ashore on the
basis of knowledge which applied to the Khanate. But
it was not the Khanate. It was another world.

Orcadai said, 'I don't see the point of trying to
dissuade you if you have made up your minds to go.
How many men do you intend to take?'

Alexei sat back. 'Half a company or thereabouts.
We ought to travel in some style, in case we find
someone we want to talk to. We will have to feed
ourselves, and so we will need a pack train and the
men to guard it.'

'Leaving the crew and the remainder of the guard
to defend the ship if it is attacked,' Sidacai
commented. He was sitting with his chair propped
against the bulwark. He tossed his head, and his top-
knot caught the gentle breeze which came off the
land. 'Do you think that's wise?'

'Given what we have seen here,' Jehan said, 'we
think the risk is a reasonable one.' He gave Sidacai a
look. 'It was you who said that ambassadors are
expendable.'

'I'm not an ambassador.' Sidacai sat forward, and

400

the front legs of his chair crashed onto the deck. 'Or do you want me to command your escort?'

They had already discussed Sidacai's role. Alexei shook his head. 'If we are attacked on land, all the skill in the world probably won't preserve us. You stay with the ship.'

C'zinsit was examining the map. 'It will take you about ten days to ride across to the west coast,' he observed.

'Longer if we are delayed.' Jehan nodded.

'The journey around the coast will take longer,' Orcadai said thoughtfully. He caught Ch'un Chu's eye. 'Twelve days maybe?'

The Losani tugged at an earlobe. 'Given fair weather, Noyon.' He nodded slowly. 'About that.'

'Then we will be able to rest our animals,' Jehan said. He laid a finger on a point on the map which marked part of the western coastline. 'We will await you here.'

Ch'un Chu dipped a stylus in a bottle of ink, and he circled the spot.

'If you're not there, we'll wait a month,' Orcadai said.

Alexei produced a twisted smile. 'You'll wait as long as it takes,' he said. 'Have you anything better to do?'

'I'm taking Jehana,' Alexei said.

Jehan nodded. 'She told me. I think you're mad.'

They had transferred the st'lyan ashore that morning. Now the p'tar were being lowered in slings from the deck of the ship into the waiting boats. Most of the beasts sat down in the bottom of the boat as soon as the slings were removed, and Jehan reflected that this was one time when a p'tar's notorious stubbornness was a distinct asset.

401

The offworlder scuffed one booted foot across the sand, turning over the particles so that they glittered in the red light of the late sun. 'It isn't going to be dangerous,' he said.

The weight of the p'tar was causing the boats to ground in shallow water some way from the beach. Troopers struggled to lead them up onto the sand. The p'tar screamed, displaying mouths full of yellow teeth. Jehan watched one which had its forelegs in the water, but its rear in the boat. The boat tipped, and the members of the crew who had been employed as rowers cried out in alarm. 'It's no justification,' Jehan said.

Alexei shrugged. 'She's tired of the ship. The motion makes her feel ill.'

Jehan looked round. It was probably too soon for Jehana to be pregnant, even if that was her intent. Idly Jehan wondered if Alexei knew that a Yek woman could control her menstrual cycle if she chose.

The offworlder's face displayed only normal concern. It was the kind of expression usually seen on the features of married men preoccupied with minor matters, and held no hint of the trepidation sometimes shown by an expectant father.

'If we have to fight, she will be in the way,' Jehan said.

Neither of them really thought that the journey west was destined to be dangerous. Jehan saw Alexei adjusting his features to conceal a frown of impatience.

'The ship will be far more at risk than we are,' the offworlder said.

At least on land they would be able to scout ahead as they rode. If the way in which the country was governed changed from place to place, they would be forewarned. Aboard ship there would always be the element of the unknown. The sea to the south-west of the continent was marked on the chart as the Gulf of Storms. The narrows between the continents might conceal treacherous reefs, or there might be more pirates.

Jehan produced a condescending sigh. 'She's your wife,' he said.

'I'm glad you're mindful of that,' Alexei responded. He gave Jehan a level stare.

A line of st'lyan were tethered to a rope stretched between two posts embedded in the hard-packed sand. Boys from the village were watching fascinated from the tops of the dunes. A trooper walking sentry between the dunes and the tether line ignored the boys.

'They behave as if they have never seen soldiers before,' Jehan said. The boys were amazed by the st'lyan, but they were only amused by the armed trooper.

'Maybe they have not.' Alexei glanced round.

It was possible of course. Jehan sat down on his heels. 'We have always dealt with people who are as warlike as we are.'

Alexei was wearing a loose figured coat which had a high stiff collar. He brushed aside the skirts of the coat and rested a hand on his sword hilt. 'You're not sure we can rule here.'

'You mean you are?' Jehan looked up. 'Can we convince them that our notion of order is best? If we cannot, we face chaos.' There was a heat haze rising above the dunes, and the roofs of the buildings on the outskirts of Patris seemed to shimmer and waver, suspended above them. Jehan struggled against a feeling of lethargy. He was still bewildered by what he had seen. Uncertainty dulled his senses, and he was amazed that the offworlder seemed so calm and confident.

'You know the Yasa,' Alexei said. 'There can be but one Lord upon the Earth.'

Jehan laughed unhappily. 'You say that to me?'

A p'tar broke loose from a line of beasts which were being led up out of the water. Oars splashed as the boats pulled back towards the ship. The p'tar trotted past the tether line, heading for a gap in the dunes. Two troopers dropped the bundles they were carrying and ran in pursuit. The offworlder gestured around at the piles of stores and the lines of animals. 'It's why we're here,' he said.

The troopers lined the beach to watch the *Sunstealer* depart. Every man had been given some time on land before sailing, although they had been restricted to the beach. Now it seemed as if those who had been detailed to ride as escort envied those who were still on board, and Jehan guessed that most of them wondered if they would ever see the vessel again. They shaded their eyes from the sun with their hands, staring silently as the anchors were raised.

'How were they selected?' Alexei came up to Jehan's side. He surveyed the line of men.

'Oh.' Jehan turned. 'They cast lots.' Sidacai had arranged it, and Jehan was not sure if the winners were those who were on the ship, or if they were the men who now stood along the sand. He glanced sideways at Alexei. 'I expected you to bring Kadan. Why did you leave him on board?'

The offworlder did not turn. 'For the same reason you left Sidacai,' he responded calmly. 'We can trust them to keep looking for us long after Orcadai and C'zinsit will have given up.'

Jehan was annoyed that his motives were so transparent. 'I am fighting Sidacai,' he said. 'Or hadn't you noticed?'

The corner of Alexei's mouth twitched. 'I heard you had agreed a truce. Don't you trust him?'

It was a difficult question to answer. Jehan shrugged. 'As much as I trust anyone,' he said finally. 'Sidacai will be true to himself. If we are lost he will strive to find us. He will never rest until what lies within our feud is settled.'

Jehana came out of a tent which had been pitched in the shelter of the tallest dune. She had obtained cloth from the village – or Kadan had obtained it for her – and she had fashioned it into the comfortable riding trousers which women wore as an alternative to breeches. Over the trousers she wore Alexei's altered coat.

Alexei bowed to her. 'My Lady, good morning.'

She smiled. 'It is a fine morning, my Lord.' She stared past him at the vessel which was pulling away.

The offworlder took her hand. 'You are happy to be on the land,' he said. He looked amused.

Jehan saw his sister flush. 'I think we all are,' he said into the pause.

The copper plating on the *Sunstealer*'s sides had weathered, and it was beginning to turn green. The wake created by the propeller broke up the reflection of the sun in the water so that it was as if the sea was a pool of molten metal which was being stirred before pouring.

'It looks strange without sails,' Jehana said, her eyes still on the ship.

Alexei looked as if he was about to say something. His mouth opened, and then he seemed to change his mind. He gazed after the *Sunstealer*, and then he turned to meet Jehan's eyes. 'New things are always strange,' he said.

It was not what the offworlder had first intended to say. Jehan pursed his lips. 'One day we will be

405

comfortable with machines,' he said, 'but not yet. You must bear with us until then.'

They rode through a countryside patchworked with neat fields. There was little uncultivated land, and Jehan supposed that this part of the continent was the most settled. If all the ground was in use there would be no room for the population to grow, and there would be signs of starvation. Because the inhabitants they saw looked prosperous Jehan reasoned that this was the area where the conditions for farming were best.

It was hard for the scouts to find unfenced grassland for an evening campsite, and the fourth night on the road they occupied a field which was being grazed by cattle. Alexei ignored the farmer who came to protest, and after a time the man went away.

'What will you do if he has gone for help?' Jehan watched the farmer out of sight. He turned.

Alexei was seated on a camp stool. He stretched out his legs and then looked up. 'If he has I will be surprised,' he remarked.

If there was something which would make the people of this land fight, they had yet to find it. Jehan stroked his moustaches. 'I'm not sure it's the answer.'

Jehana was leading her st'lyan in a circle in the middle of the field to cool it. The offworlder watched her for a moment, a thoughtful expression on his face. Then he turned to face Jehan again. 'It's not intended to be. Either we must invade this land in great numbers, so that the people have no alternative but to learn to live with us, or we must find a new way to deal with them – a way we have never tried before.'

It would not be impossible to transport an army across the Great Sea, but it would involve a logistical exercise on a scale never before attempted. Jehan made a face. 'If we try conquest, we will end up with a land piled high with the dead. You have seen how the people are. They will bare their breasts to our arrows before they will submit to us.'

There was nothing in the Yasa to cover the case of an enemy who simply refused to fight. The Yek had killed noncombatants before – even women and children – but only when it had been impossible to avoid it, or when they were the occupants of a resisting city and it was judged that the Yasa had been broken.

The embassy had ridden for four days without seeing a settlement of significant size. Most of the places where people lived in groups were villages like Patris. None were fortified. They were not even sited to provide the advantage of ground in case of attack, but lay instead nestled between hills or at river crossings.

'Maybe we will find a city,' Jehan said, knowing that they would not.

Alexei said nothing. Troopers were driving the farmer's beasts over to one side of the field so that they could be enclosed with ropes away from the camp. St'lyan trotted loose on the lush green grass. They screamed and tossed their heads, and the p'tar being driven in off the road brayed back at them. An orderly came through a gap in the hedge, his arms full of dry kindling. He managed a half bow in Jehan's direction as he went past, twigs dropping from his bundle in a trail behind him as he walked towards the place where the cook fire was being constructed. Jehan slid the scabbard of his sword out of his sash. He propped it against his saddle which was on the ground at his feet. Jehana was unsaddling her mare. She removed the st'lyan's bridle. As soon as the mare was released it kicked up its heels and trotted off to join the other loose animals. A trooper ran over and picked up Jehana's saddle. He was little more than a boy, and he blushed crimson when Jehana thanked him.

'We had to make this journey,' Alexei said at last. 'Would you have believed a land where people lived by such principles if you had not seen it for yourself?'

Jehan shook his head. 'I still don't quite believe it. The only masters are men who employ others to work for them.'

The offworlder showed his teeth. 'On some worlds they call that democracy.'

It was intended for humour. Jehan scowled. 'We are here to deliver an embassy to whoever rules this land,' he pointed out severely.

There were no rulers, and there was no identifiable system of government. Instead there were communities of individuals – people who adhered to no specific code of laws, and who survived as far as Jehan could tell because they respected the right of others to do the same. He suppressed a surge of irritation. The idea was alien without a doubt, and yet he was not sure in his heart that it was wrong.

Troopers were erecting a tent at Alexei's back. It was a military lean-to, the kind made of the coated fabric which was designed to reflect away the worst heat of the sun. Jehana came across the grass. She passed behind Alexei and stopped, resting a hand on his shoulder. She eyed Jehan. 'Brother, how out of countenance you look.'

The under-officer in charge of the troopers uttered a word of command. The troopers strained on the ropes, and the tent rose as if by magic into position. Mallets thumped on tent pegs.

Alexei glanced around to see the source of the sound. He lifted a hand and placed it on Jehana's. 'He

408

is contemplating the problems which he will encounter when he comes to rule this land,' he said.

Jehan restrained the urge to glare. He knew he was being baited. Alexei was watching, his expression amused. Jehan adjusted his features, preparing to make a dismissive remark, but Jehana only laughed. She let go of the offworlder's hand and went inside the tent.

An orderly was moving items of camp furniture and baggage in under the tent awning. Jehan pulled his shirt over his head and tossed it across his saddle. The late afternoon sun was still warm. He stretched, enjoying the sensation of it on his shoulders.

The offworlder was watching calmly. Jehan met his eyes, and then he looked away again. He gestured at the orderly. 'Find me something to drink.'

The orderly rummaged through the heap of bags and boxes on the ground outside the tent. He produced a k'miss flask, offering it to Jehan with a bow. 'Lord, the cups have not been unpacked yet.'

'It doesn't matter.' Jehan uncorked the flask and drank. The k'miss was light and sweet. It ran cold across his tongue, but in his stomach it was warm, like a small fire. Jehan held out the flask towards Alexei. The offworlder shook his head.

The last of the p'tar were being herded into the field. Jehan watched as their panniers were unloaded. He rammed the cork back into the mouth of the flask, then dropped it on the grass at his feet. He glanced at Alexei out of the corner of one eye.

'You're trying to think of a way to find out how I know that it may be your problem to rule this land,' Alexei said. His expression did not waver.

Jehan frowned. 'It isn't settled yet.' He sat down on his saddle. 'It's my father's idea.'

The offworlder nodded. 'Jehana told me.'

It was hard for Jehan to conceal his surprise. 'She isn't supposed to know,' he said foolishly. He saw the look on Alexei's face. 'Jotan should not have told her, and she should not have told you.'

Alexei snorted. 'If she had got it from him, she might have known it was secret. It was common knowledge around the court before Artai left for Pantai.'

'Oh.' Jehan tugged at a moustache. 'No one mentioned it to me.'

'Burun might have, if he knew,' Alexei said obliquely.

Jehan gave the offworlder a sharp stare.

'Your father has influence with the Kha-Khan.' Alexei returned the stare.

It was a reasonable enough deduction, Jehan supposed. He pondered the rift which had developed between his father and grandfather. There was no way to know if it was real. After a moment he shook his head. 'No. If there is an intrigue, it is Burun's. And as for this land, it will be years before it will be fit to be ruled by anyone.'

The offworlder pretended to be deceived. 'A rumour is too easily spread,' he observed impassively. The flash of comprehension which had appeared in his eyes was hidden. He looked away, and Jehan wondered if he understood how readily he could alter the course of the events in which he was taking part.

Joden came round the side of the tent. He bowed politely to Jehan, then saluted Alexei. 'Khan, I have given orders for the sentries to be posted.'

Jehan scooped up the k'miss flask from the grass. 'Are we under threat?' He offered the flask to Joden, who took it.

Alexei was taking off his boots. He looked up. 'Not exactly. But there is at least one man out of those who

410

live here who has a reason to be offended by our presence.'

'And you are concerned?' Jehan opened his eyes wide, not trying to hide the mockery in his voice.

The guard commander was drinking deeply from the k'miss flask. He spat into the grass. 'It's not the Khan's responsibility to be concerned, Noyon,' he remarked tartly. 'It's mine.'

'Oh.' Jehan flushed.

The offworlder was hiding a smile. Joden recorked the flask. He dropped it on the ground at his feet. Then he saluted again and strode away.

'Damn him.' Jehan stared after Joden. 'He never leaves me the last word.'

Alexei chuckled. 'I had a tutor like that – a long time ago, and far from here.' He stood up. 'One day we will be clever old men, and then it will be our turn.'

Jehan was not certain that age and wisdom went hand in hand, but he said nothing. He stood up and stared around. Beyond the hedges which enclosed the field there were other fields – oblong patches of green or gold dotted with occasional trees. Low hills proceeded in rows into the distance, and to the east the setting sun sat redly upon them.

'This will be a good land to rule if we can establish order,' Alexei said.

The offworlder had always opposed Yek ideas about what was proper before. Jehan raised his eyebrows, but Alexei did not appear to think that he had said anything unusual.

Jehan picked up his shirt. 'Artai is only the fifth of his line,' he observed. 'The Khanate will always stand, and one day we will rule everywhere.'

Loose st'lyan moved along the hedgerow, tearing at the foliage with their white teeth. Beyond them the farmer's cattle lowed uncertainly.

'– And after we rule the earth?' Alexei pulled off his hose, not sitting down, but hopping first on one foot and then on the other. He dropped the hose on top of his boots.

The significance of the question eluded Jehan at first. He wrinkled his nose. 'Then we will stop,' he said. 'What else?'

There were nails like plates of horn at the ends of the offworlder's toes, and his feet were hairless. Jehan tried not to stare.

'The people in this land are not of this world,' Alexei said. 'They speak the language of the Empire. Their customs are strange, even to me.'

Jehan frowned. 'You think they came here as you did,' he said.

'A long time ago.' Alexei nodded. 'The Empire which my father served has existed for less than a thousand years. Before that there was chaos for a long time, but once there was a race of man which populated the stars. These could be their descendants.'

They were treading on dangerous ground – moving into an area of knowledge which existed so far as Jehan was concerned only by virtue of the fact that it was known to the offworlders. Because it lay outside the experience of the Sechem, it was hard to dispute. Jehan stirred uncomfortably. 'Maybe the people of this land came from the stars once,' he said. 'But whoever was their lord, he is long dead.'

If there was truly an Empire, then its people were likewise the descendants of those long ago people from the stars. Jehan was not sure that the relationship was of any consequence, but he guessed that the masters of the Empire would see matters differently.

'Do you remember how this land was named on the maps?' Alexei asked suddenly.

412

Jehan chewed the end of his moustache, and then spat it out. 'Y'vrope, was it not?'

The offworlder nodded. He brushed his bare feet through the grass, then looked up. 'One of the ships of the Imperial Navy is called the *Yevropieska*,' he said. 'The name is of Terran origin, and is said to relate to one of the continents of Old Earth.'

Men who migrated to new lands quite often gave places familiar names. It was the means by which they maintained their identity, or eased the pain of separation from home. The connection was not conclusive, but Jehan felt troubled. He looked up.

'I talk about men, and so do you,' he said. 'But we mean different things.'

Alexei nodded slowly. He said, 'What separates us is our perception of what is human. Our notions of civilisation are different, and yet both the Khanate and the Empire use the principle of establishing order as an excuse for conquest. In that we are much alike.'

Jehan had guessed where the exposition was leading. 'I think you mean to suggest that we ought to extend the Khanate beyond this earth,' he said. 'Otherwise one day the Empire may claim this world as it has claimed others.'

The offworlder looked amused. 'I only asked what you would do when the conquest has to stop.'

The land could be ruled, Jehan realised. The principles by which the inhabitants of Y'vrope lived were alien, but by them they could be defeated. He felt the offworlder's eyes on his face and stared away. 'It won't be my decision,' he said. He was unable to meet Alexei's stare for fear of the knowledge he would see there.

They reached the western coast after a journey of eleven days. The coastline was rocky, and the beaches

413

were covered with pebbles instead of sand. A stiff wind blew in off the sea, and white-capped waves washed against the shore. There was no sign of the ship.

'Build a signal fire,' Alexei said. 'Build several.' If he was worried, it did not show.

They had travelled for over a day through country which was sparsely populated. Here the grassland was grazed by herds of shaggy cattle which were attended by boys or old men who rode their equines bare-backed. The trees were small, and their twisted boughs were covered by fine needles which were dark and oily. When the wood was burned, the needles flared and spat. The land presented such a contrast to the pleasant farming country through which they had passed before that there was no aspect of it which did not seem harsh and forbidding. The troopers who were working to erect the camp looked depressed and unhappy, and Jehan guessed that they were troubled by the *Sunstealer*'s absence.

Nowhere had they encountered a settlement which could be said to contain more than a thousand inhabitants, and none of the people to whom they had spoken had displayed any knowledge of a city, or of any form of overlordship or government.

Jehan inspected the shore and eyed the waves. A boat might land here, but transhipping their baggage, not to mention the st'lyan and p'tar, would be an exercise fraught with difficulty.

'We might have chosen better,' Joden said critically at Jehan's side.

'Yes.' Jehan nodded. 'Send scouts north and south. Find an inlet or a haven where we can land the boats with ease.'

Joden looked up at the sky. 'There's a storm coming,' he said.

There was a strong current running south down the coastline now. The waves were pushed by it, and the wind was veering. Jehan watched the clouds. It was not the season for bad weather, or not in the Khanate at least. Kinsai would be bathed in sunshine, and only in the dead of the night would there be any moisture in the air. He said, 'Do as I command. I will speak to the Khan.'

'Yes, Lord.' Joden saluted. He turned and started to scramble away over the rocks which barred the path to the plateau above.

Jehan picked up a pebble. The rocks here were old, washed by the sea, rolled and smoothed by constant tides. He tossed the pebble thoughtfully, then threw it seaward. It bounced and skipped across the wave caps. He picked up another, flatter this time. Thrown with a spin it went much further.

There were shallow pools between some of the larger rocks. Small creatures moved in them – skeletal shellfish with oddly shaped tails. A long-legged sea bird fished for them, its beak dipping the water with delicate precision. It looked up at Jehan's approach, but did not attempt to escape. Jehan stared at it, wondering if it was capable of flight. Its feathers were tiny, like down, and it was impossible to tell if it had wings. There was a patch of red on its breast, but elsewhere it was coloured pale blue.

Rain came down suddenly on the wind. Jehan glanced up at the sky. The clouds were heavy, black in places. A rumble of thunder sounded in the distance. He pulled his tunic closed. The bird gave a single squawk, and then it lifted scaly yellow feet high as it stepped out of the pool and walked away.

Jehan stared out to sea. The vague shape moving against the grey of the waves might be a vessel, but if it was the *Sunstealer* it would be all they could do to establish contact with it until the passing of the storm.

The *Sunstealer* came up at the height of the gale. The wind whipped away the smoke from the signal fires, and it was probably only the size of the pyres and the flaring of the oily foliage which attracted the attention of the lookouts on board.

'They are stopping,' Alexei said. He focused a spyglass, a delicate instrument bound in brass. Then he snapped it shut in anger. 'Damn them. They are trying to launch a boat.'

The wave crests were advancing towards the beach in rows. They crashed down onto the rocks on the shore, throwing spray high in the air. Jehan pulled his cloak right around him and peered into the gathering gloom. A flash of lightning illuminated the scene. The *Sunstealer*'s boat was in the water, moving away from the falls. He made out the ripple of the oars, and then the boat was lost in a trough between the waves. 'Maybe they are afraid to lie at anchor,' Jehan said. 'If the ship is carried in against the shore, it will be wrecked.' He heard Alexei give a snort of disapproval.

'Then they should continue to sail north against the current,' the offworlder observed sourly. 'There will be time enough for them to find us again when the storm has abated.'

Of the men of officer rank on board, only Ch'un Chu had experience of the sea. Faced with a command from Orcadai and C'zinsit, the sons of a Khan, he might feel it was his duty to obey. Even the objections of Sidacai and Kadan might be to no purpose. 'One of us should have stayed with the ship,' Jehan said.

Alexei grunted. It was a sound which might have indicated agreement.

416

The boat was halfway to the shore now. At one instant it rose on the crest of a wave, and at the next it had disappeared from sight. The troopers of the escort were lining the edge of the plateau, watching expressionlessly. Jehan tapped the six strongest on the shoulder. 'Get ropes. Go down to the beach. The men in the boat will need help when they try to land.'

Jehana emerged from the door of the tent. She wore a long military cloak, and when she came up to Alexei's side he eyed her. 'Where do you think you are going, my Lady?'

The men Jehan had selected were already starting down the path to the shore, ropes coiled on their shoulders. They had shed their cloaks, and they were quickly soaked by the lashing rain.

'My Lord,' Jehana said, 'Where you go, there I go also.'

It was nonsense of course. Jehan waited for Alexei to make his opinion plain. The offworlder's mouth closed in a thin line. Jehana was used to too much independence. Now she would learn that there was little place for a woman in the affairs of men. It was the way of the world.

Wind rattled the canvas. The awning under which they stood vibrated, and a seam dripped rainwater. Alexei seemed to take a breath, gathering an argument. Then he said, 'Lady, if it is your desire to assist me, take command of the men who remain here on the plateau. Direct them as you see fit. It may be that we will need assistance, but I see no point in sending more men than necessary into danger.'

Jehan gaped. Of all the things he had expected Alexei to say, it was the most unlikely. Suddenly he registered the implication behind the words. 'You're going down to the beach?'

'Aren't you?'

417

'Yes, but that's different. It was my idea.'

The offworlder snorted. Jehan turned to watch his sister. It was as if she was assessing the value of the role she had been offered. She glanced at the troopers. Jehan saw that Joden was standing off to one side. The guard commander's features looked as if they were carved from stone.

'Very well, my Lord.' Jehana nodded. Then a thought seemed to strike her. Jehan guessed she had observed Joden's expression. 'Will your men accept my orders?'

Alexei raised an eyebrow at Joden.

Joden said, 'Khatun, that's up to you.'

The offworlder produced a bark of laughter. 'That's true.'

Jehana made a face at him. She said, 'Go then, my Lord. I shall do well enough here I think.'

A gust of wind lifted the front of the awning, and men leapt to secure loose ropes. The offworlder's expression remained good-humoured. He nodded, looking satisfied. Turning, he went so suddenly out into the rain that Jehan was taken by surprise. He hesitated, and then followed. They began to descend the path.

Although it was only the middle of the afternoon, the sky was dark. Jehan stumbled at Alexei's shoulder. The offworlder's head came round. Jehan said, 'She is only a woman. I would have told her to stay out of the way.'

'I know you would.' Alexei's tone indicated that he had no intention of discussing the matter. He stopped at a bend in the path, wiping rain out of his eyes. Jehan bumped into him. They swayed together and almost fell.

It was probably not the moment to argue the subject of women's rights. Jehan was not even certain that he thought there was a place for women other than that which was assigned by custom. He had heard men talk about equality between the sexes, but it was a phrase which seemed to make no sense. The nature of a woman was altogether different from that of a man. It would not admit treatment which assumed otherwise.

Jehan stared at the heaving grey sea. The *Sun-stealer*'s boat was rising on the crest of a wave about forty drem from the shore. It pitched bow first down into the next trough. The face of the oncoming wave was so steep that Jehan did not expect the boat to reappear. When it came into view again, he saw that some of the oars were missing.

'Can you see who is in the boat?' Alexei put his hand up to shield his face from the rain.

'No.'

They started down the path again. The rain draining off the plateau was washing down the steep slope in torrents. A river of mud and slurry ran across the path, carrying away rock and soil. Jehan lost his footing. He grabbed at Alexei's arm for support. 'This is madness.'

'It was your idea. Blame the fool who sent that boat.'

The beach was a narrow strand of pebbles which was being attacked by the incoming waves. The men who had descended the path ahead of Jehan and Alexei were crouched for shelter behind a large boulder. They ducked as a wave crashed down. Spray was flung high into the air.

Alexei scrambled ahead of Jehan across the rocks towards the boulder. The ledges where the rock strata had been etched by the tide were like steps, but they were green and slippery with weed and slime. A new wave burst against the boulder. A downpour of

419

icy salt water drenched them, and Jehan flinched. He slid along the final ledge, falling headlong among the men who huddled behind the safety of the rock.

The boat was on the crest of a wave which was racing in from the sea. The oarsmen were rowing madly, desperate to keep pace with the tide race. Jehan saw that Kadan was in the stern, his hand on the tiller, and he heard Alexei swear softly.

Jehan took the rope from a trooper's shoulder. He looped the end around his chest at the level of his armpits and tied it. A burly under-officer said something in an undertone to the man beside him, and then he stood up and began to do the same.

The offworlder was staring. 'I didn't know you could swim,' he said.

The swell which was running ahead of the wave was climbing the beach. 'I doubt if I can in that,' Jehan responded. He edged around the side of the boulder, leaning into the wind. The under-officer was moving into the open on the other side of the rock, his head down.

Jehan looked back. The troopers were paying out the ropes under Alexei's direction. Jehan gathered a coil in his hand and forged forward. The water was thigh deep. Suddenly it seemed to be moving back out to sea. It pulled at Jehan, and he struggled against the force of the undertow. He looked up. The oncoming wave was above the level of his head. The ebb of the water was only a freak caused by the suction of the wall of water as it curled over and started to descend. The prow of the *Sunstealer*'s boat emerged through the crest. The wave smashed down on Jehan, lifting him off his feet. He swallowed water and floundered, spluttering. Something struck his arm, and he grabbed at it. An oar. His feet found rock and he stood. He let the oar go. The drag of the current pulled it past him.

The boat was in pieces on the rocks. Men sprawled in the water, fighting the tide race which sought to pull them out to sea. Jehan looked for the under-officer and saw that he was climbing to his feet. They surged towards the wreck. Jehan pulled a man up off his knees and put his hands on the rope. 'Get to shelter.' He caught the shoulder of another whose face was covered in blood. 'Can you walk?' The oarsman nodded. He started along the rope, hauling himself hand over hand towards the boulders. Jehan ploughed through deepening water towards the stern of the boat. Kadan lay face down across what remained of the tiller.

A new wave was rearing up above their heads. Jehan got a hand to Kadan's collar. He twisted, securing his grip, and then the wave crashed down. The whole stern section of the boat was lifted and overturned. Boards banged down on Jehan's head and shoulders. His mouth opened and he swallowed more water. He struggled to remain afloat. He thrashed, but his feet found no purchase. The rope jerked tight around his chest and he was towed backwards. Suddenly he was sitting in shallow water, his hand still twisted into Kadan's collar. Kadan stirred. A wound in his scalp oozed bright blood. Jehan struggled to his feet.

The under-officer waded up to Jehan's side. Together they lifted Kadan. They staggered up the beach, the waves washing at them. Bits of wood were pulled past them, but if there were men who had not gained the shore, there was no sign of them.

Alexei led men out of the shelter of the rocks. The offworlder's hair was plastered down across his fore-head. He loosened the rope around Jehan's chest and cast it aside. The troopers lifted Kadan and bore him away towards the foot of the path. More troopers were running knotted lines down the slope. Jehan saw that seamen were using them to pull themselves up the path. He stared at Alexei.

'How many men did we lose?'

'Not one.' Alexei looked out to sea. 'It's amazing.'

The wind was easing. Jehan stripped off his sodden tunic, ignoring the rain and spray. 'We were lucky.'

The offworlder nodded slowly. He wiped his hair out of his eyes. 'C'zinsit owes Kadan a fine,' he said.

Jehan hawked and spat. He had known that Orcadai and C'zinsit would be to blame. He said, 'Were I Kadan, I would take my recompense out of C'zinsit's hide.'

Alexei's expression changed. 'Even if Kadan does not,' he said sternly, 'you may be sure I shall.'

Suddenly Jehan realised that Orcadai and C'zinsit had been included as members of the embassy as a test. He said, 'C'zinsit is my uncle. Let me deal with him.'

Alexei was still staring out to sea. His head came round sharply. 'It is Kadan you ought to ask for that favour,' he observed.

Water sluiced across the pebbles at Jehan's feet. He said, 'Kadan is my vassal it is true, but he is your brother. Cede your right in the matter to me and I swear I will make C'zinsit pay.'

The offworlder frowned. Then he gave Jehan a hard look. 'It won't be for Kadan's sake if you do.'

Jehan showed his teeth. 'The result will be the same.'

'Will it?' It was apparent that Alexei was not convinced. He said, 'This is not an embassy at all. It is one of your grandfather's games.'

'You are angry.' Jehan avoided the offworlder's eyes. 'That's understandable.'

Alexei snorted, and he turned away. Jehan looked

422

at the sky. The wind was pushing the black clouds south, and the sun sat on a horizon which was touched everywhere with streaks of red and orange. Beyond the breakers which were rolling in against the beach lay the ship. Its anchors were out.

Jehan made his way over the rock ledges to the bottom of the path. The water in his boots squelched as he walked, and his breeches clung uncomfortably to his legs.

'The storm is abating,' Alexei said. 'There was no need for any of this.' He started up the path, and Jehan followed wetly behind him.

Joden's scouts located an inlet several verst to the north. The rain stopped shortly after, and Alexei ordered a move. Everything which had not been protected by canvas during the storm had been soaked. The troopers worked naked around the new campsite, and the trees and the ropes which supported the tents were festooned with their drying clothes. A stiff wind was blowing, but fortunately it was not cold.

By morning the sea was calm again. It was not necessary to signal the *Sunstealer* concerning their move. A second boat was despatched about the third hour of the night watch, and it reached the shore without incident. The comite who was in command carried a brief letter from Sidacai, and he was sent back to the ship with instructions which were explicit. Neither Orcadai nor C'zinsit had cared to face Alexei's quite predictable anger. Probably they were assembling excuses, and Jehan smiled grimly when he marked their absence, looking forward to the encounter which was to come.

The inlet in which they were camped was also the

mouth of a river. Here sediments had been laid down over a period of years, and these had been eroded by wind and tide so that there was now a fertile plain across which the river at its height had excavated a deep channel to the sea. The bay beyond was quite shallow, for it was filling gradually with silt washed down from the plateau. It was protected by headlands however, and was thus an ideal anchorage for their purpose. Jehan was surprised that a settlement had not been established, and he concluded that the population in this western part of the land was of no great size. Certainly the people were not seafarers. The rowers rescued the previous day had seen no boats during their journey around the continent's southern extremes; neither had they observed any kind of harbour.

'I think we are finished here,' Alexei said. He tossed Sidacai's letter into an open chest. He had given it scarcely more than a cursory inspection, and it was apparent that it contained little of importance.

The front walls of the offworlder's tent had been brailed up. Troopers led unsaddled st'lyan across the lush grass which separated the camp from the river, and somewhere out of sight a p'tar brayed.

'You mean to go on and investigate Marakan,' Jehan said. The name of the continent which lay west across the sea came easily into his mind.

Jehana was sitting at Alexei's feet on a carpet which had been spread out to cover the ground which was the floor of the tent. She looked up. 'You sound as if you disapprove,' she remarked.

Jehan pulled at his moustache. 'We could sail south and then east,' he said finally. 'There is land there.'

'Islands.' Alexei nodded. 'A place no larger than Dr'gasia.' He gestured towards the west. 'There is a whole continent over there.'

If they continued west, eventually they would reach the Khanate again. The prospect filled Jehan with foreboding. He said, 'You will do as you think fit of course.'

Alexei frowned. 'It would take forever to explore the Unknown Lands completely,' he said. 'And anyway exploration is not our task. This is supposed to be an embassy.'

Kadan came out of the rear portion of the tent. The wound on his scalp had closed, but there was still a livid bruise around the socket of his right eye. His hair had been combed out, and it was gathered together with a clasp which drew it away from the side of his head which had sustained injury. He stopped at Alexei's shoulder. 'Are you arguing?' he asked.

'If we are, you are obliged to take my part,' Jehan told him ungraciously.

'Because I'm your vassal?' Kadan looked amused. 'That's no reason.'

'We're not arguing.' Alexei stood up abruptly. He glared at Kadan. '– And if we were, it would not be your concern. Have you recovered? If so, you should attend to your duties.'

Kadan's expression did not alter. 'Brother, I'm quite well,' he said.

It was an ill-judged reply, even though Kadan could not be expected to understand why. Jehan grimaced. He saw his sister look up sharply. She stirred.

Alexei flushed. He said, 'If you had more care for yourself –'

Jehana stood up quickly. She caught Alexei by the hand, and went into the rear chamber of the tent, pulling him protesting behind her.

Kadan stared after them. He turned and looked enquiringly at Jehan, his features displaying his perplexity.

Jehan said, 'If Alexei is short with you, it is because of his concern for your safety.'

'Oh?' Kadan raised his eyebrows, his disbelief apparent.

It was probably insufficient explanation. Jehan wondered if Kadan realised that his life had been in danger. Probably he did not. Jehan said, 'I have asked him to let me deal with C'zinsit.'

Kadan's nose wrinkled. 'I think I'm capable of that.'

'Are you?' Jehan teased at his moustaches. He had got into the habit of chewing at them during moments of stress, and one end was sparser than the other. He said, 'C'zinsit was unwise to risk your life by allowing you to go ashore with the boat. If the journey had been necessary it would be another matter, but it was not.'

At the very least the decision had been a stupid one. Jehan had already spent some time considering the possibility that there had been a darker purpose, but now he thought not.

'Without someone to command them, the men in the boat would have been killed,' Kadan said.

They had almost been killed, even though Kadan had gone with them. A low murmur of voices from behind the partition at the rear of the tent made Jehan look up. He heard Alexei say something in an annoyed tone. Jehana responded calmly, insistently, soothing his temper, and Jehan hid a smile. He glanced at Kadan. 'If I don't make C'zinsit suffer for endangering you, your brother will kill him for the sake of revenge.'

Kadan sat down on the stool which had been vacated by Alexei. 'That would not be proper.' He tugged at his loose scalp lock. 'He is not of the race of the True People. He has no recourse under the law.'

'He is a Khan,' Jehan observed. 'And anyway I doubt

if he will allow the law to prevent him, even though he is concerned to preserve it.' He saw the partition stir, and knew that he ought to finish before Alexei emerged. He said, 'I came to your aid because Alexei could not. In the same way that a standard-bearer is not permitted to leave his post in battle, even to rescue a fallen comrade, so an ambassador is prohibited by the Yasa from risking his life when one of his officers is in danger. The duty of his office is paramount.' Jehan gestured dismissively with one hand, then met Kadan's stare. 'No allowance is made for the fact that the officer may be the ambassador's younger brother.'

'Oh.' Kadan digested the explanation. 'I thought I had angered him.' He gave Jehan a shrewd glance. 'Was I so much at risk?'

Jehan was unsure how to answer. He was reluctant to magnify his part. At last he said, 'You might have died.'

Kadan made a face. 'Then I owe you a life.'

'Hunh.' Jehan grinned. 'Pay me when you can.'

A trooper outside the tent shouted and pointed towards the bay. Jehan turned and saw that the *Sun-stealer* was sailing around a headland. Kadan stood up. 'Are we going to explore further before we move on?'

'No.' Jehan shook his head.

A boat was already being lowered down the side of the ship. The rowers held their oars up vertically until the falls had been cast away. Then they lowered them into position and began to pull energetically towards the shore. The water in the bay was as calm as a mill pond.

Kadan came up to Jehan's side. 'This voyage has been a waste of time.'

They had learned that they were going to have to

427

control the seas as well as the land in order to rule the world. That would require a navy. 'We are not explorers,' Jehan said. He thought about the people he had encountered during the journey across Y'vrope, and realised that he had also learned that there were situations to which the Yasa could not be applied. It was a conclusion which troubled him, and he knew that he was going to keep the knowledge to himself.

'Tell me what you are going to do about C'zinsit.' Kadan put a hand on the rolled-up tent wall.

Jehan looked round. 'Only if you will promise to stay out of it.'

C'zinsit was seated in the stern of the boat which was pulling towards the shore. Jehan eyed the muscles rippling under the skin of Kadan's arm. Whoever Kadan chose to fight, it would be no contest.

'Can't I even help?' Kadan was watching the boat. It was clear that he had seen who it contained. A predatory look appeared on his face.

'I don't want him hurt,' Jehan said warningly. 'He is my uncle after all.'

'Well.' Kadan stroked a finger across his cheek. 'I might discomfort him a little.'

Alexei emerged suddenly from the back of the tent. He came up to Jehan's side. His mouth tightened when he saw the boat and who was in it.

Jehan caught Kadan's eye. 'You can have C'zinsit when I have finished with him,' he said quickly. 'Don't kill him, that's all.'

The offworlder's head went back. Then he met Jehan's stare and nodded shortly, as if acknowledging a courtesy.

'Oh.' Kadan showed his teeth. 'Killing C'zinsit would be too easy. I only mean to amuse myself.' He slapped Alexei affectionately on the shoulder and then walked off through the camp, ignoring the boat which was coming in to land.

PART FIVE

The Place of the Dragon

Several of the crystals in the portside reflector had been loosened from their mountings during the storm. The beam from the reflector had become distorted, and the lining of the tube to the boiler had suffered damage. Alexei surveyed the unbolted sections which lay on the deck. Then he rounded on the Sechem. 'How long?'

Parin's hands and the front of his tunic were covered with ceramic powder, the result of stripping the lining blocks out of the tubes to examine them. He looked up. 'A day at least, Khan,' he said placidly. 'We must set new blocks and allow the cement to dry. Then we can reassemble the tubes.'

'And the reflector?'

The clam shell had been dismounted and taken ashore. Alexei was not sure how it could be worked on without exposing the men concerned to danger. The settings were accessible from the back of the reflector, but adjusting them was not a task he thought he would care to undertake.

The Sechem appeared to consider. 'Khan, I have only one man who is capable of the work, and he is ashore. You ought to ask him that.'

It had not occurred to Alexei that the reflectors would require maintenance or repair. He chided himself for the omission. Primitive machines broke down or wore out. Because the sunstone technology was outside his experience he had made the mistake of assigning it a value which placed it in the same category as starship drive. An Infinity generator was incapable of breaking down. It was indestructible, and there were examples which had been built during the lifetime of the Second Empire which had been installed in navy vessels.

Which powered the vessels I knew. The thought struck Alexei forcibly.

A period of roughly fifteen standard years had passed he supposed since he had been marooned on this world. Without astro-navigational equipment it was impossible to be accurate about the passage of time. Time was not something which meant a great deal to the Yek. They recorded the cycle of the years – but even that was based upon the simple count of the frequency of the rising and setting of the sun. Every month contained the same number of days, and no attempt was made to adjust the calendar to allow for orbital variation.

Alexei nodded acknowledgement and turned away. Ch'un Chu was supervising the laying out of additional mooring cables – the weather had already proved itself changeable and untrustworthy – and he sketched a salute in Alexei's direction, clearly unwilling to be distracted from the task in hand.

The water in the bay was bright azure blue. The colour was a freak caused so far as Alexei could tell by the quality of the minerals being washed down from the plateau. The bottom lay almost thirty drem below the *Sunstealer*'s keel, but it was clearly visible. Mostly it was fine sand and silt, all of which was tinged with blue. A few plants grew, rooted in crevices in the visible rocks, and thin eel-like fish wound through them in tight schools.

They were yet to discover anything in the sea which was predatory to the extent that it was a danger to man. Few of the creatures inhabiting even the deepest water were large enough to trouble a swimming human. There were the grey-skinned beasts which daily followed the ship when it was at sea – they could not be fish, because they breathed air through a vent in their foreheads and had no scales – but they seemed friendly, and made no attempt to attack the crewmen when they bathed.

Alexei gazed over the side at the activity taking place there. The comite was in a boat which was being rowed around the ship by two crewmen – so that he could inspect the plates which sheathed the hull. The water was so transparent that it was not necessary to dive. Alexei did not expect damage. They had not been at sea long enough for the copper to suffer serious corrosion, and he had observed only a few of the marine growths which were caused by the shellfish which attached themselves to any submerged surface.

The comite was dark-skinned and hairless, an oddity among those of his race. He had eyes which appeared almost yellow beneath the epicanthic fold which denoted his N'pani origin, and his talons grew so dark that they gleamed like ebony where they protruded from their sheaths. Alexei waited until he glanced up.

'What do you see?'

On another world the comite would have ranked as master's mate. He stood up in the boat. 'Khan, I can find no damage, but if we are to remain long at sea we should careen.'

Careening would entail beaching the ship so that the exposed plates could be scraped clean of marine encrustations. Alexei frowned. The thought of a vessel so completely disabled was unwelcome. He waved one hand. 'Very well.'

The *Sunstealer* now contained only cargo and crew. All the animals had been moved ashore the previous day to allow them to pasture. Alexei weighed the alternatives thoughtfully, aware of the urge to complete the embassy quickly. The Khanate was where the real task lay.

He swung himself over the side and descended to the waiting boat.

'Take me ashore.'

The oarsmen were Ch'kasians. All of them were stripped to the waist. They strained at the oars, and the boat shot away from the ship. The cadet at the tiller wore a bright blue shirt which was open to his navel. His scalp lock was freshly oiled, and the wisps of dark hair around his upper lip indicated that he was attempting to grow a moustache.

Alexei sat down on the thwart. 'Beach the boat when we land.'

The cadet ducked his head. 'The Khan wishes.'

Another boat was leaving the landing place, heading for the *Sunstealer*. It swept past, and Alexei saw that C'zinsit was sitting in the stern. They pretended to ignore one another, although Alexei watched out of the corner of one eye and saw C'zinsit scowl.

C'zinsit was under what amountd to house arrest, confined for the remainder of the voyage to his cabin except when he was engaged on assigned duties.

The cadet spat insolently into the water. C'zinsit's disgrace had been so public that there was no one in the camp who was not aware of it. Jehan had conducted an open court of enquiry, and the noise of the argument which had flared when he had given his judgement had echoed across the campsite.

Alexei wrinkled his nose. As a punishment, it was scarcely enough. He turned his head to watch the other boat, and was conscious of the heat of the anger which swelled suddenly inside his chest.

The desire for revenge was an emotion so strong

that it took Alexei by surprise. Primitive instincts were foreign to his nature, or so he had supposed.

It had been a mistake to allow Jehan to deal with C'zinsit's offence. Alexei stared at the back of C'zinsit's head, willing him to turn. He did not, and Alexei followed the boat's progress intently until it disappeared around the stern of the ship.

'If we careen, it will give us a chance to explore further,' Jehan said.

It was nonsense, as they both knew. Alexei glanced at Sidacai, who shrugged.

'We need fresh meat,' he said.

Jehan sat up. 'Yes.' He nodded.

Alexei made a face. 'There are herds everywhere,' he pointed out. 'We can take what meat we need in a day.'

Sidacai looked amused. 'You don't mean take, do you, Khan?'

'Don't I?' Alexei glared at him.

Kadan was sitting at the end of the table. He took an apple out of a bowl and pared away the skin with his talons. There was a dark soft patch on one side of the fruit, but he ignored it, biting through to the core. 'If we rob the people, they will remember,' he said cheerfully.

It would be years before they returned to conquer Y'vrope, Alexei was certain. He said, 'One day they will be our slaves.'

Jehan raised his eyebrows. 'You sound like my grandfather.'

'Like a Yek Khan,' Sidacai amended.

'Yes.' Jehan nodded thoughtfully. He met Alexei's stare. 'You know we cannot conquer here.'

Whether or not they used traditional methods, the Will of Heaven would eventually prevail. Alexei was

437

not sure when he had become convinced of the fact, but now that he was, it was much easier to reason what he had to say. He said, 'But we will rule this land.'

A flash of something passed across Jehan's face – a hint of knowledge which was his alone. After a moment he showed his teeth. 'Of course.'

'Then whatever we do, it does not matter.' Alexei stared around the table. 'Am I not in command?'

Kadan's mouth was open. Sidacai sat back, chuckling. 'Oh, certainly,' he said.

'Then we will move on as soon as we are able,' Alexei said, allowing them to hear the finality in his tone. He glanced at Sidacai. 'If we need meat, go take it.'

There were herds of cattle grazing the lush grass further up the river estuary. Probably there was a town or a village somewhere, but its location did not interest Alexei.

Sidacai stood up. 'I'll take Kadan,' he said.

Kadan looked pleased. He started to rise, looking at Alexei for permission.

Alexei nodded. 'As you wish.' He waited until Kadan and Sidacai had left the tent, then gestured to the orderly who was waiting outside the awning. The orderly poured wine into two cups, offering the first to Jehan. Jehan gestured it away. He said, 'Serve your Khan before me.'

It would have taken a court arbiter from Kinsai to decide precedence. Jehan was Altun of course, but he was not a Khan. Alexei took both cups. He handed one to Jehan, and they drank together, meeting one another's eyes. When Jehan laid his cup aside he was grinning. He said, 'That was clever.'

'I wouldn't care to offend you.' Alexei drank more of the wine, then set his cup down on the table.

Sidacai and Kadan were mounting st'lyan outside the tent. A crowd of mounted troopers rode up. Jehan glanced at them. 'They were ready,' he observed.

Alexei nodded. Sidacai had probably guessed the outcome of the council, and had prepared accordingly.

Kadan's st'lyan was a bay with one white foot. It reared while he was still only half in the saddle, but he controlled it. Sidacai reached across and caught at the bay's bridle. Kadan settled himself, and they rode off together.

Jehan picked up his cup. 'Sidacai and Kadan spend much time together.'

Alexei controlled the urge to turn at once. He watched Kadan out of sight, and then waved the hovering orderly away. 'They are friends,' he said.

It was still early in the day. The shadows cast by the tent and by the standards which had been raised on poles in front of the awning were long on the ground, and pointed to the west. Alexei stared at them, waiting for Jehan to say what was on his mind.

'I have a feud to resolve with Sidacai,' Jehan said after a moment.

'I know that.' Alexei sat back in his chair. He said, 'Kadan is your vassal, not mine. Forbid him from Sidacai's company if you doubt his loyalty.'

He knew Jehan would not do it, for it would appear mean.

Jehan frowned. 'It is Sidacai I mistrust,' he said. 'Kadan is my friend, not his.'

Alexei lifted his cup to hide his smile. Jehan had more in common with Sidacai than he had with the members of his own family, and he knew it. 'Sidacai could learn to serve you,' he suggested.

It was clear that Jehan did not think much of the idea. He tugged at his moustaches. 'He hates all Merkuts,' he responded.

439

Sidacai was a realist, Alexei thought, and would soon recognise the futility of his feud. He emptied his cup and placed it carefully on the table. An orderly passed by the tent, his arms full of firewood. He saw Jehan and bowed in mid-stride.

Jehan drank. He had not noticed the orderly, even though his head was turned in the man's direction. He swirled the wine in his cup, and then let it drain into the grass at his feet. He looked up. 'I wonder what Artai will do when we return,' he said.

Alexei produced a flat stare. 'Openly he can do nothing.'

If Artai was wise, he would not make an issue of the means he had tried to employ to control Burun. Admitting that he had been outwitted would only make matters worse. Alexei thought of Jehana in Artai's hands, and he clenched his teeth. He remembered that he had sworn an oath to Artai to serve him, but it was valueless now.

The facings of Jehan's coat were frayed from wear. Jehan brushed absently at them with his free hand. He stretched out blindly towards the table with the hand which held his empty cup, and missed. The cup fell on the carpet under the table and rolled away.

He is drunk, Alexei thought, surprised. It was the first time he had ever seen Jehan taken with wine.

Jehan leaned back in his chair. He gave Alexei a sightless stare. 'If you were human,' he said, 'it would be your lot to oppose him, and not mine.'

Alexei was not certain he understood. Artai's attempt to use Jehana as a hostage was a technical offence against the honour of her family; but since the offence could never be made public, there was surely no recourse in law. He said, 'Artai is the Lord of the Earth, and his will is supreme. How can any man oppose him?'

440

'No one can, and live,' Jehan said. He got to his feet and staggered away.

Sidacai returned with a small herd of the long-horned cattle which grazed the plain. If he had encountered opposition nothing was said about it, and the troopers looked as if they had enjoyed the exercise.

The beasts were butchered, and most of the meat was set to smoke over slow-burning fires. The troopers had scoured the hinterland to find oak, and p'tar trains moved constantly back and forward between the camp and the plateau to feed the fires.

The portside reflector was mounted in place again after three days. Parin pronounced himself satisfied with the tube repairs and with the realignment of the crystals, and it was with a degree of relief that Alexei gave orders for the transfer of baggage to the ship to commence.

C'zinsit was still being excluded from the daily councils. Orcadai likewise seemed to sense that he was in disfavour, and stayed away. No one appeared to miss him.

The chart of Marakan, the continent which lay to the west, was a copy. Alexei had seen the original, and thought that no observable detail had been omitted. The markings showed a large land mass which was split almost into two by a rift which ran in a south-westerly direction across it. A line of islands protected the approaches to the east coast, but there was a clear channel which appeared to provide access to the mouth of the river which ran most of the length of the rift valley. He tapped it with his index finger.

'If there is a settlement of any size, we will find it there.'

The west coast of Marakan was only a short

distance from N'pan, and yet there was no record of contact between the peoples of the two lands. The knowledge troubled Alexei, and he took pains to conceal the fact.

Ch'un Chu had been summoned to the council. He examined the chart, then nodded slowly. 'If those soundings are correct, Lord, then it is navigable,' he said.

'But you advise caution,' Jehan commented, his tone mocking.

Alexei saw Ch'un Chu flush. He said, 'It is the captain's responsibility to bring us safe to X'nadu.'

Jehan sat back. He stared up at the roof of the tent, and then produced a bark of laughter. 'I am behaving like a child,' he said. He switched with obvious ease into the sing-song Losani dialect. 'Honourable Chu, if I have offended you, I ask your pardon,' he said. He bowed from his seat to Ch'un Chu, and then raised an eyebrow at Alexei.

The Losani flushed again, this time apparently with pleasure at the compliment he was being paid. 'Lord,' he said, 'you do me honour.'

If he had the time, Jehan had the ability to win every man in the Khanate to his favour. Alexei frowned at the implications of the thought. He said, 'Then we are agreed.'

It would be strange indeed if a land the size of that shown on the chart were to be uninhabited. There might be radiation poisoning, Alexei thought, and he scratched a note with his stylus on the pad of fouled paper which he was using as an aide-memoire.

'And afterwards?' It was Sidacai who spoke.

A tent within sight of the open front of the awning beneath which they sat was being struck. Troopers eased the tension on the ropes, and the canvas folded neatly at the midpoint, and then sagged to the ground. Alexei's attention was distracted momentarily. He glanced away, and then back again. Jehan's face had paled, although he was quite sober.

'After Marakan, we will go home,' Alexei said.

The sea journey from Marakan to X'nadu was as long and potentially perilous as that which they had undertaken from Pantai to their first landfall on the coast of Y'vrope, but everyone save Jehan smiled.

'We will be heroes,' Kadan said ingenuously.

Sidacai laughed softly. 'Maybe,' he said.

Jehana was beside the shore, watching the baggage being loaded into the boats. Alexei did not approach her at once, but stood instead watching her, analysing his feelings.

No one would have understood his emotions. He scarcely understood them himself, and reflected that if he felt a degree of ambivalence about his marriage, it was the product of his arguably unique situation. Above all he was not sure if he had been selected to marry Jehana because he had occupied at the right moment what amounted to a pinnacle of recognition in this alien world. Certainly it was hard for him to accept at face value the reasons which he had been offered to justify the match, for they were flawed by the background of intrigue which touched everything which took place in Kinsai.

The marriage was a success it was true, but that had little bearing on what now ran through his mind. He knew he could never be certain what motivated Jehana in a given situation – she was after all at the same time Merkut and Altun, and she therefore concealed as a matter of instinct the truth of what she knew. The relationship worked well on an intimate level partly for that reason – it was the one area in which there was trust. Elsewhere Alexei was not sure that he was not allowing himself to be led or directed through events which he barely comprehended.

And he was not certain that it mattered.

It was quite confusing.

Jehana turned and saw him, and she smiled. 'Your face betrays your thoughts, my Lord,' she said.

He was instantly on guard. 'My Lady, I hope not.'

Her lips twitched, a familiar sign of inner amusement which might or might not be at his expense, and he knew he was behaving predictably.

'You wonder what our tomorrow will be,' she said.

'I mistrust its quality,' he responded seriously.

Boats were pulling away from the landing place. They were heavily laden, and sat low in the water. Alexei watched them move past.

Jehana said, 'Whatever occurs when we return to Kinsai, you must remember that you are a Khan.'

Alexei guessed that she was referring to the confrontation which seemed destined to take place between the Merkuts and Artai. He took her hand. 'If it concerns your honour, I am already involved.'

He saw her frown. They began to walk together along the river bank. The water moved sluggishly, and ripples and eddies stirred the surface where irregularities in the riverbed below disturbed the flow. Jehana was wearing a loose skirt which she had fashioned out of material which had been obtained by barter during their journey across Y'vrope. Over it she had on a man's shirt, and she wore boots. It was an unusual style, and Alexei wondered what they would think of it in Kinsai.

She said, 'If I knew my grandfather's intent, I would tell you.'

It was difficult to know how to reply. Whatever was at the core of Burun's intrigues, it was beyond normal understanding. Alexei suspected a plan on the grand scale, the elements of which would continue long after Burun's death, but he had no evidence, and knew that it was suspicion alone which fuelled his mistrust.

Usually Jehana avoided all mention of Burun's hand in their situation. Now Alexei wondered if her frankness was a true sign of her concern. He lifted her hand to his lips. 'This is a strange conversation,' he observed lightly.

Her smile became solemn. 'My Lord, I know it,' she said. She moved against him, and he glanced around to see who was watching. Alone there was no awkwardness to their intimacy. Under the gaze of others it was instinct to dissemble.

They came without much incident to their landfall in Marakan. The seas they encountered were no longer calm, and strong currents opposed the ship's progress. A vessel with masts and sails would have made headway only with difficulty. Alexei saw that Parin noted the fact, and he smiled grimly.

The land which they observed while they still headed north was stark and bare, and the islands which were strung out in a line along Marakan's east coast formed a barrier to passage. Ch'un Chu steered to within half a verst of one chain, and then resisted all entreaties to take the ship closer. He pointed without words at the white-capped waves and broken water which indicated the presence of rocks and shoals, and Alexei guessed that the two continents had once been joined as one. The cliffs he saw with the aid of his glass were very like the ones which edged Y'vrope's western plateau. They had not weathered away to form beaches or a coastal plain, but had fragmented instead so that jagged columns rose up out of a sea which washed against jutting crags. There

445

was no sign of habitation, and after a time they sailed out again into the relative safety of the main channel.

'The coast on the western side is the same by all accounts,' Jehan said. 'No wonder the N'pani avoid it.'

Alexei made a face. There had to be places where rivers drained through the rock, and even though the current scoured the coastline it made sense to expect inlets where sediments might be laid.

Orcadai was in command of the deck watch. He had set up a chair in the shelter of the bulwark, and sat stretched out in it. He said, 'If there is no place to land, our journey will have been wasted.'

It was already apparent that the failure of the embassy was a prospect pleasing to Jehan's uncles, although it was not clear why. The final responsibility would not be theirs, and they would be able to avoid blame.

Alexei saw Jehan's face darken. Jehan said, 'If we have to, we can send in a boat to find harbour.'

Orcadai looked up sharply. 'That would be dangerous.'

'Exactly.' Jehan nodded. He showed his teeth. 'I'm glad you comprehend me, Uncle.'

On the third day they reached the latitude where the coastline was broken by the continental rift. A large island lay across the mouth of the inlet from the sea, and all attempts to find a passage to the south of it failed. Broken water ran in an uninterrupted line from the chain of islands to the south, and the strength of the current was such that they were reluctant to investigate more closely. Any other ship would have been carried down onto the rocks.

Ch'un Chu sailed the *Sunstealer* north. The chart showed a narrow channel running between the island and the coast, and he nosed the vessel cautiously up into it.

446

The tide race ripped past the keel. Jehan stared over the side. He said, 'We ought to be heading south now, but we cannot turn here.'

The Losani looked amused. 'Lord, I have no such intention,' he said. He glanced back over the stern, and then nodded to the comite.

'Reduce speed.'

The engine noise lessened by a fraction. The comite was poised in the hatchway leading to the engine space. He was watching Ch'un Chu intently. The captain eyed the coastline, and then he gazed across at the shore of the island. He extended his arm, palm downward, and waved it as if he was pressing an invisible something down onto the deck.

'Slower.'

The two helmsmen were struggling to keep the bow pointing into the oncoming current. Alexei watched the coastline. A grey crag projecting out into the water was a stationary object in line with the wheel. Then it was as if it was sliding on past.

'We are being pulled backwards,' Jehan said.

Alexei nodded thoughtfully. If the engines failed now, they would be carried down onto the promontory of rock which was the southern headland of the inlet.

The coastline to port was one of sheer cliffs. Sea birds dipped and circled above them. The sea washed past grey and angry, and there was no sign of a suitable landing place.

They were slipping backwards down the channel more quickly now. Ch'un Chu watched the landmarks slide past. He turned. 'Increase speed.'

The comite shouted the command down through the open hatchway. Alexei eyed the headland towards which they were being drawn. There was less than a verst of open water now, and the gap was closing fast.

He marked a pale splash of lighter rock which was in line with the wheel. It slid past the quarterdeck, and then slowed. The *Sunstealer* was gaining headway once more.

'Hard a starboard!'

The helmsmen spun the wheel. The comite ran across the quarterdeck and added his weight to the effort. Alexei looked towards the bow and saw that the ship's head was coming round hard towards the island. The shore line reeled past. Wavelets caught the vessel broadside, and it shuddered.

Suddenly they were round, running with the current. The rocky headland was much closer.

'Ease helm.'

The wheel spun. Alexei was able to distinguish individual rocks now. Waves were bursting against them, throwing spray high into the air. He looked at Ch'un Chu anxiously. The Losani appeared unconcerned. He glanced once at the wheel, and then leaned out across the portside rail.

'A point to starboard. Steady as she goes.'

They were less than half a verst from disaster. Alexei felt the ship heel as it was caught by the force of the current. The troopers lining the main deck were hanging onto rails and fittings. Alexei saw a man vomit over the side, and experienced a moment of nausea. He stared at the headland. In their path lay a tall crag which was split by a deep vertical cleft. When he looked at it again it was infinitesimally to port.

'Increase speed!'

Ch'un Chu's voice rang out. The comite rushed to the hatchway, but already the engine noise was increasing. A thin Ch'kasian popped his head out of the hatch. He bellowed, and the engineers tending the reflector controls cranked their wheels. Alexei

448

listened for the faint noise which accompanied the beam's expansion, and heard it on the very edge of his perception. The *Sunstealer* lurched in the choppy water, and then it was moving sedately into the slack calm which lay beyond the tide race. They had entered the inlet.

'Leadsmen to the bows!'

The comite's command was drowned by the cheer which was raised by the men on deck. Ch'un Chu glanced casually at the headland. It was almost astern now. The Losani strolled to his customary place behind the helm. He looked pleased with himself.

'Name of God,' Jehan said, 'I hope it will be easier to sail out again.' He had not moved from the rail.

Emerging from the inlet they would be heading directly into the current, and they would require full power. Alexei thought that he did not trust himself to reply. He observed Kadan and Sidacai standing among the men on the main deck. Both of them looked pale, and appeared to be attempting to hide the relief they probably felt now that the immediate danger was past.

If Orcadai and C'zinsit were on deck, Alexei could not see them. His thoughts dwelled briefly on Jehana, who was below. Had she been awake, the seas they had encountered would have caused her discomfort. Parin had undertaken to concoct a sedative to allow her to rest, but there had been no time to go to her cabin to see if it had taken effect.

The shore line on either side of the inlet was an unbroken vista of towering grey rock. The cliffs were less jagged than before – probably because they were sheltered from the wind and waves. Instead there were huge masses of dark stone which loomed above calm water, and these had been weathered smooth during the passage of time. The surface of the inlet was like a dark pool. The leadsmen could not find a bottom.

Alexei had anticipated signs of habitation, but he could see nothing on the tops of the cliffs except isolated stands of tall trees. It occurred to him that the current beyond the headlands was so strong that even if this part of Marakan was inhabited, the nautical ability of its people must be restricted. Maybe boats sailed this waterway, but if there was a settlement then probably it was upriver where sediments from the interior would have been deposited to form a plain.

A movement at the edge of his field of vision made Alexei look round. Parin was emerging from the companionway which led to the cabins. Alexei caught the Sechem's eye. 'My wife?'

'Khan, she is well.' Parin's expression displayed an air of confidence. 'She sleeps.'

'Good.'

It was as if the weight of responsibility for Jehana's presence was lessened somehow. Alexei pursed his lips. He was doing his best to accord her equality, but it was difficult at times to suppress the instinct to shield her from conditions which would have been accepted without comment by a man.

The Sechem was gowned in the robes of his office, and the crewmen who were working on the quarter-deck saluted respectfully. The wealth of knowledge which the cult of Sechem embodied in each of its individuals was regarded by ordinary men with a combination of awe and reverence. Even men of rank and position deferred to them when it came to the application of technology, and their word in matters which concerned interpretation of the law was final.

They were sailing around a curve in the inlet. The rocks on one side had fallen, or they had been eroded by streams draining off the plateau above, and there was a steep-sided gorge in a cleft. It was filled with vegetation.

Something moved among the trees. Maybe it was a man. Alexei trained his glass on the spot. The creature was at least humanoid, but its body was covered with dark fur. Ears stood up on either side of the head in alert points, the eyes glowed, and a pair of fangs were displayed in a gaping mouth. It moved, as if it sensed that it was being watched. At one moment it was poised immobile, and at the next there was a blur of speed which defied the imagination. Alexei scanned the trees, but whatever he had seen, it had gone.

He turned away from the rail. Ch'un Chu had his glass to one eye, surveying the gorge. After a moment he lowered it, looking thoughtful. He met Alexei's stare, but said nothing.

Jehan was staring towards the opposite shore. His head came round. 'How much further do you think we will be able to sail?'

The chart indicated an inlet of roughly constant width extending many verst into the interior.

'If it is all navigable, we can continue for at least another day,' Alexei said.

When the water became too shallow they would have to find a place to land. Alexei was determined to visit the country around the rift, even if it meant scaling the cliffs to reach the plateau.

An expanse of rock face slid past to port. Jehan said, 'I don't like this place.'

'Why not?' Alexei stared at the vertical cliff. They were sailing quite close to it now, but the water under the keel had not diminished in depth. He trained his glass on the opposite shore line. It was not much different in character.

'There should be people,' Jehan said.

'Maybe there are.'

If there were no people, there would be a reason. Alexei glanced at the baked white clay disc which was attached to the facing of his tunic by a leather thong. The constituents of the disc would cause it to darken in the presence of radiation. Its colour was still unchanged.

There might be settlements in the interior. The coastline was clearly so inhospitable that the Marakani, if they existed, might see no profit in establishing towns within range of the sea.

There were tidal marks on some of the rocks at the base of the near cliff. The high water mark was about fifteen drem above the level of the water in the inlet, and Alexei wondered if the conjunction of the two moons was responsible for the apparent strength of tide and current, and for the violence of the seas around the coast.

If the inhabitants of Marakan lived isolated from the rest of the world, then it was possible that they had reverted to barbarism. Had they been technologically advanced, they would have found ways to break their isolation. He gave up the attempt to imagine what the embassy would find, for it was certainly pointless.

The height of the cliff to port was such that it blotted out the image of the sun. They travelled in shadow, and beyond it there was only the constant and now cloudless blue of the sky. It made Alexei's eyes ache to stare at it for too long.

By late afternoon the rock along the shore had reduced to become an escarpment, and it was much weathered and seamed. There were still only occasional patches of grass and other vegetation along the inlet sides. Apparently the force of the tides scoured the trough between the rift, carrying away sediments and detritus. The leadsmen found bottom occasionally, and so probably there were places where a freak of the current allowed mud to be laid down. Nowhere was the water so shallow that they were forced to detour.

Alexei climbed to the mast head in the hope of surveying the end of the inlet, but it was too far away for him to see much. The escarpments which marked the edge of the rift did not appear to meet completely, and there was a patch of green between them which indicated that there was a narrow plain providing access to the interior. The throb of the engines decreased suddenly, and the ship's progress through the water began to slow. Alexei descended to the deck. 'Why are we stopping?'

Ch'un Chu was the centre of an anxious group which consisted of Jehan, Sidacai, Kadan, and most of the other officers. Orcadai and C'zinsit were hovering in the background.

The Losani said, 'Lord, we think we should anchor for the night, and travel on again when there is light to see.'

Alexei frowned. He saw that the junior officers were avoiding his eyes. He said, 'Surely we can continue.'

It was nonsense to suggest that there would be insufficient light by which to steer. Even on moonless nights, the sky at this time of year was never completely dark. Alexei glanced east, and saw that the smaller of the world's two moons was already rising.

An officer of Sidacai's guard took a hesitant pace forward. He was Yek, a tall man with vivid blue eye shading which indicated that he was a member of the Obul clan. His top-knot hung down across one shoulder, and he tugged at it before speaking, selecting phrases. 'Lord,' he said finally, 'my men don't like this place. They say it has been abandoned by God.'

The officer was expressing the superstitious fears which must have been voiced by ordinary troopers, Alexei thought. He laughed harshly. 'Have you ever seen a place where God would feel comfortable?'

Sidacai grinned. Kadan said something to him in a low voice, and they both laughed. The faces of the other men remained set in a mould of unhappiness.

Alexei remembered that he had once tried to argue the subject of God's interest in the affairs of earth with Burun. It had been before the Alan campaign, and he had still thought that belief in God was necessary to sanctify right acts. Alexei remembered what Burun had said at the time, and he repeated the words.

'Are you saying that God is concerned with the Earth? Is He not the Lord of Heaven?'

'Khan, yes. But –'

'The Earth is an imperfect creation, as all men know.' Alexei ignored the interjection. 'Whereas Heaven is a paradise. If this place troubles you, the fear is in yourselves. God has nothing to do with it.'

Several men nodded, accepting the logic of the argument. Jehan was staring at his feet. After a moment he looked up. 'Still we would prefer to anchor,' he said.

The night was falling fast. The sky was a deep blue, and the horizon where the moon was rising was tinged with silver. A bird circled overhead, then flew away towards the east. The water in the inlet seemed scarcely to move.

To ignore the petition would gain only hours. Suddenly it seemed pointless, and Alexei shrugged. 'As you wish,' he said coldly. He did not look at Jehan as he spoke.

The landing was tucked in against a rock face which

454

was over a hundred drem in height. It was constructed of stone, and loomed above them at a height which was almost level with the mast head. A flight of stairs descended to the water.

Jehan said, 'There is no way for us to raise the st'lyan so high. We will have to go on foot.'

Alexei eyed the face of the stonework against which they were moored. The blocks had been cut and matched to one another with absolute precision. He had only ever seen comparable work where Imperial technology had been employed.

The construction was Second Empire. The conviction grew inside him.

'There should be people,' Jehan said, his tone worried.

They were three or four verst from the head of the inlet. A river flowed into the inlet between the escarpments, and where it had laid down sediments there was a salt marsh. The marsh was occupied by wildlife, but there was no sign of the presence of man.

Sidacai stared up at the top of the landing. 'This must have been made when the water was higher,' he said. 'Maybe it is deserted because it cannot be used.'

The exit ports of an Imperial lander would be at about the right level. Alexei pictured one of the bulbous craft which were used to carry cargo and passengers between starships and the worlds of the Imperium. Water was the preferred landing medium because a non-stellar drive employed hydrogen conversion. The design favoured by the Empire was a copy of a vessel which had first been built thousands of years before.

Kadan came down the stairs. He said, 'There are tunnels through the cliffs, but they are blocked by falls of rock.'

The Second Empire had ceased to exist millennia

455

ago. All that would remain would be deserted buildings and corroded machinery. Alexei forced himself to speak. 'Can the cliff be scaled?'

'Yes.' Kadan nodded. 'There are stairs cut into the rocks, though they are worn.'

'Good.' Alexei looked at Sidacai. 'I want half a company, armed. Jehan and I will go.'

'Me too,' Kadan said.

'No.' Alexei shook his head. 'You stay with Sidacai.'

Kadan looked disappointed. Jehan said, 'You don't trust my uncles.'

'Do you?'

'No.'

Burun had sent Orcadai and C'zinsit with the embassy to get them out of the way. The realisation came unbidden into Alexei's mind. Suddenly the significance of events which he had thought were unconnected formed a pattern. He remembered the assassination attempts, and knew at once who had been behind them.

He said, 'If we are going on foot, we won't venture far. We'll leave men on the landing, and at the top of the cliffs. We can signal if we need help.'

Sidacai nodded. 'If we have to leave the ship, we'll put Orcadai and C'zinsit in chains.'

Jehan did not look as though the proposal troubled him. He said, 'Kill them if you have to.'

Kadan gaped. He fidgeted on the stairs. Sidacai motioned to him, and he clambered onto the rail of the ship, then jumped down onto the deck.

Sidacai gave Jehan a polite nod. He said, 'Noyon, I'm honoured by your trust.' He dragged Kadan away by one arm, shouting for the captains of the guard.

The rope fender which had been put out over the side creaked as it rubbed between the hull of the ship and the wall. Jehan chewed at the end of his mous-

456

tache, then spat it out. 'You don't really expect to find anything.'

'I'm not sure what I expect.' Alexei avoided Jehan's eyes. He leaned over the rail, staring at the oily water at the base of the stonework. Dead rushes and loose weed washed around a floating log. A creature of some kind swam through the mess, its fur slimed and matted. It dived beneath the log with a splash.

'If we cannot land the st'lyan, we might as well go home,' Jehan said.

'Maybe we can land them from the boats.' Alexei turned. 'There must be some solid ground around the river mouth.'

Jehan reached out and brushed a hand across the stone of the landing. 'This is very old. I wonder who built it.'

Alexei snorted softly. 'Men built it.'

'Men like us?'

It was a clever question. Alexei stroked the gold caste mark on his cheek and smiled. 'I don't think they were like us,' he said.

The top of the landing had been stripped clean. There were signs that there had once been structures – the outlines of several sets of foundations could be seen – and there were marks which might have been what remained of the mountings for lifters or passenger gantries. Nothing had been left behind. The drainage gulley at the base of the cliff was choked with what Alexei guessed was the result of thousands of years of deposits of wind-blown soil and dust. The seeds of grasses and strange plants had taken root there, but nothing of any size had managed to grow. The area was in almost permanent shadow, and the leaves of the plants were pale, almost translucent.

Piles of rock obscured the line of tunnel mouths.

Alexei examined one blockage and was unable to decide if it had occurred accidentally, or if perhaps the men responsible for stripping the dock of its fittings had also decided to plug the passageways through the cliffs to whatever lay beyond.

The troopers stared without a great deal of interest along the desolate extent of the level surface at the head of the stairs. One or two walked to the edge and peered over at the water below. Most men carried uncased bows – Sidacai had judged that lances would be awkward and unwieldy. Scouts were already climbing the steep staircase which was cut into the cliff face above. At one time there must have been handrails embedded in the rock, but they had long since eroded away.

'It's like the old tale,' Jehan said.

'Which tale?' Alexei knew his tone sounded impatient.

'The one about the place of the dragon.' Jehan gestured around.

> 'There is a crab above a pool,
> A dragon place;
> And on the rocks in nests of stone
> Great dragons lie,'

he quoted. 'All we need are the dragons.'

There was a complex mythology which few adult Yek professed to believe relating to the origin of the True People – supposedly from the eggs of golden dragons. Alexei had heard the songs, but it was not an area of knowledge which figured conspicuously in his experience. He gave Jehan a disapproving stare. 'If you have finished gawking, we'll move on.'

The staircase up the cliffs was treacherous, the stone steps covered with a layer of silver-grey lichen.

Alexei slung his bow over his shoulder so as to keep his hands free. He climbed steadily, ignoring the sheer drop to the landing below.

A rampart had been constructed at some time in the past along the cliff top. Parts of it had collapsed or had been weathered away, but what remained was wide enough to accommodate twice their number.

At their backs stretched the inlet – an expanse of black water which lay like a great ribbon between sheer escarpments of grey rock. The *Sunstealer* at its mooring looked insignificant by comparison with the size and grandeur of the landscape. Ripples in the centre of the channel reflected the sun. Alexei could not see the place where they had entered it from the sea.

He said, 'I want ropes down those stairs by the time we return. See to it.'

Joden saluted. 'Yes, Khan.'

Alexei looked past the side of the rampart at what lay beyond. It was too much to take in at once. Deliberately he turned away again. 'And post a guard – a maniple at least.'

Jehan was coming up the final flight of steps. He pulled himself onto the rampart, breathing hard. Then he straightened and gazed around. 'Name of God,' he said, awed.

The most immediate impression Alexei received was of a huge basin – the cliff on top of which they stood was part of the outer edge. Alexei could not see the other side, but he guessed that it must be thousands of verst away. Maybe the basin stretched all the way to the west coast.

Beyond the rampart there was a gentle downslope towards a broad plain. The depression which was the centre was invisible beneath a heat haze. To left and right the rock rim curved away out of sight. The rampart appeared to continue all the way along. The first half-verst or so of the slope to the plain was covered with black granular rock which Alexei thought must once have been a kind of basalt sheet. Suddenly he realised that the whole area resembled a huge crater. He glanced quickly at the radiation-sensitive disc attached to his tunic, but it remained unstained.

A causeway had been constructed from the rampart towards the centre of the basin. In the distance to his right Alexei saw what seemed to be another. The causeways were like the spokes of a wheel running in off the rim, and he wondered if they continued at intervals all the way around the basin, and why they had been constructed. The causeways passed on supports over terraces cut in layers along the slope. It was impossible to tell at this distance if the terraces were under cultivation, but the green carpet covering them looked too uniform to be the result of wild vegetation.

Alexei swallowed. If there were people, they were the descendants of the people who had built this.

Jehan said, 'Do you suppose this rampart is for defence?'

People who desired to protect their territory from invaders might have gone to such lengths. Certainly it would explain the blocked tunnels. Alexei eyed the crumbling stonework of the rampart. 'Maybe it was once,' he said.

Alexei remembered that the Second Empire had fought itself to collapse against a race of mutated superbeings. It was possible that one of the last battles had been fought here – or maybe the people had learned of the conflict which was taking place elsewhere, and had isolated themselves. He imagined them maintaining a watch from the ramparts. With

460

the passage of time successive generations would have ceased to believe that a threat existed, and the defences would have been allowed to fall into disrepair.

'If there are people,' Jehan observed, 'they have not noticed that we are here.'

There was a hollow feeling inside Alexei's chest. He stared at the causeway and realised that he was not sure what he wanted to find there. The remnants of a Second Empire civilisation might possess the ability to re-establish communication with the rest of the Empire; but a community of technologically advanced humans would represent a threat to the Khanate. He felt confused and uncertain.

A freak of the wind or a fluctuation in air temperature cleared the haze off a section of the plain below, and in it Alexei saw the apparently intact shell of a suspensor canopy – the kind of shelter used on Knossos and other worlds to protect public buildings and parks from the weather. He could not tell if the permaglass was unbroken, and if the canopy was floating, or merely resting on the ground. The troopers who had seen it were pointing.

Jehan came up to Alexei's side. He said, 'Remember the Will of Heaven.'

Alexei met Jehan's eyes. He licked his lips. 'One Lord upon the Earth,' he said.

'And you are his ambassador,' Jehan commented. He did not look away.

People advanced enough to use technology would have ventured beyond the boundaries of this land. Alexei nodded slowly. 'I am glad you reminded me,' he said.

Figures moved among the terraces. Most did not even look up when they were hailed. Alexei could see no

461

way to descend from the causeway, and he stood beside Jehan while troopers shouted down at a pair who were tending vines directly below.

They were farm workers, Alexei supposed, although they were not human. The two figures wore only loincloths, and their upper bodies were lightly furred. One turned at last and looked up, and Alexei stared at the feline features. He remembered the creature he had seen during the *Sunstealer*'s voyage along the inlet, and thought that what he was looking at now was probably a domesticated form of the same animal.

'Do you think they understand language?' Jehan asked. There was a roughly thirty-drem drop from the level of the causeway to the terrace below. The causeway wall had crumbled to nothing, and Jehan set his booted feet gingerly on the top of a support pylon. He cupped his hands around his mouth and shouted a greeting in Yek, then in Anglic. Finally he tried a range of the dialects common around the Khanate. The creature below stared back expressionlessly. Jehan threw up his hands in exasperation. He stepped back onto the solid part of the causeway. The furred face among the vines turned away.

If they were capable of farm work, they possessed at least limited intelligence. They would have to understand signs or simple instructions, or their masters would be incapable of communicating with them.

'There are languages other than ours,' Alexei said. He turned and followed the troopers who were already moving down the causeway. They were over a verst from the rim of the basin now, but there was still no sign of stairs down to the ground. He gazed ahead, but if there was a place where the causeway came to an end, it was lost in the haze.

They continued walking. Alexei looked up at the sun, and he estimated that most of the morning had passed. Occasional rooftops were visible among the trees on the agricultural terraces, and he supposed that they were either barns or the dwelling places of the workers. If there were roads joining the different levels, they were on another part of the slope and hidden from view. How produce was moved to the basin Alexei could not imagine. Maybe other causeways were constructed closer to the ground, and had ramps or stairs connecting them with what lay below.

'This is fertile land,' Jehan said.

Alexei nodded absently. He wondered if the whole basin was under cultivation, and thought not. The population could not be so large.

They had already encountered places where the causeway was in such disrepair that little of the travelling surface remained. Stretchers of what Alexei recognised as a kind of permacrete ran like tightropes from one pylon to the next, and the troopers balanced agilely along them, ignoring the drop.

About midday they stopped to rest. The rim from which they had travelled was now barely visible through the haze. The sky above was cloudless, and the sun was huge. Even the Yek were oppressed by the heat.

Alexei sent a trooper back along the causeway to tell Sidacai that he intended to continue on.

Jehan waited until the trooper had departed. Then he said, 'We have little food, and our water will only last the day.'

There was no shade, and some of the troopers were sitting with their legs hanging over the edge of the causeway. Alexei gazed towards them. 'If we have not found a way down to the ground by nightfall, we will go back,' he said. He did not believe that the builders

463

of the structure had not allowed for the need to descend in an emergency.

Jehan made a face. He looked along the causeway. 'I think it goes on forever,' he said.

Alexei perched on a section of the causeway wall. The brickwork was brittle and flaking. He gestured at the rows of neat terracing. 'Somebody must rule all this,' he said. 'We ought to find him.'

Jehan pulled his shirt over his head. His chest was hairless, and he had grown so lean during the embassy that his pectoral muscles stood out like two pads above the definition of his ribcage. He said, 'Maybe we should go back and try by the river. We could land the st'lyan at the end of the marsh, and look for a way inland.'

Alexei stared at him. 'I never knew you so easily discouraged before.'

'I was never on foot so far from home before,' Jehan commented drily. He rolled his shirt and used the sleeves to fasten it around his waist. Then he looked round. 'Do you have wine?'

'Water only.' Alexei picked up the leather bottle he had carried from the clifftop.

'Then that will have to do.' Jehan reached out. He took the bottle and uncorked it, then drank. For a moment he seemed to be gazing up at the sky. He looked at Alexei suddenly. 'You have seen a causeway like this somewhere else.'

A tiny bird swooped towards them, wings extended. It wheeled, calling, and then dropped out of sight among the trees below. Alexei stared after it. 'Not like this,' he responded finally. 'Although I have seen structures of the same kind.'

Jehan digested the reply. 'It's very old.'

'Older than the Khanate.' Alexei nodded.

'Hunh.' Jehan corked the bottle. He held it out and

Alexei took it. 'Then the people who raised it are long dead.'

'I expect so.'

'Whoever rules here must be descended from them,' Jehan observed. 'But if the people had the knowledge, surely they would keep the causeways repaired?'

It was a sensible observation. Alexei shrugged. 'They may not all be in use,' he said. 'This one seems to serve no purpose other than to provide a way up to the rampart.'

'Which likewise seems to be unused.' Jehan frowned. 'Unless there is another way to enter the interior of the country, this land will be difficult to conquer.'

Natural barriers were sometimes more effective against invasion than physical resistance. Alexei recalled the campaign which the Yek had conducted the year after he had become marooned on Tarvaras. They had been prevented for years from attacking the Alan, who inhabited the south-western corner of the Khanate, because of the barrier formed by the G'bai desert. Only when the Sechem had worked out how to identify the areas of the wasteland which were still saturated with radiation had the Yek campaign been able to proceed.

Alexei pursed his lips. The Alan had made few real preparations to withstand an invasion, because they had believed that the G'bai was impassable. Now they were the subjects of the Kha-Khan.

The abandoned suspensor canopy dominated the landscape. Its conical framework rested on a level piece of ground to one side of the causeway – a circular base three or four hundred drem in diameter which had a cover of only partially intact permaglass at least a hundred drem high. Birds flew in and out of the spaces left by missing panels, and Alexei was able to see that the floor inside was choked with the kind of vegetation which he would have expected to see in an Imperial hothouse.

Jehan looked disbelieving when the function of the structure was explained.

'All that to keep the rain off?' He shook his head. 'Ridiculous.'

Probably it had looked quite majestic once, hovering on contragrav lifters above some park or palace, the sun sparkling on clean panels. Now it was a grimy derelict, the deserted relic of Imperial former glory. Alexei grimaced. The inhabitants of Marakan had lost all but the most basic technological ability, that was clear. The abandoned canopy was confirmation of that, for the lifters were quite simple to build, given the facilities, and they required almost no maintenance.

The sun was by now low in the west. The horizon behind the canopy was streaked with red, and a wind was springing up. It lifted the haze so that the landscape became clear.

There were two more terraces, and then the ground levelled out into a plain. It stretched off into the distance. Alexei saw the outline of another causeway structure which appeared to intersect the one down which they were travelling. It curved away, following the contour of the final terrace, and he guessed that it had been laid out in a circle and probably crossed each of the other causeways in turn.

Beneath the pylons of the new causeway were stone pyramids in a row. Alexei supposed they could be residential, although it made sense to expect that if they were buildings they formed some kind of administrative facility to do with the management of the agricultural land. A winding ribbon of road ran across the plain past the pyramids towards the first terrace. Nothing moved on it.

Jehan shaded his eyes with one hand. He said, 'If those are buildings, there should be a way to get down.'

Alexei remembered that on some worlds the pyramid was connected with religion, and on others with astronomy. He said, 'If there is not, we have walked a long way for nothing.'

'As embassies go, we don't look very impressive.' Jehan ran a hand across his scalp. 'If we are going to encounter the rulers of this land, we ought to be properly dressed. We should have brought the standard.'

'I don't think we could have got it up the stairs from the landing.' Alexei shook his head, amused. 'I suppose it would help if you put your shirt back on. Apart from that they will have to take us as they find us.'

They strode along the causeway. Probably they were visible from the ground, Alexei thought, but if the news of their presence had been communicated ahead, there was no one who thought that a reception was necessary.

'There are stairs.' Jehan pointed. He started to put on his shirt.

'I see them.'

The causeway was widening out into a kind of staging. A broad flight of stairs descended from it to the ground. It was apparent from their condition that they were seldom used, although the edge of a step near the top had been repaired at some time in the recent past.

Joden harried the troopers into orderly ranks. A man on an equine similar to those Alexei had seen in Y'vrope rode past the foot of the staircase. He caught

467

sight of the assembling troopers and stared, but did not stop.

'At least someone knows we are here.' Alexei adjusted the angle of his sword in his sash. It had been too hot to wear a tunic. He brushed dust from his breeches.

No alarm was being raised, so even if the Marakani had once feared attack, they no longer thought that the presence of armed strangers in their land represented a threat. Alexei eyed the outline of the nearest pyramid. In fact the structure had a flat top, and now that he was closer to it he could see that every layer had a multitude of openings, as if there were apartments inside, and that around each layer there were open balconies and walkways. The building material was not natural stone, but some kind of composite. It reflected the late sun so that Alexei was forced to shield his eyes to study it. If there were people watching from the shadows inside the apartments in the stepped tiers, he could not see them.

The troopers stared, unimpressed. One of the under-officers was engaged in re-winding his waist sash. He caught Alexei's eye. 'Lord, if these are castles, they will be easy to storm.'

In fact there was no sign of defensive measures. Probably the Marakani had relied in the past on the effectiveness of the perimeter barrier to counter invasion. Alexei started down the stairs, Jehan at his side. A flagged precinct occupied the area at the foot of the staircase. Beyond it there was a road. The surface looked as if it had been pounded flat or rolled, and the light-brown granular material from which it was made absorbed the sound of every footstep. Alexei found the lack of noise quite disconcerting.

They were several hundred drem from the nearest pyramid. A cart came into view. It was made of wood, and had weathered to a nondescript grey colour. A shaggy bullock was yoked to the vehicle, and it was being driven by one of the feline agricultural workers. The driver looked at the troopers as they passed, but no discernible expression appeared in the amber eyes.

The driver's appearance excited a murmur of comment. Jehan muttered something under his breath, and he spat to right and left. Alexei turned and watched the cart as it continued down the road. The driver's eyes had been empty, without life or expression, and he wondered if the creatures were taken from the wild, and had to be pacified with drugs before they became docile.

There should be people. Alexei surveyed the pyramids. They were quite clearly residential. Even if they were used to house no more than an area administration, there ought to be signs of life. The man who had ridden past the foot of the staircase had disappeared.

Alexei's pace slowed. The western rim of the basin was like a curved black wall a long way ahead, thrown into deep shadow by the setting sun. Across the plain the changing currents of air pushed heat like an advancing wave towards them. Images wavered in an atmosphere so dense that it appeared to have substance. A cricket chirped. The sound grated on Alexei's nerves. He watched the pyramid tiers for movement. His eyes caught the at first almost imperceptible signs of decay – a missing rail on one of the levels, stained stonework, weeds sprouting from a joint between two flagstones. Workers were digging on the grass verge which curved past the side of the pyramid. The heat and silence pressed down on Alexei's senses. He began to suspect that the towering structures were no longer occupied or even in use, and stopped.

Jehan said, 'Aren't we going inside?'

It was hard for Alexei to concentrate on the embassy's purpose. He gestured at their escort. 'I am, certainly. You can if you wish. I don't think we need all these.'

'Hunh.' Jehan rested a hand on his sword hilt. 'We aren't going anywhere without a guard.'

If there was danger, it would have appeared by now. Alexei shrugged. 'As you will.'

They compromised. The majority of the troopers were left outside under Joden's command. An officer and four men followed Alexei and Jehan.

The entrance to the pyramid was not immediately apparent. Then Alexei realised that one section of the base layer wall overlapped another. The space between was barely wide enough for a man to pass. Alexei wondered if there was another way in on one of the other sides. Unless there was, the builders must have put everything the inhabitants would need inside the pyramid and then closed it up until only men could enter. The space separating the two walls was not even wide enough for a chair to be carried through it.

Inside there was a huge hallway with a floor which looked as if it had been poured in a continuous expanse. It gleamed like polished marble.

There were metal doors along both sides, but Alexei could see no way to open them. He supposed there might be sensors, and approached the nearest door. Nothing happened. If there was a mechanism controlling entry, it had ceased to operate or was locked.

Jehan and the others were staring around the hall. The ceiling above their heads was low, and it glowed faintly. Probably there was a permanent power source – photocells or the like, Alexei guessed – on the building exterior.

There were no stairs. Maybe they were behind one of the doors. Alexei was about to turn away towards the entrance again when he noticed a faint seam down one section of the floor. The quality of the lighting made it difficult to see anything clearly. He moved to one side to avoid a patch of reflected luminescence, and traced the outline.

He said, 'There is a trapdoor or something similar in the floor.'

'There is no way to open it,' Jehan said, peering.

It might be opened from within of course, but Alexei could see no way for someone who wanted to gain entry to communicate the fact of his presence. He said, 'There is a way. We just can't see it.'

Jehan made a face. 'Puzzles are for children.' He cocked his head on one side, watching Alexei's expression. 'Is it so important?'

Alexei was not sure why Jehan was being obstructive. He said, 'We could try forcing the doors, I suppose.'

'Hunh.' Jehan moved the toe of his boot in a slow circle on the floor. 'Somebody keeps this clean.'

Even if the surfaces were somehow anti-static, there ought to be dust in the corners of the room. Alexei looked up at the ceiling, looking for spider webs. There were none.

'No one has come to find out who we are or what we want,' Jehan observed. 'We're not invisible.'

The only human they had seen had not stopped. Alexei ignored a sense of disquiet. He said, 'I think we ought to explore this place. If somebody comes, and we have offended, we can apologise.'

Jehan looked amused. He said, 'Alexei, I would agree if I did not doubt your motives. If these people use machines, we have seen no sign of it.'

Alexei flushed. 'If they use machines, they threaten

the Khanate,' he responded. He saw Jehan blink.

'I did not think of that,' Jehan said. 'Is the science you expect to find here so powerful?'

'Ask the Sechem.' Alexei snorted. 'If our ship was not powered by engines, we could not sail the seas.'

There was a sudden whisper of sound. It was as if a gear had moved in some mechanism embedded in the floor beneath their feet. Alexei strained his ears to hear it again.

Jehan stared at the floor. 'You have made your point,' he said.

They moved along the walls, searching for anything which might control access to whatever lay below. There were places where what might have been touch-sensitive plates had been removed – door controls, Alexei thought.

Jehan said, 'Maybe it opens if it is pushed.'

It seemed too simple. Alexei located the seam which marked one side of the rectangular outline. He put a foot on the surface which he judged must be capable of movement and pushed. Nothing happened. He stepped onto the outline. Still it did not move. Jehan had found the other side. He stepped onto it and jumped up and down, but there was no hint of movement. 'Maybe it isn't a door at all,' he said.

An inset panel would have been a different shade. Alexei looked down at his feet, pondering. One of the troopers came across the floor from the entrance. He walked onto the outline from one end, and his foot disappeared through what appeared to be solid marble. The trooper yelled and jumped back.

If the Third Empire had developed force-field science to this extent, Alexei was not aware of it. He went round to the place where the trooper's foot had gone through the floor. The surface looked perfectly firm. Gingerly he put one foot across the line and pressed. His boot encountered solid resistance. Puzzled he drew back. He gestured to the trooper. 'Show me what you did just now.'

The trooper backed off, eyeing the floor warily. He walked four or five paces towards the outline and stepped onto it. His feet went through the surface and he came to a halt, standing up to his ankles in what seemed to be solid marble. His face went white. 'Lord,' he said, 'this is magic.' He made a sign to ward off the evil eye.

However the opening worked, it only recognised someone who walked directly into it from one end. Alexei looked for sensors on the walls on either side, but he could see nothing. A person who wished to descend to the level below would have to break a beam – or maybe the floor itself was sensitised. He went around to the end of the outline, backed off, and walked towards it. It was as if the marble did not exist. He could feel the steps on which he was standing, even though he could not see them. He halted at the trooper's side. 'Go back up.'

The trooper licked his lips. He lifted his leg as if he expected to find that his foot had become detached. When his boot emerged from the field he looked relieved. He trotted back up onto the solid floor again.

Alexei went down a step. He was up to his calves in the field now, but he could feel no sensation. Jehan walked around to the side of the opening and stepped out onto the field. He came up to Alexei's side and stood above him. 'This is clever,' he said. 'How is it done?'

'I'm not sure,' Alexei temporised. 'If you go round to the end, you can come down.'

'Do I want to?' Jehan knelt down. He put his hand on the floor at Alexei's side and pressed against the resistance he found there. 'It's remarkable,' he said. 'I wonder what would happen if I tried to lift you?'

'This isn't a game.' Alexei descended another step. His feet felt cold. 'Are you coming?'

It was clear that the troopers were reluctant. Jehan said, 'If you are going down there, then so will I.' He went round to the end of the field and started down the stairs.

Alexei was conscious that he was feeling with his feet for each step. His head passed below floor level and his vision blurred, then cleared again. Apparently the field had no actual thickness, and he wondered why he had expected otherwise.

They were descending into a chamber which occupied a space large enough to be the whole basement area of the pyramid. A dais stood in the centre, and on the dais lay a metal cylinder. Alexei was reminded of a starship escape pod. He looked around the chamber, but there were only blank walls. He got up onto the dais and looked down into it.

The being inside the capsule was immeasurably old. The features were human.

Jehan scrambled up onto the platform at Alexei's side. He got to his feet. 'God's Name,' he said, staring at the capsule's contents. 'Is it alive?'

The capsule was some kind of maintenance system. It was filled with clear fluid, and the creature inside was floating in it. The top of the capsule was transparent, and Alexei guessed another force field. He stared through the transparent flesh at the tracery of veins and arteries below. The bone structure was odd — as if much of the skeleton had been partially dissolved away. The heart pumped obscenely, but the lungs did not appear to be moving at all. The stomach and bowels had been removed, and in their place wound the tubes through which the bodily fluids circulated. Apparently the dais itself contained the life-support mechanism. Alexei said, 'I think so.' He willed the creature's eyes to open, but they did not.

Someone was descending into the chamber through another opening. Alexei could not see the stairs, although his reason told him they were there. First the feet appeared, and then the legs. A man came into view. He stopped when he saw them.

'A stranger,' he said. He did not appear to be troubled by the discovery. 'Come you to look at the Old One?'

The speaker was human; of that much Alexei was certain. He adjusted to the fact that he had been addressed in Old Anglic. 'Sir, I offer greeting,' he said. He stepped away from the capsule, drawing Jehan with him so that it would be clear that they meant no harm.

The Marakani was tall and slender, hairless, and he was gowned richly in red and yellow. Alexei guessed that the blazon on the facings of his coat indicated his house, or maybe his rank or office. The man seemed to see Jehan for the first time. His head went back. 'Sir, you do not require your guardbeast here,' he said, his tone offended.

If Jehan understood, he gave no sign. Alexei hesitated. He saw that there were steps down from the dais on the side from which the Marakani had entered the chamber. He descended them, and Jehan followed.

Alexei bowed, court fashion. He said, 'Sir, as you have observed, I am a stranger here. I do not know your customs, and I ask pardon if I have offended. As to my companion, he is of rank among his own people, being the son of a most noble house.'

'He is a beast nevertheless,' the Marakani said tartly. 'I am Keeper here, and so I can tell you that no beast has ever been admitted to the lower levels.'

'Then we will depart,' Alexei said politely. 'The nature of your office I do not understand, I confess, but I would not willingly offend you. Perhaps you will allow me the privilege of speech with you when you have completed your duties.' He touched Jehan's arm, and together they walked towards the stairs by which they had entered the chamber.

'What did he call me?' Jehan asked softly in Yek.

'A guardbeast.' Alexei put his hand quickly on Jehan's sword arm. 'Don't turn. He doesn't know you understand.'

The muscles of Jehan's forearm tightened. He said, 'The day we conquer this land, I will decorate the Merkut totem with his head.' His pace did not falter, and Alexei grinned. They began to ascend the stairs.

'Wait!'

The Marakani's command came suddenly. Alexei stopped and turned. He watched the other man come round the curve of the dais to the foot of the stairway. A light was shining there. The Marakani emerged into it, his features clearly visible for the first time. Alexei saw the blood vessels which were now apparent below the exposed flesh of the face, neck and hands. The Keeper was in the early stages of the condition which afflicted the occupant of the capsule.

The Keeper said, 'Sir, I do not think that you were quickened in Eden.'

'Eden?' Alexei allowed his eyebrows to rise. 'We call it Marakan.'

'Indeed.' The Marakani looked thoughtful. He started to ascend the stairs towards them. He inspected Alexei, and then examined Jehan. What he saw seemed to arouse surprise. Alexei saw his eyes widen.

At close range the progress towards complete

transparency of the flesh was even more obvious. Alexei wondered if the condition was the result of a genetic disorder, and he strove to avoid showing by his expression that he found the result unsightly. Jehan was staring openly, but he was being ignored.

They went up into the hallway. The waiting troopers saluted Alexei and Jehan, then eyed the Marakani and muttered to one another in low voices. In the Khanate, they would have assumed that the Keeper was a mutant, and they would have avoided contact with him.

'You are well attended,' the Marakani said drily. He went out through the narrow opening between the walls without giving Alexei time to reply.

Alexei watched the expression on Jehan's face. He said, 'Whatever I say to him, pretend that you do not understand.'

Jehan sniffed, but he said nothing.

In the last light of the sun Alexei was able to see that the Keeper's eyelids were lashless. The eyes themselves were almost pink in colour. Alexei said, 'Sir, it is the custom for one of my rank to travel with attendants.'

The Keeper had already noticed the remainder of their escort. The troopers were resting on the grass which bordered the road running between the pyramids. 'They are well armed,' he observed. 'In Eden that is unnecessary. The workbeasts are tame, and there have been no escapes in my memory.'

The Marakani had gestured towards the workers digging on the verge as he spoke. Alexei saw that the feline species had claws or talons, and he guessed that it was for that reason that the Yek had been identified as beasts. He opened his mouth to rectify the impression, then closed it again. It might be of advantage for the Keeper to believe that he was dealing

477

with a human who was served by animals – especially since it was now clear that it was normal in Eden. He shrugged. 'I have travelled far, and every land is not as peaceful as this.'

The Marakani's eyes flickered. He said, 'We knew of course that there were other continents.'

'But did not seek to contact them?' Alexei said gently.

'Why should we?' The Keeper's head came round. He looked surprised. 'We are self-sufficient here, as you can see. It has always been our policy to leave the species of the earth to work out their own destiny. Clearly men are once more dominant.'

Alexei saw Jehan smile. He avoided the Marakani's gaze. 'Sir, as you may have surmised, I am the ambassador of the rulers of the land which lies across the sea to the west. Our country is settled and at peace, and we wish to establish links with other parts of our world.'

'A laudable enterprise.' The Keeper's smile was condescending. Then he eyed the Yek. 'I see no baggage. Have you left others of your party beyond our borders? Perhaps we should send for them.'

It would be unwise to reveal too much, Alexei judged. He considered how to reply, and knew at once that it was important to make it clear that he was neither alone nor cut off from aid should it be required. He said, 'Sir, we found it difficult to enter your land by the usual means.' He saw a look of satisfaction cross the Marakani's face. 'We left our baggage on board our ship, a day's march away.'

The Keeper appeared to be trying to hide the fact that he was impressed. 'No one has sailed our seas within my memory,' he said. 'The currents are too swift.'

Alexei was suddenly certain that it would be a

mistake to mention the fact that the *Sunstealer* was engine-powered. 'We were fortunate,' he said dismissively.

The sun was setting. The light from the hall inside the pyramid filtered out of the entrance. Jehan emerged suddenly at the head of the men. He bowed to Alexei, and then they all went over to join Joden. The workers rose and started to walk away down the road towards the first of the agricultural terraces. Alexei had not seen anyone giving them the command to finish work, but it was as if they had each heard the same signal. He watched them out of sight.

'You may lodge your beasts in our dormitories if you wish,' the Keeper said at Alexei's side. 'They eat meat as ours do, I imagine. It will be our pleasure to feed them for you.'

The offer implied the presence of other men, although Alexei had seen none. He did not glance towards Jehan and the others. 'Sir, you are generous. My escort are unused to your customs, as I am, and would be better camped in the open, I think. Is there a place they may use? Your gift of meat I accept with thanks. Also I would be grateful for water.'

The Marakani seemed at first disappointed. Then he seemed to register the fact that part of his offer had been accepted. He nodded and smiled. 'You are a guest in our land.' He waved a hand to indicate the fields beyond the road. 'Camp your beasts where you will.' He bowed to Alexei and walked away.

Alexei stared after him. 'Beasts indeed,' he said, and he spat derisively onto the flagged paving.

The meat was brought to the camp in cauldrons. It had been minced, and the troopers who lifted the cauldrons down from the carts looked unhappy. One of them said something low-voiced to Joden. The guard commander scooped up some of the meat in a bowl, and he came quickly to where Alexei sat talking with Jehan. 'Khan,' he said, 'this meat is bad.'

'Oh?' Alexei sniffed at the contents of the bowl. The sweet smell made his nose wrinkle. He took the bowl out of Joden's hand and passed it to Jehan. 'What do you think?'

Jehan held the bowl to his nose. He said, 'I don't think it's bad. Bad meat doesn't smell like that.' He gave back the bowl. 'There's something strange about it though.'

Something tugged at a chord in Alexei's memory, and he struggled for recollection. Joden said, 'Bad or not, Noyon, my men say they won't eat it.'

They were in the middle of fields, but it was dark. Alexei raised his head and stared around. 'If they can find game, they can hunt,' he said. 'But tell them to remember this isn't our land.'

Joden nodded approvingly. He said, 'The field across the road is full of young corn. These are Yek, and if they can't find a pig or a few fowl, they deserve to starve.' He strode away.

The pyramids were vague outlines against the night sky. It was not cold, but Alexei stretched out his hands to the small fire the orderly had lit a short time before. The nearest woodland was almost a verst away, but somehow fuel had been found.

Jehan said, 'I sent another man back along the causeway to tell Sidacai we would be here until tomorrow.'

Alexei looked round sharply. 'Indeed.'

'You must see that we can achieve nothing here,' Jehan said. 'The Marakani think we are like the creatures who work in their fields. They will never come to terms with us.'

It was probably true. Alexei stared at the flames

480

licking up around the log on the fire. 'I did not tell the man I spoke to that you are the rulers of our land.'

Jehan laughed softly. 'I know that.' He squatted on his heels beside the fire, and then suddenly he looked up. 'There is something wrong with this place,' he said. 'Where are all the people? Remember we have seen but one man.'

There could be towns or even cities closer to the centre of the basin, but if they were there, they were invisible behind the heat haze which shielded the plain by day. Alexei glanced at the nearest pyramid, trying to divine its purpose. It seemed to him inconceivable that such a structure could have been built to preserve the body of one man.

A line of troopers sauntered out of the camp towards the road. Most of them carried their bows, although few had more than two or three arrows.

'Joden went up onto the causeway,' Jehan persisted. 'He says he can see no lights to the west. If there is a settlement, it must be far in the distance.'

Alexei straightened. The troopers were indistinct figures moving through the corn in the field on the other side of the road. He heard someone whistle softly. A bird cried alarm. Alexei turned. 'Jehan, don't press me on this. We are staying until I am satisfied. If there is a mystery, we will uncover it.'

An orderly was carrying one of the cauldrons towards the road. Alexei watched him go. Jehan said, 'There is a ditch along the side of the road.'

'I know.'

'If there are wolves or scavengers, they will have a feast,' Jehan observed. 'What will you tell the Marakani?'

'About the meat?'

'No.' Jehan snorted. 'About the Khanate.'

481

'Oh.' Alexei looked round. He showed his teeth. 'As little as possible.'

'I thought so,' Jehan said.

The troopers were roasting wildfowl and a deer the size of a dog over fires when the Marakani rode up. There were three men, all dressed in the red and yellow which Alexei now guessed was the uniform of the Keepers. They led a saddled but riderless equine.

Alexei went out to meet them, relieved that the troopers were no longer hunting in the fields. If the Marakani noticed that the meat which was being cooked was unminced, they said nothing. The empty cauldrons were lying on the ground near the road. The Marakani were led by the man Alexei had already met at the pyramid. He dismounted and bowed. 'Sir, we come to offer you the hospitality of the Keep,' he said.

It had not occurred to Alexei that the title by which the Marakani had referred to himself related to something other than rank or office. He returned the bow. 'Sir, I thank you.' He could think of nothing else to say.

Jehan came up to Alexei's side. 'What do they want?' he asked in Yek.

'They are offering me hospitality. A meal and a place to sleep I imagine.'

'Do you think you should accept? It may be a trap.'

The possibility had already occurred to Alexei. He frowned. 'If I hope to be admitted into their confidence, I must go with them.'

The Marakani seemed to grow impatient. The man who had dismounted said, 'Sir, if it troubles you to leave your beasts unmastered, they can be enclosed.'

Alexei saw Jehan stiffen. He gave him a warning glance, and then turned and bowed again. 'Sir, I thank

482

you for your concern, but that is unnecessary.' He walked steadily towards the waiting equine, taking the reins from the hand of the man who had been leading it.

'My name is Vlad Travtravnya,' the Keeper said. He got up into the saddle and walked his equine up beside Alexei.

In Old Anglic the last name was the number thirty-three. It struck Alexei as strange, but he hid his re-action, supposing that the Marakani had forgotten the use of patronymics during their isolation from the Empire. He said, 'I am Alexei Sergeivitch, Khan of Khitai.' He mounted. The equine was a grey, and it was much smaller than the st'lyan which he had grown used to.

Jehan was standing watching. He came up to the equine's side and put his hand on Alexei's reins. 'Don't trust them.'

None of the mounted men understood Yek, or there would have been a reaction. Alexei said, 'If I do not return, come and find me.' He saw Jehan give the Marakani a stare of cool assessment.

'If you do not return, we will kill them all,' Jehan said.

Alexei nodded. He reined around and rode up onto the road.

The road surface was faintly luminous under the moonlight. The Keeper riding at Alexei's side held his reins with only one hand. He glanced back towards the camp, then turned towards Alexei as if he was about to say something. Suddenly he seemed to change his mind. They rode in silence along the road. Alexei saw that they were passing the pyramids. The last structure had a lower level which was lit by torches and cressets. Feline servants waited outside in silent ranks.

Alexei said, 'I thought all these buildings were the same.'

'They are,' his companion responded, his expression preoccupied.

The man in the lead was wheeling his equine onto the flagstones in front of the pyramid entrance. Alexei saw that the feline servants were so alike that they must have been selected according to colouring and stature. He reined in and dismounted. A servant took the equine's bridle and led it away.

Alexei glanced round at the Keeper who had ridden at his side. 'These creatures are well trained,' he observed.

The Keeper looked amused. 'They are bred for service,' he said.

Even if the felines were not a wild species which had been domesticated, they were clearly little more than slaves. Alexei stared around. He had expected to see other people – this pyramid was apparently in use as living quarters – but there was no one.

Travtravnya was ushering him through the narrow entrance. The hall inside was wide, and if there were doors along the walls they were hidden by the hangings which covered them from floor to ceiling. Now that they were revealed in the interior light, it was clear that both of the other men were quite similar in appearance – they were slender and had the same lashless eyes, and their flesh exhibited the early stages of transparency.

Both men bowed. Travtravnya said, 'Sir, I present Lech Dvatravnya and Sacha Zvatravnya. Along with myself they are Keepers of the Fourth Quadrant of Eden.'

Alexei nodded politely. He supposed that sons were named after their fathers, and that the last name signified the generation. To ask at this stage might be considered impolite.

A long table was laid at one end of the chamber. There were only four chairs around it, so no other diners were expected. Alexei wondered if Marakani women were kept in seclusion in separate quarters. If they were, it was a practice which extended to the servants. He tried to remember if he had seen a female member of the feline species, but could not.

It was apparent that he was expected to sit first. Alexei went towards the nearest place, hoping that precedence was not assigned according to table position. He felt inhibited by the need to avoid giving offence, and was suddenly aware that it had been easier to deal at first encounter with the Yek, who were aliens, than it was with these men who were survivors of the Empire.

The moment they sat they were served. The courses were the kind traditional on worlds of Terran origin – soup, a kind of fish, a meat course accompanied by vegetables. Alexei realised that he had grown used to Yek fare, and he missed the kva which was used like rice as a base upon which meat was served. The vegetables were strange, and he guessed that they were mutated Terran stock. He was aware that he was under scrutiny, and concentrated on the meal, responding politely and as far as possible non-committally to enquiries relating to his journey to Marakan.

There was no sweet, but servants brought a beverage which Alexei thought was similar to coffee, and poured glasses of some kind of spirit. The number of servants had by now reduced to only two, and these retired to the end of the room where they hovered, awaiting summons by one of the men.

Alexei sipped at the coffee. It was bitter and unsweetened. The spirit was like brandy, though it was very sharp. He saw that his hosts were taking alternate sips of beverage and spirit, and followed suit. The sharpness of one counteracted the bitterness of the other, and both became palatable. Alexei tried to relax, and he sat back, waiting to see who would ask an important question first.

He was not particularly surprised when it was Travtravnya who spoke. The Keeper said, 'Sir, it is clear that both of us are anxious to avoid offending one another's customs and beliefs. Let us therefore be direct about what concerns us. For our part we have noticed that your guardbeasts employ language. That is unusual, for it is apparent that they are descended from a species which originated here long ago.'

'Here?' Alexei was not sure that he understood.

'You were not aware that the workbeasts were made by man?' one of the other Keepers asked.

If he admitted how much he knew, they would cease to be so open. Alexei shrugged. 'I am not from this world,' he said. 'I have seen many kinds of creatures. Some of them employ language.'

The Keepers looked quickly at one another. 'You are from offworld?' Travtravnya demanded. 'We did not know that communication with the Empire had been re-established.'

It would not assist his purpose to tell them the truth. Alexei raised his eyebrows. 'You are the descendants of an Imperial colony; that much I know. Tell me how many of you survive. Are you the rulers of this land?'

Travtravnya looked distracted. It was as if the news that Alexei was from another world had disturbed him beyond all belief. He looked up. 'Your pardon, sir. As to our numbers, there are Keepers in every quadrant. I am the thirty-third of my kind to be quickened.'

It was the term Alexei had heard the Keeper use

before, but it held no significance for him. He sipped coffee, then lowered his cup. 'Sir, I meant the population of the continent.'

'We are the population,' one of the others said.

They guided Alexei to the basement. Once more the access was by an opening in the floor which was controlled by a force field.

Alexei had expected another capsule, but instead there were machines – a holographic projector and a bank of viewscreens, along with other equipment he did not at once recognise. 'These we have been able to maintain,' Travtravnya said. 'Every Keeper passes on his knowledge of the skills to the next of his line.'

The maintenance tasks would be simple enough, Alexei realised. He nodded silently, understanding why no other technology had survived. The Keepers had dedicated themselves to the task of keeping the system alive – the reason for the preservation of the being in the life support he did not for the moment comprehend – and they had passed on from one to the other only what appeared to be necessary for that purpose.

'We were never a colony,' Travtravnya said. 'Eden was an Imperial Research Station; it was the most important of all, for this is Terra.'

Alexei did not believe him, and he allowed his disbelief to show on his face. He said, 'How can you be sure?'

One of the other Keepers went to a console. He pressed a series of keys. The projector bay threw an image of the world into the centre of the chamber. It revolved slowly.

Travtravnya said, 'This was the world as our ancestors knew it. You will be able to tell us if it is much changed.'

The continental outlines were only a little different, and Alexei supposed that five thousand years earlier the ice cap had been smaller. He said, 'Go on.'

The image was already altering. Travtravnya went out into the middle of the floor. The hologram revolved around him. He gestured. 'We have reversed the program. This traces the way the land masses moved to form what exists now.'

'It must have taken a long time.' Alexei watched, unconvinced.

The Keeper shrugged as if time was of no moment. 'A million years or more. Man has existed beyond memory.'

The shapes of the continents were moving apart. The ice cap enlarged and another appeared at the base of the sphere. Alexei wrinkled his nose. He knew almost nothing of Terra beyond its name. He struggled to recall one fact which would tend to prove or disprove the truth of what he was being told. A scrap of knowledge surfaced in his mind, and he said, 'Terra had but one moon.'

The Keeper at the console nodded. He said, 'There were nine planets in orbit around the Terran sun once. Men mined them before they colonised space. Maybe there was an accident, but our records show that one planet was moved. That was what caused this world to change so much. Its passage around the sun is quite different now from that which it followed then.'

Second Empire scientists had kept records of everything. It was that fact which had allowed the Empire of Alexei's time to re-establish itself so quickly. The explanation made sense. He stared at the projection, not sure that what he had learned mattered.

Suddenly he realised that if this was Terra, then the

Yek were not native species as they believed. The knowledge troubled him, and he wondered if it was necessary for the others to discover it. He said, 'My escort then are a species created here. Are there others of their kind?'

The Keepers looked unhappy. 'There are none that we know of,' Travtravnya said. He gestured abruptly to the man at the console, and the image revolving in the centre of the chamber vanished.

Alexei said, 'There are names of places in the land whose ambassador I am which are Terran in origin, but I thought nothing of it until now. All men were Terran once, and took their language to the worlds they colonised.'

Travtravnya said, 'Sir, as you are an offworlder, tell us if you will of the Empire.'

It was an awkward question, for to answer with absolute honesty would be to admit that this was a quarantine world. Alexei hesitated, then said, 'The Empire your ancestors knew collapsed years ago. Now there is a new Imperial tradition. The Emperor is called Priam, and he is the second of that name.'

'Ah.' Travtravnya nodded as if he understood. He paused delicately. '– And may we enquire, sir, your rank and station? Your title is of the new Empire I imagine, and means nothing to us.'

There was no reason to lie. Alexei gazed down his nose. 'My mother is the Emperor's niece, and so I am of royal blood.' He touched the gold caste mark on his cheek. 'I would not expect you to recognise it, but this is the mark of my rank.'

The Keepers looked from one to the other. Then it was as if they had arrived at a simultaneous decision. As one man they bowed. 'The Name of the Emperor be praised,' Travtravnya said, and made some kind of sign with both hands, 'for our task is now fulfilled.'

Alexei was taken completely by surprise. He stared at them. 'What task is this?'

If the Keepers were maintaining the records of a research station so that they could be transferred to the Empire, they were going to be disappointed. Travtravnya smoothed his veined hands down the facings of his coat. It was apparent that he did not know how to start to explain. He glanced at the man beside the console. 'Lech?'

The other Keeper made a face. A blood vessel at the side of his forehead showed dark through the transparency of his skin. He said, 'Exalted sir, we hoped you would know of it.'

'I do not.' Alexei surveyed the speaker.

It was obvious that they were disappointed by his response. Travtravnya sighed. 'Sir, we are ashamed to speak of it, and yet it is our reason for being. We are Keepers of the Condemned. Now we ask you to relieve us of that responsibility.'

Alexei saw that there was a chair facing a bank of screens. He went and sat down on it, facing them. 'I know nothing of your task; but if it is of importance to you, tell me of it.'

The man named Lech gestured encouragingly at Travtravnya. The Keeper ran a hand across his hairless scalp. He said, 'Sir, you mentioned your servants. It is true that there are none like them in Eden, but we know their origin, for they are from the same stock as the beasts who labour in our fields.'

'I find that hard to believe,' Alexei said steadily. He was not sure where this was leading, but determined to maintain an encouraging expression.

The Keeper's hands moved convulsively, a sign of his nervousness. He said, 'Nevertheless, it is the truth. We told you that Eden was once a research station. The men who worked here thought they were above

490

the law, and they tampered with the creatures they had been instructed to breed for re-introduction.'

Alexei pursed his lips. 'I know of an animal which is to be found in the land from which I have come,' he observed. 'It is like an equine, but it is larger and has a horn.'

Travtravnya nodded. 'The unicorn,' he said. 'There is a record of it here. It at least was designed to be of benefit to man, for it is strong and can withstand the extremes of climate.'

'But there were others,' Alexei prompted.

'Yes.' It was the third Keeper who answered. He gestured. 'Sir, you must understand that what was done here shocked our ancestors when they discovered it. They came late to this world – after the war against the Destroyers – and they knew the folly of tampering with genetic stock.'

Alexei remembered an old Second Empire account of the war which had resulted in its collapse, and recognised the name which ordinary people had applied to the superbeings against whom they had fought. He nodded slowly.

'They were too late,' Travtravnya said. 'By the time they knew the extent of what had been done the mutations had been dispersed, and they were multiplying. The man responsible for the beasts from which your own servants are descended was no longer interested in developing a creature which would serve humankind. Instead he dreamed of a species which would replace man. He ensured that they would breed true, and left caches of law and knowledge for them to discover.'

It must have taken a lifetime, Alexei thought. He was at the same time horrified and fascinated. It occurred to him to be glad that Jehan was not present. He gave Travtravnya a hard stare. 'You yourselves make use of the same kind of creature,' he commented. 'Elsewhere on this world it is assumed that they are people. But here they are slaves.'

All the Keepers looked offended. 'Without them we could not fulfil our task,' Travtravnya protested.

'What task?'

'To keep the Condemned for the Emperor's disposal.' Travtravnya seemed to imagine that the answer was obvious. 'And as to our workbeasts, our ancestors were not told to cease their use.' He waved a hand. 'They are only animals.'

'Their existence breaks Imperial law,' Alexei said coldly. It was a law which the Empire would never enforce, but that was beside the point.

Travtravnya said, 'Sir, it was our ancestors' decision to await the Emperor's further command.'

And they had waited, and waited. Such insignificant beginnings had provided the basis on which whole societies were organised. Alexei thought about the odd systems of government he had encountered – like Heaven, where only elders of the church were entitled to own land, or Ceres, where there was a matriarchy which consigned all men over thirty to worker status because they were assumed to be too old for breeding.

Alexei suddenly made a connection. 'The Condemned are the beings you maintain under life support.' He could scarcely believe it.

The Keepers nodded. 'The technology of the station was capable of it,' Travtravnya said. 'We are the descendants of the men who sat in tribunal over them.'

They had said that they were the only population of Eden. Alexei said, 'How are you born?'

The man called Lech looked down at his feet. 'There were no women with the station,' he said sadly.

Clones. That was why they were numbered. Alexei looked away, and did not hear the faltering explanation when it was given. After a while he turned back. 'There are humans on many parts of this word,' he observed.

Something whirred softly in one of the consoles. One of the Keepers turned. He depressed a number of keys. Travtravnya did not look round. 'The stock was not considered – suitable,' he said, embarrassed.

Or in other words they were the remnants of old settlements; people who had reverted to barbarism, living on a land contaminated by radiation. The C'zaki were barely medieval now. Five thousand years ago they must have been practically Neanderthal. Alexci wondered if the condition of the planet had been the reason the research station had been established. Probably the genetic experiments had been sanctioned at first. The world was out of the way – removed from centres of government – and so there had been no interference. Then had come the wars. The tribunal must have been set up at the time when the communication between worlds was actually failing. Maybe they had expected to be picked up, but they had been forgotten.

Alexei stood. 'I understand,' he said.

The cloning tank would be an adjunct to one of the life-support systems. The principles were quite similar.

Travtravnya looked relieved. 'Then we ask you to recognise that we have fulfilled the task which was assigned to us.'

'What?' Alexei found that he was staring into the middle distance. He focused on the Keeper's face. 'Oh. You have I suppose been faithful to the task which was set out for you.' He turned and walked towards the stairway to the level above.

Travtravnya said, 'Sir, as a person of rank, you must instruct us. Will you order the Condemned to be removed for inquisition?'

It would be strange if the creatures in the life-support tanks still had the ability to sense anything, Alexei thought. He looked back. 'Name of God, no,' he said. 'Let them sleep.'

The morning was misty. The troopers filed towards the stairs up to the causeway. It was apparent from the expression on their faces that they were glad that they were returning to the ship.

Travtravnya escorted Alexei along the road. He said, 'Sir, I would come with you to our border, but I have duties –' He waved a hand in the direction of the nearest pyramid.

A cart was coming down the road towards them. The smell from it made Alexei's head turn, and he knew what the meat had reminded him of the night before. He looked over the tail of the cart as it passed at the blocks of resin, each perhaps ten diram in weight. 'You grow the Imperial poppy.'

The Keeper nodded. 'Of course. It is the drug which makes it possible for us to maintain the Condemned. They cannot die.'

Somewhere in one of the fields in the distance there would be an expanse of blue seed pods streaked with purple on tall blue-green stalks. *Papaver Longiverus*, the Imperial poppy. Cut the pods and gather the sap; dissolve the resin in hot water, and precipitate it by adding lime; filter the precipitate and allow it to dry. Taken bi-annually as a thirty per cent solution it would prolong life almost indefinitely.

Except that no one in the Third Empire had been taking Longivex for more than three hundred years, and so the term was a relative one thus far.

'There are side effects,' Alexei said, remembering transparent flesh and wasted bones.

'Unfortunately, yes.' Travtravnya shrugged. He held up one hand. 'I am nearly five hundred years old. Soon my bones will start to dissolve.'

'You could stop taking the drug,' Alexei suggested.

The Keeper laughed painfully. 'Your Empire must be new indeed,' he said. 'Taken past a certain point it is addictive, I fear. One dies without it.'

'Or lives in life support.' Alexei grimaced. He glanced at the pyramid on his left. 'If it is possible, they ought to be allowed to die.'

Travtravnya's eyes opened wide. He said, 'Without the Condemned there would be no purpose to our lives. We realised that after we had spoken to you.'

As a reason for being, it was barely sufficient. 'There are the beasts,' Alexei said. 'Without direction they would become wild animals.'

If the Yek were not to learn about their origins, the records Alexei had seen would have to be destroyed and the Keepers would have to cease to exist. The conclusion he had reached the previous night came once more to the forefront of Alexei's mind, and he was afraid to look Travtravnya in the face in case he saw the truth.

The Keeper shrugged. 'It is the Empire's problem now,' he said. 'Will it be your task to return to direct us, or may we expect another?'

'One day I will return,' Alexei said. It was a kind of truth.

A line of troopers began to climb the stairs. They were talking quietly and Travtravnya watched them. He said, 'Our ancestors always feared them. Are you truly their Lord?'

Alexei was unable to lie further. 'Not as you would understand the word,' he responded at last.

495

'I thought not.' Travtravnya's eyes were wise.

Alexei knew it was time to leave. Then a thought struck him. He said, 'You never told me how men like these were bred from beasts.'

A vein in Travtravnya's forehead pulsed, and he looked away. 'The man who designed them was the one you saw in the tank,' he said. 'He bred females and mated with them to produce a more human strain. He must have been mad.'

'Or lonely,' Alexei said, considering.

'Yes.' The Keeper bowed. 'Sir, I wish you well.' He turned and walked away.

'Tell me what they told you.' Jehan sipped water and spat it over the side of the causeway.

Alexei had known that he would have to say something. He turned. 'The thing we saw in the pyramid was a prisoner. I think there are others, though I did not ask. The men are jailers of a kind. They keep the prisoners alive.'

'To what end?' Jehan's expression showed his disbelief.

'Because it was the last command the jailers' ancestors received,' Alexei said shortly. 'Believe it or not, as you will, but the prisoners have been kept alive for five thousand years.'

They had come halfway along the causeway. The rim was just visible through the haze. Jehan stared. 'Is it possible?'

Alexei met his eyes. 'There is a way.'

Jehan looked away. He tugged at one end of his moustaches. 'Their crime must have been very great,' he said at last. 'What of the people?'

'There are no people.'

The terrace below them was covered with fruit trees. Workers moved among them, their manner docile. Alexei remembered the smell of the meat. Poppy resin could be chewed or smoked before it was converted, and it induced in humans an almost trance-like state. Here it was added to the workers' food as a pacifier – maybe they were trained to add it themselves – and Alexei wondered if the meat brought to the Yek camp had been drugged because the beasts who brought it had received no other instruction, or if it had been the Keepers' attempt to render the troopers helpless.

'If there are no people, then this land is ours for the taking,' Jehan said.

'Oh?' Alexei stared. 'We will have to find an easier way to journey into it first.'

Jehan made a face. 'That's true.'

If they had to, they could blast the cliffs along the east coast. It would take years, but the Yek were patient where conquest was concerned. Once a coastal plain had been created, they could fill the narrows between the reefs and the land. Eventually the coastline would become navigable.

The Keepers would wait as they had always waited for the kind of contact with the Empire which ignored the need for ships. Suddenly Alexei knew that the basin would have to be explored further. Some kinds of technology were indestructible and might be awaiting discovery, neglected because the inhabitants of Eden neither knew nor cared about their purpose.

'The workers have talons,' Jehan said softly. 'Have you noticed?'

'Yes.'

The pyramids could be sealed or destroyed. Once the Keepers ceased to exist, the beasts would revert to a wild state. Alexei remembered the creature he had seen in the gorge during the journey up the inlet, and supposed that it was a worker which had escaped, or its descendant. Left to themselves the beasts would evolve. He wondered if he could persuade the Kha-Khan that Marakan should be left untouched, and thought not.

'One might almost imagine them to be our ancestors.' Jehan did not look round as he spoke. He stared down at the terrace below, leaning out over the causeway wall. Suddenly he turned. 'Do you think they could be made to understand the law?'

Conquered races had to accept the Yasa. If the felines could not, the Yek would consider them animals. If they were a nuisance, they would be hunted to extermination.

'I don't know,' Alexei said. 'It could take some time.'

Jehana was angry that she had been sedated for so long. It was Parin who had been forced to bear the brunt of her displeasure, and Jehan was amused when he heard of it.

He said, 'It might be necessary for the practice to become universal.'

'I think not.' Jehana glared at him.

Jehan laughed at her. 'A silent wife is a prize,' he quoted.

It was obvious that Parin had misjudged the dosage which was required, for Jehana had woken only the previous day. 'Lady,' Alexei said quickly, 'it was the Sechem's desire and mine to spare you the discomfort you experience at sea.'

'My Lord, I would rather the discomfort,' she responded tartly.

The *Sunstealer* was moving down the inlet towards the open sea. Word had spread among the crew that they were now going home, and it was clear that even the peril to be endured during a sea passage around

498

the northern coast of Marakan was regarded by most with equanimity.

Alexei dismissed Parin with a nod of his head. Then he looked at Jehan. 'Brother, go and make trouble elsewhere.'

A flicker of amusement crossed Jehan's features. He held up his hands. 'By all means.'

Jehana watched him depart, frowning. She sat down in the chair which was lashed to the rail near the wheel, then looked up at Alexei. 'My Lord, I am not sure how to be angry with you,' she said.

'Lady, I did not mean to offend you.' Alexei met her eyes. He saw what he judged was a look of frustration appear on her face. She said, 'I should not have agreed to it, but I knew you were concerned.'

She was still annoyed, but it was now a kind of helpless irritation which she could not bear to expend lest it do harm to their feeling for one another. Alexei smiled at her. 'Soon our voyage will be ended,' he said.

He had expected her to return the smile, but instead she frowned. 'Would that we could sail forever,' she said soberly.

And so at last they came to the Khanate. Around Marakan the seas were rough, and everyone was uncomfortable. After a time, however, they passed south of N'pan into the Eastern Sea. Here the weather was calm, the days long and hot. The ship forged ahead, the boilers straining, for there seemed to be no good reason to delay.

Their first landfall was at a place some way north of the port of X'nadu. Here both Alexei and Jehan sent messengers to travel overland to Kinsai. That which Alexei despatched was a respectful salutation to Artai, and announced the embassy's safe return. Jehan's, he guessed, was to Burun, and Alexei supposed it to concern the confrontation between the Kha-Khan and the Merkuts which must surely now be brewing.

X'nadu was the principal seaport on the eastern coast. It had expanded over a period so that it stretched beyond the bay around which it had at first been built. Artificial headlands curved around enclosing the harbour, and Alexei saw ships of every description anchored there. The southern part of the city was reserved for trade, and here also were the wharves and shipyards. To the north of them were lines of neat tall houses roofed with bronze tiles in which the merchants and tradespeople lived. The mansions of the Khans and other nobles lay beyond on higher ground, and they were roofed with gold.

It was apparent from the first that the *Sunstealer* was not unexpected. Clearly their progress down the coast had been reported, and space had been made for the vessel at the stone wharf which extended the length of the dredged inner channel.

The crew had washed their clothes and dressed their hair, and Ch'un Chu and the other officers were wearing their best coats. The troopers had found it harder to achieve the kind of appearance calculated to arouse respect – the salt carried on board by the spray and even in the air had attacked leather harness and steel alike, and Sidacai and Joden had spent several frantic days attempting to ensure that the worst effects were eradicated. Everyone was on deck save the men employed in the engine space. The troopers lined the rails, and even the st'lyan in the hold seemed to sense that they were approaching land, and screamed and stamped in their stalls.

'There are men waiting,' Jehan said at Alexei's side. He pointed.

It was an unnecessary observation. In fact the sea

front was packed with people. Alexei looked where Jehan had indicated and saw what he had meant. The orderly ranks of troopers in livery stood out from the mass of ordinary humanity. He said, 'I don't see a totem.'

Sidacai was on Jehan's other side. He shaded his eyes with his hand. 'I do.'

Kadan was perched on the rail. 'It's Jotan,' he said quietly.

Alexei was not surprised. He glanced at Jehan. He said, 'He is here on Artai's business.'

Jehan nodded shortly. 'Now we will see,' he said. His expression was calm.

They were being warped in against the dockside. People swarmed forward, but the troopers held them back so that those at the back created a press. The extended lances were like rails, and Jotan and his attendants stood in a space which would have accommodated several hundred.

Jotan was wearing court dress – a long coat of midnight-blue silk, its facings stiff with gold wire embroidery. Alexei saw that he had grown a beard. Above Jotan's head was a standard decorated with white st'lyan tails. Alexei did not recognise the totem. He said, 'That's not a Merkut blazon.' He saw Jehan shrug.

'My father is a provincial governor,' he said. 'It is that design you can see.'

Probably it was not a good omen. Jotan was surrounded by his officers, but there were members of the Kha-Khan's court with him as well. Two proctors hovered on the edge of the small crowd, their gilt tunics reflecting the light.

It was late morning. The sun was almost directly overhead, and everything seemed to mirror the glare. Alexei watched what was happening on the wharf.

501

'They intend to come aboard,' he said.

A gangway was being run up to the ship's side. It was hoisted up, and at once a line of troopers trotted up it. They formed up across the deck, facing towards the stern.

Jotan strode up the inclined planking. He paused at the rail. An officer barked a command, and the troopers saluted.

'Such ceremony,' Sidacai murmured, his tone mocking. 'Are we to be impressed?'

Alexei adjusted the angle of his sword in his sash. He felt unkempt, even in his ambassador's coat. He said, 'Let's do this properly.'

Sidacai raised his eyebrows, and then he nodded. He waved to Joden. The guard commander seemed to be prepared. His voice carried high and clear above the noise from the crowd on the dockside. The troopers of the embassy escort moved without fuss into two lines. One was behind that which had been formed by the men who had come aboard ahead of Jotan. The other faced them.

Jehana was standing at the entrance to the companionway which led to the cabins below deck. Parin was with her. As Alexei passed she said, 'My Lord, remember what I told you.'

Alexei nodded absently. He started towards the main deck. Jehan followed. 'What did Jehana tell you?' he asked quietly.

'Oh.' Alexei thought for a moment. 'It was the day we sailed from Y'vrope. She said that whatever happened when we returned, I should remember that I am a Khan.'

'Hunh.' Jehan nodded thoughtfully. 'It is sound advice.'

The members of Jotan's entourage were filing onto the main deck. They ranged themselves about, staring haughtily at the members of the crew who were crowded to watch.

Jehan said, 'They don't look pleased to see us.'

At least a few of them would be surprised that the *Sunstealer* had returned at all. The mortality rate for embassies had been high in the past. Alexei scanned the men at Jehan's back for faces he knew well enough to acknowledge, and saw none. He stepped through the ranks of the troopers.

'Father, good day,' Jehan said.

Jotan gave him a frosty stare. He snapped his fingers at one of the proctors, and the official produced a scroll which was plastered with seals. He offered it, bowing.

'Alexei Khan, on behalf of your master the Kha-Khan I greet you,' Jotan said. He spoke the words as if he had rehearsed them, and there was no hint of welcome in his eyes. 'I come as his representative. Witness this my commission.' Jotan shook the scroll so that it unrolled. He waved it, and then tossed it negligently to the proctor.

'I think I should like to have read that,' Jehan murmured.

Alexei frowned him to silence. He gave Jotan the kind of bow one would offer an equal, and said, 'I am the Kha-Khan's servant.'

'That remains to be seen,' Jotan responded distantly. He hung one hand upon the facing of his coat. 'The Kha-Khan sends me to enquire the success of your embassy. Know that it is his word that as you have returned he anticipates your success, for failing, you should not be here. What submissions have you taken, and from whom?'

A movement of the water under the keel caused the ship to drag at the cables which moored it to the wharf. The cables creaked. Alexei rested a hand upon

503

the hilt of his sword. The noise from the spectators along the sea front had not completely died away. 'As to that, I found none whose homage it would have pleased Artai to accept,' Alexei said easily.

The statement aroused mutters of comment from the court dignitaries who stood around Jotan. Jotan said, 'I find that hard to believe. Such continents as we know exist must be ruled by someone. Or are they wastelands?'

'No, indeed.' Alexei smiled cheerfully at Jotan, inviting him to take offence at the manner in which he was being addressed. 'They are fair and fertile.'

'And inhabited?'

'Yes.'

'But still you found no lord to whom you could deliver the word of your master.' Jotan made the observation flatly. 'Did you visit every part of the countries you found?'

Jehan snorted softly. Alexei ignored him. 'I confess I did not,' he said. 'It would have taken a lifetime.'

Sidacai and Kadan had worked around the end of the rank of troopers and were standing at the rail. A movement among the troopers of Jotan's guard caught Alexei's eye, and he saw that Orcadai and C'zinsit were forcing their way between the ranks to join Jotan.

Jotan seemed to study the deck planks between his feet. Slowly he looked up. 'Your life is the Kha-Khan's,' he said. 'Did you have anything else to do?'

Alexei stared at him. At his side Jehan stirred. 'We have circumnavigated the earth,' he commented. 'Is this to be our welcome? What Alexei says is the truth. It was his judgement that there was nothing to be gained – no purpose to be served – by journeying longer. I concurred with that judgement, and if it was contrary to the Kha-Khan's will, then we are equal in blame.'

'Indeed.' Jotan glared at the interruption. Then he seemed to collect himself. He said, 'And yet it seems to me that the patent was issued to Alexei Khan alone.'

Jehan's head went forward. He said, 'Had we searched a lifetime, we would have found no one from whom submission could have been demanded. You have not enquired what we found.'

If Artai had sent Jotan, it was because he had made up his mind how to deal with their return. Even if they had obtained homage from all the peoples they had encountered, a fault would have been found.

Jotan wrinkled his nose. 'What you found will be a matter for the Kha-Khan's court,' he said. 'It is clear that Alexei Khan has failed to fulfil the terms of the ambassador's patent granted to him, and he must answer for it.'

Alexei saw Kadan's hand move towards his sword. Sidacai saw it, and he placed a hand on Kadan's arm, restraining him. He shook his head, and then said something in a low voice. Kadan looked startled. Then he nodded slowly.

'Alexei Khan, I call upon you to surrender to the Kha-Khan's justice,' Jotan said loudly. His voice carried across the deck of the ship. Some of the troopers of the embassy guard growled and moved in their ranks, and Alexei heard Joden issuing commands in an angry voice. Orcadai and C'zinsit both had satisfied looks on their faces. They stared straight at Alexei, and he saw the malice in their eyes.

Jotan had not moved. He gazed down his nose at Alexei. 'Khan, do you yield?'

Alexei showed his teeth. 'Is this Artai's will?' he asked insultingly. 'Or is it yours?'

'I am the servant of the Universal Khan.' Jotan smiled grimly. He gestured to the troopers of his escort. 'Take him.'

The troopers were not Merkuts. They moved forward, and Alexei knew that they had been expecting the command.

Jehan said, 'If you fight, they will kill you. We can deal with this before the assembly of the Khans.'

A trooper jerked Alexei's sword from his sash and tossed it aside. Alexei felt himself being jostled with brutal efficiency, and he knew that they had orders to provoke resistance. One man had a d'jaga concealed in his hand. He jabbed it into Alexei's side. Alexei gritted his teeth. He stared over their heads at Jotan, and saw a look which was something like calculation in Jotan's eyes.

Someone had produced a rope. They bound Alexei's arms to his sides and began to hustle him towards the gangway.

Jehan thrust himself suddenly up to Alexei's side. He knocked one of the troopers aside, and the man fell. The others swung round. 'Claim your rights,' Jehan hissed. 'Remember you are a Khan.'

Alexei planted his feet astride the gangway. The people along the dockside were staring, a sea of faces transfixed by the spectacle of the arrest. He looked back at Jotan, resisting the men who were trying to force him down to the wharf. Jehan was turning. He shouted, 'You cannot do this. He is a Khan.'

Jotan raised his eyebrows. 'He is an alien,' he said. 'He has no rights under the law.'

The noise from the wharf had suddenly lessened. Alexei saw his opportunity. He called out, 'I call those here present to witness; this man denies me the right to the treatment due my rank.' He saw Jotan flush angrily.

506

Jehan said, 'The Yasa says that a Khan may not be bound or shackled until he has been condemned. Alexei is a Khan.'

There was a moment of silence while Jotan seemed to consider. One of the proctors came up to his side. He said something, his manner agitated. Jotan nodded, looking all the time towards Alexei and Jehan as if he was weighing what he could risk. Then his face closed. He gestured at the troopers. 'Unbind him.'

A collective sign ran round the wharfside. Jehan looked back at Alexei. 'I told you it was good advice,' he said.

Alexei could feel a trickle of blood running down his side, soaking into the waistband of his breeches. The troopers still crowded him, but more warily. He glanced back over the heads of the people on deck to see if Jehana was watching, and saw that she was in the centre of a protective ring of Sidacai's men.

Jehan's face was pale. He looked towards his father again, then said, 'I will speak to him. He has to agree to release you into my custody.' He pushed through the troopers and went up to Jotan. There was a sharp exchange of words.

'No.' Jotan's reply was perfectly audible. 'Only a Khan is eligible to stand surety for him. You are not a Khan.'

Jotan had thought he would be able to control Jehan, Alexei thought. Now he was being embarrassed by his son's willingness to offer public opposition to what was occurring.

Jehan seemed to gather himself. He spoke what was clearly an appeal. Jotan shook his head.

'He will not release you.' Jehan came back to Alexei's side. He stared around the crowd. 'Burun should have been here.'

If Burun had stayed away, Alexei reflected, it was for a reason.

Jehan said, 'I will travel with you. He cannot deny me that.'

A Noyon was entitled to a personal guard, and so the troopers who were now his guards would be watched all the time. Alexei nodded gratefully.

Jotan had turned away. The nobles of the court gathered around him, fawning on him. Orcadai and C'zinsit were attempting to gain his attention, and Alexei saw Sidacai watching them, the intent plain in his eyes.

Jehan waved to summon Joden. He spoke quickly to him, and Joden nodded. He turned and pointed to several troopers, and they moved at once to his side. The men who had arrested Alexei seemed to realise that they were being surrounded, and they looked nervously towards their comrades who were still ranged across the main deck.

'He has chosen Artai because he does not think that we can control him,' Jehan said. He stared after Jotan. 'He was ever wary of my grandfather's intrigues.'

Alexei thought that there had been more to Jotan's conduct than mere service to Artai. He said nothing. A cloud passed across the face of the sun, throwing the harbour into shadow. The gloom advanced across the quayside, and people glanced up quickly, as if they feared to be out of the light.

'You must not blame Jotan,' Jehan said. 'He fears Artai's nature.'

They were riding in cavalcade up the trunk road to Kinsai. At every town and village the people had come out to see who was passing. Jotan they saluted because he was the Kha-Khan's envoy, but when they saw Jehan and Alexei they cheered.

'Are you saying that you do not?' Alexei enquired. He let his reins fall loose on his st'lyan's neck. Jotan

508

had tried to insist that because he was a prisoner he should ride in a cart, but to little avail. The wagon produced the first day had suffered a broken lynch pin; its replacement had caught fire during a break in the journey. When the third had lost a wheel less than a verst after they had resumed travelling, Jotan had retired in defeat.

Jehan gazed away into the distance. His st'lyan tossed its head, and the gilding on the horn glittered. 'We should never have elected Artai,' he said softly.

Artai had been elevated to the Dragon Throne because Burun had supported him, and like everything which originated from Burun's hand, it was hard to know the true purpose.

They were being escorted by troopers of Jehan's personal guard. The men who had been involved in Alexei's arrest were riding in an unhappy group at the rear of the column. Every time they came closer they were crowded, and a few had fallen or been pushed from the saddle. Jehan stood in the stirrups and looked back the way they had come. Then he sat down again and gathered in his reins. 'I sent Jehana to Khitai. Sidacai undertook to guard her.'

Alexei pursed his lips. 'Your father wanted her at Kinsai.' He had heard Jotan issue the invitation. The wording had amounted to a command.

'I think he was expressing Artai's wish,' Jehan said. 'They still think to use her.'

Jehana widowed would become a ward of the Kha-Khan's court. Alexei stared ahead. It meant that Artai probably intended to encompass his death.

'Why do you think I am riding with you?' Jehan sidestepped his mare so that he was riding at Alexei's shoulder. 'If you are killed, it will all have been for nothing.'

'I could be condemned anyway,' Alexei said soberly.

509

Jehan shook his head. 'Your judges will be the Khans,' he said. 'It was never intended that you reach Kinsai.'

They entered the city very early in the morning, and Alexei guessed that Artai wished their arrival to pass unnoticed. If that was his desire, it was frustrated. Everyone in Kinsai seemed to be on the streets, and the troopers had to force a path through the crowd.

'It's like a festival,' Kadan said. He had ridden down to the column the previous day with a message for Jehan, having used the system of courier way-stations to complete a journey from X'nadu which had taken less than half the time required by their cavalcade. Alexei supposed that Kadan had been sent to speak to Burun, and that the letter he had returned with was the answer, though he did not know its content.

The reception was Burun's doing, Alexei guessed. He remembered the enthusiasm of the people in the places through which they had passed during the journey from X'nadu, and wondered how many of them had cheered because they owed service, or had been paid.

Jehan grinned at Kadan. 'You said we would return heroes.'

Alexei saw Kadan blush, and he smiled. Kadan reined across until he was a little way in front. Then he turned and looked back. 'Even if Artai tries to have you condemned,' he said, 'no one will support it now.'

They were moving up one of the principal streets which radiated from the centre of Kinsai like the spokes of a wheel. A Shaman stood at a corner surrounded by his acolytes. He did not bow as they rode past, and Jehan frowned. It was the fourth or

510

fifth time they had encountered a priest since entering the city.

Kadan had reined in so that he was riding level with them again. He glanced at the spinning prayer wheels which were set up at the side of the road. 'We will find the cities much changed,' he observed blandly. 'The mystics are everywhere.'

'Oh?' Jehan turned. 'They were restricted before.'

The Shamen had been trying for years to establish themselves as priests of Yek mysticism, but the cult of Sufi had never been widespread. The Yasa was too specific for organised religion to gain influence.

They passed a line of tall houses. Outside each the guards saluted Alexei and Jehan when they rode by. 'There are strange stories,' Kadan said. He ran a hand up under the facing of his open coat, easing it away from the shoulder. 'I spoke to a man who said that the Shamen are hailing Artai as a god.'

The implications made Alexei grimace. Jehan snorted. 'How can the son of a man be a god?' he demanded. 'I wonder what Tulagai has to say about that.'

The Kha-Khan's father was not noted for his tact, and the relationship between the two had never been good. Alexei smiled grimly at the thought of Tulagai's reaction. Then he said, 'I'd rather know how Artai feels about it.'

Jehan looked thoughtful. 'As honey is to a bee, so flattery is to Artai,' he said.

Artai was capable of convincing himself that it was proper for the occupant of the Dragon Throne to be worshipped as a god. Alexei wondered if the Sufi had thought up the notion, or if one of the nobles of the court was behind it. Now that he knew that the basis for the Yasa was a code originated by a man, Alexei was able to appreciate how much thought had been

511

given to the factors which tended to divert a developing society. The Yek were lacking in superstition, simplistic because they had been made so by the nature of the inheritance passed on to them. Their philosophy did not require the prop of religion, and reflecting on the fact Alexei was surprised that Sufi had been able to grow at all.

The column had been forced to come to a halt because the way ahead was blocked by people. Troopers of several guard companies were attempting to work their way forward to clear the street, but it was apparent that they had been instructed to avoid the use of much force, and so progress was slow.

Alexei said, 'Whatever Artai thinks about it, it is contrary to the Yasa.'

Kadan kicked his feet out of his stirrups, and he crossed one leg over the other, sitting at his ease. His st'lyan was an enormous chestnut with a light mane, and it stood patiently, ignoring the crowds pressing around it. 'Oh, well,' Kadan said. 'It's only a rumour.'

Jotan rode up the side of the column, two officers clearing his path. He barely glanced at them as he passed, and Alexei saw that his expression was preoccupied.

'I did not expect that we would go straight to the Golden Yurt.' Jehan stared after his father's departing back as he spoke. He looked troubled. 'There should have been more time.'

Probably Artai thought that if he rushed the enquiry, the judges would do whatever he wanted. Alexei made a face. 'Now or later,' he said. 'Does it make a difference?'

Jehan frowned again. 'The outcome affects us all,' he said after a moment's pause.

The open concourse in front of the Kha-Khan's palace was decorated with the banners of the Khans.

Small groups of guardsmen stood in protective screens around standards and totems on poles, and Alexei looked at the emblems to see which of the important families had stayed away. Merkuts thronged the steps to the entrance, and they cheered Jehan when they saw him. Alexei stared around. He felt as if he had a bare exposed place between his shoulder blades. If Artai intended to prevent a trial from taking place, this was probably the last opportunity for an assassin to make his attempt.

People were breaking through the line of troopers who were engaged in crowd control. They ran forward, streaming past the startled guards and standard-bearers. Alexei saw that there were no women among them, and he felt a prickle of apprehension. He tightened his grip on his reins. A loose st'lyan reared and screamed. The crowd surged around him, shouting and waving. A hand came out of nowhere to jerk at the st'lyan's bridle. The mare side-stepped, and almost at once Alexei was isolated. He saw the flash of a blade as his reins were slashed, and he grabbed a handful of mane and hung on. The press of men against the st'lyan's side was actually lifting the animal off its feet. Hooves rattled, and Alexei realised that he was intended to be the victim of a staged accident. Should he be toppled from the saddle and trampled, no blame could be ascribed to Artai. The crowd of men shouted and surged again, separating him still further from the escort, and Alexei heard Jehan swearing in a high clear voice.

Suddenly more men were joining the throng. Several of them got up and ran lightly across the heads and shoulders of the press which surrounded Alexei. Someone was trying to work his foot out of the stirrup. He kicked out hard, connecting with something solid, and a man cried out and fell away.

513

The men running across the top of the crowd were all Merkuts. One of them got a hand to the st'lyan's head. He lashed out with his feet at the faces within range. The men attacking Alexei seemed to realise that they were themselves under attack. They turned, reacting to the threat. The Merkuts moved forward with brutal efficiency. Three or four had reached Alexei now, and they had ranged themselves around him. None of them appeared to be armed, but whoever had organised the incident had made the mistake of employing humans. The Merkuts had talons, and used them without hesitation. The noise grew in intensity, and then began to fade. Part of the mob was dispersing, the men running towards the anonymity of the main crowd. Jehan shouted at the troopers, who rode to intercept. Alexei saw a sword blade flash, and a fleeing man screamed and fell.

Jehan forced his st'lyan up to Alexei's side. 'I am a fool,' he said. He reached out and took Alexei's bridle out of the hand of the grinning Merkut who was guarding it. 'I never thought they would try here.'

Alexei found that he was breathing hard, as if from great exertion. He took several deep breaths. A man lay on the paving nearby. A Merkut went and turned him over, looked at him, and then raised his head and said something in an amused voice to the others who were grouped around. They laughed. 'I expected an arrow,' Alexei said.

A file of troopers trotted across the concourse. One of Burun's officers was leading them. Several captives were led away.

'We will find out who is responsible.' Jehan released the st'lyan's bridle.

'I am sure we will,' Alexei said. He waited for Jehan to look away, and smiled grimly when he did so.

*

Artai said, 'We are here to sit in judgement upon a man who has betrayed my trust.'

Jehan was standing at Alexei's side. He stirred. 'Are we indeed?' He made no attempt to lower his voice.

Alexei saw the Kha-Khan glare, and he concealed a smile. The audience chamber was crowded, and only small sections of the gold-embossed floor were visible. Reflections jostled one another, and it was apparent that there were places where the planks would have to be redecorated once the hearing was over.

Artai was standing on a raised dais near the centre of the room. Behind him were rows of attendants, along with the men who were the captains of his personal guard. Most of the Khans present had brought their principal advisers, and they were grouped about on both sides of the chamber. At the front on the right stood Burun, with Suragai at his shoulder. Directly across from him stood Siban, Sidacai's father, on his own. The Kha-Khan's father and his uncles were off to one side, and near them were most of the Arcutt Khans. The men who stood around Burun were clearly his supporters. Alexei judged that they outnumbered Siban and the Arcutt. He looked for Jotan, and saw him among the members of the court.

Burun said, 'Lord, I was not aware that we were assembled for any purpose other than enquiry.' His voice was a bass rumble. Heads turned, and the men who were whispering to one another fell silent.

The Kha-Khan looked as if he had eaten bad meat. 'It is our prerogative to decide the purpose,' he said.

The corners of Burun's mouth twitched. 'Lord, if this is a trial, who is the accuser, and what is the charge?'

Artai was wearing a floor-length coat of straw-

515

coloured silk. It was embroidered over all in gold, and there were gold threads woven through his unbound hair. His eyes enlarged as he stared at Burun. 'Khan, we are the accuser,' he said flatly. 'Alexei Khan was our ambassador to the lands across the Great Sea, with our patent to deliver demands to the rulers of those lands so that they might submit to the Will of Heaven. By his own admission to our envoy, he failed in that task. He obtained no submissions, and gives as his excuse a reason which is in our judgement false.'

'As to the matter of the truth or otherwise of the excuse,' Burun said, 'that is surely a matter for the judges; and since you are the accuser, Lord, you cannot be one of those.'

A number of the older men nodded sagely. Artai looked angry and frustrated. Then one of the Arcutt took a pace forward. 'That would be the case were we trying a human,' he said. 'Alexei is an alien, and he had no right to trial by an assembly of Khans.'

Burun looked at the floor as if deep in thought. He turned without a word and gestured to someone who was standing at the back of the crowd of Merkut retainers. Men moved respectfully to one side, and a man in Sechem's robes came to Burun's side. Alexei saw that it was Parin, who had been left with the ship, and he wondered how he had been brought to Kinsai so quickly.

Parin was performing a ceremonial bow towards Artai. He did not look at Alexei.

At Alexei's side Jehan said, 'The *Sunstealer* brought him from X'nadu. Two days sailing at full speed. He landed on the coast last night.' He looked pleased with himself.

It was clear that the Kha-Khan was annoyed. He ignored the Sechem's bow. 'All men here know the Yasa,' he said petulantly. 'We need no lesson in law.'

'– And yet, Lord, it seems that there is a question of law here,' Parin said placidly, 'and so I will resolve it. The right to trial by assembly is open to all Khans. There are no exclusions.'

'But humans have no rights under the law,' someone on the Arcutt side said swiftly.

The Sechem glanced once towards the source of the objection. He said, 'It was the Kha-Khan's right to ennoble Alexei, according to the provisions of the second *sura* of the Yasa. Thus Alexei is no longer an alien under the law. He may not be human, but he is a Khan.'

'– And has rights accordingly,' Burun said smoothly. He nodded to Parin, who drew back, bowing.

There was no one who was willing to deny the Sechem's right to arbitrate the Yasa. A few men were muttering to their near neighbours, arguing the matter, but gradually the murmur ceased.

'It's neat, you must agree,' Jehan said cheerfully. 'Artai made you a Khan, and he can't unmake it unless he is a judge, but he can't be, because he made you a Khan.'

Artai seemed to look for inspiration towards his courtiers. Suddenly he turned. 'Then let judges be chosen,' he said. 'Burun Khan, since you have knowledge of this we make you chief of judges in our stead.'

Burun bowed. 'Lord, I am your servant.'

'And for the others –' The Kha-Khan appeared to ponder. He glanced towards the court again. '– Jotan Khan, how say you? Will you judge this matter faithfully?'

Jotan bowed, expressionless. 'Lord, I will,' he said.

Jehan looked stricken. 'He makes it seem a panel fair to your interests,' he said low-voiced. 'But my father will decide the way he is told.'

517

'– And for the third, Sulagai,' Artai said.

An Arcutt bowed, looking pleased. Burun was looking at Alexei, his expression remote. He turned. 'Lord, as I am chief judge I say that we must enquire the circumstances of the charge before we can decide. That will take time.'

The Kha-Khan looked down his nose. 'Khan, your own son made enquiry on our behalf, and it was by his hand that Alexei was brought here.'

Burun stared past the dais at Jotan. Then he faced Artai. He said, 'Lord, I would condemn no man on an uncorroborated word, for that would indeed be contrary to the law.'

Alexei saw Artai's mouth tighten. Jotan's face was frozen immobile, but he had gone pale.

'Very well.' The Kha-Khan seemed suddenly to lose interest. He waved a dismissive hand. 'We agree an adjournment. Alexei Khan shall be detained meantime.'

The casual tone did not deceive Alexei. In prison he would be at Artai's mercy. He glanced quickly towards Burun.

'Alexei is a Khan,' Burun said calmly, 'and his offence is not treason. Let him be released on surety.'

'Oh?' The Kha-Khan looked amused. 'Only the head of a clan may provide such a guarantee. You are one of the judges, Khan, and so you cannot.' He gestured around. 'If there is anyone else who will accept the responsibility, let him speak.'

The heads of the principal clans were Arcutt, or their friends, or else they were related to Artai by blood, and could not therefore be seen to oppose him directly.

'I will,' Siban said ponderously.

Only Burun did not appear surprised. Artai gaped. 'What's that? Siban Khan, do you stand surety for Alexei?'

518

And, 'I do,' Siban said.

The effect was shattering. The Kha-Khan's eyes seemed to expand. His face went crimson, and he stared at Siban with an expression which suggested that he was trying to will him to fall dead on the spot. Siban ignored the look. He caught Alexei's eye, and bowed to him. The Arcutt watched Siban nervously, as if they thought madness had suddenly overtaken him.

Burun said, 'Then it is settled. Alexei is released, Siban acting as surety for his behaviour. The Kha-Khan's complaint against Alexei will be judged in due course, myself and the other judges having examined the evidence.'

Jehan took a pace forward. 'There is another matter.'

Artai's head came round. 'Jehan Noyon has no right to speak here,' he said distantly.

'I think I do,' Jehan said. He exchanged a look with Burun, and Alexei saw Burun's nod. Jehan's face seemed to close. He walked to the front of the dais. He said, 'Artai, son of Tulagai, son of Khotan, I call kanly against you. I call on those here present to witness that my grievance is just, for you have wronged me and my house.'

There was dead silence in the chamber. Jotan was staring at Jehan as if he did not believe what he had heard him say. The faces of the members of the court were frozen. Alexei glanced at Burun, and he saw that he was watching Artai. There was a speculative expression on his face.

Artai started to laugh. It was the only sound in the room, and most men stared, their attitudes strained. 'You challenge me?' Artai tucked his hands inside his sleeves. The only sign that he was unsure of himself was his use of the personal pronoun instead of the royal plural. He said, 'This is treason.' He gestured to one of the captains of his guard. 'Arrest him.'

The captain was a big man – the guardsmen who served the Kha-Khan were chosen for their size and strength – and his hair was iron grey. He inclined his head politely. 'Lord, I cannot,' he said. 'For no man may be imprisoned who challenges another justly.'

'I am the Universal Khan.' Artai looked around. 'The man who defies my will breaks the Yasa.'

Siban stirred. 'Lord, you have been challenged. You must answer,' he said.

Alexei could not see Jehan's face, but he saw that he was standing motionless, waiting for a response. Suddenly he knew that this was what Jehan had meant when he had said that it would be his lot to oppose Artai, and he realised why Jehan had got drunk the day before they left Y'vrope.

'Men who desire to engage against one another require our permission,' Artai observed austerely. He seemed to have regained his self-possession. 'Jehan Noyon, will you speak of your grievance?' he demanded.

The attempt to use Jehana as a hostage could not be brought into the open, and the Kha-Khan knew that. Jehan said, 'Lord, I will, but to the Universal Khan alone as is my right.'

Artai snorted. 'Either we are your lord or we are your adversary. It does not seem to us that we can be both.'

The Sechem was still standing a little way behind Burun. He looked thoughtful. Burun turned and glanced at him. He said, 'Sechem?'

Parin seemed to consider. Then he said, 'Lord, the forms have been observed. You are both of the race of the True People. A challenge has been issued, and it is the right of the challenger to speak of it only in front of the Kha-Khan. Here the Kha-Khan is also the recipient of the challenge. Are you saying, Lord, that you do not know the Noyon's cause?'

Artai was caught by his own cleverness. His mouth opened, and then closed again. To admit knowledge would be to admit the act. He said, 'It is not a just kanly. I refuse it.'

'Lord,' Parin said, 'were your only part in this to judge, you could refuse it. But you are the challenged. How can you decide what is right or wrong when your interest is concerned? Remember that the Yasa says that no man can judge his own cause.'

Further protest would make it seem as if Artai was afraid to respond in the proper form. He looked around the chamber as if seeking support for a further refusal. Alexei turned, and he saw only set faces and steady eyes. Even those who had supported Artai thought he had to accept now.

'Lord?' Siban prompted gently.

The Kha-Khan seemed to take a deep breath. He looked at Jehan. 'Noyon, I acknowledge your declaration of kanly and your cause,' he said. 'As I have offended you, so will I meet you – body to body, claw to claw.'

Alexei saw Jehan's shoulders drop abruptly. It was as if he had released the breath he had been holding. 'Then it is done,' Jehan said. He turned and walked blindly past everyone out of the chamber.

Siban and Burun walked towards one another across the floor. They bowed simultaneously, ignoring Artai, and turned to face the part of the room in which Alexei stood.

Siban said, 'The kanly will take place within three days, for that is the law. I am the son of Daijin and the oldest of all the Altun. I claim the right of witness.'

Burun did not even look at Siban. 'On behalf of

521

Jehan I recognise Siban's right,' he said. 'The Yasa allows three witnesses. I claim the right to be one. Alexei will be the other.'

Alexei felt himself flush. Someone said, 'He cannot be a witness. He is not human.'

'He is a Khan,' Burun responded coldly. He stared towards the Arcutt, and then turned his head and looked at Artai's father and uncles. 'Does any man dispute the right I claim for him?'

The Arcutt scowled. T'zin was standing on Tulagai's right. He gestured. 'If Artai wins, Alexei is a dead man,' he said. 'If he desires it, let him witness. His fate rests upon it, and that is price enough.'

It was as if the Kha-Khan was no longer present in the chamber. Burun and Siban had their backs to him, and it was towards them that all men looked. No one else appeared to want to offer an argument. Burun nodded, satisfied. 'It is well,' he said. He nodded curtly to Artai, and then he walked from the room.

'You are mad.' Jotan took several agitated paces across the hall floor and turned. 'If Artai wins he will destroy us.'

'Artai will destroy us anyway,' Burun observed calmly. 'At least this way there is some doubt about the outcome.'

Jotan was still wearing court dress, but he no longer looked poised or contained. They had been sitting down to eat when he had arrived at Burun's house, and it had been Burun's choice to go out into the hall so that they could talk. The other guests included Siban and Jehan, but Burun had only gestured to Alexei to follow him. Jotan went across to the fireplace. He rested his hands on the shelf which ran along the wall above it, his head down. Suddenly he turned round. 'Only talk to Artai,' he appealed. 'If you turn Jehan from his intent there is nothing the Kha-Khan will not give you for a reward.'

Burun raised an eyebrow. 'Does he fear kanly so much?'

'You know he does not.' Jotan's lips compressed. 'But what you want can be gained without risking so much.'

'I am Khan of the Merkuts,' Burun said blandly. 'I have everything I want.'

Jotan opened his mouth to speak, then glanced towards Alexei. He said, 'Does he have to be here?'

Alexei watched Burun's reaction. Burun wrinkled his nose. He seemed to be selecting phrases. Alexei said, 'Your son thinks you want the next Kha-Khan to be a Merkut, Khan.' He saw Jotan flinch.

The silence seemed to grow and expand, and Alexei wondered who would be the first to break it. Finally Jotan said, 'Jehan could be Kha-Khan one day, but not like this.'

Burun did not say anything. He sat back in his chair.

Jotan gestured again. 'Use Artai,' he said. 'Make him trust you and he will do anything you ask.'

'You mean flatter him.' Burun was watching Jotan steadily.

'If that is what it takes, then yes.'

Even fawned upon, Artai could not be trusted, Alexei thought. He remembered conversations, and how the Kha-Khan's mood could change from one instant to the next. If Artai lived he might will the Khanate to Jehan, if Jehan was alive. He might equally consign it on a whim.

The roof of the hall was also the roof of the house. Alexei stared up at the beams which supported it. They were blackened with age, and it was hard to tell where the shadows began.

'Khan, tell me what you think of my son's words,' Burun said.

Alexei made a face. 'I would trust a snake before I would trust Artai,' he said. He saw Jotan flush.

'Alexei's opinion is influenced by his situation,' Jotan said. He gave Alexei a distant stare.

'That's true.' Alexei showed his teeth. 'I offered him honest service, and he has tried to kill me for a reward.'

Jotan snorted. 'You hold yourself too high. Whether you live or die, it is of no moment to Artai.'

'It obviously matters to someone,' Burun observed mildly. He gave Alexei a piercing stare, his eyes reflecting the light from the cressets around the walls.

Alexei had wondered until now how much Burun knew or had guessed about the source of the assassination attempts. He said, 'It would suit Artai very well to have Jehana a widow, but I do not accuse him of attempting to bring about my death.'

'How generous.' Jotan sneered, his colour high.

'Not at all.' Alexei stood. 'The organising was not Artai's at all.'

Burun was wearing a flowing coat of dark-green silk over loose trousers. He crossed one leg over the other. 'You can hardly blame the Arcutt for today's attempt,' he said.

'I don't.' Alexei moved his chair so that it was out of direct light. He sat down again. A shadow of something like expectation crossed Burun's features, and Alexei guessed why he had been brought out to the hall. 'Khan, it is Jotan your son who has been trying to kill me,' Alexei said. He looked steadily at Burun as he spoke. 'For I have threatened his plans from the first.'

It was not to be expected that Jotan would lose control. Alexei waited until Burun looked away, and then he turned his head. Jotan's face changed slowly, as if he was digesting the accusation. He said, 'This is nonsense.'

'Is it?' Alexei leaned back in his chair. 'I wonder whose planning it was that caused Artai's attention to light on Jehana, so that he desired her for his wife.'

Jotan looked down his nose. 'She was a lady of his court,' he said. 'A suitable match.'

'And through her you might have controlled the Dragon Throne,' Alexei commented prosaically. 'Her child would have been yours to govern had Artai died.'

The chances were that the Kha-Khan would not live past thirty. He had inherited the genetic disorder which cursed many of the Altun, and only those who were born free of it lived long.

Burun was watching Jotan. He uncrossed his legs and sat forward. 'I hear a theory,' he said. He glanced at Alexei. 'Do you have proof?'

Alexei shrugged negligently. 'A little. It was a blow to Jotan's aspirations to discover that you had no intention of allowing Jehana to marry the throne, but I suppose he thought he might have circumvented your opposition in time. When you selected me as an alternative match, however, he became desperate. He decided to have me killed, and he tried twice on the day of Artai's enthronement – once while we were on the way to his house, and again later the same night. On the first occasion I was simply lucky. The second time Jotan determined to lead me into the assassin's hands. He dismissed his escort on the pretext that they were to wait to intercept the attack which he pretended to suspect. He had arranged for a dwarf who had been involved in the first attempt to be seen in your courtyard, and this was intended to provide a clear link between the events. He gave the guard captain misleading directions so that the way was left clear for the men who were waiting for us. His actions at your house and on the staging when he took the dwarf captive were calculated to convince everyone that he was concerned for my safety.'

Jotan brushed his coat. 'And to achieve that I was prepared to risk not only my own life, but also that of my wife and daughter,' he observed. He shook his head. 'I must have been desperate indeed.'

'I think you were,' Alexei said seriously. 'Although the risk was small in fact. There were three occasions when you tried to isolate me. Unfortunately for you Jehana chose to remain behind with me when I stopped to delay pursuit. I doubt if the assassins would have injured her, but it meant that in the end you were forced to work at our escape so that your part in the incident would escape detection.' Alexei waited for Jotan's stare to drop, and then he caught Burun's eye. 'Of course none of the men involved were ever found alive.'

Burun got up from his chair. He went to a table which was against the wall. On it was a tray with a k'miss flask and cups. He lifted the flask, then turned as if he had suddenly thought of something. 'I seem to remember that it was Jotan who suggested that we avoid the crowds on enthronement day by using the stagings to cross the city.'

'But you selected our route,' Jotan said quickly. 'You don't take any of this seriously?'

'I have heard nothing convincing so far.' Burun produced a tight little smile. He looked towards Alexei. 'Is there more?'

Alexei nodded. 'I asked Kadan to find the man who captained Jotan's guard,' he said. 'Jotan had him disgraced and turned off, but he still swore that Jotan had misdirected him.'

'He would.' Jotan snorted. 'He used the same

excuse when I questioned him.'

'And he was not believed.' Burun nodded thoughtfully. He gave Alexei a stare. 'Go on.'

'So long as Jehana remained unmarried, there was a chance that she might be made available for Artai,' Alexei said. 'The Arcutt were blamed for the attempts on enthronement day. A third one at Pantai almost succeeded, but by that time Jotan was aware that you suspected him.'

Burun smiled innocently. 'Did I?'

Jotan opened his mouth as if to speak. Then he waved his hands in disgust and walked across the room to the fireplace again. Alexei watched him, but Jotan did not turn. Burun's expression was inscrutable. A draught from somewhere made the cresset flames waver, and the flickering light threw the planes of his face into relief so that there appeared to be movement where in fact there was none.

Alexei said, 'It must have been about that time that Jotan realised that there was another way to control Artai. I was by now so closely guarded that further attempts to kill me were pointless. He persuaded Artai to promote the marriage by telling him that Jehana could be used as a hostage against your conduct. His intent had been all the time to supplant you in Artai's favour, something which he seems to have achieved quite effectively.'

Burun's head came up.

'I think Jotan probably originated the coup which was aimed at taking control of Kinsai,' Alexei said. He stopped to gather his thoughts. 'Sidacai was blamed of course, because everything was done through intermediaries. That has been Jotan's problem throughout, for he could never be seen to be involved in intrigue. Always it had to appear that he was honest and straightforward, so that Artai would never doubt that

527

he was to be trusted. It was easy to convince Artai that your influence threatened the throne, Khan,' Alexei commented. 'The method Jotan suggested to counter that threat appealed to Artai so much that he agreed to travel to Pantai to set it in motion.'

The door to the room in which the meal was being served opened suddenly, and Kadan poked his head out. He said, 'Khan, we have got Jehan drunk.'

Burun looked round. 'Good.' He nodded. Kadan withdrew his head, and the door closed. Burun poured k'miss into a cup. He held it up, offering it to Alexei, and when Alexei shook his head Burun came back to his chair and sat down. He did not look at Jotan.

'Khan, I think you were surprised when Artai pressed you to allow Jehana's marriage to go ahead,' Alexei prompted.

'I could not see his motive at first.' Burun lifted the cup and sipped at the k'miss.

'But then you worked it out.' Alexei watched Jotan out of the corner of his eye, and he wondered why he did not storm out of the house or at least protest what was being said. A scent like honeysuckle was filling the room, and Alexei realised that someone had put incense in the cressets. He caught Burun's eye. 'You arranged for Orcadai and C'zinsit to be appointed to the embassy because you knew that Jotan had persuaded them that he could deal with Artai, and so you could no longer trust them. You also made arrangements for Jehana to be brought aboard ship at the last moment. In the final event Artai was unable to restrain himself. He announced that he intended to make her his ward during my absence – I think maybe Jotan had convinced him that we were not likely to return.'

Alexei saw Burun's mouth twitch. The mortality

rate among ambassadors was high, since their principal task was to demand submission from often hostile states so that there would be an excuse to wage war on those who responded with rejection.

'It meant that Jehana's departure had to be contrived so that it looked as if she had joined me on the spur of the moment,' Alexei continued. 'That way Artai would think only that he had been thwarted, and would never realise that you were anticipating every move he and Jotan made.'

Jotan looked round sharply. He gave Alexei a glare of pure animosity. 'So much theory, so little proof.'

'Maybe so.' Alexei forced himself to speak calmly. 'But that's how it happened. The embassy's return gave you a second chance to persuade Artai that Jehana could be used as a hostage. There was the added opportunity to have me condemned and killed. You had already made him believe that I had betrayed him, and was serving Burun. You came to X'nadu determined to arrange my death so that it would look as if I had been killed resisting. Failing that I was to have an accident. Jehan prevented both.'

The lamps on the wall behind Jotan flared, and Alexei saw him flush before he turned away. Burun was toying with his cup. He rolled the bowl between his hands, saying nothing. Alexei waited until he looked up, then said, 'Khan, I'm not sure how much Jehan knows of this. He has tried to make me believe that Jotan's actions have been influenced by his desire to dissociate himself from your intrigues. That's what Jotan has always expected me to think.'

'Hunh.' Burun looked down at the cup in his hands, and then met Alexei's eyes. 'Whatever Jehan thinks,' he observed, 'he is preserving your life at the risk of his own.'

Alexei knew that he was being offered a diversion.

529

'Say rather that Jehan knows that the only way to deal with Artai now is to supplant him.' He watched as Burun emptied the cup, then said, 'You must know that he does not want to be Kha-Khan.'

Jehan feared the weight of the throne, and it was the knowledge of what lay ahead which had made him act strangely at times.

Burun laid the cup aside. 'Only a fool would desire the throne,' he said soberly.

'Maybe Jotan is right,' Alexei suggested lightly. 'Artai would still take Jehana to wife were she free, and her children would rule the world.' He saw Burun blink.

'Are you so anxious for death?'

'No.' Alexei shook his head. He stood up. 'Jehana is my wife, Khan, and remains so while I am alive. If Jehan is killed then it will be as Jotan says. Artai will destroy us all.'

'And if Jehan lives, so will you,' Burun observed gently. 'You cannot be convicted if your accuser no longer lives.'

Alexei thought that his fate was entirely incidental to Jehan's challenge to Artai, but he did not say so. He glanced at Jotan.

Jotan's expression was brooding. He said, 'Were you human, Alexei, I would have to fight you, for your words have dishonoured me.'

Burun said, 'If Alexei's accusations are true, you have dishonoured yourself.' He stared steadily at Jotan.

Probably Burun knew the truth of the matter – had known it even before he had heard it spoken – but he would never admit it. Alexei gestured. 'Jotan, I will fight you if that is what you desire. It will not change anything.'

'I came here to entreat you not to destroy us.' Jotan

530

did not flinch from Burun's gaze. 'The aliens have poisoned your mind. Think of the Yasa, and what it means to oppose Artai.'

'I love order, not Artai.' Burun showed his teeth. 'Go back to your master. You have my leave.'

Jotan went pale. 'There is no proof against me.'

'Go.'

After Jotan left Alexei sat down again. He remembered the times Jotan had appeared to be a friend, and the laughter they had shared at Artai's enthronement, and wondered if he could be wrong. He glanced at Burun. 'Khan, you knew everything.'

Burun shrugged. 'It was necessary for him to hear you say it.'

He did not intend to disgrace Jotan, Alexei realised. He thought about what would happen if Jehan was killed at kanly. Jotan was afraid the issue was in the balance, or he would have kept his own counsel. If Artai won, all the Merkuts would suffer. Jotan feared to be coloured by Artai's knowledge that he was of Merkut blood. Alexei said, 'You wanted him to know that you were using him all the time – that you never trusted him.' It made the effort of exposing Jotan appear so pointless.

A remote look appeared on Burun's face. Suddenly his head came round. He met Alexei's stare. 'In one thing alone he was right,' he said. 'Jehana's children will rule the world.'

Alexei raised his eyebrows. 'Jehana's children will be mine.'

Burun did not look away. 'That's what I meant,' he said.

Jehan was pretending he was still asleep, but Alexei was not deceived. He said, 'What did you tell Burun about Y'vrope?'

A bird called in the tree above their heads. Jehan opened his eyes abruptly. He sat up, his naked upper torso glistening with the oil the slaves had applied while he had slept. The bird flew down out of the branches of the tree. It darted away towards the eaves of the house.

'I told him they would die before they would submit to us,' Jehan said. He turned and stared at Alexei.

Burun had spoken to every member of the embassy who was available. He had even sent to Sidacai in Khitai for his opinion. Alexei wrinkled his nose. 'I said it would be your problem one day.'

Jehan became very still. There was grass on his shoulders and across his chest, for he had been lying face down. He brushed absently at it. 'Not if Artai kills me,' he observed.

The kanly was set for the day following. Jehan's talons had been honed to needle points in preparation for it. Even those which grew from his toes had been filed to provide a weapon. Alexei moved so that his back was against the trunk of the tree. 'You are heavier and stronger.'

'Artai is younger and faster,' Jehan said shortly. 'Alexei, you have never seen how we fight at kanly. It will shock you.'

Alexei raised his eyebrows. He supposed that humans must once have attempted to tear one another limb from limb. Then someone had picked up a stone, or the branch of a tree, and so had begun the progression of arms.

The garden was practically all in shade because of the height of the wall around it. Alexei's half-sister, Irina, was sitting on the low wall around a fish pond. Sitting on the grass at her feet was D'mitri, the Alan who captained one of the Merkut guard companies. He was not much taller than the average Merkut, but he was broad and muscled like an ox. Irina was stroking his fair hair.

'You are set to gain a brother if that goes on.' Jehan was looking down the garden towards them as he spoke.

'Hunh.' Alexei nodded. Irina was probably too young to marry. He thought about how Kadan, although still a youth in years, was a man in stature, and wondered if she had inherited similar genes. The mixture of Yek and offworld blood might be producing a new strain of being. Alexei looked at Irina again. She had grown considerably during his absence with the embassy, and now possessed the air a woman adopted when she was aware of her sex. It was the blink of an eye for him to move from consideration of Irina to thoughts of Jehana. Alexei touched the letter in his sash, and he longed for her.

Jehan rolled over onto his stomach again. 'You spoke last night to my father,' he said casually.

Alexei gave him a sharp look. 'You were getting drunk at the time.' He heard Jehan laugh softly.

He said, 'It's Burun's answer to all this. He thinks that if I'm drunk I'll forget what I will have to do.'

Jehan was not talking only about his combat with Artai, Alexei realised. If Artai was killed, Jehan was almost certain to be elected to the Dragon Throne. Alexei thought about Jotan's treachery, and of the mischief Orcadai and C'zinsit had made on Jotan's behalf. Jehan knew about them of course. They were his blood, but as Kha-Khan he would have to ignore that. Briefly Alexei wondered what he would do in Jehan's place. Probably he would try to use their guilt as Jehan would to force them to exert themselves in the service of the Khanate. Every man involved in Jotan's intrigue would be trying to avoid Jehan's displeasure once he ascended the throne. They would die to prove that they were loyal. Jehan would use that. Alexei stared down the garden again. 'When all this is over, I will go to Khitai,' he said.

'Hawks and hounds and country pastimes.' Jehan smiled. 'You were bred for other things, Alexei.'

As a servant of the Empire, Alexei thought, he would be part of an artificial system of privilege which took no account of merit. In the Khanate, however, merit was the only measure of the right of one man to rule another. He made a face. 'I have a wife to discover, and my embassy is done.'

Jehan grinned. 'There is Marakan to conquer. Tell me how you would go about it.'

Alexei pursed his lips. 'The Keepers will have to be removed. Let the beasts develop until they are capable of submitting to our rule.'

Jehan looked thoughtful. 'That could take years.'

'Yes.' Alexei did not look at him. 'But there is time.'

'Not if Artai remains Kha-Khan.'

Artai would order the beasts hunted to extinction. Alexei pictured it, and then realised that if Artai lived to order it, he and Jehan would not be alive to care. He said, 'Now tell me what you intend for Y'vrope.'

A sparkle of amusement appeared in Jehan's eyes. 'Maybe I will let them be.'

It was unlikely, for it would not accord with the Yasa. Alexei gave Jehan a disbelieving stare. Jehan shrugged. 'In Y'vrope the land belongs to whoever works it. I will settle our people where it is un-occupied. As they multiply, so there will be order in the land, for they will live according to the law.'

In both cases they were talking about policies which would take many years. Alexei said, 'They might convert our people to their ways. Their customs are not all wrong.'

'I know it,' Jehan said seriously. He got to his feet. Then he stared down at Alexei. 'But that would make a nonsense of everything.'

The place of kanly was a circular arena of hard-packed earth which was exactly fifty drem across. It was surrounded by a high stone wall to which there were but two entrances. No other building stood near enough to provide a view inside.

Outside there were crowds, for everyone wanted to see who would emerge as victor, but within the walls there was almost no sound. Alexei stared at the grey stones. They had been slotted into one another like the pieces of a jigsaw, and the joints were lines which were only visible to the eye because some stones had weathered to darker shades than those upon which they were set. Siban and Burun were circling the arena, examining the surface to ensure that nothing had been buried or concealed. Both were naked. Alexei looked down at his own exposed torso, and he pursed his lips. Of all the Yek customs and traditions, kanly was probably the strangest.

'Body to body, claw to claw,' the form of acknowledgement ran, and it meant precisely that. The participants entered the circle of stone naked, and fought only with the weapons provided by nature – hands and feet, teeth and claws. The winner was the one who remained alive, and he had to be capable of walking away.

Burun and Siban had just drawn lots to decide who would administer the death stroke in the event that one or other of the fighters required it, and Siban had won – or lost according to the point of view – which was to say that the task was to be his. For the first time since entering the place Alexei was glad that he was not human by Yek standards. He was only now starting to comprehend the nature of what he had come to witness. He looked up at the midday sun. It hung brooding overhead, baking the soil of the arena so that it was hot to the touch. He waited for Burun to complete his circuit and then went to join him. Siban was standing on the far side of the arena near one of the doors.

'It is nearly time,' Burun said.

Alexei was not sure how Burun could tell. There was no discernible alteration in the level of noise from outside. What little Alexei could hear was like the sound made by geese on a salt marsh during migration. It had no form, and defied the ear.

The kanly would begin as soon as Artai and Jehan entered. There were no preliminaries, no formalities. Their only purpose in coming to this place was to try to kill one another. Alexei glanced towards the nearby door. It was a solid chunk of wood with no handle or other fittings. To enter the killing ground it was necessary to lift it out of its frame. A pair of braces held it in place once it was shut. The guards outside had the authority to kill anyone who tried to enter unless he was naked and unarmed.

The doors were supposed to be opened at the exact same moment, and there was a connecting rope strung around outside the wall so that the sentries on one side could communicate with their comrades on the other. Alexei stared at the surface of the wood. 'What should we do when they start?'

'We should stay out of the way,' Burun responded drily.

Burun was bulky without being fat. His back was covered with hair. Alexei looked quickly away. They were naked so that they could bring nothing into the arena which could conceivably be used by the participants. Even a piece of clothing could be employed as a weapon.

536

Alexei said, 'I feel ridiculous.'

Burun's head came round. 'It is the Yasa. Our people came into this world naked. Before we used weapons, this was how we fought. If there is a test of our manhood, it is this.'

It was a startling concept, for it suggested that the Yek were far more aware of their origins than anyone would have imagined.

'This is what we are,' Burun said. 'I claimed the right of witness for you because I wanted you to understand.'

The door was opening. Artai came through it. Alexei looked across the arena, and he saw that Jehan was framed in the opposite door space. The covers were rammed back into place, and Alexei heard the thump of the mallets as the wedges were driven home.

Artai looked as if he had been bathed in gold. His unbound hair stood out around his head like a p'ntar's mane, and his skin was bronzed and glistened with oil. He started to run lightly and swiftly across the arena, clearly intending to take the initiative. His talons were fully extended, and the gold sheaths caught the light as his arms swung.

Jehan was motionless. He looked around the arena, first towards Siban and then over at Burun and Alexei, and he seemed not to notice Artai's charge.

'What is he doing?' Alexei realised he was straining forward.

'Be silent.'

Burun's response was low. He held one arm cupped inside the other in front of him. The talons of the cradled hand were out, glinting silver.

Artai's stride was lengthening, becoming the bound of an animal which was coming upon its prey. The soil was so hard-packed that the sound as his feet struck the ground was clearly audible. The distance closed so quickly that Alexei had no time to take it in. The bound became in the same instant a leap, and Artai went headlong at Jehan, his claws outstretched.

Alexei had not known that anything could move so fast. Jehan was a blur sliding past Artai, and Alexei was suddenly reminded of the beast he had seen in the inlet at Marakan. Jehan raked Artai with the talons of his left hand as he sprang out of the way. Artai screamed, a wordless high-voiced cry of pain and anger, and he turned impossibly in mid-air and landed on all fours facing Jehan. He leaped upon him, and they rolled together, clawing and snarling.

They are like wildcats, Alexei thought. He remembered what Travtravnya had said about the origins of the Yek, and knew that he had been told the truth.

It was Jehan who drew back first. There were bloody furrows down his back and along both of his flanks. He disengaged and slid to one side like a wrestler, watching Artai. The separation was so violent it pitched Artai onto the ground. He twisted and rose in one movement, and Alexei saw muscles he had never suspected rippling beneath Artai's flesh.

They screamed at one another – there was no other way to describe the sound. Fangs seemed to gleam in Artai's open mouth, which was surely impossible. Jehan's roar was deeper-throated. He struck out, and his arm seemed to lengthen to cover the distance which separated him from Artai. Artai was too late to move away, and the slashes down his shoulder and upper arm gaped, then erupted in blood.

The fact that their wounds would close almost as soon as they were inflicted would extend the combat, Alexei realised. Artai was circling warily, and dust rose from the dry ground at his feet. He sprang at

538

Jehan, and Jehan seemed to arch backward, striking up with both hands and feet at Artai as he went past. Artai landed badly, and when he straightened there was torn flesh down his chest. One of the tears ran all the way down across the stomach. It gaped horribly.

'Now,' Burun said. Except that he spoke Yek, it was barely a human sound at all.

Artai backed away. He had one arm across his stomach as if to hold himself together. Jehan moved towards him, stalking him.

Suddenly Artai attacked. He leapt at Jehan, landing on his shoulders. His talons embedded in flesh and he bit down at Jehan's neck.

Jehan dropped on all fours. He rolled on top of Artai, dislodging him, and Alexei saw one hand come up amid the dust, the talons glinting. Then it fell and rose and fell again until Artai was finally still.

Jehan stood up. He paced in an arrogant half-circle around Artai's body, watching him. His arms were limp at his sides, and the extended talons dripped fresh blood. He threw back his head and roared deep-throated at the sky. Then he turned away.

Siban started forward.

'Come,' Burun said. He went towards Artai.

Alexei followed. Jehan was still moving around the arena, and he seemed to be unaware of them.

They reached the body together. Artai's head hung at an impossible angle. The flesh around his neck had been torn away to expose the spinal column, and the ground was black with his blood.

Burun knelt down. He lifted Artai's head, then grunted and looked up. 'I knew he was not human,' he said.

Alexei stared. Artai's mouth was open, and the fangs which overlapped top and bottom jaw were exposed. Siban bent to see. 'Name of God,' he breathed. He gave Burun a hard look. 'No one else must know of this.'

It was clearly impossible for Artai to be alive, and yet his eyes now opened. Burun saw it. He looked up at Alexei. 'You are a witness,' he said. 'He cannot survive.'

They could not allow Artai to survive. Alexei drew a breath, then nodded. 'I am a witness,' he responded.

Siban's talons went in quickly and mercifully. The body in Burun's hands shuddered, and then it went limp. He stood up. Siban was already walking towards one of the doors. Alexei stared after him. 'I meant to ask why he stood surety for me.' It was suddenly important to know.

Burun was looking down at the carcase at his feet, his face expressionless. He raised his head. 'Siban owed you a debt,' he said. 'Artai would have killed Sidacai, had you not intervened.'

Alexei remembered how Burun had intrigued to ensure Sidacai's release. Even then he had known about Jotan's betrayal. Burun started to walk towards the door which was now opening for Siban. Alexei went after him. He said, 'What about Jehan?'

Jehan was crouched by the wall midway around the arena. His back was to the stones, and he was staring up blindly into the sun.

'Leave him until he comes to himself again.' Burun did not look back. He gave Alexei a flat stare. 'Did you think you were alone in knowing what we are?' he asked. 'Now that Jehan has tasted Artai's blood, it is not safe to approach him.'

In the Golden Circle, the centre of the centre of Kinsai, the nobility of the Khanate were assembled to pay their final respects to Artai the Golden, Fifth Kha-

Khan. His body had been wrapped in layers of tissue of gold, and now it lay on a funeral pyre of oil-soaked wood in the great oval ceremonial cremation bowl. On the beaten gold of the dais four gates had been erected. They faced north towards the Khirgiz, south to the G'bai, east to the coast and N'pan, and west towards Khitai and the setting sun.

The western gate had been left unsealed. Alexei did not look towards it, for he did not believe that Artai's spirit still remained in his body, and thought the ritual meaningless.

The Khans were standing in a group under an awning which extended the cover provided by the portico giving access to the vestibule of the Golden Yurt. Alexei was in the centre of the front rank, and to his left stood Artai's father and his uncles, their expressions sombre. Everyone wore the crimson scarf which signified mourning. The women in the arcade on the eastern side of the courtyard wore red gowns, and the setting sun cast a haze over the whole scene so that it was easy to understand why red was the colour for death.

Burun was laying Artai's totem on the dais along with the seals and insignia of his reign. The emblems had been defaced on the instant of the Kha-Khan's death, and now official communications originating from the Golden Yurt were sealed with the talisman of the vacant throne.

Alexei glanced towards the canopy under which should have stood the Kha-Khan elect. It was surrounded by courtiers and attendants, but the space for Jehan was empty, for he had refused at the last moment to occupy it and stood instead at Alexei's right hand. Alexei turned and stared at him, but Jehan did not look round. He was gowned as befitted one who had been nominated for election, but if he was

541

aware of the attention he was receiving he gave no sign.

The gongs of Kinsai were being struck now. At first the noise was confused, a clamour which had no form. Gradually the beat steadied. It became a metallic throb which enfolded everything in the city so that it was possible to imagine that the heartbeat of every living creature pulsed in time. Wherever they were and whatever they were doing, the people would be turning now to gaze in the direction of the setting sun.

Burun accepted a torch from a servant. A Shaman would have lit the pyre in times past, but there were none in Kinsai, for they had been excluded by Jehan's order, and Sufi had been declared outlawed. Burun walked thrice round the bowl, and then he touched the pyre with the torch. The wood exploded and a puff of grey smoke rose on a current of hot air. It was blown west on the breeze and dispersed.

Men were making the invocation. Alexei did not speak, and he saw that Jehan's lips did not move either. If Artai had a spirit, it was probably in hell. Certainly it was not winging its way towards the sun, or Heaven which was supposed to lie beyond.

Burun bowed to Jehan. He dropped the torch on the pyre and walked off to the side of the dais. Nobody was supposed to leave before the Kha-Khan elect.

Alexei saw that everyone was waiting. He nudged Jehan. 'We should go now.'

The courtiers who saw Alexei's action looked outraged, but Jehan turned slowly, and then he smiled. 'Is it over?'

'It was over yesterday.' Alexei met Jehan's stare without flinching. He saw a look appear in Jehan's eyes – as if he was trying to recall a faint but lingering

542

memory. Finally Jehan nodded. He started towards the vestibule gate.

Alexei looked back at the pyre. The flames had engulfed the wood, and hid the shape of the tissue-wrapped body on the wood. Thick smoke rose into the evening air. It blew away to the west, obscuring the setting sun.

THE EARTH IS THE LORD'S

Book One of the Sunfall Trilogy

William James

Tarvaras – a barren, harsh land, scorched by an
unforgiving sun. A land dominated by the Yek, a
quarrelsome race, bred for war. And the Yek are about to
wage war again, on the Alan, one of the few peoples not
subject to their rule.

Admiral Rostov of the Imperial Navy, on a routine
survey mission, suddenly finds himself marooned on this
strange world, the prisoner of Burun Khan, one of the
Yek warlords. Rostov quickly realizes that he has little
choice: become a slave, or be trained as a soldier of the
Yek and learn their language, laws and ways.

AN ORBIT BOOK
1 85723 084 1

And look out for *Before the Sun Falls*, the triumphant
conclusion of the Sunfall Trilogy.

THE DRAGON REBORN

Book Three of The Wheel of Time

Robert Jordan

The Dragon Reborn – the leader long prophesied who will save the world, but in the saving destroy it; the saviour who will run mad and kill all those dearest to him – is on the run from destiny. Able to touch the One Power, but unable to control it, and with no one to teach him how – for no man has done it in three thousand years – Rand al'Thor knows only that he must face the Dark One. But how?

AN ORBIT BOOK
1 85723 065 5

THE BROOCH OF AZURE MIDNIGHT

Anne Gay

Spiderglass is a vast, interplanetary combine, ruled by the Tjerssen family. Karel is the youngest member of the Board, and learned early – on the day his grandmother died – to trust his family even less than outsiders. Looking to the future when he plans to rule the corporation, Karel creates a double-edged weapon . . . Jezrael and Chesarynth Brown, sisters born on the asteroid cluster of Witwaterstrand. Jez the rebel and Ches the brilliant scholar. Unknown to either of them Karel moulds their lives throughout the Solar System so that they will be ready when his time comes to strike.

But then the Gate is discovered.

At first simply a rumour. Instantaneous matter-transmission. No more never-ending interstellar journeys, no more starving colonies. And no more monopolies. In their different ways, Jezrael and Chesarynth will be utterly changed by Karel's manipulation – although not as he expected.

And the Gate will change humanity itself.

Anne Gay, author of the highly-praised MINDSAIL, moves onto another level with this intricate, fast-moving novel, both colourful and sophisticated. She is a major addition to the world of science fiction.

AN ORBIT BOOK
1 85723 037 X

ETERNAL LIGHT
Paul J. McAuley

In the aftermath of an interstellar war an enigmatic star is discovered, travelling towards the Solar System from the galactic core. Its appearance is a new and dangerous factor in the turbulent politics of the inhabited worlds as rival factions – the power-holders of the ReUnited Nations; the rebels who secretly oppose their power; the religious Witnesses – all see advantages to be gained.

But what awesome technology started the star on its journey half a million years ago? And why? Caught up in the quest to discover its secret are Dorthy Yoshida, whose empathic talent places her in danger from those greedy to use it; Suzy Falcon, an ace flier on the run from her unwitting part in a conspiracy that went wrong; Robot, an artist/terrorist with computer circuitry implanted in his brain; and Talbeck, one of the Golden – the immensely rich élite whose lives have been extended to near-immortality. They each have their own motives. Each will experience events that will change them forever.

Huge in scope, breathtaking in ideas, ETERNAL LIGHT is packed with life, character, atmosphere and incident. To read it is to rediscover science fiction's sense of wonder.

AN ORBIT BOOK
1 85723 015 9

THE ENCYCLOPEDIA OF SCIENCE FICTION

John Clute and *Peter Nicholls*

When the first edition of *The Encyclopedia of Science Fiction* was published in 1979, it was immediately hailed as a classic work of reference. Frank Herbert described it as 'the most valuable science fiction source book ever written' and Isaac Asimov said 'It will become the Bible for all science fiction fans.'

This new edition has taken years to prepare and is much more than a simple updating. The world of science fiction in the 1990s is much more complex than it was back in the late 1970s. The advent of game worlds, shared worlds, graphic novels, film and TV spin-offs, technothrillers, survivalist fiction, sf horror novels and fantasy novels with sf centres has necessitated a radical revision, and this has allowed the inclusion of related subjects, such as magic realism. Accordingly, the book has expanded dramatically in order to cope with the complexities and changes. It now contains well over 4,300 entries – a staggering 1,500 more than the original – and, at 1.2 million words, it is nearly half a million words longer than the first edition.

This is the indispensable reference work not only for every reader who loves, uses and wishes to know more about science fiction, but for every reader of imaginative fiction at the end of this century.

AN ORBIT BOOK
1 85723 124 4

☐	The Earth is the Lord's	William James	£4.99
☐	The Dragon Reborn	Robert Jordan	£5.99
☐	The Brooch of Azure Midnight	Anne Gay	£4.99
☐	Eternal Light	Paul J. McAuley	£4.99
☐	The Encyclopedia of Science Fiction	John Clute and Peter Nicholls	£45.00

Orbit now offers an exciting range of quality titles by both established and new authors which can be ordered from the following address:

Little, Brown and Company (UK) Limited,
P.O. Box 11,
Falmouth,
Cornwall TR10 9EN.

Alternatively you may fax your order to the above address. Fax No. 0326 376423.

Payments can be made as follows: cheque, postal order (payable to Little, Brown and Company) or by credit cards, Visa/Access. Do not send cash or currency. UK customers and B.F.P.O. please allow £1.00 for postage and packing for the first book, plus 50p for the second book, plus 30p for each additional book up to a maximum charge of £3.00 (7 books plus).

Overseas customers including Ireland, please allow £2.00 for the first book plus £1.00 for the second book, plus 50p for each additional book.

NAME (Block Letters) ....

....

ADDRESS ....

....

....

☐ I enclose my remittance for _____

☐ I wish to pay by Access/Visa Card

Number | | | | | | | | | | | | | | | | | | |

Card Expiry Date | | | | |